"What is it you desire?" he asked.

♡

Jenna began to back away from him. The silence was broken by the gentle slap of water against the muddy bank. A silver fish arched above the water and smacked the surface in a dive to a deeper pool.

Jenna turned toward the river. "I want to know," she whispered into the wind, hoping the words would be carried away and leave her alone.

Ian approached her. "Such honesty carries a price." He pulled her to him and kissed her tenderly, longingly. The night's growth of his beard scraped across her cheek as they embraced, his hands roaming her back. There was only the scent and the press of his body against her. Her own hands stroked the width of his chest, slipping under his shirt, absorbing the solid heat of his body.

He pushed her away gently and began to unbutton the bodice of her riding habit. She stayed his hand, hesitating, wanting to slow down the pounding of her heart, slow down this journey that would change her forever. But his lips crushed hers with a hunger that set a pace of its own.

In a minute, her bodice was open...

Dare I Love?

Dare I Love?

Gillian Wyeth

POPULAR LIBRARY

An Imprint of Warner Books, Inc.

A Warner Communications Company

While references are made within *Dare I Love?* to real places and events, the setting, characters and situations are complete fiction.

POPULAR LIBRARY EDITION

Popular Library ® and the fanciful P design are registered trademarks of Warner Books, Inc.

Cover illustration by Morgan Kane

Popular Library books are published by
Warner Books, Inc.
666 Fifth Avenue
New York, N.Y. 10103

 A Warner Communications Company

Printed in the United States of America

First Printing: December, 1987

10 9 8 7 6 5 4 3 2 1

Chapter 1

Jenna's boots made no sound on the dew-soaked grass. Her steps grew more hesitant as she entered the vale and moved down close to the hiding place—a brush-covered outcrop above the stream.

A twig snapped somewhere on the hill above her. Jenna stopped immediately, steadying the bow slung over her shoulder with her gloved hand. She scanned the oaks and scrub brush of the slope to her left, searching for a shape out of place. She did not move until a hare scampered from behind a tree and ran across the crest of the hill, on its way to the fields. Or maybe, she smiled, it was heading straight for the early shoots in her friend Leona's garden.

Jenna relaxed and made her way quickly to the rocky overhang. Clad in the dark breeches and overshirt of a village boy, Jenna crouched behind a thick rhododendron bush. She laid her rifle on the ground and exhaled with relief. Her left arm ached from the gun's weight. It would be used only in an emergency—if her arrow missed. She could not afford to bring noisy attention to her shocking state of dress and her even more eccentric mission. Lady Jenna Thornton was willfully breaking the law of the lord of the manor. Again.

Slowly she slipped the longbow off her shoulder, pulled two arrows from her quiver and fitted a shaft into the nocking point of the drawstring. Her left thumb and forefinger formed a steady shelf for the arrowhead snug against the bow grip. Jenna flexed the cold fingers of her right hand to restore circulation, then she pulled the floppy brown plow-boy's hat lower to cover her neck.

She had begun her approach to the deer crossing carefully downwind. That meant a long, steep walk up the ridge from the manor house to the south edge of Shadow Glen's thick woods. The sun was still only a misty promise above a can-opied ridge of elm, spruce and chestnut trees. Jenna yawned and arched her tired back. Stolley should be in position downstream by now.

How he hated this. The deaf-mute had an almost mystical communication with creatures of the forest and field. "But it is necessary," Jenna had said in the sign language she and Leona had created to communicate with him. "You would have my father serve porridge to the arrogant baronet who's coming to dine tonight?" Stolley had struggled and given her a sign that said, more or less, "Skewer the baronet."

Jenna listened for hooved steps, but she heard only the trickle of water against rocks. When struck, the wounded deer would bound down the open path of the stream until faint from loss of blood. When the animal took to the woods to hide, Stolley would follow the trail of blood.

Her father, Lord Arthur Thornton, sixth Earl of Glen Manor and its tenant estates, had forbidden the killing of deer at Shadow Glen during the fawning season. But Jenna had to find a substitute for the joint of beef to be served at the manor's formal dinner tonight. Her father was adamant that the meal be perfect. She could not afford such a horrible lapse of hospitality, especially since this sudden dinner seemed to be pulling her father out of his long depression.

The fault was hers, of course. She had acted against the

earl's orders. "You should support the strikers—um—indirectly," her father had said. Secretly, though, she made sure the joint was delivered to a famished group of fifteen coal miners' families camped at the edge of the village of Glencur on her father's property.

Fortunately, old Cook had not cried thief when she discovered the joint missing. She went straight to Jenna. "Ya been feedin' the strikers ag'in, ain't cha?" said the Irishwoman, looking mad enough to pluck a live chicken. "Fergive the impertinence, but 'tis too much ya've given this time. 'Twas the only beef we had for the gran' dinner tomorrow."

Jenna tried to make her nineteen-year-old face look detached and unconcerned.

"Y'know how much yer father was countin' on this dinner to impress his new neighbor," Cook scowled.

"You shall have your meat tomorrow morning," Jenna said calmly.

"Meat, is it? I need tender beef for braisin'! And there's no one in the valley butcherin' this week. I will not be held responsible for ruining the bill o' fare." Cook crossed her arms and pursed her grim lips.

"I do not owe you an explanation. You know those families were starving. They cannot even poach a hare or a pigeon. Lord Parrish is just aching for an excuse to call the magistrate and arrest as many of the men as he can. He means to break the strike and break it soon. Even if it means bringing down Scots from the north or poor men from the south."

"I know that," Cook said, softening a little. "But good hearts don't rule this world. Especially hearts just hopin' for vengeance as they're spoutin' out virtues."

Color rose to Jenna's cheeks and she carefully kept her

hands unclenched. She loved this abrasive old woman, but she could not take the insult. Especially since it rang true. As usual. "My dislike of Lord Parrish and his whole family is well-known, Frances Mary, but my concern for the tenants and commoners living on Thornton property is also well-known and has never been questioned. Until now."

The old woman sighed in resignation.

"You will prepare an entrée with the meat I bring to you tomorrow. God willing, it'll be cow. If He's not willing, then we'll eat something else. Three downtrodden families of His children can live a week on one joint of beef. And there's not a menu on earth worth more than that."

"Aye, m'lady." Cook had made a stiff little curtsy and turned to leave. "May the Red Bow come soon," she said over her shoulder, "so that a lady can tend to the problems of the pantry instead of politics."

Jenna shook her head. The Red Bow was a century-old legend in Lancashire, a champion and avenger whose name was invoked each time the monied class had the common man under siege. Perhaps the striking miners needed their belief in the Bandit's deliverance more than they needed Lord Thornton's beef. I doubt it, though, Jenna thought.

The ache in her legs warned her to shift her crouching position in the damp brush. Why was her father so stubborn? He had no sense of timing. Each week more miners fled the homelessness they faced in the strike at Bolton Colliery near Manchester. The drifters only increased the burden and fed the tempers of the strikers at Lord Parrish's colliery outside Glencur. Why, at a time when violence between mine owners and laborers seemed imminent, would her father arrange a dinner party with well-bred neighbors he had ignored for twenty years?

Oh, if there were only more money, she thought, she

could rehire the gamekeeper. If there were only more money, she could restock the herds on the tenants' farms and install good drainage systems. She could replace the sun-rotted curtain in the morning room and . . .

Snap! Two small deer treaded cautiously down the brackened slope toward the shallow stream. Brown tufts of tail flicked nervously. Stubs of antlers jutted from their heads. Bucks! Thank God it wasn't a nursing doe! Jenna thought. Surely a small yearling buck wouldn't be missed.

Hidden behind a black-barked oak tree not thirty yards up the slope, a stranger watched the hunter and the hunted.

He had thought the poacher a boy at first, perhaps the son of a hungry striker. But as she moved cautiously down the hill, he saw she was too clean to be a miner's brat. Closer still and he knew the contour of the breeches could not be rounded so fully by the hard flanks of a boy. A heavy leather vest hid her bosom. Small, he judged. But he had been fooled before by slight-figured women.

Sir Ian Stonebridge relaxed against the tree, intrigued. The minx was obviously concerned about being caught, yet there was a cool self-possession about her movements, a decisiveness in her manner. As if she had done this before.

He released his handhold on the English revolver at his belt, eased his arm back to his side and silently expelled a long breath. Just minutes before he had been drinking at the muddy edge of the stream, grateful for the sting of icy water across his face. It bit easily through the dusty fatigue of the night's fourteen-mile ride. He glanced to the crest of the hill. His horse grazed unseen on the other side.

Stonebridge carefully stretched his lean body against the wide oak trunks so that he could better see the young poacher. Stiff muscles in his thighs and calves protested. He had been too long at sea, and not enough in the saddle since his return to England.

He was dressed comfortably in a wrinkled waistcoat over docksman's togs, but his jaw itched with the roughness of two days' growth of beard.

The sour lightheadedness he felt made him even more impatient to take care of the poacher soon. Good French brandy from the card room didn't mix well with the raw whiskey he'd tossed down at the Bull and Mount Tavern. But the ungodly pounding in his head was worth the information.

The Red Bow Bandit was real. At least to the common folk of mining villages like Turton Bottoms and Bolton.

Last night Stonebridge had sat on a coal-blackened bench while day laborers and miners shared tankards of ale and joked about the Bandit, who would come and toss shillings to their children. The reckless guffaws were half-hearted, half hoping, because their children were at home asking for more than bread and broth. The miners' strike for safety in the pits was into its second month with no end in sight.

Stonebridge had drunk his whiskey alone, his thoughts tuned to their tipsy laughter. The proper Church of England and the Wesleyans could no more replace the poor folk's legends with scripture than they could turn thin potato soup to kidney pie. One was always available to the poor. The other was not.

And when there was no meat, there were the squire's game fields, Stonebridge thought, watching the poacher silently shift in her cramped space behind the brush.

The poacher posed a moral problem for him. As an English gentleman, Sir Ian Stonebridge was bound by law to abhor theft of a lord's game. But as a renegade privateer, he was more wont to cheer on the common man's struggle against hunger. Stonebridge smiled thoughtfully as he watched the two deer lower their heads to drink. His ships had been sold. He was landed gentry now, locked into a much different game of survival, one which depended on compliance with the established order.

There was only one response to a young poacher. Turning her in would add credence to his new position at the manor.

Suddenly the girl below lifted the bow and drew the string tight back, level with her ear. Stonebridge felt his body tense and his breath stop instinctively in sympathy with the hunt.

If she got her buck, she would be prosecuted. If he caught her trespassing, she would be warned.

Quickly he shrilled the sharp, warning peal of a bobwhite.

The nervous deer bobbed up instantly, their heads raised high to sniff the air—giving the hunter a clear shot at broad chests. The arrow found its mark near the heart. The buck stepped backward, then both creatures bounded away downstream.

Damn her for an alert little bugger! She turned the bobwhite's warning into a good shot. If the crime of poaching yearlings were not so odious, he would have found a grudging admiration for the girl's reflexes. As it was, it was time to nip the little schemer's success, lest she carry the theft just eight miles northeast of these woods onto land belonging to Stonebridge himself.

On the outcropping Jenna stooped to retrieve the rifle and the extra arrow she no longer needed. With a leisurely swing, she slipped the bow over her shoulder and headed down toward the stream to track the wounded deer.

Stonebridge saw his chance and bounded quickly down the slope. The noise of crackling underbrush made Jenna start. She whirled and found a tall, unkempt stranger almost upon her. Her eyes widened in fear as his right hand reached for the handle of a pistol in his belt. She dropped to one knee and leveled her rifle at his chest, praying that she would not have to fire. She opened her mouth to yell, "Stop!" but the man fell and rolled out of sight.

Silence.

Jenna tried to slow her ragged breathing and pinpoint where her attacker lay hidden. A rifle shot, she knew, would bring the villagers running into the glen. Should she fire now, just to bring help? Or had the stranger run scared at the sight of a rif—

"Ooooooffff!"

Stonebridge heard a high-pitched gasp as his weight knocked her off balance. She scrambled quickly off the outcrop as he grabbed a handhold on her shirt. The fabric tore and she fell forward with the sudden release. The gun clattered down the hill. She landed with a cry of pain against the blunt edge of a rock.

Stonebridge straddled her quickly and grabbed the small hand that reached for the leather-sheathed hunting blade at her waist. A cascade of thick black hair spilled from the plowboy hat as she fought. She tried to twist away, kicking and writhing for leverage to get out from under him. But she stopped suddenly, hatred welling, as she realized how carefully his thighs pinned her, giving her just enough room to struggle with no chance of escape. Bastard! She lay back gasping, unable to speak.

God in heaven, she was a fine catch, Stonebridge swore to himself. The urchin's eyes raged a royal, haughty blue. She was well-kept. A lady's maid, perhaps. Stonebridge smiled and settled more comfortably across her abdomen.

"I had no idea Shadow Glen had such comely thieves," Stonebridge said, lifting her long tresses in one hand.

"Get off!" Jenna hissed, raising herself up to claw at the

villain's face. He grabbed both wrists and pinned them above her head. Jenna moaned, aware of a stabbing pain in her right side.

"You're hurt?" he asked, using his free hand to tear open the rough leather vest that covered her thin shirt.

Jenna screamed, wide-eyed with terror.

"Quiet. I'm not going to hurt you." Gently, his fingers probed her injured side.

The outrage of this stranger's hand upon her body hurt more than the ribs he had bruised. "You rotter!" she said through gritted teeth. "You dirty animal! You may not touch me! I am Lady Jenna Ashley Thornton, mistress of Glen Manor. Leave me unharmed, else the entire village will search you out and hang up your empty hide for the wild dogs."

Stonebridge laughed as he gazed down at the disheveled village girl with the highborn manners. "A wit as sharp as your marksmanship. Lady Jenna? The Ice Maiden herself? Traipsing the woods in boy's breeches?" He smiled. "You entertain the ears as well as the eyes. What else are you good at?" he mused.

He could feel her body grow tense, more wary underneath him. He released her left hand and drew her right hand down to lay across her middle, cradling her side.

"A bruised rib, cracked maybe, not broken. You're fortunate. Could have been much worse."

"Fortunate? You madman! Let me up!"

"You're in much trouble, you know." He said the words softly, but they carried a chill to Jenna's heart. "Caught stealing your lord's game. Even worse, you threatened to shoot a Lancashire gentleman right through the heart."

"Gentlemen do not dress like penniless vagabonds. Nor do they stink of brandy at dawn. And they never lay hands

Gillian Wyeth

on a lady, you slime-rotted bastard." Jenna felt her eyes sting with tears.

"True, perhaps," Stonebridge said. "Neither does a lady dress like a boy, shoot as straight as a poacher or swear like a prostitute. All in all, your manners are quite barbaric," he said, catching Jenna's fist as it landed against his chest. "How do you plead, 'm'lady'?" His eyes flicked downward to the open neck of her loose shirt, and Jenna felt panic rise in her throat.

"Leave me alone!" she cried, beating against his shoulders as he leaned his face closer to hers. His dark eyes, almost black, caught hers. He stopped a moment. "Perhaps, my thief, both of us have stolen liberties not allowed us. There comes a time for everyone to pay." His lips brushed hers suddenly, a kiss gentle, not harsh, a sensation so light and strange that Jenna caught her breath.

A huge rock slammed against the back of her attacker's head like a sledgehammer seating a peg. Stonebridge rolled unconscious to the ground. Quickly Stolley pulled Jenna to her feet, growling in concern.

"I'm fine," she gestured. Her head was reeling, though, with dizziness and worry. If Stolley had killed the man, she was to blame. It was her own, stupid folly which had led to the masquerade and the hunt.

When Jenna's hands steadied, she knelt and felt for a pulse in the ruffian's neck. His heartbeat seemed regular, but his breathing was shallow. Probably normal for a blow to the head, Jenna hoped. "He's not dead," she signed to Stolley. Relief flooded the boy's sensitive face like a fresh rain. He smiled and pointed downstream toward the bloody deer trail.

"I have to stay," Jenna said, "until he wakes up."

Stolley shook his head vigorously and pounded his fists in the air, imitating Jenna's struggle.

"I'll wait up there on the ridge." She pointed. "When I see that he's able to stand and walk away, I'll run home. Now go," she gestured. "Put the deer in the pushcart and take it to Cook. She doesn't have much time to dress it for the dinner."

Stolley didn't leave, however, until Jenna had picked up her weapons and climbed slowly to the top of the hill. The pain in her side made each step uncomfortable. Behind a clump of bracken she stretched out carefully in a patch of low-growing heather just below the crown of the ridge.

The stranger lay unmoving for nearly an hour. Perhaps he was dead. Perhaps her unorthodox manners had finally cost her serious trouble. This is a sign, she thought. A sign to stop sympathizing with colliery workers just so she could eke out a little vengeance against arrogant lords like the Parrishes. A sign to give up her piteous, penny-pinching efforts to save her father's declining estate.

Time, even, to swallow her fear and accept a marriage proposal. Connell Parrish, son of Viscount Hutton Parrish, was her most hated and persistent suitor. But with him Glen Manor could be saved. The miners would have an ally in the Parrish house. Only she would be the loser.

Jenna's head sank to the grass and she nearly screamed into the silence: "Get up, you stupid oaf! You cannot die!"

Leaves rustled. She looked up. The man rose to his knees, holding his head. Finally he stood and leaned against a tree for support. His dark eyes scoured the hillside north and south, as if somehow he knew she was there. She controlled an urge to flee. There was a danger about this man. Finally he turned and made his way slowly up the hill on the other side of the glen.

The sun had fully risen now, casting tree shadows over the stream where she had shot the young deer. Thank God there was only one death on her conscience this day. Stiffly, she got to her feet.

A quick glance to her left took in the green ruggedness of the Forest of Bowland, which bordered Shadow Glen. Straight ahead she could see across the moor to the rocky, bracken-covered foothills of the Pennines, the mountain chain that separated Lancashire from its neighboring county of Yorkshire.

Her eyes swept upward to the daunting white cliff face of Pennines Peak. The view was marred by the tall metal frames of the colliery cranes. To Jenna, they rose like black skeletons, a warning to those who sought the peace of country living.

But the miners would think differently, Jenna knew. It was their only livelihood. Rows of their tiny thatched cottages lay in a lowland dip a mile from the mine portal.

To her right, along the winding River Ribble, the tile roofs of Glencur's shops rose neatly from a hilly slope. A small village now, it had once boasted three taverns and a cramped haberdashery with a big glass window. But when the Parrish vein began to play itself out, miners had left the valley.

Last fall the vein became reborn. And Jenna had hopes that the village would revive. It would mean more rent money for the Thornton estate. The earl was a lenient squire and never demanded rent payments in hard times.

After the strike, she sighed. Things would be different after the strike.

She headed down the ridge to the grassy pastures and tenant farms of Glen Manor. Home.

Chapter 2

"Ellen!" Jenna called from the top of the curved staircase. "Did you dust the drawing room yet?"

"No, mum!" yelled the woman, craning her neck and tossing the words forcefully over her posterior and up the spindled bannister. The servant was on hands and knees, scrubbing the blond beechwood floor of the entrance hall and was in no mood to hear of chores yet to do.

"Make that the first thing you do when you finish the floors," Jenna said, closer now, her arm casually bracing her rib as she crept down the worn green Brussels carpet on the stairs.

"Scrub the floors! Air the parlor! Freshen the linen! Tend the grates!" The middle-aged woman muttered and scrubbed. "Lords comin' to call only make more work for a tired body deservin' better. 'Twould be better to live with a bunch of hermits. . . ."

"Poor Ellen." Jenna tsked. "It's a mess to scrub, isn't it?"

The short, wispy-haired woman sat back on her heels and sighed. "'Tis that, m'lady."

"Well, you wouldn't have a foot of filth there if you cleaned it every morning." Jenna said. "That would make it much easier on you in the long run, I'm sure."

Ellen pursed her lips tight. "I don't believe you've said

that, m'lady! Threatenin' to put an ailin' old woman on her hands and knees everyday," she muttered and dipped her brush in the pail, slamming it against the floor.

"Mean I am," Jenna said, "especially when I pinch."

Ellen turned quickly to see if the threat were real. She found her mistress's even, white teeth parted in a grin. Ellen smiled back, a little unsure of herself. "You can be a devil when you want to."

"Lucky for you I'm feeling angelic today."

"I'll be done soon, m'lady."

"I know," Jenna said. She walked down the entrance hall, past the tall-case Byzantine clock, which had stopped at half past four. The servants like the joke. It was always teatime in the hallway, even though the Thornton mistress rarely called for it in the drawing room. Ornate brass lanterns on the wall hung like mile-post warnings in the dim light of the corridor.

"Snuff these, Ellen!" she called. "It's full daylight now." At the end of the corridor, Jenna turned at the bare wooden stairwell leading down to the kitchen. Her worn brown morning dress hung limply on her slender frame. The garment had been washed and worn too often.

Ellen paused, looking after her. The young lady worked too hard for her fool of a father and that sot of a brother. She only had three or four dresses worth primping over.

But having a mistress who dressed like a mouse wasn't so bad. There was many a lady who would rather buy frocks than pay servants. Fortunately, this girl had better sense. A queer one, she was, though. Common as an old shoe one minute and haughty as a queen the next. As quick to take tea from a cracked pot in a cottage as she was to sip the champagne of the London lords she was kin to. Always flying away on horseback to check on sick villagers. Sure, she was kindly, but she should have thought of how it looked, her acting like a common nurse. And then there was the time she talked cattle breeding to Squire Ames. Like a farmer, she was. Yet you get the least bit uppity and she'd freeze you solid with one look. The time she got in a temper about Mrs. Searle cuffing Stolley, the deaf and dumb boy, my God, you never heard such language. And from a lady! Ellen giggled and scrubbed harder.

The cavernous kitchen downstairs was a stone-floored sanctuary of steaming broths and clanking pots. A giant hearth trimmed in an arch of blackened brick took up an entire wall. At the far side of the room the wall was lost behind strong oak shelves stained dark by decades of smoke. Rows of plates and platters, crocks, tureens and pitchers were collected in uneven lines. Underneath, just above the flagstone floor were implements of Cook's trade: knife block, vegetable mill, lard press, meat grinder, sausage stuffer, apple parer, rolling pins, cast-iron coffee mill and black-crusted pots.

Peggy, the scullery maid, a miner's daughter of about fifteen, sat sleepily in an alcove, pumping the handle of the wooden butter press. Just around the corner from her a marble-topped table of ancient oak squatted against the wall. Cook was bent there, up to her elbows in bread dough.

"Did Stolley bring you the meat we found?" Jenna asked.

"The meat you 'found,' is it?" said the wiry Irishwoman, brushing a stray string of hair off her forehead with floured fingers. "Like a gift from providence, yer sayin'? Like a big, hairy lump of manna itself landin' square into Stolley's cart with the arrow of God stickin' in its heart? That the meat you mean?"

"Hush up!" Jenna said. "Someday God's going to get tired

of hearing your profanities and he'll sour every sweet scone you put in your oven!"

"Never happen and you know it," said Cook, unperturbed. She pummeled the bread dough with rhythmic thumps. "Not to my scones. Would ya like to explain to me how I'm gonna turn a flank of venison into a joint of beef by dinnertime?"

"I don't know. Didn't that French husband of yours teach you any tricks in the kitchen?" Jenna asked.

Cook whomped the dough down so hard the table shuddered. "Doncha dare invoke the mem'ry of that hairy little Frog!" She choked. "That cheatin' deserter and snaketongue. Tricks, ya want to know, do ye? The only tricks he knew in the kitchen can't be repeated to virgin ears like yours, that's fer sure. Tricks. Pshaw. That bastard was full of 'em." Cook punched the dough decisively.

"He may not have been worth much as a husband, but he was a chef!"

"As good a chef as I am a shoemaker, pttuuii!" Cook spat. "Of course," she said, turning thoughtful, "there was one time we had a tough, stringy chunk of stew meat and he had me soak it in buttermilk. Seems to me it turned tender as veal, although I've forgotten what it tasted like. The horny little toad never did let us finish a meal," she grinned.

"Cook!" Jenna admonished with a smile. "Will it work?"

"I don't know. I'll try. Yearling meat is tender anyway. Soaking it might make it fall apart in the pan."

"Or it might make it taste like seasoned beef, you old nay sayer. However it turns out, I'm going to call it a classic French recipe prepared especially for our honored guests. And if it turns out badly, I'm going to offer your services to a grim old fishhead—Lord Parrish."

Cook stopped and pursed her lips. "Doncha joke about

filthy slavers like the Parrishes. Ole Hutton's an evil one, lord or no. Gall for his brain and stone for a heart. I know for a fact God won't bother about a foul-mouthed old woman that makes wonderful bread when he's got a house full of devil Parrishes to toast right next door."

"Think he can also overlook a daughter who lies to her father?" Jenna asked.

"Depends on how good the lie," Cook said, wrestling the dough into a huge glazed bowl for rising.

"How about this? Stolley was gathering kindling and came upon a pack of wild dogs tearing at the throat of a yearling. Stolley chased the dogs away and brought the dead deer home, knowing that Father might want to distribute it to the poor. That'll explain the carcass hanging in the cellar."

"It'll do for an old gullible like yer father." Cook moved to the stove to stir a pot full of potatoes. "Now, if yer not gonna help me dress that bloody animal for dinner, go and sit down and play the grand lady," Cook said. "Yer lookin' tired. Like you've been wrestlin' wild boars in the woods."

Jenna looked sharply at the old woman, whose eyes were fastened on the steaming broth. "I don't wrestle."

"You're a lot safer if ya don't, I always say." Cook adjusted her fire. "But 'tis best to stay clear o' the woods so yer not such a temptin' little morsel."

"Cook," Jenna said, her voice dipping cool and clear with warning.

"Yes, m'lady?" The old woman calmly arched her eyebrow.

"If I didn't know you were so discreet, I'd mistake you for a gossip."

"Just because I gather doesn't mean I spread it." She inhaled a deafening slurp from the wooden ladle. "I wancha ta be careful. So don't waste yer ice voice on me. Save it for

the arrogant bastard who'll be suppin' on poached deer tonight."

"Sshhhhhh!" Jenna nearly screamed in exasperation and
fled.

She found Eaton, the butler, in his pantry. He was supervising young Martha Bricks, the parlor maid, as she polished the silver tea service with a pasty, green-tinged rag.

The smooth mahogany dining table had been lemon
waxed to a mirrored glow. Cobwebs had been cleared from
the rosettes in the plaster molding of the ceiling. To Jenna's
right, just inside the columned entrance arch, the ebony,
claw-foot sideboard her grandfather had brought home from
the Orient hulked against the wall like a protective beast.

With luck, the eclectic collection from five generations
would distract their guests from the worn silk upholstery of
the chairs. And dim lighting would hide the saw-toothed
gaps in the fringe of the gold brocade drapes.

"How's Father today, Eaton?"

"Rather good, I think, m'lady. Seemed to grumble more
than he coughed when I took him up his tea this morning."

"A good sign, I'm sure," Jenna smiled. "Eaton, is there
any way Mrs. Searle can come back from Buxton to help us
tonight?" The housekeeper had left two days ago.

"'Fraid not, m'lady. Her father's funeral is not till tomorrow. She said she would be back by nightfall."

"Are you sure we have enough help to attend a formal
dinner? Maybe Ellen could serve."

Eaton's eyebrows rose in judgment. "Ellen is too rough in
her manners to be serving gentlemen, ma'am." He rubbed
vigorously at a tarnished spot on the tea tray. "Do it over,"
he said to the timid Bricks.

"I will have to find someone else, then," Jenna said,

frowning. It would be a small enough expense, nothing really when added to the cost of running the forty-room mansion with a skeleton staff of sixteen indoor servants and seven gardeners, grooms and stablemen.

She reminded Eaton to make sure all coal scuttles were refilled for tonight. Then she left the house through the servants' entrance.

Jenna closed the warped plank door to the outside, and it groaned on loosened hinges. She kept a sharp eye on the ground as she made her way to the stable. There were missing cobblestones on the path, leaving many holes to twist an ankle.

The rolling swales of Glen Manor's grassy western exposure lay before her. The hawthorn hedges of Squire Ames farm began just over the hill.

All the extra money Jenna could muster was reinvested to maintain tenant properties on the six-hundred-acre estate. The earl had never been adept as a manager. His eye was always on the bigger picture, the grander scheme. Lord Thornton's ideals and love of the public life led him straight to his seat in the House of Lords soon after he married Jenna's mother, Charlotte Ashley.

The earl's booming theatrics in the halls of Parliament were memorable: "If we mean to make a man work like a mole in the wet, stinking bowels of the earth," he would thunder, "we had damn better remember he's a child of God and accord him the right to safety and livelihood that every one of His children deserve!"

With charm and subtle drawing-room politics, Lord Thornton formed a powerful lobby of statesmen who supported passage of community health standards and a strict mine-safety act.

Then, three years ago, as his victory seemed assured, the

scandal of his wife's suicide destroyed the life they knew. When the countess took her own life, Lord Thornton's political dreams were buried with her. Gone also, many said, was the earl's grasp on reality.

Independent colliery owners rallied fiercely to defeat the bill which would have cost them thousands in capital improvements. The coal industrialists were led by the Thorntons' country neighbor, Hutton Parrish, third Viscount of Tyne. When the oratory was over and the votes cast, Parrish had won.

That was three long years ago. A simple story, really, Jenna thought. A rise and fall in politics, with a little social addendum: the personal disintegration of a titled family. Jenna, in the bloom of her sixteenth year, was left with no mother and, in many ways, no father. Lord Thornton had retreated in shock to his country estate to nurse his grief and anger.

Jenna found it was left to her to nurse her father's sickly financial affairs. A blessing in disguise, it had given her little time to grieve for a mother who had destroyed her family.

Angry tears threatened and she reached quickly to throw the bolt on the stable door. Jenna groaned aloud as the muscles of her rib cage were stretched painfully tight. She would have to guard the use of her right arm tonight.

She glanced about for Stolley in the dim, musty barn. The earthy smell of straw and horse dung seemed to close around her. Bright slats of sunlight painted yellow stripes on the broad gray flanks of the carriage horses.

Dulcy whinnied at her approach. Jenna reached up with her left arm to stroke the snow-white marking on the nose of her chestnut mare. "No riding today," she smiled. "Your step's not light enough for these ribs."

Stolley appeared in the back door of the stable, pitchfork in hand. "You're all right?" he signed quickly.

"Yes," she assured him. "But I cannot ride to your mother's house." She ran her hand along her rib cage and grimaced. "I need her to help serve at the dinner tonight."

He nodded. "I'll go. She can tend to your side."

"If we have time." Jenna shrugged.

She returned to the house with the intention of confronting her father. This sudden dinner plan of his was completely out of character. For years now he had been an addled old fool of an earl whose wits had died along with his wife. They had even been politely shunned in social circles out of deference to her father's "condition." Now the Thorntons were about to host an intimate dinner party. Why?

In the main hall Jenna reached for the frayed rope of the bell tassel and rang for Eaton.

"Is Father dressed?" she asked.

"He rode out to the cemetery, m'lady."

"Tell him I need to see him when he returns," she said, irritated. "I'm going to rest."

She made her way up the stairs and past the room of her half brother Phillip. He was sleeping late as usual. The card games and claret had taken their toll again. She wondered just how much Phillip had lost this time. He was ruining their monthly accounts. As Jenna scrimped and juggled tenants' needs against the disrepair of the manor house, Phillip dallied at the gaming table—and, it was rumored, with an Italian-born tart in Lancaster who loved fine frocks.

Her side ached. Her head hurt. And her ledger would be bloody red by the time Phillip ended this mouth. Damn him!

She opened his door and went straight to the windows of the sour-smelling room. She yanked open the dusty muslin curtain liners and let the light glare white against his puffy eyelids.

"For God's sake, Jen," he moaned.

"How much did you lose this time, Phillip?" She fought to control the anger.

"Lower your voice," he mumbled. "'Twas only a few pounds." One hand scratched sleepily at his tousled brown hair.

"How much is 'a few'? And when are the notes due?"

"God, what a shrew you are! No wonder you're not married yet! I don't remember how much. It was mostly Connell's win. Go ask him how much I owe! Good Lord, my head's rolling. Send Eaton with a powder for me." He sank back down into his pillows, looking more like a debauched clerk of forty than the twenty-nine-year-old heir to an earl's estate.

She closed the door, trembling with rage, and went down the hall to her room. Her brother's friendship with the greedy House of Parrish was unforgivable. Phillip waved the relationship like a red flag in every conversation. Jenna had long ago learned to talk with her brother only when necessary, in short sessions. It was the only way she could keep her temper.

She slammed the door to her room and stood still, breathing deeply, controlling anger and anxiety about the toll Phillip had added to his debt with his dismal skill at cards last night.

She walked to the window and waited for the room to work its peace. Her bedroom was a private, airy haven in the musty expanse of the Elizabethan manor. Light, ivory-patterned stripes were printed on yellow-flowered wallpaper. A light blue canopy with white ruffled trim hung from her corniced four-poster bed. A gleaming writing table of inlaid rosewood and gilt drawers took the wall nearest the window. A huge oak armoire loomed in the darkest corner of the room, its plain wood doors trimmed with etched bronze mounts. Her washstand was a four-legged chest of drawers with the porcelain basin sunk in the top.

A long wooden trunk with battered deerskin hinges sat in another corner. The maid Ellen insisted on calling it Jenna's dowry chest. But Jenna called it her book trunk and stored the cherished books and ship's diaries of her grandfather, Papa John.

The room showed little clutter. "Too much space in 'ere," Ellen always accused. "Looks like you 'aven't got money enough for bric-a-brac."

"We ''aven't,'" Jenna sighed, sitting down on her bed. She let her head sink back into the pillows and laid her right arm across her stomach, just as the ruffian had placed it, lessening the tension on her rib. It felt better that way.

As gradually as the sun warms a chill window, Jenna grew aware of a strange tenseness taking hold in her belly at the point where he had straddled her.

Her outrage returned, and along with it the feeling of his weight across her, a massive warmth holding her snugly against the ground. The feeling traveled up to her face and sent color to her cheeks.

Oppressive, arrogant, he had touched her bare skin. Without encouragement. Or permission. Touched her as simply as if she were a common chit.

As if it were the natural thing to do.

She closed her eyes against the memory of his dark, searching face. He was, she knew, a man who would always do the natural thing.

Sleep was a long time coming.

* * *

In his bedroom four miles away, Hutton Parrish pulled his eyes away from the window. He had been gazing long and hard across the lowland of miners' cottages to the rolling ridge beyond which Glen Manor sat hidden.

He looked down at the naked woman he held pressed to the wall.

"She's preparing for guests, no doubt," he said, thrusting hard. His slim fingers let loose the edge of the fine brocade curtain. It fell back toward the pane with a heavy flap, like a cupboard door clicking shut.

Carolina's moan was small and distant to him, as always. But her flesh remained firm, fresh and near. He rammed again and her body flattened against the wall, his weight bearing hard. A small plaster lion teetered on the shelf near her head.

"My true love would not cry so soon," he said, close to her ear, pulling back a lock of her copper hair. "Would she?"

Carolina, her chest barely able to rise with each breath, could not shake her head. "No," she whispered, barely audible.

"So you are not performing well for me, are you?"

She swallowed, her mouth open to catch a shallow breath.

He thrust again and again. "Answer me!" he hissed in a grimace that placed his yellow teeth smooth against her pale cheek.

Her full red lips formed the word "no."

He relaxed then, and watched the tears squeeze like luminous gems from the edge of her tightly closed eyes. He licked upward to catch the sweet salt, marveling, as always, at the perfect temperature the body provides for its effluents.

He released the pressure on her. "Then you will come to me again tonight."

He did not wait for her affirmation. He stroked his hand slowly down her perfectly rounded, silken flank and withdrew his weight. The anger began to ebb, along with the deep ache inside the delicate sac that fed his desire.

He would wait. Slowly he pulled her near and embraced her. "You may get dressed, my love," he whispered. "I am finished."

Her eyes glistening, Caroline stepped away and raised her arms expectantly toward him.

He smiled and picked up the pearl-handled stiletto that lay on the small guéridon table by the bed.

The slim blade slipped between the rawhide strips that bound her wrists, and with one upward twist of Hutton's wrist, the razor edge freed her hands.

She moved quickly from him and grabbed her gown from the back of a chair.

"No, Carolina," Parrish said. "You know better. Begin with the stockings." He went to the bow-front chest near the fireplace and picked up a ruby-studded cigarette case. From here he could see her reflected in the gilded pier glass mirror above the mantel. "And go slowly," he reminded, striking a match and lighting a long, thin cigarette.

She stepped stiffly into the flickering glow of the hearth, her rounded curves catching the uneven shadows. Rose-colored stockings hung limp from her hand. She turned her back to him. The fresh, symmetrical finger marks high on her buttocks were highlighted by the fire.

He shook his head slightly and folded his tall, naked body into the soft tuftedness of a silver-blue armchair. "You amuse me, Carolina." Thin lips sucked forcefully on the slender tube, then pursed in a long exhalation. "Always hoping to force some conscience into the aftermath, my dear? All women do. But, in actuality, we are all where we choose to be. Are we not?" His eyes waited for hers to look up.

She nodded once, quickly.

Parrish smiled. "Good."

There was a sudden pounding at the great oak door of the bedroom. "Father!" It was his son, Connell.

Parrish rose unhurriedly from his chair and went through the anteroom. He unbolted the door. Connell entered, wineglass in hand, cravat untied and his day coat half off his shoulders.

He averted his eyes from his father's naked body. "The strikers have meat again, damn them!" he said, taking Parrish's chair in front of the undressed girl. "A joint of beef, fer Christ's sake!"

Parrish drew close to him. "Get up, Connell. You're interrupting."

The pudgy, red-haired Connell angrily jerked himself out of the chair. "For God's sake, put on some trousers."

Parrish sat on his bed and smiled. "Come and help me, Carolina." The girl held each trouser leg and helped him button the waist above slim, hard hips. "It's amazing to think I sired a prudish Puritan, isn't it?" He stroked the girl's long, straight hair.

"And how do you expect me to win the hand of Lady Jenna with as sordid a reputation as yours?" Connell stared into the fire and downed the last of his wine.

"My reputation is selectively sordid. I'm very discriminating. That's why I chose Lady Jenna for you."

Connell watched his father select a large white overshirt and pull it over his narrow, firmly muscled chest. The man was fifty-five and fleeced as white as a new lamb. Yet he was more virile a specimen than Connell had ever been.

Connell smashed his wineglass into the grate. Carolina flinched as she quickly pulled a petticoat over her head.

"You've chosen Jenna not for *me*, but for *us*." Connell whirled to face his father. "For the land she'll bring, for the earl's heirs she'll bear. We keep Phillip so sotted and debt-ridden he'll never marry. Jenna's the next step on the ladder of nobility you cherish so much. And she will bring us Shadow Glen. Everything, everything depends on Jenna!"

"And she despises us. I know." Parrish calmly lit another dark cigarette.

"With good reason," Connell muttered.

His father's voice grew soft and sinuous, a tone that Connell knew and hated. "There is no evidence to link us with her mother's death. Lady Thornton took her own life."

"But you—"

"A woman does not die of that," Parrish laughed.

"The old bugger knows, Father."

"But the earl cannot prove it. It's the advantage of the peerage. You cannot be lightly accused."

"But she doesn't want me. And it's because of you."

The grim-lipped lord walked over to his son and grabbed him by the shirtfront. "People change, you idiot! They forget. Especially when a crisis appears. We hold Phillip's notes in the palm of our hand. We will bargain for Jenna and Shadow Glen."

Connell pushed his father's hand away. "Have you forgotten the miners?" he asked through set teeth. "What will happen if the new inspection act passes?"

A nervous tic began to pulse at the edge of his father's slim jaw. "It won't," Parrish said. "We will break the strike. With two hundred farmhands from the south. And it'll only cost us a week's pay for each. Our own filthy moles will run screaming back to work to save their jobs."

"And at a half cut in their pay, no doubt." Connell grabbed the neck of a crystal claret bottle on the bureau.

Parrish smiled. "You understand more about business than I give you credit for, Connell." He pulled the bell rope next to the ornate, burnished panels of the bedstead and summoned his valet.

"There's something you must know, Father." Connell clicked Parrish's gold cigarette case closed and lit the slender tube of expensive Turkish tobacco. "If I win her, I will not share her."

Parrish gazed thoughtfully out the window, seeming unconcerned. "I share with you, Connell," Parrish smiled.

"Jenna is different."

"Yes, she is," Parrish said, eyes on the horizon of Glen Manor. "Quite special."

"Bequeathing me the bed of a submissive whore is not largesse, Father. Generosity is not an attribute either of us care to claim." Connell exhaled, lost in thought. "She will be mine."

"I see." Parrish reached for the pocket watch he had looped over the florid scrollwork of his writing desk.

Inwardly, he smiled. By the time Jenna joined the Parrish household, he would have something precious for which Connell might trade.

His future.

Chapter 3

"Jenna. Wake up." The older woman lightly grasped Jenna's arm.

"Leona?" Jenna sat up slowly, brushing wisps of dark hair from her cheeks. "Is Father back yet?"

"No," Leona said, climbing a small wooden step stool to sit by Jenna's side. "So the deer wasn't the only one felled by the hunt."

Jenna smiled at her friend. "I don't know who attacked me. Some vagabond. I'm fine. Except for a bruised rib." Jenna winced as she reached back to undo the buttons of her dress.

"Let me help," Leona said.

"He claimed to be a gentleman of the shire. At the least he was someone who took my masquerade very seriously. He thought he was nabbing a poacher."

"He was."

"Oh, not you, too! I can hardly defend my actions to my own cook, let alone a good friend. I was so foolish. I nearly got Stolley in trouble. He saved me."

"I know." Leona smiled away the apology in Jenna's voice. "Let's see what we can do for that ache in your side."

Jenna peeled her dress from her shoulders and then removed her thin chemise. Leona bent to examine the swelling.

"You're right. It's not broken. But I'll need some strips to bind you tightly. And the time to do it in. Cook's calling for somebody to help her orchestrate this madness."

"A corset will be support enough for tonight," Jenna said. "Then you can tie me up after the grand dinner. I'll plead a monstrous headache brought on by all the activity, and retire early. Very ladylike."

"Are you sure?"

Jenna nodded.

"At least soak it in some cool water. It'll help the swelling. And for God's sake don't let Ellen pull the stays too tight."

"Leona?"

"Yes?" She turned in the doorway, a trim composed figure in black serving dress and immaculate white apron. Her soft gray hair was pulled back into a classic chignon.

"Thank you for doing this. It's not something that belongs to your station in life. . . ."

"Good work is beneath no one's station, Jenna. And you know the money will be welcome." She smiled and left.

Thank God for Leona, Jenna thought as she edged slowly off the bed. She had been the only steady rock in Jenna's life since Lady Thornton's suicide.

Though unshakably calm and quiet, Leona Brockmeir had endured a less than tranquil life, Jenna knew. Disowned by her father, a gentleman, for falling in love with a working-man, Leona had long ago shed an existence of drawing-room chatter and boat rides on the lake at her Yorkshire home. She had run away with a house carpenter to live in a small cottage.

"Was it worth it?" Jenna once asked. It was a bold question, one that had burned in Jenna ever since she had been pulled behind brocade curtains and thoroughly kissed by a young architect at her cousin's ball.

Leona had stopped peeling a turnip and looked at her young friend. "He gave me a freedom that was priceless. No one can judge its worth but me."

Jenna took Leona's thin hand.

"Someday you'll have the chance to judge for yourself," Leona said. "When the time comes, go slowly."

"As you did?" Jenna asked.

"Feed the fire in the cookstove," Leona smiled. "You should be making bread, not indelicate queries."

Curious, thought Jenna as the maid Ellen dropped a soft chemise over her head. The judicious Leona had made a rash decision in the matter of love, and soon after Stolley's birth she had lost the husband for whom she had given up so much. Yet she was richer in her lonely love than any married couple Jenna knew. Except for her father and moth—

Jenna shook her head to dispel the image of her mother's face and set a cane-backed chair as near to the fire as she dared. There she combed black, tangled tresses still damp from the bath. Ellen laid out her petticoats, good stockings and shoes.

Then it was time for the corset. "Your waist's barely the size of a dinner plate," Ellen chattered, lacing the stays. "Seems to me a body oughtn't put 'erself through all the torture with a figure like yours. 'Specially since you hardly ever wear low-neck gowns. For a slight-figured girl you've got a nice bit o' trim at the top. You shouldn't let it go to waste."

"Don't be impertinent! My green silk is appropriate and serviceable. And, please"—she tried not to scream as Ellen pulled the corset strings tight—"loosen it so that I can breathe. If I'm as shapely as you say," she breathed out raggedly, "then you don't have to truss me up like one of Cook's roast chickens."

Ellen giggled. "That better, mum?"

"Much. Now I won't faint into my soup."

Ellen opened the door to the cedar-lined armoire to find the tailored high-necked silk her mistress preferred to wear to dinner.

Jenna sat down with relief on the tufted cushion of her dressing-table stool. She heard Ellen exclaim.

"What's wrong?"

"The green silk has a tear in the waist."

"Ellen! You were to make sure it was ready."

"I pressed it after you wore it at Christmas, mum."

Jenna sighed. What next?

"What about the new blue frock your uncle sent from London? The latest fashion, mum. You'll look so grand."

"All right. It doesn't matter," Jenna said.

The servant carefully slid the dress over Jenna's head.

"If I didn't know better, I would think you had planned this."

"Pshaw. 'Twas fated for you to wear this frock tonight," Ellen replied, fastening the bodice. Jenna could not see the devilish grin on her broad face.

Quickly, before Jenna could look in the mirror, Ellen began brushing and smoothing Jenna's hair.

"The neckline seems very low. I—"

"It's not low atall, compared with what the gaudy Lady Saundra'll be sportin' tonight."

"Ellen!"

"Sorry. Just tilt your head back a little. You've got your Irish grandmother's hair, you know. So beautiful and thick, it's a handful, mum. Got a mind of its own."

"Pull it back and pin it up and be done with it. I'm awfully tired."

"I'll only be a minute. You've got to have something different tonight. I've got a gift with hair. Mrs. Searle has me dress hers, you know. Here now, we'll just sweep it back and to the side like this and then the ringlets will hang right over your shoulder like a goddess's. Don't forget your necklace."

Ellen fastened the strand of pearls around Jenna's neck. She stood back. "Ready, mum." The servant's eyes softened and met Jenna's in the mirror. "You're such a grand young lady. Take a look at yourself."

Jenna stood up, marveling at how much better her side felt supported by the corset. A little snug, but it would be fine.

Then she looked in the full-length mirror and was mildly surprised to see a stranger.

The young woman was elegantly dressed in light turquoise, a color which made her eyes deepen to sea blue. The gown swooped low off her creamy shoulders to a froth of soft, ruffled lace which barely covered the upward swell of her bosom. The dress came in at her waist, then flared outward, the curve of her hips accentuated by layers of starched petticoat underneath. The bustle was small, designed just to enhance the elegant drape of the modest train. Light, puffy sleeves tucked daintily into pearl-button cuffs. Her hair cascaded to the side in a mass of black ringlets.

"You're beautiful, m'lady," Ellen sighed. "Mark my words. That high-nosed Sir Ian will be struck dumb as a stone. You wait and see."

Jenna awaited the arrival of her guests in the archival mustiness of her father's upstairs library. She had hoped for a chance to talk to him. But he had returned too late from his ride.

"I'm not ready! Can't talk now," he muttered, running his pale, puffy hands through the gray frizz which even Eaton's hair grease hadn't managed to tame.

"The baronet and his brother will be here soon," the earl said. "There's important business to discuss." He unbuttoned his vest coat and checked his pocket watch.

"What business do you mean, Father?"

"Where's my good silk cravat? Eaton! Where is that man?"

"He's downstairs readying the house for the guests you foisted on us! Why? What's so important about the new master of Stonebridge?" She grabbed his hands and stood in front of him, forcing his attention on her.

His nervous brown eyes seemed to still for a moment. He glanced at the door and then pulled Jenna over to the window.

"It's part of the plan," he whispered.

"Plan?"

"To save Glen Manor and the miners."

"Whose plan, Father? How can you save both? Who have you—?"

"Shhhhh! Jenna, my dear Jenna, I'm going to save you, too! Everything's going to be all right. Finally. After three long years, I'm going to avenge your mother's murder. Those blackguards will be hurt to their very core. The Bandit will finally come and Hutton Parrish will be destroyed." Arthur Thornton had become very calm in his speech, which made his statements all the more shocking to Jenna.

"For God's sake, what are you talking about? The Bandit? The plan? What do you mean? Everything's *not* all right!

How can Glen Manor survive when Phillip's debts keep rising and we cannot pay!"

"Phillip is not important. What he does is not important. He's not the only Parrish spy in our house. You are important. I'm doing this for you, dear one. And for your mother, whom I loved with all my heart. Oh, Jenna, I have to be so careful tonight."

There was a knock at the door. "Shhhhh." The nervous flutter of his eyelids returned and he pulled his vest coat halfway off, then answered the door.

"Shall I summon Timman to help you finish dressing, sir?" Eaton said.

"Yes, yes," Lord Thornton said, leaving the room. Then he turned quickly. "I'm so excited, Jenna," he smiled. "It's going to be a wonderful evening. You look so lovely. You are my pride and my joy." He kissed her forehead and roughly wiped a tear from his cheek.

When he left her alone in the study, Jenna felt drained. She had no energy to think or to feel. Her father was mad. He had to be. What else could his nonsense mean? Why else would he begin to forge ties with a high-placed neighbor he did not know? How could he save the strikers when he didn't even have the wits to recognize that Jenna had smuggled food and clothing to them for weeks—all in his name —making sure they knew that Lord Arthur Thornton was still their ally?

Oh, Father, Jenna sighed as she gazed out the window, how can you save the manor? You have lost yourself.

Beyond the ancient oaks that guarded the fenced entrance to Glen Manor, she could see a black coach drawn by four matched whites churn dust on the roadway. Two riders followed behind. On the carriage itself she counted a driver clad in full-skirted coat and two footmen with powdered, pigtail wigs. He had money for show, this new, titled Stone-bridge.

Perhaps her father had a mad plan to borrow some.

"They've arrived," Leona said. She stepped inside the library and closed the door. "But something's amiss with Stolley. He signaled danger for you. You must be careful tonight."

"The young squires of Stonebridge may be dandified and arrogant, but surely not dangerous," Jenna said. "Why, Robert rarely stays at the country manor long enough to remember his housekeeper's name, and the older brother left England years ago after a terrible fight with his father. He only returned to assume the title when his father died this past winter. It could have been their female companion who set poor Stolley trembling. They say the Lady Saundra O'Rourke is a devastating beauty."

"Stolley was not shaken by beauty. He was frightened— The door! Receive them on the landing. And please be careful." Leona kissed her quickly on the cheek and hurried down the hallway to the servants' stairs.

Jenna waited until she heard the commotion of Eaton and her father greeting the guests in the front hall. She descended to the first landing and waited there, hand poised on the glistening cherrywood bannister, a study, she thought wryly, in the cool reserve of Queen Victoria herself.

"My dear Jenna!" her father said loudly. All eyes raised to her. Jenna smiled warmly, waiting to receive the group as they ascended to the drawing room. She glanced from Saundra in her peacock finery, to Robert, a dandy and friend of her brother's, and at last to the tall, dark man she had not met.

Her heart began to pound.

Carelessly, the man threw topcoat and hat across the servant's outstretched arms. He immediately took the stairs two at a time, frowning and slowing his climb as he grew near to study her.

"Whoa there, Ian!" his brother called, laughing, from the bottom of the steps.

Jenna swallowed.

His eyes were dark as mink, but they held no sign of softness. They fixed on her face, demanding her attention.

His black hair was not disheveled now. It was brushed back, smooth, correct. Nor were his clothes torn and poor. The brushed-velvet vest and light wool pants were well-cut, his formal dinner jacket perfectly tailored to broad shoulders and narrow waist.

His firm, square jaw, so bristly this morning, was clean-shaven, his sideburns trimmed but full. Jenna glanced once at his lips, held tight together. They gave the fine, angled planes of his face a grim look.

She closed her eyes. He had caught her weaponless now. Only strength of will kept her rooted to the landing.

"It is you." The intensity of his voice carried no farther than her ears. "Upright, you look different to me." His gaze was level, hard. "I believe we have a kiss to finish, my thief."

Before she could slap his face, he stepped backward and bowed. "Lady Jenna Ashley Thornton, mistress of Glen Manor, I presume?" said the vagabond whose hand had roamed inside her bodice that morning.

"See how unmannered my elder brother is!" Robert Stonebridge called from the bottom of the stairs. "Rushing ahead to steal the lady's attention! Ian's afraid I will awe you with my more civilized charm!" He crooked an arm for the smiling Lady Saundra and ascended slowly.

"I am smitten, m'lady," Ian Stonebridge said softly. "Quite literally." His gloved hand reached back to slide gingerly down the back of his head. "Your friend—and I hope to meet him sometime—has a cowardly hand. But an effective aim."

His hand was outstretched, waiting for Jenna to place her right hand in his. His glance lingered on the swell of her breasts. Jenna's throat tightened as she remembered the careful pressure of his fingers searching underneath a light shirt.

"M'lady?" he smiled.

Robert approached. "He doesn't bite, Lady Jenna," he joked.

"That remains to be seen, Robert," she smiled. "Sir Ian?" She extended her arm, appearing gracious and unconcerned. But Stonebridge could feel the tension in her small hand as his lips touched her skin.

Phillip emerged from a downstairs room and heartily yelled his greetings to Robert and the Lady Saundra.

In the noisy distraction, Jenna pulled her hand down, away from the lips of the arrogant baronet. But Stonebridge held firm and watched her wince when the sore muscles of her rib tightened in response.

He frowned. "You did not see a physician?"

"It's my turn, you selfish renegade!" Robert interrupted. He had turned back to her, tsking at Phillip's lusty eagerness to escort Lady Saundra up the steps. Gracefully, he gave Jenna's hand a light peck and, with a self-mocking flair, raised his elbow high, hand extended. "Will you rescue me and take my arm, dear lady? I fear your brother has stolen my companion."

The group gathered somewhat awkwardly on the stairs, waiting for Jenna to lead the way to the drawing room. Apprehensively, she raised her right arm high enough to place it atop Robert's. With a theatrical smile of triumph at his titled brother, he covered her hand with his. "Shall we go?"

Jenna gathered her skirt to take the stair, but Robert stepped one higher, pulling her arm upward. It was too much. Jenna gave a small cry and jerked away, stumbling backward into the arms of Ian Stonebridge.

"Jenna!" her father cried.

"Excuse me, Lord Thornton, for my sudden hold on your lovely daughter. Just now she made brief mention of her riding accident today, which made her hesitant to take my hand a moment ago."

"I am so sorry!" Robert said, all joviality gone.

"Please," Jenna said in a low voice, forcefully pushing herself away from Stonebridge, "I am fine. Please proceed to the drawing room. It is nothing. I apologize for the trouble. . . ."

"My sister, the stoic," Phillip chided. "Come, Lady Saundra. Jenna will rally her considerable strength as usual, and beat us intellectually to a pulp with her wicked tongue. We must get a head start on the claret."

"Forgive the impropriety," Jenna said evenly to Stonebridge, her look clearly indicating whose misstep she found unacceptable.

Her color had returned with a vengeance, Stonebridge mused. It brought a fighting flush to pale, fine cheekbones set high in an oval face.

"I shall escort the lady," Stonebridge said quietly, urging the group ahead to the drawing room.

Robert smiled once more in apology. "This has been an unfortunate day for my brother, too, you know." He turned to the earl and they climbed the steps. "He was set upon by thieves in the streets of Turton Bottoms last night. Knocked unconscious. He was somewhat disoriented—after a long evening in the card room, you know. They surprised him—"

As the others entered the drawing room, Stonebridge extended his hand.

"Don't touch me," Jenna said.

"So you told me before."

"You didn't tell them you were chasing a 'poacher' in Shadow Glen this morning. Why not?"

"I trust my instincts and lie accordingly."

"And quickly. I—I must thank you," she said slowly. "The story of the riding accident rang quite true."

"You wished it were true, little thief."

"I am not your diminutive anything. Leave me now."

"No," he said, taking her left elbow firmly in his hand. "I will see you safely up the steps. You were foolish to think your corset would serve—"

"God's eyes on you in hell! You do not have leave to remark on my undergarments or speculate on the state of my—my—person! And I refuse to accompany you to the drawing room!"

He released her arm. "As you wish. I accede to your tongue and your temper. For now. But if you do not join us in ten minutes, you will have a dexterous 'vagabond' in your bedchamber tending the injury. You have my word."

"Your word? The word of a mannerless ruffian!"

"Perhaps," he smiled strangely. "But you may not dismiss yourself from this most—interesting—evening. Fate—and your father—have thrust us together, mademoiselle, in more ways than one," he said wearily, his eyes closed, rubbing his temples with thumb and forefinger. "And, of all our meetings to come, that brief tryst on the forest floor may be the least painful of all our exchanges. Ten minutes." He bowed and walked slowly up the stairs.

She held herself erect until the dark tails of his evening coat were out of sight. Then she slowly sat down on the steps.

Stolley had been right. Danger.

Chapter 4

"The wounded horsewoman returns," Phillip said, pouring his sister a glass of sherry as she entered the drawing room.

"Are you feeling better?" Robert rose.

"Yes, thank you. I apologize for the incident," she said, nodding at her guests. Her glance carefully excluded Stonebridge.

"Oh, no need to apologize, my dear," said Lady Saundra from her seat on the couch. "'Twas a most novel way to draw attention away from the grand entrance of a guest who had spent a fortune on her finery and all day in preparation —all to no avail," she mocked sadly.

"I give you leave to try my method," Jenna said with a smile. "But you may find it's better to be temporarily ignored than thrown for a fall."

"No one ignores Lady Saundra for long, do they, my sweet?" Phillip said, walking over to the bosomy blonde whose voluminous skirts filled the brocade sofa.

"Sit here, Jenna," her father said, pointing to a faded, blue-fringed armchair near the fireplace. "I think we should call Dr. Falmon tomorrow."

"Thank you, Father. And no thank you to Dr. Falmon."

"Jenna hates physicians," Phillip said. "Goes back to when her mother died in—"

"Phillip!" her father warned.

Jenna stared at the earl. It was the first time in years her father had uttered an admonition to her brother.

The edgy silence that followed amused Stonebridge.

He stepped forward casually with a smooth admission. "I must confess that I was trained for the 'hated' profession, Lady Jenna. Studied in France. I found myself more interested in scientific study than actual treatment."

"Too much blood and guts, eh, Stonebridge?" Phillip asked.

"No." The tall man eyed him and sipped his wine. "Too many people in pain."

"There are many people in pain right now in our own valley," Jenna said coolly. "The striking families are malnourished. Their children are succumbing to disease. Regardless of whatever stand you take on the rights of laborers, it would be a sign of Christian charity to share the excesses of your kitchen with the poor."

"That would be false kindness. If obstinate strikers need food, they should return to work in the mines." His black-brown eyes met hers in challenge.

"Their stubbornness is the only attribute that allows them to survive the hellish conditions at the Parrish Colliery. Perhaps you would want to talk to them sometime. Purely in the interests of scientific research, of course. You could study how the foul, mephitic gases affect the twelve-year-old boys who work in the pit. Learn how the constant cold and damp cripple the joints. Marvel how the spine curves after twelve hours of picking and digging in a shaft just four feet high."

"What awful things to talk about," gasped Lady Saundra.

"Despite her quite feminine and charming appearance tonight, Jenna actually has the brain of a democrat," Phillip drawled.

There was silence. It was a dangerous label, even to be made in jest.

"Surely," Jenna replied, calmly smoothing the skirt of her gown, "you can distinguish my humane concern for the poor and downcast from the anarchic threat of democracy, Phillip. Even you, with your limited reading, know the Bible."

"Don't worry, Phillip!" Robert interrupted. "Even I have found the book a trifle dreary as literature."

Lady Saundra tittered. "Robert! I shall tell the vicar you said that Sunday next!"

The group began to chuckle lightly, awkwardly, grateful for a lessening of the tension.

"Let's discuss something interesting," Lady Saundra suggested. She opened her green eyes wide to gaze at Stonebridge. "Like Ian's travels to America and the islands."

"My brother's actually had a hard time finding the gentleman's calling that suits him," Robert said. "He even tried the military at father's insistence. Lasted a few months. Said the country's defense was led by insipid drunkards and babyish peacocks who didn't know the end of a cannon from—"

"Robert!" Lady Saundra giggled.

"Well, from anything," he grinned.

Phillip downed the contents of his glass and slapped it on the table. "I was a lieutenant in the infantry, Stonebridge. I have a different view." He reached for the decanter.

"As seen through the bottom of a wine bottle," Jenna said. She met her brother's eyes, not bothering to veil her anger.

"Interesting," Stonebridge mused. "While I was out of the country, family feuds must have become acceptable drawing-room melodrama."

The group again went silent as color rose hotly to Jenna's face. She stood and faced the tall baronet. "My apologies," she said, her voice sharp-edged. "I beg the understanding of a man whose own feud made him run simpering from the reality of a situation and desert his father."

The dark-haired man moved toward her like a descending hawk.

"Ian—" Robert interjected.

Stonebridge stopped in front of her, so close that she could smell the sweet hint of wine on his lips, so close she could see the pulse at his sun-browned throat. Details that spoke too intimately for comfort.

Uneasy but unafraid, she looked up at him. Her breath caught in her throat as she sensed the contained anger behind his words.

"A cruel bite, for a lady."

"But befitting the provocation," she said softly.

Slowly, he reached for her hand. His warm fingers enclosed the small ones which lay curled round the delicate stem of a crystal cup. He pulled her wrist upward, just high enough for her to feel the twinge of impending pain in her side, then he stopped.

Softly, he clinked his glass against hers. "I salute your tongue and your courage. May only one of them be blunted."

Phillip guffawed and the group followed in uneasy laughter. "Not many recover from Jenna's lash so adeptly," Phillip grinned. "I could have used your tutelage over the years. Where've you been, anyway?"

"Traveling," Stonebridge said.

"The rumors had you privateering in the Caribbean and trading in America. A little mercantile-minded for landed gentry, wouldn't you say?"

"Depends on how averse a gentleman is to having money. I've expanded the family resources. Our heirs will have more, not less. We've no debts. That's not a position everyone can boast of."

Phillip choked on his wine.

Eaton appeared in the doorway. "Her ladyship is served."

Stonebridge approached Jenna. "My lady?" Carefully, he offered Jenna his arm.

She hesitated, weighing what effect her refusal would have on her father's expectations of the evening. Then she nodded once. "Sir."

They walked out, chatting woodenly, a striking couple. The conservatively dressed privateer, dark from the sun, and the fair, blue-eyed Jenna. Both unconventional to a fault.

Lord Thornton coughed nervously and wiped his forehead with a crumpled handkerchief. God help me, he thought, fiddling with the chain of his pocket watch. The plan depended entirely on their ability to get along.

As Stonebridge and Jenna descended the stairs well ahead of the others, the baronet leaned close to her. "We must talk privately after dinner."

"Impossible," she said icily.

"By the bloom in the silver locket, make it possible," he said.

Jenna stopped, her hand grasping the polished bannister. "Who gave you those words?" she asked. Her voice seemed small to her, as distant as the memory buried three summers ago. She had taken a single, stunted rosebud from the funeral wreath on her mother's casket before the death carriage bore her mother slowly up the hill to Shadow Glen. And she had pressed the dead bloom carefully into the frame of Lady Thornton's favorite locket.

"Your father," Stonebridge said softly, aware of the hurt

that moistened her eyes. "He said to utter those words if I ever needed to gain your trust."

"He is surely a witless old man if he entrusts such precious words to a blackguard like you!" she said, stepping down to the first landing.

Stonebridge quickly, firmly, grasped her arm. "He is not as muddled as you think. And his plans are very delicate. He needs you," Stonebridge said, beginning their descent to the ground floor. "And, for God's sake, will you pretend we're chatting socially? Eaton is a Parrish spy and he's watching every move you make."

The information began to overwhelm her. She reached out to Stonebridge for support, and Eaton, from his stance at the bottom of the stairs, saw a touching scene—Stonebridge protectively supporting the beautiful Jenna, helping her descend the stairs.

"Thank you, Sir Ian," Jenna said, removing his hand. "I fear the throw from my horse hurt my balance as well as my arm."

Stonebridge bowed and they both followed a grim-faced Eaton into the frescoed dining room.

Jenna smoothed the linen napkin on her lap and glanced at the baronet. I will have to meet with him, she thought.

He turned and smiled, as if in agreement.

The meal began with sea turtle soup, a great delicacy. Then followed soft-shell crabs and sweetbreads in a rich sauce. The game course was next, young pheasant with spinach.

Although convention forbade the guests from praising the meal, it was obvious that they enjoyed it. Cook truly had outdone herself this time, Jenna thought. The wily Irishwoman had obviously learned more from her French bantam than she would ever admit.

Thank heaven. Jenna's eyes shut for a moment. She had no energy to worry about the dinner. She was seated next to the menacing baronet, who had gained her father's trust. And he knew more about her own household than she. Eaton was a spy and her father was puttering about with a risky scheme of vengeance.

Jenna found herself toying with the bird, her stomach tensely awaiting the next course, the fillet of "beef."

Leona smiled reassuringly as she offered a serving dish to Jenna. Small, delicate cutlets lay in a hollandaise sauce. As she cut the meat, she looked up to find Stonebridge watching her.

"A marvelous texture and delicate taste," he said. "May I ask what cut of beef it is?"

"Cook had been saving this new French recipe for a special occasion," Jenna said carefully. "Medallions of veal Versailles."

"We are honored," said Lady Saundra, stabbing the last tender cutlet on her plate. "Do you think your cook would part with the recipe? You are so fortunate to have a foreign culinary influence in your kitchen. The last time I visited Paris I could barely keep myself from overindulging. . . ."

"At the dinner table, I presume?" Phillip broke in.

"Phillip! You're wicked!" Lady Saundra admonished him.

"And that's his most appealing trait!" said Robert.

Jenna listened politely to the banter. Robert was a quick-witted tease who pounced constantly on the conversational gaffes of Phillip and Saundra. Stonebridge was quiet, unconcerned with making dinner chitchat, no matter how hard Saundra tried to engage him.

"Saundra, don't bother," Robert teased. "Ian lived on a

lovely tropical island with—well, with company of his choosing. I have not yet reinitiated him to polite society."

"I find polite society very akin to muddy puddles, Lady Saundra," Stonebridge smiled, preoccupied. "I sidestep both when they're in my path." He drained his cup and looked at Jenna. "A marvelous dinner. My compliments to your cook. And to your gamekeeper." He gave a small smile.

Jenna nodded and rose. She and Saundra left the gentlemen to their port and cigars.

Lady Saundra gathered the drapes and ruffles of her full skirt in front of her and chattered happily as she and Jenna ascended to the drawing room.

Lady Saundra confided that she had been a bit leary of accepting tonight's invitation. Her father had been unable to escort her, and with Jenna's own father "ill" for so long, she was concerned about the propriety. But with the unpredictable Ian guaranteed to attend such an intimate affair, she just couldn't resist. "Robert and his brother are just like night and day. But rumor has it they're not even half brothers, you know."

Lady Saundra lowered her voice and chattered on. Ian's mother was an adultress, the gossips said, and Ian was not the old baronet's true son. But the old man had groomed him as heir all the same. Then they had a bitter fight when Ian was eighteen, and the young Stonebridge had left England suddenly—near death.

"I thought Ian was going to explode when you made that cheeky remark before dinner," Saundra said.

Jenna stiffened. "I was only responding to his provocation."

"But can you imagine? Thirteen years and he never once returned to see his father. Not until he was dead and gone," Saundra said, tsking. "But the old baronet did not disown

Ian as his son. And Robert's never pressed the case. Mysterious, isn't it?"

"Interesting," Jenna smiled. The corset bit persistently into her swollen rib. "Where do you gather all your— news?"

"Everywhere. On my calls to friends, after the church services, when I have the vicar's son to dinner. That young man knows everything about anybody. Just like his father. And he's got breathtaking eyes."

"Do you play, Saundra?" Jenna indicated the harpsichord, her voice tight. She grasped the top of a court cupboard for support. The throbbing ache was getting worse. The corset had to go.

"Rather badly."

"Well, I can't play at all tonight. In truth, I need to have a servant tend to my injury. Would you mind playing while I excuse myself? If the gentlemen rejoin us early, please tell them I shall be here directly."

"I'll practice a waltz I know," Saundra said, sitting down on the round, polished wood stool and carefully arranging the drape of her skirt.

"Thank you," Jenna said with her arm crooked across her stomach.

"Take your time," Saundra said with a thunderous, dissonant attempt at a tonic major chord. "This might take some time."

Jenna went to her bedroom to wait for Leona. She lit the oil lamp on her dressing table, but the draft from her open window blew out the flame, leaving Jenna with the bright moon light.

With careful contortions, she removed her gown. The corset knots were too intricate and out of reach. Jenna bent over her mirrored washstand and bathed her face in the clean water Ellen had left in the porcelain basin. The cool wetness streamed down the skin of her cheeks, a welcome awakening. The evening's events had created the feeling she was not on solid ground. The baronet's arrogant presence itself was enough to give her a sense she was slipping. She patted the hand towel to her cheeks with relief, then dabbed the soft curve of her neck.

The dark shape appeared suddenly behind her in the mirror. Jenna whirled and opened her mouth to scream.

The baronet's hand stilled the sound.

"Don't struggle. When you're calm, I'll remove my hand."

She nodded assent, eyes cold with anger and outrage.

"Let me remind you how devastating it would be for your reputation if you drew attention to my presence in your bedroom. Chemise and pantalets are fashionable for only one kind of entertaining."

He removed his hand slowly. Jenna's left hand caught him smartly on the cheek. "You madman," she hissed. "If you are caught in my bedroom it is you who will lose. Your prized bachelorhood will be forfeited. My father would force you to marry me!"

He stroked his cheek, one eyebrow raised. "There is more irony in the statement than you know. I am your intended. Your father accepted my offer for your hand."

"How ridiculous! Father would not do such a thing without my agreement!" she cried.

"Lower your voice. Else we'll be discovered tonight and wed in the morning. That's not what your father has in mind."

Jenna turned and marched to her armoire, snatching a dressing gown from the cedar-lined cupboard. "Pray tell, what does my father have in mind? And why did he not tell me himself!" Containing her anger, she tied the satin ribbon at her throat and sat down stiffly on the edge of a chair.

"You must let me bind your side while I explain," he said quietly.

Jenna could not summon more anger. She closed her eyes and bent her head wearily. "Are you without any sense? We are unchaperoned, two strangers in my bedchamber, talking about a nebulous affair I am somehow part of, and I am not even dressed! Does the impropriety not impress you?"

Stonebridge turned to face her fully. "Your state of dress does indeed impress me. But I have no time to appreciate it. To be truthful, neither you nor I give a hairy fig for the stuffy conventionalities we live by. And it is dangerous to run 'simpering from the reality of a situation,' as a wise but impertinent woman once told me. Our time is short. If you want answers, you will let me tend to your bruised rib. Your father wants you to ride with us tonight."

"Where?" she asked. Her eyes followed him to her bed, where he stripped a top sheet. With a long, sharp blade he pulled from his boot, he ripped the sheet into long strips.

"We go to meet a group of miners. We are resurrecting the famous Red Bow Bandit."

"To what end? Why a thief? Whom will he rob?" she asked, incredulous.

"He will relieve Hutton Parrish of a payroll being sent to recruit strikebreakers from the south. Stand up."

Jenna rose. His hands were at her throat, softly loosening the tie of her gown. Her hands flew to stop him, but the fabric slipped like cream from her shoulders.

She backed away. "You cannot do this. It is not right. My friend Leona will be here soon. She can—"

"She is not a physician," he said calmly, knife in hand. "Turn around."

Jenna had no time and no room to protest. He was upon her, grasping her two hands in one of his, turning her around gently and cutting the stays with one upward sweep of the knife. He pulled the corset away from her body. "Torturous contraption. Sit down." He indicated a straight-backed chair and laid the torn strips on the floor beside it.

Jenna bent and sank slowly into the chair.

"I don't suppose you would entertain a physician's request to remove your chemise?"

"You're not a physician. You're a thieving trader," she said wearily. "I'm paying for information and getting none."

"Information can be painful," he said softly. Stonebridge knelt on the floor before her and leaned close to reach around her waist.

Jenna pushed against his chest with both hands. "You are too close."

"I am your fiancé. I will be closer than this by the time our charade ends."

"It's not yet begun, you presumptuous fool." She let her hands slide away.

Ian took his chance to wind a length of bandage around her. "We will be publicly engaged from tomorrow onward. But it is a ruse to enrage Connell Parrish."

"I am bait in a snare?"

"You are the one woman Connell must have, or so your father says."

Involuntarily, Jenna shivered at the thought of marrying the pudgy-faced Parrish cur.

"Did I hurt you?" Stonebridge asked.

She shook her head. "The Parrishes are cruel. And clever. Is my father sure he wants to taunt them?"

"Yes," Stonebridge said, bringing a quilt from the bed and

draping it around her. "The earl says he has proof that Hutton Parrish caused your mother's death."

Jenna closed her eyes. With deliberation she repeated the litany she had carried for three years. "My mother took her life during a decline." She realized how vague that sounded. She had suffered a difficult miscarriage. There was no reason to imagine the Parrishes played any part.

Stonebridge resumed his bandaging. "Your mother committed suicide after returning from an alleged meeting with a Lancashire mine leader," he said. "The ensuing scandal—"

"Ruined both the mine safety act and my father's career," Jenna said bitterly. "You needn't remind me. I bear the loss daily. Our estate is struggling, my brother is debt-ridden, and my father plays a fool."

"And you? You're the Ice Maiden of the shire, famous for chilling the advances of peach-faced dandies who want to wed the befuddled earl's daughter," he said.

She pushed his hands away from her, voice hissing. "And you, you arrogant dog! How in the devil's name do you know so much? It's unthinkable that my father would confide to you what he withholds from me!"

Stonebridge looked down at his hand and raised a questioning eyebrow. Jenna's nails had pressed half circles in his palms.

Jenna frowned and looked away. "I'm sorry. . . ."

"Your father wants your knowledge of the scheme limited so that you will be innocent."

"That means there's a high probability he will be caught and prosecuted."

"But there is a better chance that Parrish will be branded a murdering thief. That is worth the risk."

Stonebridge felt her sharp intake of breath as he wound the strip nearer her breasts. She grew very still, like a marble statue. He was careful to keep his distance as he worked higher. She would bolt angrily, and soon, he thought. Stonebridge felt his own breath stilling, his hands slowing their pace.

"Why you?" she asked softly. "Why did my father choose you?"

"Your father and I chose each other," he said. "I have my own vengeance to seek."

"But why—?"

"There is no more time." He cinched the strips under her arm, near the curve of her breast. He was careful not to touch her filmy garment, nor the soft hidden crevice under her arm. A subtle lilac scent hovered around her body.

Uneasy, Jenna thought about the many ways she would destroy his reputation if he touched her improperly. But she found nothing wrong. His touch was gentle and sure, like that of a good surgeon. But as she glanced into dark, stormy eyes, she could not find the paternal disinterest of a doctor.

She began to lean back, away from him. "You are finished?"

His broad hands left the bandage and fell, one to each side, to fit in the sharp curve of her waist. "No," he said softly. "But I will go." His thumbs began to slide along the firm line of her stomach, the thin fabric of her chemise bunching and smoothing with the slide of his hand, tightening, thinning, until the material seemed erased and she could feel the warmth of his thumb under her breast.

She shook her head slowly, warning him, warning herself. He stopped but kept his hands firmly around her. Slowly he rose, bringing her with him.

"Do not trust me again," he said.

She stepped back from him.

"You are much too rare to be handled with diffidence."

His hand reached down as if to brush back a lock of her hair, but she stepped back. Stonebridge smiled, his lips a humorless twist caught in a stream of moonlight. "Virgins frighten so easily. I had forgotten," he said softly.

Jenna's hand rose to slap his face, but he grabbed her wrist and held it tightly in front of him. The silence gathered round them, enclosing. He searched her face, and her breath slowed in confusion as she tried to mask whatever he was seeking.

Slowly his lips lowered to the thin silken skin that pulsed inside her wrist. His mouth pressed against the delicate vein, and when he withdrew, his lips left a burning memory on her skin.

"We had best stay in public as long as we play this game," he said.

The knock at the door startled them both. "Jenna!" Leona called.

"In a moment!" Jenna said, keeping the panic out of her voice.

Stonebridge ran to the open window.

"You're mad!" Jenna whispered.

"Not as handy as a ship's rigging, but a drainpipe serves," he said, and climbed over the sill, finding a foothold on the dormer outside.

"I have been walking in the garden, airing my overindulgence in good port," Stonebridge said in a rush.

Her cheeks warm, Jenna quickly gathered her gown and opened the door for Leona.

"Please help me with the dress, Leona."

"But how did you bind your—?"

"It was very—difficult. Hurry. And remake the bed for me. I shall explain another time."

Chapter 5

Jenna leaned against the arched entry outside the drawing room, afraid to enter. She pushed her fingertips against her temples, tried to control the questions that churned in her mind. She wanted nothing more than to pull her father out of his precious social affair and demand answers.

How could Hutton Parrish have caused her mother's suicide? What proof could her father have? And why did she suddenly find herself blessed with a rich, arrogant suitor who was as stealthy and light-fingered as a rookery thief?

Even now the phantom pressure of the baronet's touch traveled across her stomach. She closed her eyes against the feeling, then entered the drawing room, a cool, careful mask over her feelings, a too-warm flush in her cheeks.

The baronet sat slumped in a chair, looking wine-worn and taking little notice of her presence. Relieved, Jenna stood talking with Robert. He told her of the new public bathhouse at Ashton-under-Lyne that boasted Turkish baths and an immense chimney built like an Italian bell tower. Jenna asked about the season's meager theater offerings in Liverpool and Manchester. She had not been to a gala since her mother's death and wondered what was current.

All went smoothly, until she shifted the conversation to something more important to her. Politics. Prime Minister

Gladstone was campaigning for abolition of the income tax. The government's levy was hardly significant: seven pence per pound for incomes over 150 pounds. "Can a government serve its citizens if it has no money?" Jenna put this question to Robert.

At that, the baronet rose from his chair.

As Ian approached Jenna, Robert excused himself and indicated he would rescue the earl from Phillip and Saundra, who were discussing London fashion. As Robert moved away, Jenna turned to follow him.

"Why do you flee?" Stonebridge asked, stepping in front of her.

"You are a bold and unnerving man," she answered curtly, quietly, smiling graciously when she saw Lady Saundra glance her way.

"Who is gamely trying to be a good match for you," Stonebridge said. "You have an invigorating intellect, which I applaud." His voice grew louder. "Except, of course, for your misguided views on the politics of industry. Explain to me how the colliery workers are furthering their lot by starving their families."

The self-satisfied tone in his voice sparked a cold anger in Jenna. His arrogance with women must be surpassed only by his blind insolence toward the rights of the less fortunate. "The miners sacrifice so much because they have so much to gain. Any fool can see that."

"Lord Parrish has a business to manage," Stonebridge said.

"Of course. And backs to break, pennies to pinch—"

"Jenna!" Phillip said, joining the argument. "I will not hear such criticism of our neighbor."

"It's not his business you defend, Phillip. It's the abundance of claret on his card table."

"Jenna!"

"You soft-bellied gentlemen know nothing of heaving a pickax and shovel for hours. You fill an iron cart with coal, yet you do not get paid because it is one stone underweight. You squires of the nobility know nothing of leaving God's sweet air and sinking four hundred feet under the ground to breathe the devil's gas. The stench and the mephitic vapors cause your lungs to ache. Your joints cramp. Firedamp—methane—seeps through the seams you have cut. One day it explodes. And there is no place to run. Lord Parrish has no escape shaft. It is much easier to find other men to replace the dead."

"Merciful God, Jenna, this is a drawing room, not the House of Lords," Phillip said.

"Miners already have the right to organize and petition Parliament for redress," Stonebridge said. "They don't need the strike."

"You are truly naive. The strike was engineered by Lord Parrish. He cut wages, increased work quotas and forced the grievances to a head. His timing is perfect. The union's great leader, Alexander McBryde, is right now before Parliament, lobbying to force regular government inspections of hellholes like Parrish's. But now the striking miners at Bolton and Glencur have been made to look like hotheads undeserving of protective legislation."

"Lord Parrish is a clever man," Stonebridge said, then frowned, one forefinger massaging his right temple. He set his glass carelessly near the edge of a cabriole-leg table beside her. His hand reached back slowly to cup the nape of his neck.

Jenna shook her head. "I do not understand you." She remembered the urgency of his words in her bedchamber: *I have my own vengeance to seek.*

"Well, the young squire Connell Parrish understands Jenna perfectly," Phillip said. "He knows that all she needs is a strong man to knock some sense into her overwrought brain."

Jenna glared at Phillip.

"Connell is paying court to Jenna." Phillip turned to Stonebridge. "Why he should invite such a vixen's torture, I do not know. She has yet to acknowledge his suit. But she will."

The assurance in his voice caused an involuntary shudder which Jenna disguised by turning away to face the fireplace.

"Perhaps he is simply a brave man," she heard Stonebridge say. "Or else he is astute enough to grasp a treasure when he sees one."

Phillip, indeed all the group, grew silent at the baronet's serious tone. Stonebridge looked at Jenna, her back still turned. "I consider myself an astute gentleman also."

Jenna's shoulders stiffened at the compliment.

Lady Saundra began to dab her sweaty hands with her lace handkerchief. Did this mean that the rich and forbidding head of the Stonebridge house fancied a match? Was this titled commoner choosing the Ice Maiden of Glen Manor? Oh, God, what a delightful gush of details she'd have for the vicar's son at dinner this week.

Phillip frowned. "Of course, Connell has already—"

"Beg pardon, Phillip." Stonebridge pressed his hand to his head with a tight grimace. "I suddenly feel—" The baronet staggered and caught himself against the small mahogany table. His wineglass tipped and spilled dark claret over the back of his hand.

Jenna turned at the clatter.

"Dear lady—" His voice was hoarse as he stepped toward her. "I beg your leave—" Stonebridge reached quickly for the back of a satinwood settee, but toppled against it, rolling limp to the floor.

Lady Saundra screamed.

"Quick," said Robert, rushing to his brother. "Grab his feet, Phillip. Get him on the chesterfield. The blow to his head last night—he is unconscious—"

Jenna rang for Eaton and told him to bring smelling salts and a basin of cool water. "Perhaps we should send for a physician, Robert," she said calmly. Inwardly her stomach churned. She was the cause of the baronet's head wound.

"Let's see if we can rouse him first," Robert said. Eaton returned and Jenna quickly wrung a cool cloth and pressed it to the baronet's forehead. Robert passed the smelling salts under his nose and Jenna was relieved to see Stonebridge open his eyes.

"Enough, damn you," he said weakly, waving the salts away. "I am dizzy."

"How is your head?" Robert asked.

"Terrible," he grumbled.

"You cannot travel, Ian," the earl said. "I insist that you stay the night with us. We shall call for the doctor in the morning." There was an air of authority in his voice Jenna had not heard since his days in London.

The reason for Stonebridge's fainting spell suddenly became clear to Jenna. She removed the cloth from his head and dipped it in the cool water.

"Robert, both you and Lady Saundra are also welcome to stay over, of course," Jenna said as she bent over the prone man. His eyes remained closed, but she saw him crook a forefinger in warning to Robert.

"But I have an extremely important appointment tomorrow morning," Robert said. "I'm afraid I must go. In truth, I would not leave if I felt Ian were in danger. But he will be well attended here. I'll send the carriage for him tomorrow."

"Eaton, prepare the guest room next to my bedchamber," the earl said.

Robert invited Phillip to ride with him. "It would give us a chance to continue our conversation so rudely interrupted by my brother."

"It would be an honor to escort Lady Saundra." Phillip bowed.

"Perhaps a game of cards at Stonebridge Hall before dawn?" Robert added. "You can return when the carriage comes for Ian. I'm sure you will be much better company than an aging brother who finds little fun in billiards or cards."

"Coward," Stonebridge said, his voice low and his eyes covered by the cloth. "I become your 'aged' brother only when I am flat on my back, unable to knock the impudence off your tongue."

"You are not the only Stonebridge known for taking advantage of a situation." Robert smiled as he pulled his brother up and slipped an arm under his shoulder.

"God's eyes, man, you're heavier than you look," Phillip groaned as he and Robert supported the tall man down the hall and into a dark bedroom. The baronet's valet, a Scotsman named Ross, appeared at the top of the servants' stairs, bowed to Jenna, then hurried to his master.

Jenna smiled and nodded distractedly as Lady Saundra chattered on about the early, but dramatic, end to her evening at the Thorntons'.

Remembering the baronet's remark about a ride and the mythical Red Bow Bandit, Jenna worried that her own evening was just beginning.

Preoccupied, Jenna escorted Saundra and Robert down the

curving staircase to the ground-floor foyer, where Eaton waited with their traveling coats. Her father followed silently. Jenna glanced up at him as he paused on the landing. He had stumbled clumsily against the bannister. It was then that she noticed the feverish gleam in the earl's eyes and the white cast of his face. She was about to go to his aid, but he shook his head once in warning. He obviously wanted the travelers gone without delay.

Jenna swallowed her fear and turned to make her good-byes to Robert and Saundra. Phillip held Saundra's floor-length blue cloak. She made a show of needing help to button the fox fur collar. Phillip was quick to oblige. "It wouldn't be seemly," Saundra protested sweetly and asked for Jenna's maid.

"I am faster than my maid, Lady Saundra," Jenna said, fastening the white bone cylinders through their loops. "And we do not want to delay Phillip." She smiled as Saundra's kohl-colored lashes lowered demurely. "It seems he cannot wait to leave home."

As soon as the Stonebridge coach and attendants pulled away, Lord Thornton collapsed at the bottom of the stairs.

Jenna rushed to his side.

"Rest," he whispered weakly. "I just need some rest."

Father, Jenna thought, what have you done to yourself—and to us? She signaled to Eaton, and the butler helped the earl up the stairs to his room.

When Eaton left, the earl motioned Jenna nearer. "Not much time." Her father's voice was rough, clotted with phlegm. "You must represent me tonight. An important meeting. Fifty gold sovereigns for Bilpo Grawlin." The breathless earl fished weakly in the drawer beside his bed and withdrew a sack of coins.

"Fifty sovereigns! My God, Father, where did you—?"

"Hush. It's my reserve. It will not bankrupt us," he whispered.

"But the debts, Father!" Jenna nearly broke into tears. He had money for his plan, but none to spend on Glen Manor.

"I read the accounts. I know Phillip's notes to Parrish are nearly due. They are close to taking Shadow Glen."

"What do you mean? Shadow Glen is mine—left in Mother's trust. They cannot touch it."

"But they can touch you," the earl said. "They will press you to marry Connell, promise to clear Phillip's debts. Then they would have both you and Shadow Glen."

"Never. But why do they want Shadow Glen?"

"Coal." The sixty-year-old lord turned away from her in a spasm of coughing. "Coal underneath Shadow Glen. A fat, deep pocket. The vein surfaces—"

"We must hurry," said the deep voice behind her.

Jenna started. Stonebridge had sneaked through the connecting door as silently as a heathen beginning a hunt.

"No!" She held on to her father's arm and bent low to speak to him. "Why do you entrust this stranger with a plan that can see you both in jail?"

"Prison would be a small price to pay," the earl whispered.

"Father." Jenna leaned closer and whispered, "What did Parrish do to make Mother—?"

Tears glazed the hazel eyes of her father before he turned his head away from her. "The bastard—will—pay," the earl said through gritted teeth. Then he gestured the tall baronet closer.

The old earl spoke in broken whispers, his mouth set in a grimace of pain. Neither the miners nor Parrish would know that the House of Stonebridge supported the strike, he explained. Phillip and Saundra would spread effective gossip about Ian's pro-Parrish position in the drawing-room argument. Everyone would think that Stonebridge sided with the monied lords.

"You are my surprise," the earl smiled.

"I will keep my identity secret tonight," Stonebridge said urgently. "But we must go." He grabbed Jenna by the arm.

"I will not travel alone with him, Father." Jenna's voice was pitched low and firm. "He has gained your trust. But not mine."

"He is your intended," said her father. "Did he not explain?"

"Oh, yes, he explained it." She shook her head, trying to keep her anger in check. "Why didn't you?"

The weary man on the bed was silent a moment. "You would not have allowed it." The voice was rough with phlegm, heavy with sorrow. "You would have argued how useless, how dangerous and foolish this gesture. And I would have put it aside. And died in misery." The earl raised himself to his elbow and put his hand on Jenna's shoulder. "But it's too late now. The Red Bow will ride."

She looked deep into his tortured eyes, hoping for a glimpse of the lucid soul she had sought ever since her mother died.

"Father," she whispered, hugging him with all her might.

"Help me," he said.

"I will."

"No matter the cost?" Stonebridge asked from behind her, his voice strangely tense. "For the price will be dear for all of us."

She turned to look up into eyes so dark they seemed lost in the shadows. "I'm not afraid," she said.

"You should be." He pulled Jenna to her feet. "We can no longer delay. Ross will tend the earl."

They left by the servants' stairs. Leona had packed Jenna's riding clothes and sent them to the stable, where Stolley had saddled horses waiting.

"Hurry!" Stonebridge whispered from the barn door.

"I am trying!" she hissed from behind the slats of Dulcy's stall. There the sweet smell of hay bunched at her feet mingled with the earthy musk of the barn. She reached again for the buttons down her back and groaned.

Impatient footsteps brought the shadows of a swaying lantern closer. Stonebridge appeared, climbed over the gate and dropped into the narrow box. Jenna stifled a scream.

"May God condemn women's clothes to hellfire!" he said, reaching for her. She spun away and backed into a corner, startling the carriage horse in the next stall.

"Quiet!" Stonebridge said.

"Don't touch me!" she whispered.

He grabbed her and dragged her to him. "Timid maid, there is a time and a place for everything! And this," he said as his arms reached around behind her, "is not the time." With rhythmic jerks he ripped the line of button loops free.

The small pearllike buttons fell like a handful of grain into the hay. Jenna stood still, frozen in her anger, encircled by his arms. Slowly, he let his arms drop to his side. She crossed her arms to her shoulders to keep her bodice from falling away.

"One day your crudeness will get you killed," she said softly.

He stepped back, aware of how rigidly she stood and of how much she hated him at this moment.

"Perhaps," he agreed, "but only if I am so stupid as to allow you a weapon."

She stood within arm's reach but so distant that he wished she would move. Away from him, toward him, any motion would be a response. Her hands were spread protectively against the creamy, delicate line of her collarbone, close to the chin she held so proudly, close to the firm, full mouth he had only begun to kiss in the glen that morning.

He pulled his eyes away to break the impasse and turned from her to gain a toehold in the planks of the gate. "Fair warning to a fairer maid." In one smooth motion he hurtled up and over. "I believe it's better to die a satisfied man than a tactful one," he said from the other side.

"You will die neither," she said evenly and certainly.

"You have five minutes," he said roughly. "Then you come as you are."

She did not take longer. And she did not forget the hunting knife the cautious Leona had packed in the bundle. Quickly Jenna slipped the blade inside her boot.

"Stolley goes with us," she told Stonebridge as he tossed her into the saddle. Before he could protest, she signaled Stolley to saddle and catch up with them.

She guided Dulcy closer to the gray stallion Stonebridge rode. It was the only thoroughbred in her father's stable. Jenna pressed her lips together, trying to phrase her question calmly. "Will my father be all right?" she asked.

"For tonight." She could not see his face in the darkness.

"Is it consumption?"

"Yes."

"Curable?"

He shook his head.

"How long—?" she whispered.

"I don't know. I ordered a special syrup from the chemist. Gave it to him when we met this afternoon. It's a stronger medicine. It should help when he's very uncomfortable."

Jenna looked back toward the house. "Let's be done with this quickly."

*   *   *

The horses' hooves sounded loud as thunder as the three riders pounded down the cart path toward the outskirts of Glencur. The moon was bright, softly outlining the dark figures against the open heath.

Ahead of Jenna, Stonebridge jogged off the trail and headed for the dense cover of woodlands bordering the north side of the River Ribble. The slower pace of the horses winding through the tall trees was a relief. Her bruised rib felt battered from the full canter.

Stonebridge reined in before a stand of pines. Jenna and Stolley stopped behind him.

Stonebridge appeared on her left side and raised his arm to help her down.

"I don't need your assistance." She straightened her back until her side ached.

He grasped her hand and placed it firmly on his shoulder. "Lean on me and slide down."

Reluctantly she swung her right leg over Dulcy's head and felt Stonebridge hold her snugly as she slid to the ground. His body was hard muscled and lean, alert to the feel of her. He let her down softly and released her. She pushed away roughly.

"Tie the chestnut next to mine," he said, "and tell the boy to follow us. Bilpo's waiting."

They stepped around a thorny thicket of sparse-leaved blackberry and made their way toward a clearing. A squat, box shape jutted upward before them. The shack was rough stone and mud chinks. No light showed through the numerous cracks in its walls. That meant no fire to warm them. Jenna pulled her cloak tighter about her.

Stonebridge motioned for her and Stolley to stay back. He

pushed slowly against the door. Wood-warped creaks broke the night silence.

"The Red Bow rides," he said into the dark room.

"Then get in 'ere and close the door. We got business to tend," said a rough voice. Jenna heard the sound of a match scratching. Then candlelight bloomed in the blackness, illuminating a dark-shadowed face topped by a black wool beret.

She stepped into the room. The man quickly doffed his cap, then studied Stonebridge.

"You ain't the old earl who promised to come, now, are ye?"

"No," Stonebridge said calmly. "And you're not alone as you promised to be, either."

A tall, muscled miner stepped out of the far corner of the room into the candle glow. He was black, covered with coal dust. Only the hollows of his eyes, and the eyeballs themselves, showed white.

"The union has struck," Jenna said, eyeing the man. "You work unmindful of the cause of starving miners?"

"No, mum," the man said with a smile which added a gleam of white to an unrecognizable face. "I am one with the strikers. I just had a bit of—investigatin' ta do in one of the shafts taday. Just finished, as a matter o' fact." Jenna heard a soft Scottish burr and an educated accent in his voice.

The scruffy man at the table said, "I'm Bilpo Grawlin. Are you the old lord's daughter?"

Jenna nodded.

"The earl's been a true friend of the colliery workers." The tall Scot to her left bowed slightly. "it is a pleasure to make your acquaintance."

"Lord Thornton is still a friend of the workers and their

families." Jenna dropped the pouch of sovereigns on the table. "Fifty gold sovereigns to aid the plan on its way."

Bilpo, after a nod from his big friend, picked up the pouch and peeked inside. "God's fingers, Alex. 'Tis gold, all right."

"Our women and children will be grateful," the big miner said. He turned to Stonebridge. "And who is this patient gentleman escorting you so late at night?"

"This is my—" Jenna paused. Stonebridge's well-cut clothes and arrogant posture would belie a servant.

"—solicitor, Mr. Rockwell. He is very involved in our effort. And very discreet."

Stonebridge took the Scotsman's hand. "You are well-spoken for a colliery worker," he said. "I would mistake you for a man more used to meeting people in a great hall than in a squatter's shack."

"I talk a good yarn anywhere, Mr. Rockwell."

Stonebridge stared at him. "I heard you once in a town square at Manchester. Eloquent, testy badger you were, and two heads taller than any other orator. You're Alex McBryde."

Jenna was startled. McBryde was president of the Miners National Association of Great Britain.

The tall Scot was silent, then nodded once.

"Mr. McBryde, what are you doing here?" Jenna asked. "You're supposed to be shepherding the new mine act through the back rooms of Parliament."

"I am, m'lady. But it's here the wild dogs are tearin' at it. I'm gatherin' more petitions on the grievances against Lord Parrish. But I'm about to run out of time—if the devil gets jobless farm workers from the south to turn into coal miners."

Parrish planned to recruit hard and fast and give new employees train fare to the colliery, McBryde explained. "My miners are good people. But they're hungry ones. There'll be fights. And the older men—those with more mouths to feed—might break ranks and go back to work before the new law passes."

"Robbin' is the only way to stop 'im," piped up the little miner at the table. "The Red Bow Bandit'll take the ole devil's payroll larder from the night coach in about two weeks. That way the miners get no blame. No one gets no blame."

"Assuming no one gets caught, Mr. Grawlin," Jenna said.

"I've got me five good men sworn in blood to keep the secret. And if any die in the doin' of it, the rest of us swear to take care o' their wives and little ones. 'Tis better'n sittin' to watch 'em go hungry, ain't it?"

"Which coach will be carrying the money?" Stonebridge broke in.

"The evening coach from Clitheroe to Ribchester. From there he's to put it aboard the train for the long run to Liverpool. We've only got the twenty-six miles before Ribchester to lay it by. My men and me'll be gathered at the knoll on Three Bend Road at seven o'clock. I'm ta be the Red Bow 'imself." Bilpo smiled, showing a black gap in his front teeth.

"Do your men know the hiding place?" Stonebridge interrupted.

"Aye. The old lord told me. We'll stay there till the authorities get tired o' huntin' aroun' for us."

McBryde turned to Jenna. "Please give your father a message. Tell him it's just as he suspected. One of Parrish's northeast shafts is angled right under the southwest ridge of Shadow Glen. A pretty pocket of coal runs there, a dogleg vein from an old surface mine quarried in your great-grandfather's day. And it looks like it's been picked at long before the strike began."

"That's why the dead veins in the Parrish colliery were suddenly reborn," Jenna said. She paused. "It is an outrage. But one whose revealing must be carefully timed."

"What do you mean?" McBryde asked.

"Just that it is important ammunition in your fight," Stonebridge interjected. "Parrish is flaunting the law. And it can be proved by the existence of the shaft, verified by a surveyor's inspection."

McBryde rubbed his jaw. "I agree that we can surely use every evidence of Parrish skulduggery we find. And we'll have ta be careful. Mine shafts—and the people in them—disappear in a cloud of dust."

"We need people who will swear they were ordered to work in the Shadow Glen shaft," Stonebridge said.

"I kin find 'em," Bilpo said. "But gettin' 'em to talk is another matter. They'd lose their jobs fer sure. And Parrish's bastard manager Stiles'd make sure they're blackballed at other pits."

The door creaked. Stolley timidly entered the cabin and moved nearer to Jenna, nervously twisting his cap in his hands. "What wrong?" she sighed.

He stuffed his cap under his arm and gestured quickly. "Storm. Please go."

She put her hand on his arm and nodded.

"Stolley says we're about to have a thunderstorm here, gentlemen. He's always right about these things. Is our business about finished?" She looked to Stonebridge.

He nodded. "Bilpo, we'll meet again in two days."

"It has been a pleasure to meet you, Mr. McBryde," Jenna said. The Scotsman reached for her hand, then jerked it back quickly, realizing how sooty he was.

Jenna kept her hand extended. "I don't fear the earth's dust."

McBryde lightly took her hand. His lips left a gray smudge on her knuckles.

"Guard this lady well," he said to Stonebridge. "She is precious to many." He bowed.

Jenna pulled her warm woolen riding hood over her hair and left with Stonebridge. They walked in silence to the horses.

"You play your part well," Stonebridge finally said.

She didn't reply.

Stolley waited, already mounted, near the pines.

Stonebridge cupped his hand to help Jenna into her saddle. The rising wind blew off the riding hood she had donned. Her loose dark hair swirled around her neck like a soft, silken scarf.

Stonebridge held tight to Dulcy's bridle and studied the woman in the saddle. "You are quite extraordinary, you know," he said, almost too softly for Jenna to hear.

"You sound surprised," Jenna said. "I didn't think a man of your experience could be astonished by any female's capabilities." She gently heeled Dulcy in the side and guided the mare through the trees.

Stonebridge smiled and swung into the saddle of the skittish gray. "You have untapped capabilities, Jenna," he said. "And they will amaze even you." The wind carried his words far ahead.

Chapter 6

The raindrops became a deluge by the time the trio emerged from the forest and reached the Glencur road. Stolley gestured wildly to Jenna. His mother's cottage was the closest shelter.

"Follow Stolley!" Jenna shouted to Stonebridge above the loud hiss of the wind. Branches of oak and London plain bobbed and collided in the turbulence. A sudden gust whipped Jenna's cape off one shoulder and furled it around the other side. She groped to right it as thunder clapped again.

A grouse hen, seeking forest cover, darted across the road in front of Jenna's horse. Dulcy gave a startled squeal and reared. Jenna was pitched backward in the saddle. She threw herself forward, swaying and unbalanced. As Dulcy's front hooves struck the earth with a jarring thud, Jenna gasped and dropped the reins. Her eyes stung with pain as the skittish horse took off at a mad gallop.

Jenna bent low in the saddle, praying Dulcy's fright would soon be spent. She had taken up the reins, but Dulcy had the bit between her teeth. Surrounded by the racing darkness and the howl of the storm, Jenna was aware of little save the pain in her side.

Behind her, Stonebridge drove the big gray hard until the

horses ran flank to flank. Daringly he leaned from his saddle to grab Jenna's reins near the bit and as he slowed the gray, forced Dulcy to follow pace.

"Are you all right?" Stonebridge shouted, holding the mare's bridle firmly.

Jenna was bent in the saddle, face streaming with rain. She nodded without looking at him, one arm cradling her side.

He pulled the reins over Dulcy's head, then reached across and grasped Jenna's arm to help her raise herself upright.

Her face was hidden from him by a tangled mass of wet hair. Stonebridge swept his hand suddenly across her cheek and held the strands back high against her head.

"Are you all right?" he repeated.

She shook her head away from his grip and reached for Dulcy's reins.

"I'll lead her," Stonebridge said, turning the gray and setting off at a slow canter with Dulcy on short rein beside him. Jenna's face had told him much. Both her pride and her side hurt, but neither state gave him leave to run his hand through her hair. He smiled at her determination. And strengthened his own.

Less than a mile later, the three riders stopped their horses under weather-blackened timbers of the barn at Leona's empty cottage. The two men dismounted. Stonebridge handed his reins to Stolley, who led the horses into the barn.

Stonebridge pulled Jenna from her saddle and carried her across the threshold of the small yellow-gritstone house. He kicked a straight-backed chair over to the fireplace, sat her down gently and began to build a fire.

"Take off your cloak," he said, carefully stacking small

kindling pieces over a beginning spiral of smoke in the blackened grate.

He turned and shrugged off his own wet coat. Jenna had not moved. He reached down to untie the hood strings at her throat. With little energy left, she tried to push him away.

"I don't want a fiancée with a red nose and consumptive disposition," he said, peeling the wet, heavy cloak from her shoulders."

"You have no fiancée," she said, watching the new fire crackle hungrily through dry wood. "You have a woman trapped into helping her father."

"What I have," he said, "is a beautiful woman. Alone."

She looked up at him. Color rose to her cheeks as she sensed the target of his gaze. Stiff, cold nipples were pressed tight against the soaked bodice of her habit.

Anger rising, Jenna bent forward and slipped her fingers into the top of her right boot. She froze. The knife was gone.

"Looking for this?" Stonebridge held up her long-bladed hunting knife, turning it slowly so that it caught the glint of the rising fire.

"I noticed it when I helped you down from your horse. Looked too dangerous for a lady. But perhaps you have need of it after all. I'll find you a blanket," he said, and handed her the knife.

She grasped it firmly, the blade angled toward the baronet whose back was bent over Leona's small cotton-ticked bed in the corner.

Stonebridge returned with a worn quilt. Jenna stiffened against his touch as he draped it around her shoulders.

"You can relax," he said from behind her. "I have yet to take a woman against her will."

"Only a fool would trust you." Jenna rose from the chair. "You said as much yourself."

"Good advice," he smiled.

"From an arrogant beast whose desires are very different from my own."

"You don't know the difference between arrogance and honesty. And I doubt you know much of desire. What is it you desire, Jenna?" He said her name softly.

Her hand tightened its grip on the leather hilt of her knife. But her mind fixed on his question: what did she want? She swallowed hard, the ache of what she wanted throbbing deep at the base of her throat. She wanted him to stop speaking in the low timbre that rendered all his words intimate. She wanted him to stay at a distance, so she could not catch his thick scent of leather and sweat.

But he was close now. His breath was warm on her brow. Frightened, she pressed the knife blade to the belly of his shirt.

"Are you a prize worth blood?" he mused, his dark eyes searching hers.

She looked away. But he reached out to cup her chin and turn her face to his. With his other hand Stonebridge wrapped his fingers around the delicate hand that held the knife. With slow pressure he began to press the point further inward to his stomach.

"Stop," she whispered.

"Is it not what you want?" he asked as the point of the blade broke through his shirt.

With a small cry, Jenna reversed the pull and jerked the knife back.

"You will not slit me like a rabbit for the pot? That's comforting news."

"Not for me," she said, her voice too breathy, her face

less than a handsbreadth away from the thin cotton shirt matted to his chest by the rain.

Slowly, his lips came nearer, the plane of his face and dark halo of his hair blurring before her. As her eyes closed she felt the moist, insistent warmth of his breath along her cheek. Then his lips pressed to hers gently. His mouth began to move rhythmically, carefully, over the soft fullness of her lips, teasing her to respond. She pulled back, head swimming, her lips parted to say "No." But his lips were already there at her half-open mouth, and it was impossible to escape his tongue. He took his chance, tasting her fully, imprisoning her head with his free hand.

The kiss enraged her. She stiffened but could not break his hold. His tongue was an insistent explorer, claiming new territory with practiced strokes.

She heard a small cry, like the mew of a new kitten wrenched from its box. Her own sound, telling him to stop, warning him to stop, but the knife blade lay flat along his side and she was pressed too tightly against his lean, hard body. She tried weakly to twist away from him, but his hand only molded deeper into the small of her back, pressing so that each rounded breast met the rigid contour of his chest.

At last he stopped, knowing that if he didn't, his hands would soon begin an affront she was not ready for.

She stepped backward, out of his reach, and grasped the chair for support, out of breath, unable to speak.

The baronet, eyes strangely intense, exhaled raggedly. He watched Jenna struggle with her anger. "Perhaps I've found the secret to stilling your tongue," he said softly.

"Bastard cur." Her teeth clenched tightly to hold back a sob. She raised the knife in a trembling hand, waiting for hate and rage to well up inside her. But all she could manage was a tired pool of tears. Her senses were still swelling, uncontrolled, aching from his kiss, unwilling to reject the feel of him. "Go away," she whispered. To him. To the feelings.

The baronet smiled, a gesture apologetic but firm, and shook his head.

The door opened. Stolley entered, stomping his wet, muddy feet on the mat by the door. He stopped short when he saw the two figures framed in the firelight. They had ignored the creaking of the door and the rush of chill wind as if they were frozen in another world, cordoned off by flickering shadows.

Stolley saw Jenna, a tear gliding down her cheek, one hand braced warily on the back of the wooden chair, the other hand pointing a knife at the baronet. Stonebridge, her enemy of the woods, stood not three feet from her.

Slowly Stonebridge approached her and grabbed her abruptly by the shoulders. Jenna's mouth formed a weak, silent "No." And Stolley ran headlong to save her.

Jenna saw him rush forward and shrugged out of the baronet's grasp. "Wait!" she signed to Stolley, but Stolley's eyes were fixed on his tall target. Stonebridge turned quickly, but the force of Stolley's body hitting his midsection hit him double and they both tumbled in Jenna's direction. The chair beside her splintered and Jenna flattened against the stone wall, her knife knocked to the floor.

"Ian!" Jenna cried. "Don't hurt him!" Stolley tried to pummel the older man, who had raised himself half off the floor. Stonebridge unfolded from his crouching position and rammed a fist into Stolley's shoulder. The youth flew backward and landed on the floor.

"Damn you!" Stonebridge yelled. "Twice in one day is too much!" He started for Stolley, but Jenna stepped in front of him. "Please!"

The knife blade flashed at Jenna's feet. Jenna saw the blur of Stolley's hand as the youth grabbed the hilt. She turned to intercept Stolley's rush. "Stop! Stop!" she signed frantically, but the arc of his arm was already racing forward, aiming for Stonebridge's broad chest.

"No!" she signed, stepping into the weapon's path. She saw Stolley's eyes widen in horror as the possibility of hurting her seemed unavoidable.

With an ungentle push, Stonebridge moved Jenna aside and grabbed at Stolley's wrist as the knife blade lunged toward his shoulder. The point drove home below his collarbone, but the baronet's hold and Stolley's horror had slowed its velocity.

Stonebridge grimaced and backhanded the youth across the face. Stolley whirled and landed against a tall oak cupboard, jarring the pottery inside. He slid to the floor, his shoulders heaving, his mouth agape in the agony of silent sobs.

Stonebridge stood, fists clenched, breathing deeply to still the pounding of his heart. Then he felt a soft pressure on the throbbing wound and jerked away.

Jenna waited, then again pressed the clean towel against his shoulder to staunch the slow trickle of blood. A minute passed.

"Your wound—" she questioned.

"Is not deep," he seethed.

"Hold this," she said, grasping his left hand and pulling it gently up toward his right shoulder. Her hand was small-boned, fine. She did not tremble, but her touch, as she pressed his hand to the towel, was cold as fear.

Then she dropped slowly to her knees and gathered the shaking boy in her arms. Stolley was a year older than she, but he would always be younger, always be hurt, she knew.

She smoothed his hair and made rapid signals with her other hand. Stolley kept shaking his head, too ashamed to look her fully in the face.

Cursing under his breath, Stonebridge sat down at the small kitchen table and watched the two on the floor. Jenna's hair hung loose and wild around the pale, perfect oval of her face. Dark tendrils stretched halfway down the back of her maroon riding habit. Stolley's head lay buried in her lap. The boy was half again as big as Jenna. But she seemed to encompass him, protect him with her body, hand flying with signals, lips pursed in a comforting "Sshhhhhh."

How young she looked, Stonebridge thought, with her hair veiling her shoulders, the clear planes of her face shaded and softened by the firelight. She is too young to be part of this, he thought.

But when she looked his way, to check on the red-blotched towel he held to his shoulder, he saw storm-blue eyes that were burdened. A woman's eyes, clear, strong, vulnerable. In a young, sweet body. Wisdom and wonder.

Tania.

For a horrifying second, his lips had parted to say her name. Stonebridge jerked himself upright in the chair as if he had been caught napping. His wife's name was buried deep in his mind, like treasure on a secret island, safe as long as it was not disturbed. He stood up, senses suddenly on guard against the young woman before him.

"What are you saying to him?" Stonebridge asked roughly.

Jenna sighed. "That he didn't hurt you badly. That he misunderstood. I said that you did not hurt me. And you will not harm him."

Stonebridge pulled his shirttail out of his trousers. "I do not hurt puppies who protect their mistresses," he said, unbuttoning the collar. "Tell him you are safe with me. That I respect your wishes. And I may someday forgive him for crushing my skull in the woods this morning." The baronet wrenched his arm out of his shirt-sleeve. A stream of drying blood ran down through the dark hair of his chest.

Jenna averted her eyes and gestured to Stolley. Then she rose, pulling him up with her. Stolley walked stiffly to Stonebridge, his tousled brown hair and red eyes making him look as if he had been soundly throttled.

With deliberate slowness, he made a fist with his right hand, tapped his heart and then presented his palm, flat and open. Then his fingers flew in intricate flutters. Stonebridge looked to Jenna with a questioning brow.

"Stolley says that his heart hurts because he nearly killed you twice in one day. And he promises not to assume the worse of you anymore." She stopped.

"And?" Stonebridge prompted.

"And you must not hurt me. Because—"

Stolley gestured, his hand moving upward along his own throat, stopping with fingers pressed against Jenna's lips.

"Because I am his voice," Jenna said softly. Her hand made the sign for "tea" and Stolley hurried to set up the cooking trivet in the fireplace.

Jenna opened one of Leona's cupboards above an iron water pump perched on the edge of the sink. On tiptoe she rummaged until she grasped the neck of an amber whiskey bottle.

"You have a physician's instincts," Stonebridge said.

"It's for your shoulder."

"Bring a glass. That stuff works from the inside out."

She poured the glass a quarter full and watched him down it in a second. She poured him another and then went about the task of warming the teapot and steeping the tea.

She talked quietly as Stonebridge sipped his whiskey, covering her unsettled feelings with words and memories of another time.

Many of the happiest moments of Jenna's childhood had taken place around the polished oak table here in Leona's cottage, she told him. How many times had she poured out her soul to Leona and had it returned, safe, warm and comforted by the older woman? Leona had been a foster mother. Jenna's own mother, the countess, spent most of her time in London. In their three-story brick townhouse in the West End, she entertained, socialized and played the part of a statesman's wife with good grace and exquisite correctness. Except for that one night. When she did something incorrect. . . .

Jenna stopped abruptly. Stonebridge was staring at her. "It is all past," she said.

"But never gone," Stonebridge said softly, swirling the amber liquid in his glass.

"None of us will have a future if we're caught financing the robbery of the shire's richest coal lord," Jenna said, dipping a rag in the warm basin of water Stolley set on the table. She pressed it lightly against the dark clot of blood in the hollow of his shoulder. He did not flinch.

"We just have to divert Parrish's attention from Parliament for a while," he said.

"I am the diversion, then? I reject Connell Parrish as a suitor, openly choose a rich and—"

"Handsome," he interrupted.

"*Vain* specimen of titled stock, and—"

"—it should provide some—er—emotional cover for Bilpo and his band. The little miner will need all the help he can get," Stonebridge said.

"Bilpo is ill-suited for the role," Jenna said. "It's rumored the real Red Bow was a well-educated nobleman. An advocate for humane treatment of miners and millworkers."

Stonebridge ignored her. He downed the whiskey and set the glass down sharply on the table.

"They'll be instantly marked as the poor pitmen they are," she said. "Did my father not think of that?"

"He thinks of nothing except the downfall of Hutton Parrish."

"And you? What made you accept such a flawed plan? You must be desperate." She held the bottle of whiskey, tilted, above his shoulder.

"I'm ready," he said tersely, shoulder back.

She hesitated. It would burn like a devil's brand. "My blade was clean. Perhaps—"

"I want no infection. I have a fiancée to embrace."

His self-assurance stung. "You'll skate an ice pond in hell first," she said. Then she threw a stream of liquid fire across the open wound.

He did not move. The sun-bronzed skin around the wound glistened with the sticky wetness of the liquor. Jenna dabbed roughly at the excess which had run through the dark furrow of his chest to the waistband of his trousers. His abdomen was hard, tightly muscled. Stonebridge had downed the liquor fast and hard. But apparently his was not an excessive habit, or else he burned away the evidence with much physical activity, she thought.

She sank to her knees to sweep the towel across the breadth of his chest. Leona had taught her how to tend wounds—and told her what to expect from the man she married, but that comfortable talk had not prepared her for the touch of these hard muscles. Had not made her aware of how dark and hard the nipples lay. Had not mentioned the sweet secret smell of spicy cologne brushed idly along the dark curly hair that furred him lightly from collarbone to abdomen and—

Her eyes closed and she pulled her hand away from his chest as if she had been burned. A treacherous pulsing had begun inside her, deep and low in her loins. It was a knot of heat, tightening painfully, pulling her insides to a molten pool within her abdomen. She released the breath she held high in her chest, and it freed the warmth. It spread willfully upward on a rolling path that constricted her belly, her chest, her throat.

He said nothing, made no move as he watched her grow aware of the fire that could so easily melt them together. He had sensed the moment long before she. Had felt it build as her hand stroked more slowly and gently across him. Had watched her sweet, dry lips part naturally as she drew a deep breath of control.

The moment hung between them like a veil each could see through.

Then Jenna rose slowly. She backed away to the edge of the table, her stiffness, her guarded glance speaking a fear of him, a bewilderment that her body had answered his manliness so quickly.

As she withdrew, Stonebridge consciously slowed the pounding of his own heart. She ran on instinct, this one, no matter how quick and calculating her mind.

The screech of glass against metal behind him signaled that Stolley was filling another oil lantern. The harsh sound severed the tense thread that connected him to the haunting young woman not three feet away. Stonebridge caught the acrid smoke of a wick newly lit. He turned his head to sip his whiskey and consciously subdued the throbbing fullness in his groin.

Stolley brought the lamp to the table and Jenna began tearing a clean rag into strips for a bandage.

"You will have to sew it first," Stonebridge said softly.

Shaken, she let the bandages fall to the table. "I cannot."

"You must. It is my right arm. I have need of it. So will your father and Bilpo Grawlin."

He was right. The robbery was only two weeks away.

"Have you not done this before?" he asked.

"Never," Jenna said.

"This will be simple. Three stitches at most."

"Simple! I must sew together this night the vagabond who attacked me this morning? My body aches! It's tired! Tired to death of the trouble you make for me!" she cried.

"That is understandable. Your presence has also cost me no little pain." His voice was tight with anger. "Our trysts need to be more conventional and less bloody, don't you think?"

"I think our courtship will easily be marked for the mockery it is." Her words were bitter.

"On the contrary," he said with a humorless smile. "I think our unsettled feelings will lend a touching validity to our relationship. Are not all courtships marked by quivering trepidation?"

"There is trepidation on only one side of this courtship. And that is the crux of my concern." Angry, she signed to Stolley, asking him to find Leona's sewing box. She chose a needle, threaded it and dipped the sliver of silver into Stonebridge's newly filled glass of whiskey.

She was ready, needle poised. "Lie down and relax your shoulder."

He kept his eyes on the amber liquid in his glass. "Dear lady, in the space of an hour I have had three tall whiskeys, a short fight and a thoroughly satisfying kiss. If I lie down anywhere, I will take you with me. Now, will you get on with it?"

She did, taking time to make the stitches small and tight. Then she bandaged the shoulder, winding the strips across his chest and under his arm.

"A good job," he said, easing his shoulder up and forward, testing the flex in the bandage and the soreness of his arm. "How do I pay an unwilling surgeon?"

"With answers," Jenna said hotly, clicking shut Leona's wooden sewing box. "I will not endure one more misunderstanding until I know exactly why you are partner to my father in this foolish plan."

Stonebridge stopped the glass halfway to his lips. "It's a personal matter," he said. Sobering, he stood and went to the fire, stoking it to a hot rush of smoke and ashes.

"Most hatred is. I want to know that your stake is as great as ours."

Absently he traced the bowl of a brass lantern resting on the white, carved mantelpiece. "I promised your father Parrish would be destroyed."

"Tell me why, if you want a smitten fiancée—"

"Instead of a frigid shrew? What is it you're willing to barter?" He turned and held her eyes.

"I do not bargain with my body."

"A shame. It would make you a lethal negotiator." His drink raised, he studied her image through the bottom of his glass. He owed her nothing, not even honesty. And yet . . . She waited for his answer. Pale, lovely little fool. So coolly distant now, thinking the ember of desire had safely died. Dear God, she was so new at this. And he had neither time nor wits to waste on a stormy affair with a young innocent who was the key to vengeance.

He decided to give her much more honesty than she bargained for.

When he finally broke the silence, his voice hit her low-pitched and warm, like the edge of an undertow in a cold sea. "You must never repeat what I tell you."

She nodded agreement.

"Hutton Parrish sired me."

The fire cracked in the silence.

"Good God," she breathed. "He's your father? How can you be sure?"

He reached across the table to pour more in his glass. "My mother herself confirmed it. One cold autumn day after I'd been sent home from school. Fighting," Stonebridge said, looking into the fire. "Always fighting."

His father the baronet, Sir Roderick Stonebridge, had endured fevers as a child. "He was sterile. But he wanted an heir. My mother supplied him with one."

"Sir Roderick knew you were not his?"

Stonebridge nodded.

"Does Parrish know?"

He swirled the amber liquid in his glass. "No," he said quietly. "Being his secret bastard was torturous enough. God only knows what would await me in his good graces."

Hutton Parrish had lusted after Ian's mother, Ariel Stonebridge, ever since she moved to Stonebridge Hall as wife of the baronet. To conceive a child, Ariel spent one night with Parrish, then rejected him with a lie. She told him that she had lain with many other men, and that she found Parrish less than adequate.

Parrish was furious. Ariel left for France before her pregnancy was evident. She spent four years there, returning with falsified birth papers and a son who was half a year older than the date on the certificate.

In her absence Parrish had ruined her reputation. He kept the rumor mills churning with stories of her prowess in warming the beds of an Italian horse breeder, a Scottish barrister, a Yankee cotton merchant and a score of others in Lancashire and Lyons.

Ariel died when Ian was eight. "A sad, beautiful woman," Ian whispered. "A distant one. All she did was give my father the son he wanted. The price was branded on all of us."

But Parrish's shadow didn't fade with Ariel's death. Throughout his years at boarding school, Ian was badgered. His constant nemesis was a merchant's son, Hasting Wills. Sarcastic, gregarious and often drunk, Hasting goaded others to taunt Ian as a bastard. After many fights and threats of suspension, Ian learned to withstand the name-calling. All except one: Hasting labeled Ian's mother a bloody whore. Forever after, the phrase insured a bloody fight.

A stocky country lad, Hasting usually surrendered quickly after landing a few satisfying blows. Aside from his fervent hatred of Ian, the curious thing about Hasting was his unending supply of spending money.

"The money came from Parrish," Ian said. It was a simple scheme to harass Ian's father.

Sir Roderick owned land near Parrish's textile mills. Parrish often wished to recruit workers from the villages where Sir Roderick's tenants lived, but Sir Roderick had no wish to see the woman and children turned into wage slaves. Not only did he warn them away when Parrish's agents came by with glowing promises of employment and wages, but he also found jobs for many who fled Parrish's inhuman treatment.

Proud and principled, Sir Roderick knew that his son's troubles at school were instigated by the viscount. But he couldn't prove it. The old baronet had a soft heart for social justice, Ian said. "And a naive philosophy that justice was possible." Bitterly Sir Roderick fought Parrish's influence.

Until the murder. Hasting Wills was found bludgeoned to death in a dank alley. Less than an hour before, a dozen schoolmates had watched the seventeen-year-old Ian beat his tormentor bloody on a cobblestone street nearby.

"I was arrested," Ian said, his voice slowing. "Put in a dark cell with one other man. A huge fellow. A Swede from the Parrish pits. The best loader he had. Lindstrom was his name. Brains the size of a penny nail. Hands as big as a shovel. I was used to taking punches, but not like these. Pounded again and again, like a piece of meat that wouldn't get tender enough for him. I finally stopped screaming. I knew no one would come. When he was finished, he left me his trademark. A broken finger." Ian downed the whiskey quickly as he stared beyond Jenna. "He has a peculiar way of disjointing the middle finger. One you do not forget."

"Dear God," Jenna breathed. "Your father?"

"Sold his land to Parrish. Only then was the murder charge dismissed for lack of evidence. And I was secretly carted off to France to recover."

"Ian—" she began softly.

He seemed not to hear; his head leaned forward into his hand. "I promised then that I would create as much torment for Parrish as the bastard made for us."

"You are not the law, Ian," she said gently. "Parrish must be proved guilty."

He looked up at her with a twisted smile, his muscled back flickering with shadows.

"You truly don't know what a monster he is, do you?" He rose and approached her slowly. "What he would do if he had y—" He stopped and shook his head. Of course she could not know.

"Get dressed," she said, her eyes wide and luminous with concern. She handed him the white, bloodstained shirt he had discarded. She turned and signaled to Stolley it was time to saddle the horses. The deaf mute shut the door quietly with a last wary glance at the baronet.

Behind her she heard the silky sound of a hand sliding through a sleeve. She turned. He had one arm through, his wounded shoulder covered, as his arm crooked back to reach the other sleeve dangling behind him.

He stopped to look at her, then shrugged the garment fully on. "I don't want your sympathy. I trust these lengthy confidences have paid for a compliant companion," he said.

"No. Only an honest one," she answered, her heart beating high and shallow.

"That's even better," he said, walking slowly to her and pulling her close. "I would like an honest reaction from you."

She brought her arm up to push him away. Her hand pressed ineffectively against his bare chest, the black hair rising soft between her outspread fingers.

"You want truth, Sir Ian? You have the morals of a Cardiff dock thief and the breath of a Drury Lane sot."

"That's all?" He placed his warm hand over hers and pressed her palm flat to the hard planes of his chest.

"And the basest instincts of a rutting stag."

He guided her hand upward along his shoulder, across his

collarbone, to the strong cord of his neck. "A brave image for a young virgin to project. Are you brave or just foolish?" He removed his hand slowly.

The small one under his pulled away quickly, but he caught it easily. "I thought so." Gently he drew her hand to him again and pressed it to the firm ridge of his lips. Her fingers were finely formed and moist with her fear.

His lips traveled down to her palm then and pressed a kiss there.

Like a flower closing, her fingers folded over the secret warmth he had breathed into the soft crease of her hand. But the gentleness of his touch belied the hard, pressing line of his body that molded itself against her.

She grew uncomfortably aware of how warm she felt, of the sweet scent of the whiskey, of the thick swelling against her belly.

He released her hand and shook his head. "What do I do with you?" he whispered.

"You cannot decide," she said, "because you have no right."

"Then you choose, Jenna." He smoothed back the wild, damp hair from her face and tilted her chin high. Her lips did not welcome him, yet his mouth played there, pulling and probing gently until her lips softened to a sweet fullness. They parted then, showing a moist curiosity he wanted to satisfy. But she twisted suddenly and struggled free.

"No," she said.

"A wiser choice than I would make," he said unevenly, "since we have no time."

Jenna walked past him to get her cloak.

He began to fasten his cuffs. "Some honest advice."

Something in his voice stopped her.

"Never again step between me and a knife." He picked up her cloak. "I may not be able to save you.. And I promised your father you would survive our gambit."

"We shall all survive," she said.

"I like your confidence," Stonebridge said, holding the cape behind her. "Next time express it without the quiver."

The garment settled around her shoulders like a cold, dark shroud.

Chapter 7

Stonebridge knocked twice, then twice again. Leona raised the small cellar door at the east corner of Glen Manor's stone foundation.

Stonebridge and Jenna carefully descended the rickety wooden steps to the tiny basement hideaway Stolley had built and insulated with wood and straw.

"I was worried," Leona whispered. She held an oil lantern. Its flickers played on the tired visages of the riders.

"Stolley was with us. He is fine," Jenna assured her, her voice low.

"The meeting?" Leona asked.

"Went well. The Red Bow will ride," Stonebridge said.

Jenna had no energy for surprise. How many more of her friends would she find caught up in her father's strange crusade?

Leona led the way to wide, musty steps that ended behind a slatted door near the fireplace in Cook's kitchen. Leona scouted the big room and the servants' stairwell before signaling Stonebridge to come ahead. Then she waited at the top of the stairs on the second floor, her lantern casting black, outsized shadows in the stairwell as her young friend and Stonebridge made their way up.

Jenna, wet and shivering, mounted the steps one at a time,

her arm cradling her side. She paused on the third stair. "Go past," she whispered to Stonebridge, her shadow bending low in the small corridor.

Without warning, Stonebridge swept her into his arms. Too exhausted to protest, she clasped her hands tightly at the nape of his neck for balance. She tried to stiffen her torso away from his, but he hefted her up against his chest until she nestled in the bow of his shoulder.

"Be still. I'm only a beast of burden," he whispered, and went up the steps.

"Beast, I agree," she said. But fatigue—and his physical closeness—took the bite from her words. His long hair covered her wrist in a soft, silken ruffle. She curbed an impulse to sift a strand of his dark hair between her thumb and forefinger. "Your shoulder?"

He shook his head, dismissing it, and carried her easily up the stairs to the shadowy hallway. Her breath came as delicately as a dove's step in the crook of his neck. Her cheek brushed inadvertently against the rough black stubble on his chin and she remembered his fevered kiss in the cottage. The harsh, grinding pressure of his mouth on hers as he reached fervently for something deep inside her.

How easily she curled against him now. How hot the line of his body against hers. How slowly he walked.

She tensed. "Put me down," she said.

He ignored her.

She grasped a handful of hair at the nape of his neck and pulled hard. "Now!" she whispered, urgent.

She felt the strong arm supporting her back twist around to entangle his own hand in her waist-length hair.

He tugged just enough to tilt her head back. Her defiant eyes met his. God save him from a hurt, tired girl afraid of becoming a tart. He wanted to deride her fears, chide her for a fool. But the warmth of her, the firm but soft roundness of her breast against his chest, the curve of her waist where his fingertips lay, the fine line of her brow etched below tousled hair—all called to him. But neither he nor she could afford his answer.

He set her down without a word. She turned away so he would not see the pink flush of her cheeks, then walked slowly to her bedchamber, where Leona waited with the lamp.

Stonebridge paused at her door. "Keep her well," he said to Leona. Then he disappeared to his "sickbed" and his role of injured gentleman.

Leona helped Jenna remove her wet clothes.

"I thought someone like you too wise to be a party to this," Jenna said as Leona found a clean white nightdress in the drawer of the armoire.

Leona smiled sadly. "I have spent years exercising wisdom and reason. It did nothing to stop Parrish. And he must be repaid." Leona's voice grew soft. "Pain for pain."

Jenna reached out to grasp the older woman's arm. Leona shook her head at the questions in Jenna's eyes. "Only when you understand the hideous soul inside him will you forgive us for acting like desperate fools." She pulled away from Jenna gently and lay the cotton gown across the girl's outstretched hand.

Jenna could not speak. A tear had marred the soft, crinkled smile of her friend.

Leona gathered the wet clothes and left. Jenna went to the window, more afraid than she had ever been.

He had made Leona cry. Dear God, what had he done to her mother?

* * *

As dawn broke over the ridge of the Pennines that morning, Hutton Parrish tucked the covers around the sleeping Carolina. Last night he had given her laudanum.

Hutton could barely walk away from her, the throbbing was so fierce. She had not even tapped his need. Hutton closed his eyes, annoyed. She tried, Lord knows she tried. But she had submitted too soon, and that always made him angry. And she lacked imagination. Nothing he could do about that, Hutton sighed.

Lovemaking was the essence of a man and woman's primal relationship with each other. And Carolina refused to plumb the depths of her natural instincts. Bless her limited capacity, her primary response was fear. Even after he had spent three painstaking years teaching her the movements of each procedure. She knew her part well, like an actress practicing a craft. But he needed someone with fire and spirit to make it the art he knew it could be.

And he needed her now, while he still had years left to appreciate her.

What would she be up to this morning? he wondered. Sleeping late after her successful evening, probably. Or perhaps she rose before dawn, as he did, to fit as much work as possible into her day. Lying there in her high four-poster bed, one hand brushing dark strands of hair away from her young, unguarded eyes, her skin as sweet-scented as the rosewater in which she bathed.

He would require the simple things first. There was so much to teach. His approach would be deliciously slow, weeks in the making, to lengthen his anticipation and . . .

He yanked the bell rope with all his might. "Find Master

Connell!" he spat at the servant who answered the strangled call of the bell.

Hutton quickly took the curving grand staircase to the ground floor, stopping at the bottom to look upward. A wrought-iron chandelier the size of a dining table was suspended in the three-story stairwell. Thirty feet above him was the gilt-framed ceiling mural of Venus and Vulcan, the Roman god of fire. Vulcan gazed down on him, red-robed and stern. Hutton took a deep breath. It had cost him a fortune, but the effect was magnificent.

He went through the great hall to the library and sat down to his bookkeeping. Tabulating the sums always had a calming effect. He worked, pen in hand, until the door rocked open.

Connell lumbered in, tying the sash of his dressing gown. "You know I hate these godforsaken dialogues at daybreak," Connell grumbled. "My nightcap's not even had time to wear off."

Hutton tsked indulgently. "Just a little trouble in the miners' camp. My friend there tells me something's brewing."

"What's wrong?"

"That's what I want you to find out. You'll need an early start," Hutton said with a smile, closing his book with a soft snap of the spine. He stepped to the fireplace and tugged once on a fringed gold tassel.

"That damn well better be my tea you're ringing for," Connell groaned, holding his head in pale, freckled hands.

"Of course," Hutton sighed, eyebrows arched. "And, Connell?"

"Yes?"

"It is time to press your suit for Lady Jenna's hand. I understand she had a rich, handsome gentleman paying her compliments last night. It wouldn't do to let him get the upper hand in her affections."

"The only thing that bitch has affection for is slittin' my gullet with her tongue."

Hutton smiled and flicked a tiny dust mote off a gilt-edged plate resting on the mantlepiece. "She baits you. You must be the fisherman. Stay calm. Toss out your net. She will get tangled, fight a little. Then it's a simple matter to reel her in."

"Ha!" Connell snorted. "She's not one of your little minnows with musk glands in place of brains!"

His father's ice-blue eyes narrowed thoughtfully as his lips pursed around a slim cigarette. "I know. There's much more sport when you cast in the deep holes instead of trolling the shallows." He exhaled a long, thin stream of smoke.

Jenna awoke at sunset that day. The baronet had left that morning when her brother Phillip returned in a crested Stonebridge coach.

She crawled stiffly out of bed. The midnight ride had left her side swollen and aching. Wrapped in her dressing gown, she sat down by the fire and thought about how she could extricate her father from this mess.

There were too many innocents involved, uneducated miners like Bilpo Grawlin whose hopes for the new mine safety amendment rode on his risky masquerade as a reincarnated folk hero. Her father, too, was an innocent. A man stripped of pride and purpose by the death of her mother. Surely her mother should have known what a scandal suicide would be. Countess Thornton had lived in the political arena all her married life. She was astute, gracious, a perfect lady.

Jenna's eyes closed as she remembered what life was like before. How her mother had loved their turreted brick town home in London's West End. It was always cozy, warm, frenetic, a constant circus of meetings, dinners and soirees for Parliament's Liberal lords.

But for all the activity and warmth, Countess Thornton had never seemed truly connected to the affairs she hosted. Detached and demure, smiling at the correct moment, she was the perfect politician's wife, always awaiting her next cue to organize and orchestrate.

Beautiful. God, how beautiful her mother had been, Jenna thought. Fair golden-brown hair swept back from a heart-shaped face with hazel eyes as distinct as two green olives on fine white china. She had been a beauty courted by many, Jenna knew. But Charlotte Ashley, a baron's sister, had chosen brash and brilliant Arthur Thornton as the man to adore her. He had been a widower then; Phillip's mother had died in childbirth. The earl quickly began to shine as a star on the political horizon, his lovely Venus by his side.

"Never," Jenna said aloud. She rose and went to her mirror, gazing through lamplight at a dim and worried face. Never did she want to be so beautiful an object as her mother. To sit in a chair as the adornment to a room, to be asked no question more intriguing than who made her gown.

And yet, Jenna frowned, there was a need to be a little lovely at times. Her head tilted thoughtfully in the mirror, her hair slipping like silk over one shoulder, a soft shield over her breast. Critically she assessed her image. Soft-angled, oval face with porcelain skin accented by high cheekbones. A result of her Thornton blood. Mercurial blue eyes that hued soft and tender or intense with purpose. A trait of her high-tempered Ashley grandfather. Lips, fleshed full and pink, that were too wide to be Thornton, too firm to be Ashley. What were they? "Gyspy," her grandfather had teased. "Every family has a gypsy pass through. Lucky all she left is a winsome smile."

Jenna's reflection smiled at the memory. Beloved Papa John had taught her much during her childhood days at Glen Manor. How to hunt, to ride, to travel through the books in her father's library, how to question in order to learn, how to calculate a risk and insure a gain.

"What," she mused, "what would he advise me now?" Her only answer was an echo of her own biting words to Stonebridge. Don't run simpering from the reality of a situation, she had taunted him.

God knew that's just what she wanted to do. Pack her father off to London. Stay with Uncle Ronstead Wilkes, her mother's only brother, a shipowner who would be able to protect them until the mine act faced its destiny in Parliament, until her father let loose his vain hope of striking back at the cause of his downfall.

"Simpering . . ." She saw Stonebridge's mouth form the word uneasily, as if it were alien to his vocabulary. Jenna could not imagine the imposing baronet running like a silly fool from anything. He would always chart a sure course to his goal, test the water, measure its depth, then plunge ahead.

Two slim fingers raised en route to her lips, the girl in the mirror looked suddenly young to Jenna. Gently, so lightly, she traced a path across her half-open mouth, the trail Ian's tongue had followed so many hours ago. She swallowed. Slowly she licked her finger lightly. Then she retraced the trail Ian had marked, the moisture sticky and warm on the tip of her finger. The feelings came back, his mouth joined with hers, the helpless swoon that she could not bear yet did not want to end. The pounding ache in her groin that came from the tumult deep inside her.

Quickly Jenna closed her eyes so she could no longer see the helpless young woman in the mirror.

But head bowed, waist pressed hard against the washstand, she could still feel. Him.

"Sir Ian has asked to pay a call on us tomorrow," her father said the next morning at breakfast.

Jenna's heart beat faster. A public call. An outward show of courtship. The game was advancing and she still did not know the rules.

As the earl nibbled absently on an oatcake, Jenna noticed how wrinkled his silk dressing gown was. The black velvet trim along the collar edge was worn. He dressed with the care of a Haymarket cigar merchant, she thought.

Then she looked down at the frayed cuff of her gray day dress. Was she any better? And why, quite suddenly, did she care?

"You look better this morning, Father," she said, adding a dollop of blackberry jam to one of Cook's light, soft crumpets.

"This poultice Leona made keeps me awake," he grumbled, patting the thick linen scarf tucked into his dressing gown. "Stinks to high heaven."

"But your breathing is better. I must talk with you about—"

His hard frown stilled her inquiry. He glanced quickly at the door to the morning room and rose.

"I am fatigued. We will talk later."

"But, Father—"

He rose and patted her hand. "Come to my room," he whispered. He left with a hand to his chest and a hacking cough.

Jenna kept a tight rein on her annoyance. She chewed her

crumpet and gazed out the window. Rolling curves of soft grass met the graceful oak stands which lined the carriage road leading up to the manor portico. Her father risked all that was dear to her—her home, her family, her name.

This estate had been her most treasured world once, this room one of her havens. The morning room, with floor-to-ceiling panes, allowed streams of eastern sunlight. The plaster of the ceiling was bordered with insets of gold-edged fleurs-de-lis. The wallpaper was blue, flat, a simple and outdated design but one which Jenna liked better than the scrambled prints and raised patterns so popular now.

She and her grandfather had spent pleasant hours reading stories in the satinwood settee near the fireplace. The long, low seat was covered with a fringed yellow dustcover now. Underneath were memories. The smudge marks of her shoes as she climbed into his lap. The tiny ash burns where his pipe had sputtered. The lemonade spill which had just missed page 109 of his ship's diary. It was the entry about the whale sightings on his journey to India, and her mother, cool, poised and beautiful, had walked in on the mess. Jenna prepared herself for a scolding, but the countess merely rang for a servant and shook her head. "Both of you are cooking tall tales for breakfast again," she smiled. "I think I'll have some, too."

Her mother had sat carefully on the edge of the navy-blue davenport, arranging her unwieldy hoop skirt so that no lace edge of anklet would show. Impulsively the eight-year-old Jenna had run to her, scrambling up and across the sea of scallop-shell silk until she had her arms around her mother's neck. The countess giggled and hugged her tight.

Mrs. Searle, then a ladies' maid in white cap and apron, walked in. "My lady! She'll crush the crinoline!" she cried.

With the appearance of Mrs. Searle Jenna felt her mother withdraw to a gracious coolness. Countess Thornton slowly loosened Jenna's arms, gave her daughter's cheek a quick kiss and said: "We must be careful, Jenna."

Careful of what? Jenna thought as she looked into hazel eyes which looked as puzzled as Jenna's own. Careful of hugging? It wasn't the crinoline hoop which kept them apart. It could be scaled. It was something else.

Propriety. He mother had excelled at it. And her reward was death.

Mother. Jenna swallowed hard to keep the loneliness deep in her chest. How unfair. The hollow knot began to well in her throat. I miss you so much. There is so much to tell you, things I must ask. . . .

But she was gone long before Jenna grew woman enough to understand her distance—and forgive her.

Jenna downed the last sip of tea in her cup and set it unsteadily in its rim. Her hand was trembling. If Hutton Parrish was truly the cause of her loss, he would be punished. "Pain for pain," Leona had said in her hard and haunted voice.

"Excuse me, m'lady." Jenna froze by the table. Eaton stood in the doorway. With Connell Parrish.

"I thought Lord Thornton was still here, m'lady. The young squire said he had urgent business to discuss," Eaton explained. He bowed quickly and left.

"Forgive me." Connell walked forward and bowed, his gloved hand reaching for hers.

Jenna felt her stomach tighten. The tenseness spread through her chest, down her spine, like a shell hardening around her. The Ice Maiden extended a cool hand to her enemy.

"Connell." She felt his soft, dry lips peck the back of her hand. "This is highly irregular."

"I know. I apologize," he said. She watched his eyes flick over her casual dress, uncorseted waist and the curtain of loose black hair tumbling around her shoulders.

"I must talk to your father," he said.

She hated his eyes most of all. So light a blue they might have been two blank holes in his face. Empty. Unreadable. Exactly like his father's.

"He is sick. He cannot receive visitors today," she said, her hands clasped in front of her skirt.

"How unfortunate," he said. "It is time for me to repeat my offer of marriage and to formally ask your father for your hand. It was a mistake not to personally approach him earlier. But we were sensitive to his—infirmity." His face remained carefully inscrutable, a pale, blank mask that was neither handsome nor ugly. A pinched, chameleon's face.

"Your sensitivity is much appreciated. But the answer is the same." Jenna looked straight into his narrow-set eyes. "I will not marry you. I am already engaged."

A muscle in the hollow of his jaw jumped once, then was still. He smiled.

"I'm sure you need time to think about such a serious question. I will call again—"

"Don't. You know I would never wed a Parrish."

"Political differences do not matter when a man takes a wife," he said softly.

"I differ with you for personal reasons. You are a liar and a cruel man."

With utmost control, he kept his temper. Brazen chit, he thought. Don't let her bait you, his father's words echoed. Connell forced a laugh. "Many fascinating marriages have been built on hatred, my lady. Ours would be a stormy, fascinating affair, I'm sure."

"There will be no affair. Ever. You may take your leave."

She turned her back to him. After a full, tense minute, she heard his riding boots stride toward the door.

"Until next time," he called smoothly. She whirled, but he was gone.

Eaton had reappeared accompanied by a liveried footman and a tall man in a dull brown morning coat. Jenna recognized Ross, the Scotch servant who acted as Stonebridge's valet.

"A message from Sir Ian, my lady," Ross said. The footman bowed and presented a large velvet-covered box.

She felt Eaton's eyes absorbing all the details of the moment as she slowly opened the lid of the box.

Inside, a gleaming emerald teardrop necklace lay on a white satin cushion. "My master said to tell you these gifts have been in the Stonebridge family for four generations. He gives them to you, anticipating the fifth."

Jenna bit her lip to keep an epithet on his master's presumptive manner unsaid. "It's a breathtaking piece," she said. Gingerly, she reached for a small gold case that nested separately in a corner of the box. The case was inscribed with the Stonebridge crest—a rearing panther with the head of a falcon.

Inside, lying on a ridge of black velvet, was a diamond ring. Jenna heard Eaton's sharp intake of breath. The stone was large, perched at the center of a triangle of gold filigree. The band was delicate and thin. Jenna picked it up carefully.

"It's actually one-half of a ring, m'lady," Ross said. "There's another diamond-stud band that attaches to the setting. On the wedding day. The ring was handed down to the old sir for his marriage to Sir Ian's mother."

Jenna's eyes closed a moment. The bastard baronet was using real props in this farce. The fool. Did he truly expect her to flaunt an authentic family heirloom?

"He left a note for you," Ross prompted. A small folded card was tucked in the lid of the large box.

> Dear Jenna,
>   Wear it. We are engaged. Until tomorrow,
>   I.

Lips tight, Jenna placed the card back in the box and did as she was bid. With care she slid the ring on her finger and found it only slightly too big. She extended her arm and stretched out her hand to look at the stone. It gleamed like a beacon, calling attention to her small, fair hand.

"It's really quite beautiful," she said truthfully. "I—I am honored by the special meaning this ring bestows. Please wait while I prepare a response to your master."

As she went to her desk to find pen and paper, she pretended not to hear the hollow, diminishing clump of boot soles striding down the oak floor of the hallway to the front door. Each sharp step was a reminder to her, though: every performance has an audience.

It was early afternoon before she could make time to visit her father.

She found him drowsy and unable to answer her clearly. On the bed stand was a small brown bottle of syrup from a Lancaster chemist.

"Ian's medicine. I'm so tired," he muttered. "Don't talk," he whispered. "Eaton will hear. He spies on us, the Parrish dog. But I have a hawk, Jenna." He coughed phlegm into a handkerchief.

"What do you mean?"

"A hawk in the Parrish house, who flies back to me. Be careful, sweet. Be careful. . . ."

His gray head lay back on the pillow and his chest heaved in a restless sleep.

The earl did not come down to dinner that evening.

Mrs. Searle was home from the funeral of her father, a cobbler in Buxton. Dressed as always in black, the thin, prim woman moved from sideboard to table. Supervising an informal dinner for Jenna and Phillip, she used her long service as an excuse to talk to Jenna during the meal.

"I must apologize for my absence during a difficult time for you," Mrs. Searle said to Jenna. "I heard about your accident. I hope you are feeling better."

Jenna looked up into her round face with its narrow-set green eyes. "Leona is a good nurse. I am grateful that she could stay after helping us with the dinner."

"Of course. It sounds as if the baronet and his party went away very impressed." She sounded almost disappointed. "Your soup, my lady." Mrs. Searle placed a steaming bowl in front of her.

"Did you have a good ride to Stonebridge Hall with Robert?" Jenna asked Phillip.

"Smashing. What I remember of it," he said, tipping his bowl to scoop the last bits of "beef" in the soup. "I understand you slept the day away yesterday. Exhausted after your performance that night, no doubt," he said. Mrs. Searle removed his bowl.

Jenna was quiet a moment. "What do you mean?"

"One brief evening in which you dress like a real woman and curb your tongue—somewhat—and you snag a filthy rich baronet just like that!" He snapped his fingers.

"Why does that cause you outrage?" she asked, smiling.

"Because an honorable man has been paying court to you for three months and you have not been polite enough to give him a response."

"I did respond to Connell. I sent back his flowers, his French chocolates and his requests to call on me. I detest him and his family. Does he not understand rejection?"

"Oh, but you're an arrogant little tripe. With one little yes you could unite two houses. But instead, you become a spiteful, money-hungry little baggage and accept the suit of a bastard privateer."

"Rumors do not make a bastard," Jenna said smoothly. "Nothing is proved. Except that Ian Stonebridge is heir to the Stonebridge name. His Lancashire estate is a thousand acres. His London town home has a walled garden. He has estates on the east coast in Essex and a yacht in Brightlingsea and God knows what holdings across the ocean. It's more than you or Hutton Parrish will ever have. Tell him that, Phillip." She stood up to leave. "And tell his cur of a son that he will never rise to the rank of son-in-law to the earl."

Mrs. Searle's mouth formed a silent, shocked "Oh!" Jenna moved toward the door.

"You are more greedy than I thought." Phillip stopped her near the columned arch of the dining room. "Already you wear a token of the price Stonebridge will pay to have you in his bed." Phillip tugged at the emerald necklace that gleamed against her white throat. "Yes, I know of his gifts and his oh-so-proper request to court your hand in marriage. You are going to ruin everything." His voice had grown soft, almost pleading.

"It is you who are gambling away your birthright. Why, I don't know. But I shall find out. And in the meantime, quite by accident, I have gained new resources to save the Thornton name you so thoroughly put to shame."

Her head tilted high, defiant, she pulled the emerald strand from Phillip's fingers.

For a brief moment the Venetian chandelier above them caught a glimmer of green.

Chapter 8

Sir Ian visited Glen Manor the following afternoon for tea.

Ellen brought the tray to the drawing room. She could hardly keep from smiling. Her cool young mistress looked a bit unnerved in the company of her strapping new fiancé. Sittin' at the edge of her chair like that, Ellen thought, skittish as a doe ready to leap away.

And the earl, poor old sore-chested fool, hackin' and chokin'. Never should have got out of 'is bed. And that devilish Stonebridge squire. Looked amused, he did, like teacups and party games were a lark.

"So glad to see you feeling better, Lady Jenna," Stonebridge smiled.

Dressed conservatively for tea, he looked too handsome to be her ruffian of the woods, too sure to be the tortured confessor in the cottage. The wool of his dark brown jacket was new, impeccably brushed, his white shirt clean and crisp. He wore no obvious signs of wealth. No heavy gold watch chains crisscrossing his vest, no jeweled cuffs. But the vest buttons that lined his flat, hard stomach were carved ivory.

She avoided his gaze. "You look well also."

"I brought the gowns your seamstress sent from Liverpool," he said, and popped a strawberry tea cake into his mouth.

"Wh—?"

The earl broke in, "Oh, um, yes, Ian, thank you." The earl turned to Jenna. "Ian's tailor is affiliated with the seamstress from whom I ordered your new gowns."

"New gow—?"

"Of course. They are only now getting them finished. I sent them a deposit last month."

"Father! How much—?"

"Jenna! Ian did not travel nine miles from Stonebridge Hall to hear us discuss petty—"

"But, Father—" she whispered.

"Ian has invited us to attend the opera with him in Liverpool tomorrow evening. I said we could."

"But this is such short notice. It is a long journey by train. I have correspondence overdue, I must find a fence builder for Squire Ames, the Tiltons had a cooking fire in the room above their shop last week—"

"If you will permit, Lord Thornton, I can offer you craftsmen to attend to the jobs," Stonebridge said with a strained smile.

"I'm sure my father cannot accept your generosity."

"Yes, I can," the earl said wearily. "You two continue your visit. I must return to my bed or I shall never hear that redhead soprano warble her aria tomorrow. Excuse me."

"I believe the lady could benefit from a more soothing atmosphere. Shall we walk in the garden?" Stonebridge stood and crooked his arm, awaiting hers.

"I could benefit more from a soothing companion," she grumbled, voice low.

"I'm trying to make things easier for you."

"Then why do things seem so difficult when you're here?"

"I'm only hoping to find you clothed in something a little beyond the time of Queen Victoria's infancy!"

"You impertinent—!'

"Smile, Jenna," he whispered, turning warmly to her as Mrs. Searle hurried in. "Remember, you are smitten."

"If I had something in my hand, sir, you would be," she smiled sweetly.

They strolled to the stairs and descended. Ellen passed them on her way upstairs to finish the rooms. What a pair of lovebirds they made! she thought. They'd be off to an opera tomorrow, Mrs. Searle said. And the lady had some new gowns the earl had ordered. Maybe the old bugger was finally ridin' on two rockers ag'in. Oh, things are workin' out so fine for Lady Jenna! Ellen hummed an old love ballad as she hurried down the hallway.

"What are you singing about?" growled Eaton, hurrying along with the earl's top hat. The old man wanted it brushed and brushed right now! The birdy old loon wouldn't need it till tomorrow. From the window at the end of the upstairs hall, Eaton scowled down on the couple in the garden.

"So you find me a dowdy little bird?" she asked, coolly conversational as they walked arm in arm along the winding, daffodil-lined path. "My clothes unbefitting my rich new caller?"

"Your clothes befit a house besieged by hard times. You need better."

She had stopped, staring fixedly ahead. "I am an object of charity. A bedraggled chicken to be grandly trimmed until time for the feasting."

"You are extraordinary without any trimming at all. I know." Stonebridge tugged her ahead before she could hurl her heated response. "But you have too much pride. It is time to reclaim your family's good name. And you must start by being the gracious daughter of an earl, not the testy nursemaid to the poor and brain-addled."

"You have no idea of the financial difficulties we face, nor of the ideals I adhere to," Jenna said coldly.

"I know more than you would like, little clerk. And as for ideals, I know that they can be achieved only with money and power. And the Thorntons have their share of neither."

She jerked her arm out of his grasp and hurried ahead on the path to a gazebo shaded by a weeping willow. She stood by the rose-trellised entrance, controlling her anger.

"For a woman who espouses a love of the straightforward and honest, you're reluctant to embrace the truth when it's handed you," Stonebridge said quietly from behind her.

"It's never easy to bear, especially when it's delivered as delicately as a hammer blow," she said angrily. "You are too bloody blunt."

"It's only one of a thousand faults," he smiled.

"God save me from encountering the rest," she hissed.

He was silent. Finally, "I will save you from all that I can."

The tone of his voice struck her. She felt her anger float away like a child's balloon, untethered and forgotten. In its place was a tight throb in her abdomen, the feeling she had tried to keep at bay from the moment he had appeared in the damask-draped doorway of the drawing room.

"The game frightens me." She dared not turn to him.

"But we are committed to play." She felt his warm presence at her back.

"I want no one hurt," she said as calmly as she could.

"Not even Parrish?" he asked. He placed his hands on her shoulders and slowly turned her to face him. "You must think I'm a hired murderer."

"I don't know what you are." She searched his face.

"Of course you do," he said with a serious smile. "I am your intended. And this"—he tipped her chin upward—"is permitted."

His kiss was not proper. It went on much too long. She lost track of time. The only certainty she clung to was the nearness of his body to hers. They were alone on the steps of the trellis house, protected in a shaft of spring sunlight. Small red tea roses lent their clinging perfume to the air around her as she caught the searing, searching press of his lips. His mouth molded itself to hers, moving slowly at first, until she relented and parted her lips. His tongue slid between, questioning. Unsure, her own tongue flicked a warm, wet question of its own. He answered quickly, plunging deep into her open mouth, replacing her breath and her senses with a warm, sure fullness that lasted long and left her aching for more.

But she would not ask for more. Already she had only the barest control. Breathless, she pulled away from his mouth, from the tea-bitter taste at the base of his tongue, from the sweet musky smell hidden in his sideburns, from the thick tweed coat that she wished was not between them.

His dark eyes roamed her face intently. She shook her head, a trembling request to stop.

He exhaled a ragged sigh, eyes closed, and answered by stroking his hand upward from the small of her back until it cupped the back of her neck. With a gentle force he pushed her head forward to lay against his chest. Her hands should have pushed him away. Instead, they slipped quickly inside the flap of his coat to press hard against his warmth, the soft linen of his shirt feeling as silky as the dark hair she knew was underneath.

"Jenna—" he whispered into her hair.

Her hands clenched suddenly, nearly tearing his shirt. She

whirled away from him and went swiftly down the gazebo steps. She stood just out of reach.

He stayed on the platform, watching her through the trellis. At length he asked: "Was that for whoever is watching us? Or was that you?"

Jenna was silent. He knew the answer. "I do not perform like some trained animal panting for a tidbit."

"True," he agreed. "You have a natural spontaneity that is suited to a smaller audience. An audience of one."

Her face flushed hotly. "I do not give private showings to you or anyone else."

"That's a good rule." He straightened his coat and walked slowly to her. "As long as you keep to it, we shall both stay out of trouble. Let us go." He extended his arm.

She hesitated, wary.

"Neither of us can afford more time alone." Stiffly, she slid her arm through his and fell into step beside him, a sedate distance apart.

The silence was uncomfortable. "Tonight is your meeting with Bilpo Grawlin?" she asked finally. They were passing the tall, tiered fountain where a chipped marble cupid splashed water into a pool.

Stonebridge halted at the edge of the loud, churning water. "There might be a problem," he said.

The little miner still planned to meet, but Bilpo had sent word changing the time and the place. "It suggests he is in danger, I think," Stonebridge said.

"I hope you're wrong," Jenna shuddered. Her shawl slipped from her shoulders.

"Sometimes I am." Stonebridge draped the soft lace across her arms. "But not usually in illicit matters like these." He reached down and pulled one yellow flower from the bed of hundreds that bobbed and rippled in the strong spring breeze. "The trick is to concentrate on what will bloom, not what will die." He handed the soft-petaled flower to Jenna.

She was quiet a moment, then spoke low in the direction of the splashing water. "What did Parrish do to make my mother take her life?"

Stonebridge did not answer.

"I have a right to know."

"But you wouldn't be able to control your hatred the next time you meet him. You would endanger what we've planned."

"*We! We!* Just how many are 'we'?" Jenna exploded.

"Keep your voice down," he said through gritted teeth.

"I will not be put off." She waited in the uncomfortable silence.

Her profile was coolly adamant, but her hands gripped the fountain rail as if she were afraid of falling. Stonebridge ran a hand through his hair. He respected her right to know, but he dreaded the bitterness it would bring to the surface. He stepped away to give his words room. He would relay to her only a part of the past, but never would he tell her all that the earl's hawk had told him.

"Parrish lured your mother to a rendezvous," he said quietly. "She was told she would get vital information. Death threats had been sent to your father after his pro-union speeches in Parliament. She thought she would learn details of a planned attack. Instead, Parrish raped her."

Jenna focused her eyes and her emotions on the pounding water.

"More than once," Stonebridge said softly.

It was time to close her eyes, to wish she had not asked. Her clenched fist pounded slowly against her breastbone. There, under her worn lace bodice, the silver locket lay. The locket that kept the dead flower safe. The locket that stopped time at her mother's funeral each time Jenna opened the tiny door.

Stonebridge reached out and enclosed her small fist with his hand. To Eaton, watching from the upstairs portico, it was a lover's gesture offered to a shy young woman. Playing coy, was she, after letting him kiss her in the gazebo? The Ice Maiden was turning out to be a hot little tart. The butler pressed grim lips together and left to answer the old lord's bell summons.

At the fountain where cupid smiled, Jenna swallowed hard. There would be no tears. Only justice.

"How did you find out?"

"We have a witness who heard Parrish boast."

"Where is this witness whose conscience appeared too late to save my family's honor or my mother's life?" Jenna asked bitterly.

"It doesn't matter. There's nothing to be done legally. Parrish is too clever."

"You're wrong! She should have accused him! We will accuse him!"

Ian was silent.

Jenna turned away from his sympathy, realizing how futile her idea was. "He must be stopped," Jenna said, "before he hurts someone else."

Ian said nothing, only offered his arm. They walked slowly back to the marble terrace where their stroll had begun. It seemed, somehow, long ago.

He bowed and kissed her hand, his lips warm and soft next to the diamond he had given her.

"The ring becomes you. It is almost a perfect fit." He jostled it gently on her finger.

"You play masquerade games with valuable toys," Jenna said. "Why?"

"So that it will seem real, of course," he smiled. "Until the opera tomorrow."

He left. She twisted the ring back into position. It did fit almost perfectly.

The nightmare of her mother's assault preyed on Jenna's mind that night. She did not sleep well.

"The baronet has arranged for us to stay with an old friend of his, Lady Helen Whitston. She is a widow," Jenna's father said at their early breakfast the next day.

Jenna rubbed the back of her stiff neck and thought about the Lady Whitston, an eccentric old matron of society who adopted every titled Londoner who spent the summer in the countryside. Lady Whitston had long ago given up her dream of orchestrating a season for Liverpool. The town was England's busiest seaport. Money flowed freely, along with foreign transients. Wealth was granted indiscriminately to the industrious and the clever, and thus was bestowed on people who had no idea how to use it. The rich merchants had driven the poor blue-nosed matron crazy with their pleas to be admitted to polite society. Jenna smiled at the thought of meeting the famous Lady Whitston. "Where's Phillip?" she asked.

"Still in his dressing gown. He awoke too late for breakfast. Eaton is trying to get him packed."

"Then we must talk." She was firm, her voice low.

The earl set his teacup back on its saucer and sighed heavily. "I have not done right by you, have I?" He ran a trembling hand through the gray frizz he had forgotten to comb.

"No, you haven't." She was careful not to look at her father. "Ian told me," she said gently.

The earl did not speak for a full minute. Perhaps he did not breathe. She could not hear his labored wheezing.

"Good," he whispered. "For I could never have formed the words that would tell you how your mother was debased. It is so private a horror for me. A terrifying picture that's seared in my mind. Each day I envision it, and my vengeance grows more sure. I should have been able to keep her safe, but I had no idea." He had come around behind Jenna and placed his hands on her shoulders. She could feel the trembling in his arms.

"It is not too late to call a halt to the madness."

The old man's flushed face lit up with a tremulous smile. "Oh, but it is too late, Jenna. The mine camp is abuzz with rumors that Parrish cannot break the strike. Bilpo used my sovereigns to buy food and medicine, and he's spread word that a lord other than me has been drawn to their cause."

The union leader Alexander McBryde was back in London awaiting any evidence the earl could provide that Parrish was stealing Thornton coal. As soon as the earl could prove the trespass and theft, McBryde would pass it discreetly on to sympathetic lords in the House who were lobbying for mine safety.

"The thought of hurting him is the only thing that keeps me sane right now." His voice was soft, full of pain. "But each day I become more worried for you. The demon bastard wants you, Jenna. By my life, I won't let it happen again."

"Please," she said in the voice of someone very young, "don't let anything happen to you."

He was quiet. Then she felt him plant a kiss on the top of

her head. "Don't worry. It will be soon over. And Ian will be here to help."

The earl stepped back and ran his hand through his hair. "It is time to go. It is a relief to finally be in motion. Going somewhere after three long years. And by my side will be a beautiful young woman. You look very becoming in your new finery."

Jenna stood up in the flounced navy-blue twill. Its classic lines draped to a manageable train in the back for traveling. "You chose good colors for me."

The earl kissed her on the cheek. "I did not choose them," he smiled.

Half an hour later the Thorntons were settled in the carriage for the winding ride to Turton Bottoms. There the coach would be strapped aboard a flatcar for the train journey to Liverpool. Stonebridge had sent two liveried coachmen to tend to the luggage and the horses. But the earl insisted that it be Stolley who drove the matched speckled whites, even if he had no formal dress. The baronet had also offered to send a posh rented carriage, but the earl wanted to arrive in the aging coach with the Thornton crest of arms on the door.

The ride was jolting, boring and cold. Jenna could find nothing to say to Phillip. Her father dozed in one corner, his breathing labored. She opened a book and pretended to read.

"You are really quite a striking young woman when you dress well," Phillip said.

"Generous of you, Phillip," she said, adjusting the set of the delicate ash-colored hat. It was an elaborate basket-weave design perched lightly on a high nest of curls which Ellen had fashioned with pins and ingenuity that morning.

"But then, Connell always said you were beautiful. Said

you dressed dowdy in order to hide yourself from prying eyes. Like an innocent fawn playing at camouflage."

"Your friend is a trifle poetic. But mostly a trifle," Jenna said. The talk of Connell made her uncomfortable. She wanted to hurry the argument and be done with it.

Phillip did not rise to the bait. "I would certainly want you to stay innocent, little sister," he said casually.

"What do you imply?"

"That Stonebridge has a salacious reputation. They say he has tasted every native woman he has come across in his travels. All in the interests of scientific research, I'm sure."

Inwardly Jenna fumed. "I would venture a guess that your own—experiments—have been—varied. And they would certainly have been more numerous if you had not made love to a wine bottle first."

She watched his jaw clench shut. But he did not explode. "You have found me easy to goad. But I will be a more difficult target from now on. Connell pointed out how you bait me, belittle me. And I won't be used any longer."

Jenna sighed wearily. "Father and I are the ones being used. We are your family, not Connell, not Hutton Parrish. We are sinking under the weight of your debts."

"They are my friends. The notes are a social propriety. They make the game more interesting between us. I am getting better at the card table in Lancaster, too. I will soon win enough to put your church-mouse little soul at ease."

How had he come to trust the Parrishes so? she wondered. He obviously did not know of Hutton's role in her mother's suicide. Or did he? Phillip, who had been raised by a series of nannies after his mother's death, had always been polite but cool toward Countess Thornton. Never close. Never a genuine son. Jenna felt an apprehensive chill start at the base of her neck. "Your blindness depresses me," she said warily.

"I see clearly enough to want our house united with Connell's for the good of both estates. And I will be watching for any missteps on the part of your disreputable fiancé. Coachman!" He pounded on the roof of the carriage. "Stop here! There's a stand of trees in need of water!"

They exchanged no more words on the trip to the crossroads town of Turton Bottoms. When the carriage had been wrestled aboard the open freight bed, Jenna pleaded fatigue and rode in the covered passenger car, eschewing the grand, open view she would have had in the jostling coach.

At the Liverpool station, the coach creaked in protest as it bumped down the ramp to the ground. A pair of rented grays were harnessed quickly and the carriage wheels were soon rumbling over the cobblestones of city streets.

The driver halted in front of an unusually wide house, four stories high. In the long, wainscoted reception hall, her silk skirt rustling excitedly, a smiling Lady Whitston met her guests.

"And you are the lovely Jenna whom Ian described to me," said the elderly woman, grasping Jenna's gloved hand in her talced and wrinkled one. "You must be exhausted. And only three hours to prepare for the opera. Let us get you quickly to a room to rest," she said in a cackly, shrill voice which loved its own eccentricity. "This is Susannah. She will act as your maid for your stay. Go on now." She urged Jenna up a wide staircase posted with torchères at the landing. "Now for you gentlemen—"

"Oh, how nice, my lady!" Susannah chatted as she hung up Jenna's gowns. "You will be the prize attraction tonight, for sure! Let me help. Yer lucky, mum. Ya don't have ta draw your corset to a pop. My sister, who is a trifle heavy, you know, was once so hard-pressed by her foundation she swooned right off a bridge into the lake."

"How terrible," Jenna murmured.

"Oh, no! Matt—this sailor what's ever so sweet on her—dived right in to save her and they dried their clothes by firelight on the shore."

"Very romantic," Jenna smiled.

"Oh," Susannah rattled on, "Sir Ian is, too, mum. I'm sure yer aware o' that." The girl grinned, tucking a puffy crinoline into the cedar-lined wardrobe. "So dashin', so traveled, so generous with 'is ladies. But jealous as a ram. Once wounded a bloke just for strollin' with a mistress 'e was particularly fond—" Suddenly the fast-tongued girl stopped, red in the face.

Jenna looked at her, eyebrow raised. "And?" Jenna waited.

"Oh, m'lady." Susannah curtsied frantically. "My tongue is a curse. Me own mother said so. It's always gallopin' into trouble and never says the right thing to get me out."

"Well," Jenna smiled, "as curses go, it's not as bad as some. You could have been born with no tongue at all."

"I'd die, my lady," Susannah said, eyes wide. "Truly I would."

"Perhaps not." Jenna's eyes closed as she thought of Stolley in his silent world, running helter-skelter into trouble with no words at all.

"Could you have a tub of warm water brought up for me? I would much rather bathe than nap." Jenna rubbed her temple, tired physically and mentally.

"Of course, my lady." Susannah smiled gratefully, bobbed a lightning curtsy and left.

Jenna stood before the fire, arms crossed, absently rubbing the tense muscles in her shoulders.

So, she was engaged to a dashing, lusty gentleman who defended his mistresses like a greedy dog his bone. Just one more facet to the dark, shirtless man who had shared his anguished secret with her in Leona's cottage. A man who had treated her with blatant honesty on their garden walk. A man whose presence knotted her insides with an unspoken wish. He kissed with such hunger, like a man familiar with the feeling of being empty. Already, in only four days, she had traded him kisses and intimate touches. What more should she expect?

"Beware the hungry man that smiles at 'cha," Cook always said. "'e's lookin' to steal ya blind."

God willing, she could keep her eyes open. At least until the masquerade ended.

At last she was dressed. Patiently Jenna listened to Susannah congratulate herself on the finished product. "My lady, what a vision you make! The lords are all gathered waitin' for you now. I can't wait until they see!"

Jenna swept quickly out the door, eager to begin—and end—the evening. The long, graceful train of the watered-silk evening dress glided along the carpet and warned the drawing-room crowd of her approach.

"Lady Jenna!" Robert Stonebridge exclaimed.

"How are you?" she smiled. "So nice to see you—and I think now, Robert, we could dispose of titles."

"How is it you look even more lovely engaged than you did as a free-spirited young lady?" Robert laughed.

"Your brother challenges me to rise to his expectations."

"Dear lady." Stonebridge came forward and bowed low. "You exceed them all."

She smiled at him then, telling herself she was simply caught up in the make-believe. She saw his eyes rove from the low-cut bodice of the lilac silk to the tailored sleeves and the beaded trim of the flounced overskirt. In her hair Susannah had wound tiny sprigs of white baby's breath into the cascade of curls hanging at her neck. The baronet's gaze at last came to rest on the simple gold chain she wore around her neck.

"I have something more appropriate," he said. He held out a flat case and opened it. A sparkling diamond strand and two small earrings lay on black velvet.

Phillip gasped openly.

The Lady Whitston said, "My, my, Ian. Those are no baubles."

"Too valuable, perhaps, for one evening at the theater." Jenna looked up at him, worried.

"Not at all," he said, holding the necklace in his hand. "These are very happy, dancing gems. They deserve a night at the opera. May I?" he asked, drawing close behind her.

"Of course not. Lady Whitston can help—" Jenna nodded to the elderly woman in a nearby chair.

Stonebridge glanced her way with a questioning brow.

"Highly irregular, Ian," the old woman said with a smile, tilting a crystal wineglass to her lips. "Go right ahead."

He had already lowered the strand to rest on her neck. She felt the warmth of his breath on the fine hair at her nape. His fingers brushed her soft skin lightly as he fastened the necklace. Jenna stood with head lowered.

"Done," he said low, for her ears. "And your reputation is intact."

"It is perched on the edge of a precipice. I trust you not to dash it on the rocks."

He smiled.

"We must be on our way, gentleman." Lady Whitston rose.

They walked out into the hallway. "The lilac is most

fetching," Stonebridge said, "but why did you not choose the magenta gown?"

"I found it a little too—drafty. Perhaps your other lady friends preferred the risk of consumption. I feel I must keep up my strength. Evenings with you tend to be strenuous."

"Indeed." His tone turned serious. "One poor acquaintance of ours found it so."

"Is something wrong? Your meeting with Bilpo—"

Stonebridge suddenly leaned close and whispered: "Shhhh. Phillip comes."

His lips had brushed her ear—inadvertently? She did not know. But she was left with the sweet-strong scent of his cologne in the air between them. A reminder to her senses that he could get very close and still not get caught.

"Where's Father?" Jenna asked as Lady Whitston caught up with them at the door.

"Ill, Jenna. He sends his regrets, but he will not be able to attend with us," Lady Whitston said.

Jenna turned back toward the stairs. "Perhaps I should stay."

"No." Stonebridge's voice stopped her. "Your father would be doubly indisposed if you were to miss a special evening," he said. "His wish was that you and Phillip join us."

"Of course," she said, hating to appear obedient, yet sure her father was more comfortable here.

The group moved out to the steps. Phillip passed close to Jenna. "It only takes one diamond necklace to make you a chit that minds, eh?"

"Phillip." Stonebridge appeared suddenly behind them. "Can I have a brief word with you?"

They walked off to the side. Stonebridge spoke low and briefly. Color drained from Phillip's face and he nervously straightened his tie. He turned to walk away and Jenna heard the baronet say calmly: "I give you my word."

"Let's take a hansom cab and get there quickly," Phillip said to Robert. "We wouldn't want to crowd the others."

Robert grinned at Stonebridge and agreed.

Chapter 9

At first Jenna thought everyone was fascinated with her for a simple reason. She was the female who had trapped the elusive baronet.

But there was more than polite curiosity in the huffy greetings of other young women and the stares of the gentlemen.

"En—vy." Lady Whitston's high-pitched cadence made it two words. Doubly evil. And, to judge by her smile, a very delicious thing to accuse young ladies of. "You're beautiful. Bejeweled. Intelligent. And you have a filthy-rich Stonebridge devil tame at your side. Reason enough for the mediocre to fume, my girl." The elderly woman fanned herself contentedly, hawk-eyeing the other boxes for overt signs of jealousy.

All the cantilevered balcony boxes were richly draped in brocade and arched with rosewood tracery. The Wickham was a small theater, but all the more splendid for its recent renovation. Spires rose from the roof in deference to the Gothic revival. The marble columns in the lobby extended up to a high molded ceiling montage of lyres and masks. Underneath, Liverpool's monied class milled in rustling taffetas and fine velvets, each flounced skirt, ruffled bodice, jeweled cuff, silk cravat and kidskin glove chosen carefully to help each theatergoer read the other's status at a glance.

"Now do let me see that marvelous ring Ian's given you," Lady Whitston said. "We mustn't disappoint your audience." She raised an eyebrow toward the Italian countess playing with her fan in the neighboring box.

Jenna smiled and obliged by removing her long glove.

Phillip remained nervous throughout the entire first act, eyes flitting about the theater. Looking for what? Jenna wondered. At intermission he and Robert left the box to flirt with two boisterous Deerman cousins who were inadequately chaperoned by a small maiden aunt.

"What did you tell Phillip on the steps tonight?" Jenna leaned close to Stonebridge.

"I told him never again to imply that I buy a lady's obedience with baubles. Else I will take a knife to what he values most."

Jenna smiled. "Words are not usually so effective with Phillip."

Stonebridge shook his head. "I don't know how you abide him."

"He is my half brother. And heir to the family title. What am I to do?"

"You could have married early and escaped."

"I prefer a cage I know to one that I don't."

"Our courtship must have the distinct feel of a prison sentence to you," Stonebridge said.

"On the contrary, I take your attentions as lightly as you give them to all your other ladies."

"So I am to be dismissed as easily as a headache, like the poor marquis's son who visited last month?"

"You spy! How many skulking friends do you have gathering downstairs rumors?"

"I never accept rumors. I rely on the confirmation I find in a woman's face."

She looked away, suddenly wary of his game. "Then I must be more careful."

"Indeed, you must," his voice hardened. "We have visitors."

Jenna looked up and felt her heart grow cold.

"So nice to see you again, Lady Jenna," said Connell Parrish, pale eyes strangely intense. He reached for her hand. She stood. His touch felt as flaccid and cool as a fresh fish's belly.

"Good evening," she said. His lips brushed the back of her hand, dry and light, like the legs of a fly. She quickly cast her eyes to the side so he would not see the disdain she could not conceal. Beside Connell, a man stepped forward and intercepted her look of open contempt. Hutton Parrish smiled slowly, amused.

"It's my turn to greet our lovely neighbor." The elder Parrish bowed, back effortlessly straight, with the grace of a courtier. He lifted Jenna's hand from Connell's fingertips.

The white-haired viscount's grasp was warm and hard, so different from his son's. A patrician smile held her eyes as he pressed four firm fingers against the soft flesh at the heart line of her palm. As he raised her hand to his slightly parted lips, her fingers acceded to the pressure and folded softly down into his palm. He bent to press warm lips to the delicate skin on the back of her hand, but she withdrew her hand as soon as she felt the heat of his breath.

Smiling coolly, she inclined her head and murmured an apology. "Excuse me. I promised to meet a friend." Aware of the three men's eyes on her, she gathered her skirts quickly and eased by Hutton Parrish without another glance.

As soon as she had stepped outside the brocade curtain of

their alcove, she fell trembling against a Doric column. How dare he! she breathed, shaking with rage. How dare he think he could kiss her hand so easily!

Ian was right. Her heart was sick with hatred at the sight of Parrish. She had fought the urge to jerk away at his very touch. God help her to control herself better at their next meeting or she would endanger the whole bloody plan. She breathed deeply, straightening her shoulders before anyone could notice her disposition.

Inside, Ian had covered her sudden exit with a smooth comment about the eternal partnership between ladies and their powder rooms. He made a nodding bow to Hutton.

"I am Ian Stonebridge—"

"Baronet, and a *trader* of some renown." Hutton smiled and shook his hand. "I knew your father, Roderick, and your mother, Ariel, for some years."

Ian hoped his smile did not look as stiff as it felt. "I went abroad in my youth, before the business of country living could make us better acquaintances," Ian said.

"Do you know my son?" Hutton gestured.

Ian inclined his head in Connell's direction.

"Thornton has told me much about you," Connell said. His emotionless smile creased a face devoid of muscle tone. The stench of Scotch on his breath reached Ian across the two rows of seats that separated them. "It seems you have cornered the rare Jenna, even though I began the hunt some time ago," Connell said.

Ian felt his right fist clench. "I am not sure I can allow my fiancée to be labeled an animal to be preyed on." Ian stepped forward.

"You'll have to forgive my son, Sir Ian," Hutton stepped smoothly in front of him. "It's just that Connell had declared his intention to seek Lady Jenna's hand some months ago.

And we were all astonished at the speed at which your acquaintance became an engagement."

Grim-faced, Stonebridge forced an accepting nod and relaxed his fist. "I think it is foolish not to secure a prize of great beauty when it's within your grasp."

Stonebridge saw something flicker behind Connell's expressionless eyes, like the inner eye of a lizard adjusting to new light.

"You are right," Hutton interjected with a smile. "Timing means everything in the delicate maneuvers between men and women. Eh, Connell?"

"You appeared out of nowhere," Connell said softly to Stonebridge. "Like a—"

Hutton clamped a warning hand on his son's shoulder. "Surprise is a trademark of a good hunter, Connell. Primitive, but always effective."

"I find it safer to approach unknown situations that way, Lord Parrish," Stonebridge said. He kept his eyes locked with Connell's, but he noticed Hutton studying him with an odd smile.

"Yes, we should have pressed the earl more directly, as you did," Hutton said, reaching for his gold smoking case. "But, of course, we've been preoccupied with the strike of late. How do you feel about businessmen being besieged by lazy upstarts?" Hutton asked, drawing out a slim, dark cigarette.

"I'm on the side of profit. It's the grist that keeps all mills running," Stonebridge said.

"That's a very farsighted view for a young empire builder," Hutton said with a smile. "I must keep my eye on you. Have you a match?" Hutton asked, holding the cigarette to his lips.

Stonebridge made no move to search his pockets to oblige

the old dog's petty game of deference. The young baronet forced a smile. "No."

Hutton smiled broadly, the cigarette pinched in a corner of his mouth. He stepped closer to Ian and slowly reached up to jerk the glass flue from a lantern bracketed on the wall. He stretched forward, close enough for Ian to see the loose, crinkled skin of his neck, the only sign that he was a man on the wrong side of fifty. The tobacco singed gray and Parrish withdrew, leaving a swirl of smoke between him and Stonebridge.

"We are well matched, don't you think?"

A warning chill raised the fine hair at the base of Ian's neck. "In what sense?"

"Our resources, for one thing. We are both rich. Our interests. We both appreciate the thrill of money changing and industry, even though it is not a gentleman's calling. Even our height is evenly matched. I had your solid build once, you know. But one thins and becomes sinewy with age," Hutton smiled. "Connell here is not like me at all. He has his mother's stockiness."

Connell reddened and opened his mouth to respond, but Hutton rushed on.

"And you, young Stonebridge. You must take after your mother? That dark Norman blood shows through, I think. You certainly don't look like Sir Roderick," Hutton smiled and exhaled a stream of gray film.

Ian watched the smoke dissipate. The long silence that followed gave his words the still tension of a bowstring drawn to cheek.

"You are fishing in dangerous water," Ian said quietly. "It is juvenile sport for such an experienced man."

Hutton's chin tipped slightly, his eyes on guard. "What do you mean?"

"You very clumsily question my legitimate claim to the Stonebridge name," Ian said. "I am very certain who my father is. Your opinion on the issue is as important as a flyspeck. I could have easily called out your son for a duel for his crude remarks. But I didn't. As for you, I don't think I can overlook such direct provocation."

Neither man seemed to breathe. "I was clumsy, wasn't I?" Hutton said softly. "I get slipshod, associating with dolts so much of the time." Slowly, he narrowed his eyes and appraised Stonebridge anew. "I can understand your right to call me out. And I would accept. I have an enviable record with the dueling pistol. But I truly did not mean to disparage your parentage."

"I see," Ian said, his gaze steady. "You were just seeking background information, then. You should be more careful in your approach."

Hutton sucked deeply on his cigarette, his eyes never leaving Stonebridge.

The orchestra struck up the overture to the second act. "We must continue our discussion another time," Hutton said. The older man bowed first.

Stonebridge returned the gesture.

Parrish flicked the dark, spent butt on the floor and turned to leave.

Just then a young woman appeared silently from the shadows of the green brocade curtains surrounding the box.

"My ward, Miss Carolina Durrell," Hutton said, making an impatient introduction.

Stonebridge bowed. She was a young woman in her mid-twenties. Her auburn hair was topped with a high-fitted hairpiece of ringlets and she was corseted so tightly that her breasts bulged over the neckline of her ruffled red gown. Her lips were full and brightly rouged.

"My pleasure, Miss Durrell." Stonebridge kissed her extended hand.

The Parrishes curtly took their leave. As they walked away, Ian eased the set of his jaw. It had begun to ache with the tension.

Carefully, Ian unfolded the tiny note Miss Durrell had secretly pressed into his fingertips.

"Bilpo is dead."

Ian's eyes closed. Bilpo must have gone straight from their meeting last night to an ambush. Were they fellow miners paid by Parrish or outside ruffians bought for a night?

That didn't matter now. He had to find a replacement. A safer Bandit, one who would not act like a desperate laborer in search of glory and lead Parrish right to the miners' camp. If Bilpo's friends were still planning to ride as the Bandit's band, they would surely be traced, arrested and scapegoated by antilabor lords.

The Red Bow robbery needed new bandits. Tough. Disciplined. Untraceable. And Ian knew just where to find them —the Liverpool docks. Ian's ex-crew was fitting out a new ship for an old shipmaster and friend, Simon Oxmain. Simon would help, no questions asked. The crew would join, for a price.

Stonebridge heard a rush of skirts behind him and folded his fingers quickly over the note as he stood to allow the ladies to pass.

Jenna sat down as he greeted Lady Whitston. "Oh, I took Jenna on tour to show off your ring, Ian," Lady Whitston crowed. "Now we must settle in to hear the opera. Mozart's a delicacy up here in the cultural hinterlands, you know." She raised her long-stemmed opera glasses and set them atop her imposing, Roman nose just as the French horn sounded the forlorn introduction for the tenor in the second act.

Jenna flipped open her fan and held it to cover her conversation with Ian.

"I could not stay. I'm sorry," she said.

"You'll have to steel your stomach next time. Connell is used to your icy reception. But if you had stayed longer, Hutton would have read beyond your usual loathing," Stonebridge said.

"We must both take care around him," Jenna said.

"Indeed. The stakes have been raised." He smiled thinly. Slowly, he opened his hand and revealed the note.

"Dear God," she breathed.

"I must leave. I will tell Robert to escort you to dinner."

The chorus of singing villagers on stage reached a crescendo.

"I am going with you," she whispered.

"No." He kissed her hand and stood up. Quickly he whispered to Lady Whitston, whose gray eyebrows rose in surprise. Then she smiled and nodded her head.

With a fleeting farewell grasp of his hand on her arm, he was gone.

In a box directly across the balcony, a quiet figure also left his seat.

Jenna made herself wait five minutes. "I am going to make myself comfortable," she whispered to the elderly woman. Lady Whitston's eyebrows raised again.

Downstairs in the chandeliered glare of the lobby, Stonebridge was nowhere in sight. Jenna quickly wrote a note to Lady Whitston pleading concern for her father's welfare. She left it with an usher and called for a carriage.

As she prepared to step into the small coach, a man hastened to take her hand.

"Allow me," Connell Parrish smiled.

She was startled.

"Get in, Jenna," he said smoothly. "We must talk."

"I cannot leave with you. It would look—"

"As if I were usurping the bastard baronet's place. Quite right. Up you go." He placed his hands on her waist. She gave a small cry as he hoisted her into the shadows. Then he jumped in behind her and tossed a crown to the liveried footman who had watched curiously.

Jenna made a mad rush to unlock the door at the opposite side of the coach. She groaned as Connell neatly knocked her wrist against the wall of the coach.

"You animal!" she seethed as the coach lurched into motion. "You are mad!"

"Maddened by your beauty," he said smoothly. "And by your ability to spurn me so completely."

She could not see him well in the dark cubicle, but the thick, sickly-sour smell of liquor wafted across the small space between them, marking his presence. He reached for her hand. She jerked away from him.

He smiled. "You knew how your flirting with that bastard would affect me, didn't you?"

His arm extended from the darkness and she felt his fingers groping to free the nest of curls atop her head.

She pushed his arm away, but he lurched to her side of the carriage and grabbed her by the shoulders.

"We have planned for you for quite a long time," he said roughly. "And my father always plans well. I know so much about you. I know what you will feel like in my bed. I know how you will fight. And I know how you will scream when I bury my seed deep inside you."

A sick fear rose in her throat and cut off her breath. She shrank back, realizing she had no knife, no weapon. "I will charge you publicly with assault." Her voice was thin but steady. "A coin does not buy silence."

"Of course not. But if I am charged, I will take your reputation down the running sewer along with mine."

"No, Connell." Thank God they were passing along a well-lit street. She could see his florid, meaty face and pale, reddened eyes. "You need your reputation, what little you have," she said.

His back stiffened.

"You are burdened with an inhuman, backbiting leech for a father. He is tolerated by his peers only for his wealth."

"Is he?"

"And he is counting on you to bring a charade of respectability to a family name synonymous with tasteless, mercantile bestiality."

He grabbed a handful of her hair, yanking her close to his face. "Oh, you are such a high and mighty little witch," he said softly. "You go instinctively to the core of things. I will do the same for you—"

She opened her mouth to scream, but he pulled her head back abruptly. She struggled as his hand encircled her breast. "First, a kiss—"

A pistol shot rang in the air and Jenna heard the horses whinny in fright. The coach jostled wildly as they reared.

Connell dropped his hold on her and went to the window. "Is it a robbery?" Connell called out to the coachman.

"Indeed it is." The door was wrenched open and Ian Stonebridge yanked Connell out by his throat collar. He pushed him to the ground and leveled his pistol three inches from the pale man's belly. "It's I who was robbed of my lady. And if she's been harmed, your guts will feed the geese tomorrow. Jenna!" he called.

She had tried to collect herself, straighten her hair, smooth her gown, anything to ward off the tears.

"Jenna!" he called more urgently.

She stepped shakily out of the carriage. "I am all right," she said, her voice uncertain.

The baronet's eyes quickly took in her disheveled hair, her rumpled gown. "I should kill you now for the mad dog you are!" Stonebridge roared, twisting the barrel of the revolver deep into Connell's soft belly.

"It was the lady's plan!" Connell blurted in a high voice, edging backward with arms flailing. "She planned to get away to meet me. She wants to play us one against the other," he said, his speech growing more sure.

"You lie! My brother and I were in the lobby when you pushed her into the carriage. My God, man! Did you think you could get away with kidnapping another man's betrothed?"

The coachmen watched, enthralled, from their perches. Servants and townspeople milled in the street, vying for a clear view.

"Jenna, were you hurt?" Stonebridge turned to her.

She would have liked nothing more than to back into the coach, into the darkness. But she sensed the stage and the part she had to play.

"Verbally abused and threatened," she said haltingly. "Physically, I—" She swallowed. "He grabbed me. I am shaken but unharmed." Her eyes pleaded with Stonebridge that this be enough.

Stonebridge called to the driver of the coach he had commandeered. "Go back and tell my brother that Lady Jenna is safe. I will escort her to Lady Whitston's."

Connell had risen from the cobblestones and was slowly brushing the street filth off his coattails. Stonebridge shifted his pistol to his left hand and approached the man. Connell shrank back.

"Stand up, you slimy son of a twitching whore." Stonebridge landed a powerful right fist against Connell's soft cheek. The crack of flesh against bone reverberated in the silent street.

Ian stood over him. "There will be outrage over this. You will lose the name gentleman, if you ever had it."

Stonebridge supported Jenna as she stepped into the carriage and closed the door. The hackney-cab lurched forward and Jenna tensed against the leather seat, trying to control the trembling inside her. A musty scent hovered in the coach. The lingering presence of Connell mixed with her own smothering cloud of sweat and fear.

"Jenna." His voice was soft. He did not press.

Finally her arms reached across, then her whole body fell forward against him. Her watered-silk gown rustled warnings of the crush, but neither of them heeded the rough, scraping whispers.

"Shhhhh." He stroked her loosened hair.

She lay in silence, her eyes closed, head tight against his chest.

"I had no idea he would take up the challenge so openly." His lips brushed her hair. "It was only chance that I turned back to confer with Robert." Gently he pushed Jenna away so he could see her face. "Did he—?"

Jenna shook her head and pressed her fingers against his lips. She did not want his questions. He held her close and he could feel the sobs expand in her chest, growing like waves that dashed themselves against his shirt. Her clenched fists burrowed into his waistcoat as if she were preparing a place to hide.

How could she have been such unwitting bait? She had always been so sure of human nature, unafraid of its depths. But never had she been face to face with the secret darkness in a man's soul. It was there in Connell. And in how many others?

The hollow near his heart grew warm with the force of her choking, warm cries. "He is but a madman, Jenna. And his father, madder still. I will not let them hurt you. So help me God." He clutched her tighter.

Finally she quieted, drained. But he could feel the protective gap she had placed between them, even as she lay her head in the crook of his arm. Carefully he gathered her close. She lay unprotesting across his lap, her awareness safely distant. His finger brushed wet strands of hair away from her cheek. "It is just as Alex McBryde said in the cabin," he said. "You are precious to many."

"No more valuable than a sacrificial calf tied to a stake," she said.

He waited, prepared for her bitterness.

But her voice was soft, almost apologetic. "I am not yours, Ian," she said. "Nor my father's. I am no one's bloody sacrifice."

The coach lumbered past a ribbed iron pole, and her face was caught in a flickering shaft of lantern light. She was right. She was not his. Involuntarily his fingertip touched the fine line of hair that began at her temple and stroked back behind the curve of her ear. Her eyes were the blue of a Jamaican summer sky. The Jamaica he loved and left because he could not play at pirates' games forever. There is a time to grow up and face the past. He had not thought to envision a future. Until now, when a young woman lay like a baffling gift of quicksilver in his arms, her spirit so finely tempered that his arms ached to shift her body against him and free his hands to explore the substance underneath.

She became uneasy in the silence and tried to rise from his lap.

"Stay, Jenna," he whispered.

She turned her head away from his gaze. Her cheek met his hand and he softly ran his thumb over her fine eyebrow, her straight nose, the high cheekbone, until he had outlined all his thumb could reach. She could smell the metal of the pistol in the sweat of his palm, and the vague sweetness of his cologne. She slowly turned her head to nestle her mouth in his palm. She kissed the warm folds, and her eyes closed as a tenseness rose in the center of her abdomen.

Why did she crave the feeling this man aroused in her? She felt fear, but not the sick fright Connell had created. He had promised force and pain. Ian offered her knowledge, a deep, intimate wisdom she would acquire once in her womanhood. And she knew she would be hard-pressed, by an urgency she didn't understand, to accept this knowledge. Soon.

He lifted her face to meet his and he pressed his lips softly against hers. He went slowly this time, waiting for her mouth to move against his, waiting for the spark of instinct he knew would take hold in her. She grew warm quickly. He played with the fire, teasing it with touch and flickering tongue, until she pulled away with a breathless moan.

"Ian—"

His lips began a trail from her forehead down past the soft lobe of her ear to the nape of her neck. He licked at the fine hair hidden there.

He felt her breasts straining under the silk of her bodice. His hand ached to engulf the sweet, warm globe, but with a rough sigh, he encircled her waist instead and hugged her, breathless against his chest.

The ridge of heat that pressed tight against her belly grew fuller, wider, and its cusp arched high along her bodice, molding to her midriff.

He released her and she pushed away, warmth flooding her cheeks.

"I am actually being a gentleman," he said, eyes closed.

"Stopping before you are asked to stop?"

His hand stroked her hair. "It takes great control."

"And produces a great ache," she said, shifting her weight.

"What does a virgin know of such pain?"

She hid her face in the warm crease of his neck so that he could not see her answer. He kissed her long and hard, then filled her throat with his tongue until she writhed breathless in his lap. She arched and he felt her firm breast press hard against his hand. He caressed its fullness, halting his kiss to concentrate on the feel of her, amazed at the sweetness of his small victory. His eyes locked with hers, he gently twisted her erect nipple between his thumb and forefinger.

She pulled away quickly, eyes closed. Too late. He had seen the naked, innocent hunger hovering there. He held her gently for a moment, quieting their storm, as if she were a rosebud in danger of blooming too fast.

Then the coach stopped in front of the warm gaslight glow before Lady Whitston's house.

Chapter 10

The footman swung from his perch to open the carriage door. But a command from Stonebridge made him stop abruptly.

Jenna avoided Ian's gaze as she tugged her bodice straight and smoothed her gown. Her hair had fallen disheveled from the first cruel tug by Connell. The pins were lost.

The coachman knocked on the tall, brass-knobbed door of the brownstone house to summon a servant. The little fellow bowed low before Jenna and Ian as they stepped up to the door, so low that the pistol-wielding baronet would not see the lusty admiration in the coachman's eyes. Like a gypsy she was, he thought, her hair spillin' wild around her shoulders like that. Big haunted eyes. A positively heathen-looking piece of nobility. The driver smiled as he led the horses away.

The baronet himself had similar images in his head as he escorted Jenna inside. Her cool trust and explosive instincts had nearly led him to maul her as wantonly as her attacker, Connell Parrish. Ian breathed in deeply. Was he no better than an insane pup? God knew. He had regained control, and a guilt-ridden sensitivity, just in time.

"But your father 'as left, m'lady," a sleepy Susannah told Jenna. "An urchin came bangin' on the door with a sealed-tight envelope. Then his lordship called for us to pack 'im up." It was obvious that their early return to Lady Whitston's was a surprise.

The earl had left a note for Jenna on the polished oakwood bureau in the hall.

As Jenna read the letter, Ian studied her profile. A touch of the classic in the oval line and high cheeks. A touch of the wanton in the soft, full lips. His eyes traveled farther down to the good-sized bust, the indentation of her waist. He wanted to place his two hands there without the impediment of dress, underskirt or—

Damn! He stepped away from her. He could not be saddled with obsession tonight. The new Red Bow band had to be recruited now.

Everything was moving faster because Connell had jumped at the bait so ridiculously soon. The "game" of courtship could be played in earnest only ten more days, when the strikebreaking money was scheduled to leave Parrish Hall. After that, Jenna and Ian would need only a cool pretense of impending marriage. The earl would be in London coordinating the pro-union sympathies in Parliament's back rooms. Ian would remain in Lancashire to secretly advise the local miners and to keep a careful eye on Parrish. And Jenna? Where would Jenna be? Free of her obligation to her father. Free of her false fiancé.

He did not want her free. He wanted her warm, trusting body in his arms, twisting against his kiss, so unsure but wanting more.

As did he. . . .

Jenna looked up from the note. "Father is returning to Glen Manor. I shall have to leave very early in the morning."

"Yes, mum," Susannah said, her eyes drooping.

"You may go to bed. I'll call if I need you," Jenna said.

"Shall I call for your valet, sir?" Susannah asked.

"Not yet. I'll see myself to some brandy in the library," Stonebridge said.

The girl left them.

"Will you leave Liverpool tonight?" Jenna asked Ian.

Frowning, Ian put a finger to her lips to shush her, then grasped her arm and pulled her along the damask-covered corridor, past portraits of stern Whitston patriarchs and demure matrons, to the library at the end of the hall.

The air in the room was heavy with the musty smells of book dust and old tapestries. Ian closed the door and there was no light.

"Ian?" she whispered. Yet she knew he was close.

"Yes?" His hand rested warmly on her bare shoulders.

"Where will you go?"

"To the docks." He gently turned her to face him. In the blackness between them she could feel his heat. "To create a new Red Bow band." She could sense the breadth of his shoulders bending close to her. His lips found hers easily and claimed them a long time.

With effort she pulled herself away. "Light the lamp," she said. "I am not a trollop used to the dark."

"No, not a trollop," he said. She felt his finger begin a trail in the crease of her breasts, up across the diamond necklace, along the length of her neck until her chin raised upward on the tip of his finger. "A gypsy, perhaps."

He pulled her close. As they kissed, his hand roamed her bodice. She gave a sudden cry as he released her breast from her low-cut gown.

She tried to jerk away, but his arm held her fast against him. "Do not run," he said, "when your body tells you to stay."

As his hand pressed warm against her breast, Jenna marveled at how consciously she felt each fold in his hand, each press of his fingertips, the warm padded ridge below the thumb that rested atop her nipple.

"Your heart races," he whispered, "like a cornered doe."

"I have more resources than a trapped animal," she said. She placed her hand across his, ready to pull it from her breast.

But his own hand turned quickly and gripped hers, palm up, and pulled it gently to his lips.

"But sometimes," he said, "the poor doe is trapped by her own confusion." In the darkness she could feel his tongue glide wet and warm across the pulse point of her wrist and slide slowly down to the warm, tender fold in her forearm.

In the cool blackness the nipple of her naked breast rose harder, stinging with a longing so strong that she stepped back from him.

"No," she breathed. "Your hands trespass as freely here as they did in Shadow Glen. It is no different." She spun around and groped for the door.

He seized her waist and swept her easily into his arms. Then his mouth covered hers with a kiss that engulfed her sense of time and place. There was only the insistent suckling of his tongue as it formed a trembling trough for hers. She caught the heady, wood-clean scent of cologne as her hands stroked upward along his jaw, then around his neck. Her slim fingers crooked of their own accord, raked parallel paths through his hair, sliding back to entangle the thick swatch at his nape.

Finally he pulled away, breathing hard. "There is the difference," he whispered.

He carried her deeper into the room, using the eyes of a

cat or a smug familiarity with the house. He lowered her onto a high-backed sofa. "Don't move."

A fire had been laid in the hearth, ready for morning. Ian lit it. Then he stood and strode to the door.

Jenna heard the key click in the lock solidly. It was a decision she did not know she had made.

She knew she should bolt for the door. She could shout. They could be discovered by servants. But he is thought to be your fiancé, said a voice inside her. If it seemed he tried to take advantage of you, the pretense would end.

He is a bastard avenger, she replied, arranging her bodice.

But he is clever, said the voice. And he has such knowing hands. And you are so ignorant. Your body burns with ignorance, Jenna.

"No!" she cried.

"The fire will warm us soon," he said quietly. "We can talk."

"Your hands speak for you," she said.

"And what do they say?"

His smugness stung. "That you are taking advantage of the moment and the woman!"

"And does the woman not desire something of the moment also?" he asked. He gave her no time to answer but grasped her arms. Jenna struggled and kicked, but he sat and leaned his torso across her waist, pinioning both her hands in one of his.

"Bastard! Your lovemaking has a distinctive style," she said, angry and out of breath. "A style reminiscent of the Parrish dog that seeded you!"

His hold tightened painfully on her wrists. She heard the sharp hissing intake of his breath, and she feared she had gone too far. The firelight in the hollows of his dark face played like ripples on stormy water.

Suddenly he stood, towering over her, fists clenched. "You strike well and true! With the only weapon you have. But my heart is too far away from your tongue to be sorely wounded. Perhaps it is time to move closer."

She lay deathly still on the sofa, fearful and conscious that, as in the lightning storm, a moving target is more readily struck.

He bent over her and reached down. Slowly he slid the top of her dress down to her waist. Jenna closed her eyes so that she could not see the hunger in his as her naked breasts lay before him. She felt his finger softly trace the line of her eyebrow and down her temple. Her eyelids opened.

"There is no shame in your beauty," he whispered. "And no shame in my seeing."

Ian loosed her hands and stood. He stripped to the waist, unhurriedly, as if he had control of time, Jenna thought, as if there were not a world outside waiting for them. At last he stood above her, breeches tight and strained, chest bare.

"I would never take you against your will. But," he said softly, "I will have you." Then he bent to his knees and leaned over to kiss her forehead, her eyes, her chin, her breast. When his lips encircled the taut nipple, Jenna's breath stayed trapped in her throat, not knowing what words to form. His wet tongue painted a slick, suckled line around her pale areola and his mouth engulfed it, creating a tension that made her gasp.

The heels of her hands found his shoulders and pressed hard to push him away. He lessened the pressure but kept her nipple firmly in his teeth. As she groaned at the pleasure-pain, his head shifted to take her other nipple into his mouth, his tongue sliding rhythmically against the underside of her breast. Again and again he nursed the sweet tautness, warming it, moistening it.

The feeling was too strong, the throb in her groin too tight, unbearable. Her knees drew up and she arched sharply up against the pressure of his warm mouth. She gave an exasperated cry as she felt the arch break. Her back sank with aching slowness to the sofa.

She closed her eyes, shaken by the intensity of her reaction.

Ian pulled away and stroked her breasts, her tiny waist, her creamy shoulders. She had skin of velvet. And a sweet scent he knew. Lady-sweat. And lady-fear. His arm slipped slowly between her thighs.

"Ian, no!" she cried. He deflected her protest with a hungry kiss while his fingers slid across her flat abdomen and down to the fine, soft curls inside thin pantalets.

Jenna lay rigid as his fingers played lightly at the edge of her intimate world, guilt and fear chilling the warm turmoil she had felt.

"You cannot—" she breathed. Then his other hand found her breast, his mouth found her lips, and she did not remember the words of protest. Jenna's fingers swept through the dark matting that furred his hard chest. She made no sound until Ian's fingertips pressed gently against the taut, secret warmth of her longing.

"Jenna," he breathed, "sweet one—"

Her eyes were wide, afraid of the deft control he exercised. Then her eyes closed, lost in the motion of his touch.

A knock at the door. Then two short knocks. Then a scraping sound.

Jenna froze, her hands pressing Ian's shoulders.

"Damn," he swore through gritted teeth. "Damn." He stroked her long hair. Damn! he raged inside. He exhaled a ragged sigh. "It's Ross's signal. God, what timing. Don't move."

He pushed himself to his feet and walked away.

Immediately Jenna sat up and untwisted the bodice of her gown, disregarding the wave of sensations deep in her abdomen that had not yet subsided.

Ian's shadow, taller than the door, bent and retrieved something from the floor. The shadow spread menacingly as Ian turned, and shrank with each flickering step toward her.

He stooped in front of the fire and held the note close so he could see. "Lady Whitston's party left their dinner early. They heard about Connell's assault."

Jenna stood slowly and began to shake out the wrinkled skirt of her evening gown. "With luck, they will never hear of yours," she said softly, almost to herself.

Still bent on one knee before the fire, Ian shook his head as he watched her. "My assault? Your hypocrisy, mademoiselle. But I forget. It is a virgin's duty to deny complicity." He turned his gaze to a red, glowing ember that had fallen through the grate.

Slowly she stepped toward the kneeling figure, for once towering over the man who had cast her thoughts, her safety, her feelings into turmoil.

"I do not deny the feelings inside me." She reached down and smoothed back a strand of black hair that had hovered boyishly on his brow. "They assault my good sense. And leave me quivering. Like any of a hundred wenches whose legs open in darkened rooms."

He looked up at her. A lone tear caught the firelight on its slow journey across her cheek.

"Jenna—" He reached up to pull her down into his lap.

But she moved to the door. The key was still in the lock. It scraped gratingly as she turned it. The bolt withdrew suddenly from its socket. The click seemed to echo in the silence between them. Ian had not moved.

Jenna opened the door and was caught in a slanted shaft of light from the hall, a burst of brightness that cast a strong shadow across the straight set of her shoulders.

"But you are different," Ian said softly in the darkness. Too softly, perhaps. The shadow was gone.

Jenna was adjusting her bonnet at 5 A.M. when Susannah brought in a tray of hot tea.

"A little talcum and lotion'd help those dark circles, m'lady." Not waiting for a response, the girl dipped a cold finger into a hand-painted tin of cream on the dressing table and began to dab daintily under Jenna's eyes.

"The bastard's lucky Sir Ian didn't spill his bloody guts on the street bricks, pardon the language. Lady Whitston wants to see you before you go. Her ladyship's not even been abed yet. Too busy buzzin' about young Parrish and writin' letters to London."

"Thank you, Susannah." Jenna grabbed up her shawl and reticule.

"God spare ya more problems until yer safe and married." Susannah bobbed a curtsy as she left Jenna at the door of the morning room.

Lady Whitston was sipping warm milk by the window. "I love to see the sunrise."

"I, too, Lady Whitston."

"I think it's because these aging eyes see more clearly in daylight. Darkness isn't safe, is it, my dear?" the old woman's voice was a raspy shrill.

"No," Jenna said softly.

"I deplore what happened to you. That graceless lump of

lordship left the opera with his painted lady as soon as word got round what had happened."

"Begging your pardon," Jenna interrupted, "my carriage is wait—"

"I didn't approve, you know. At first," her voice pealed like a finger rubbing clean glass. "Ian's choosing you was too sudden. Just like him, though. Hardheaded. But I care for him. As I cared for his poor tortured mother."

"Sometimes," Jenna said softly, "one can't do what another approves of."

"You, too, eh?" The white powdered cheeks shook sternly at her. Gradually the wrinkled grooves creased upward in a thoughtful smile. "Well, whatever path you choose, my girl, stick to it. Look straight ahead. That was poor Ariel's downfall. Ian's mother looked back once too often, and she got trapped by what was past."

"Some things are impossible to forget," Jenna said, uncomfortable with the old woman's words.

"Of course, they are!" the lady said. "But we have to disregard them! In your case, well: you're a stunning young woman of common sense. But if you knew what I heard about you and your poor sick soul of a father! They say you ride a horse like a man and talk figures like a store clerk!"

"I've ridden astride only twice—in public. Emergencies in the village. No sidesaddle and a matter of getting there quickly. In one piece." Jenna smiled good-bye and moved toward the door.

"A moment," the lady called, adjusting the quilted coverlet on her lap.

"Yes?" Jenna had her hand on the brass knob of the door.

"I once rode astride." Lady Whitston's stage whisper carried across the room. "Much more balanced sensation." The elderly woman's mouth pursed approvingly. "You may go."

"Jenna!" Ian's brother Robert called. "Please wait!" He quickly took his tall silk hat and frock coat from the butler and joined her on the darkly lit stoop. Even though his clothes were fresh and his cravat straight, there was a ragged look to his dandyish appearance. He took her elbow and helped her up the carriage steps, quickly climbing in opposite her.

"Phillip—?" she asked.

"The rutter's asleep, thank God." He slammed the coach door and the horses jerked forward.

Behind them a hansom cab rounded the corner—a cab that had been waiting since sunup for a sign of Lady Jenna.

"Fortunately, Madam Babette's Game Room closes when its patrons become so drunk they can't spend money. Phillip and I were thrown out two hours ago."

The sour stench of the night's brandy had followed Robert into the coach. Robert scraped thoughtfully at the dark beard stubble sprouting on his jaw. "Didn't have time to call for a shave."

"Poor Robert. You should have opted for a less demanding role than playing nanny to my brother. And now I'm added to your protective covey?"

"Ian's orders and my pleasure," he said, lips parting over even white teeth. "Ian said he underestimated the dogs once. And he will not do it again."

"Do we all jump at Ian's request, like dogs ourselves?" Jenna mused, her tone too hard to be taken for humor.

Robert sat back and studied her. "I can only speak for myself. It is in my best interest to help my brother. Perhaps you have not yet discovered where your own best interests lie."

"You are not the empty-headed dandy you play, Robert. Forgive me for underestimating you and impugning your obedience to a 'higher order,'" she said with a weary smile.

"It is good to see you smile. I feared that my brother's company had begun to weigh on your spirit," Robert said, eyebrow raised.

She looked away. "He is different. And difficult," she said.

"And he plays by his own rules. I know," Robert smiled. "That's why it's best to let him call the shots. He is good at the sport and a fair man."

"And what sport are you talking about?" she asked, smiling in spite of herself.

"Hunting, of course." He stretched out his legs and propped his feet on the seat beside her. "Something that you also have a talent for, I hear." His hat slid down over his eyes and he yawned. "Pardon my boorishness, but I can't protect you from so much as a tea biscuit unless I get some sleep. Wake me when we get to the station."

Jenna shook her head and leaned her head against the smooth blue velvet that covered the interior wall of the Stonebridge coach. The seats were cream-softened leather of dark maroon with tufted buttons along the back. A contrast, she thought, to the cracked black seats and water-marked walls of her father's carriage.

"Robert," she said thoughtfully, knowing he only dozed. "What will you gain from the pipe dream of a vengeful old man?"

"Peace in my household," he said sleepily. "Peace for all of us."

* * *

Jenna learned much on the rail-car ride to Turton Bottoms. She learned that the jovial, fair-haired Robert was a devotee of Keats, Vivaldi—and his brother. Country life was something he endured in the patient hope that Ian would settle down soon and manage the huge estate.

When the old baronet had become deathly ill a year ago, Robert spent two months searching for Ian. He found him on an island plantation in the Caribbean. By the time they both returned, Roderick Stonebridge had died, and Ian was the new baronet.

"Strangely enough, sailing home with Ian was one of the happiest times in my life. We fought. We talked. We began to understand that the conflict was not between us. We became friends, Jenna. I felt, finally, as if I had gained a family. And the irony, of course, is that neither one of us share a drop of Stonebridge blood. My own mother was an engineer's widow from Stafford. Sir Roderick married her after Ariel died."

"So you know who your blood father is?" Jenna asked gently.

"Yes. Not that I care. I was an infant when my father died. But even if I didn't know his name, I wouldn't want to. I see what it has done to Ian. I am content with the father who raised me."

In Turton Bottoms the carriage was harnessed to four feisty matched chestnuts. The horses, new as a team and not of Stonebridge's stable, were high-tempered, nearly uncontrollable. After five miles they still ignored the pull of the rein and the snap of the whip. Jostled and battered inside the coach, Robert called for the driver to stop at the nearest inn for a change of team.

"I'd like to geld 'em m'self, the bloody bastards," the driver yelled back, arms and backside aching.

Gwyenth House was a tiny but fairly clean tavern and inn settled in a clearing about a mile from a fork in the River Ribble.

The tavernkeep, wiping ale off a black oak bar, was adamant. "Ain't got me n'other 'orses to lend ye, sir. Maybe yer topper boy wants to ride one of those brown devils back to T'rton Bot'ms 'n' rent ye some new ones." The keep poured a tankard of ale and offered it to Robert.

"I think we should just try blinders on their bridles," Jenna said.

Robert, draining his ale and flopping onto a smooth, worn bench, requested a respite for the travelers so he could sleep. Jenna was anxious to be home, but she agreed.

One trunk was unstrapped from the coach top for her. At the top of the rickety hairpin stairs, Robert gave Jenna the tidiest of the bed-and-tea-table furnished rooms and said he would be across the hall if she needed him.

She didn't. She had plans to make a secret visit, a visit that would free her, temporarily, from the weight of her worries. She was going back to "Cape Cod."

Jenna changed as quickly as she could into the close-fitting bodice and full skirt of a royal-blue riding habit. Her boots were in another trunk. Her black, high-button leather shoes would have to do.

In the stable she found the boy who rode on top with the driver and asked him to help her saddle one of the small chestnuts. "The bright one, with the white blaze mark on his nose," she said. "I know that horse," she lied. "He just needs a quick run to calm him down." As she suspected, there were no sidesaddles in the barn. The boy was too backward to be shocked when she hiked her skirt to reach the stirrup and mounted the horse astride. She smoothed her skirt over the horse's rump and trotted out of the yard.

Jenna headed for the river, reining in tightly until they were beyond the mole holes and sudden drops of the rolling grassland. Then she took off her high silk derby, its long muslin veil trailing in the wind, and shook out her hair until it, too, rode the wind. Smiling, she dropped the hat atop a guidepost bearing a rusty-nailed hand-lettered sign: CAPE COD.

The sign was still there. Ten years of wind and rain had not destroyed a childhood whim. Jenna and her grandfather had hunted the river land when she was nine, exploring, chattering and tracking game. Her grandfather had talked of his homesickness. "I'm sick of home!" he cried and Jenna laughed. "I want the sea! I want the salt crust in my beard, the sting in my eye!"

"Then pretend, Papa John," young Jenna said. "Pretend this is a pirate's cove close to Cape Cod and we can see the whales blow from the knoll."

So she and Papa John made a sign, her grandfather carving the letters, Jenna crushing blackberries to stain the grooves.

Papa John's "Cape Cod," a sheltered bank on the fork of the river, was just beyond the rise. Jenna kneed the chestnut forward and gave the high-tempered horse his head as they hit hard ground in the old river bottom.

They galloped free, Jenna bent in the saddle, knees high and tight, her mind clear of everything except the rush of wind and the animal beneath her.

She reined back near a stand of poplar and sagging willows and dismounted, allowing the horse only a brief drink from the river's edge. She tied the reins to a strong branch and walked up the rise of trees to a tiny ridge overlooking the narrow river fork. A bracken-lined trail on one side of the outcropping led her down the steep bank to the "cove" she had explored with her grandfather. It was only a grassy bank with the outcropping for a ceiling, a hideaway made secure on three sides by thick brush and trees.

Before she could enjoy its peace, she heard the brush crackle and bend on the outcrop above her. An animal? Or could someone have followed her? Quickly she stooped to grab a large, smooth river stone, then she flattened against the angular rock face that supported the ridge, listening. Footsteps brushed a pebble down the bracken trail to her left.

Silence.

Then a black shape hurtled down in front of her.

The hooded man landed on hands and knees and rushed toward her. Jenna swallowed a scream and hid the rock behind her skirt. Come *closer*, she thought, and I will crush your skull.

"You bloody little fool," hissed a familiar voice. Two black-brown eyes stared out from the mask. She dropped the rock.

Slowly, Jenna reached out and pulled off the black cloth hood.

Ian's long hair was tousled, wild. His dark lips set a grim line. And his eyes glared with such a strange intensity that a knot of fear rose high in her throat.

"You take too many chances," he said.

Chapter 11

At the anger in his voice, Jenna backed away from him, but he lunged for her and whirled her round. His arm snaked tightly around her midriff and he clamped a hand over her mouth as he pulled her back against the cool rock wall under the ridge.

Jenna kicked and struggled, grappling to loosen the hand that covered her mouth—until she heard the clopping of horse hooves nearby. She stopped then, breathing hard, her back pressed tightly to Ian's rigid body. She could feel the tension steel his abdomen, his arms, his thighs.

She relaxed against him, a signal that she would not struggle. His hand left her mouth and went to the polished wood grip of the revolver in his belt.

The hooves sounded close. Gradually the horseman came into view across the river. The tangled brush hid Jenna and Ian, but gaps in the brambles, like spidery cracks in a window, gave Jenna a limited view of the rider. She recognized him. Gault. One of Parrish's quick-tempered foremen. The stocky ex-miner was well-known to her. While drunk one night, he had beaten one of the Thorntons' tenant farmers senseless.

Gault took orders from a ferret-faced camp supervisor named Stiles. Miners in the pit had reason to fear both men,

Jenna knew. But she would take Gault's bulky stupidity over Stiles's cunning any day. The thickset Gault rode with his rifle barrel crossways on his saddle, hunched forward with the rocking motion of the horse's gait.

Jenna looked up at Ian. He shook his head. A warning. She didn't move until the horse's swishing tail went out of sight at the bend a quarter mile downriver.

Ian, still tense, let her go. Jenna moved out onto the protected grass bank.

"Who is he?" Ian asked, voice low.

Jenna explained.

Ian kept his eyes ahead on the river bend. "I knew he was a Parrish tracker. He followed me from Lady Whitston's last night. Managed to lose him in Piccadilly. I got back this morning just in time to see him in a cab following you and Robert to the train. The bastard jumped aboard. And so did I."

"You were on our train?"

"Not in a first-class compartment," he said dryly. "I changed clothes." He indicated the work jerkin and breeches. "Something more appropriate for the produce car. I've been trailing him from the rail station at Turton Bottoms. Why isn't Robert with you?"

"He's resting. And he's not my nanny," she said, temper rising.

"Well, you need one! Any other woman would take an assault by a madman as a sign to be cautious. But you," he said, shaking his head. A chill fear had roiled his stomach when he recognized the wild young woman racing the horse down to the dry river bed, just around the bend from the rifleman. He'd quickly veered his own horse over rocky, low ripples to try to intercept her.

He ran a tired hand through his hair. "So help me God, Jenna, if you ever run off unprotected like that again—"

"You would what?" she broke in angrily. "You are not my jailer."

"No, I'm not!" He grabbed her by both arms, impatient. "But Hutton Parrish would like to be."

She quieted, waiting for the pressure of his grip to ease, waiting for his senses to cool. She hoped it would be soon, for his nearness spread an uncontrolled warmth through her. Her heart began to pound harder. She shrugged out of his grasp, away from eyes that read her too easily. She turned her back, the blue velvet sweep of her riding jacket a wall she wanted to keep him behind.

"It's ludicrous to think Hutton would pull me from the streets and carry me kicking and screaming to Parrish Hall. It would do him no good," she said. "I would not marry his son nor deed him Shadow Glen."

"He has a way of presenting choices, Jenna." Ian's words were quiet, careful. "He can insure any response he wants."

"He's not the bloody Zeus you think he is!" she said, too quickly. From his position behind her he saw her shoulders rise with a deep worried breath. "I just wanted to ride free," she said. "Just for a while."

"You can't. Not until we break Parrish's hold on the colliers and your family. After the Red Bow Bandit has come and gone."

She indicated the black hood lying on the ground. "And shall I guess which country gentleman will ride as the infamous Red Bow?"

He shrugged. "It will be safer for the miners. They will not be involved. My crew is willing."

"I thought you sold your ship."

"I did. But my crewmen are still dockside. They're not

too eager to privateer on horseback. But it pays better than loading ships."

"You have people who'll do your bidding everywhere you go," she said, walking farther from him, wishing there were more than soft grass and sweet air between them.

"But I don't command your loyalty, do I?" he said.

"No." She stopped, her voice soft.

He moved close behind her. "What should I do, then, to earn the respect of a high-minded lady?" He walked around to face her and gently smoothed a soft tendril of hair away from her cheekbone.

"Leave me in peace."

He pulled her close. "That is a virgin's lament," he said softly. "Can you not offer me something less common?"

As his arms encircled her, she felt fear. A fear of what she could allow to happen here. A fear of the solid heat Ian's flesh transmitted to her each time they touched. Her breath grew light, her eyes closed. A mistake. For she could better see the chaos inside herself, a whirling firestorm of feelings she ached to explore. But she dared not with this man. He was too much in control of the fire.

He waited, not pressing her, but with his instincts on guard for the moment she would try to flee from his arms. The choice was hers. But, dear God, he would help her make the right one. He nested one hand in the soft crest of her hair. The other hand opened and closed long fingers like a slow, warming fan along the small of her back. The movement subdued an ache in him, a deep ache to touch her, stroke her from nape to buttocks, again and again, until her sweet roundness was molded tightly to his hard length.

"What do you offer in return?" she asked quickly, before the feelings raging deep inside could rush to her throat and consume the words.

He heard it. The decision in her voice. The certainty stopped his heart a moment, then it pounded with a new unevenness. But a wary intensity flashed in his eyes. She wanted a trade. "Are you asking for marriage?"

"No," she said.

That gave him pause. "Money, then? For Glen Manor?"

"I am not a whore."

"Then what is it you desire?"

She swallowed hard and reached back to loosen his embrace.

He held firm.

The silence was broken only by the gentle slap of water as it licked and eddied against the muddy bank. A silver fish arched above the water and smacked the surface in a dive to a deeper pool.

Her hands rose to his face and molded themselves to the angular line of his jaw like a sheath of warm velvet. Soft fingertips explored the high cheekbone that ridged the delicate tanned skin under his eye.

He looked down on her, the wind wisping long strands of her ebony hair riverward. He reached up to contain the escape. He wanted nothing, not even the wind, to have a part of her now.

His mouth descended on hers with a tenderness and longing that left her lips trembling. The night's growth of his beard scraped across her chin as his head turned to allow his tongue a deeper track. He ended the kiss abruptly, though, his hands stroking her back, pressing her to him.

She nuzzled her face deep in the fold of his neck, shutting out sight and sound. There was only his scent, the musky linen smell of the shirt released by the solid heat of his body underneath. Her hands slipped quickly under his rough shirt and slid across his skin with a sensual hunger that, he knew, was just beginning.

He stepped back and began to unbutton her bodice. She stayed his hand, hesitating, wanting to slow the pounding of her heart, slow this journey that would change her forever. But his lips crushed hers with a hunger that set a pace of its own. In a minute he had opened the garment. She felt his warm hand reach under the round weight of each breast, lift it gently over the lip of her thin chemise, freeing her, revealing her.

Then he began at the pulsing hollow of her throat and trailed small, hungry kisses down the creamy flesh of her bosom, leaving a pinkened path to the outstretched nipple he lifted to meet his lips.

She closed her eyes against the sight of his dark head at her breast. A heady rush of pleasure sped to the throbbing knot in her abdomen, causing it to spiral like a top in an ever-widening sweep. The feeling left her unsteady and she nearly fell against him.

His breathing shallow and fast, Ian stepped back to take off his vest and unlace the shirt. In one quick motion the shirt was over his head and on the ground. He waited, watching her.

Slowly she shrugged the jacket and shirtwaist down her slim white arms. They dropped to the ground.

He waited still.

Eyes down, she unbuttoned the waistband of her skirt. The heavy fabric slipped past slim hips to the grass. She wore no petticoat, only long pantalets. The breeze billowed its soft folds and pressed the cloth inward to the dark triangle below her navel.

"I did not bring a blanket," he said softly, his eyes following the course of the wind.

"Good," she said, turning away. "Then you were not certain I would lie with you."

Not certain when, he thought as he studied her in silence. Nor how willingly. She was a constant surprise. Enticing. Independent. And so vulnerable.

He spread her discarded skirt wide on the soft spring grass. Then he removed his boots.

She could not move. The phantom, pleasing touch of the wind teased her breasts alert, but she was unaware. She watched him discard his breeches, standing tall and unashamed, the breeze blowing dark strands of hair across his forehead.

His body was long and lean, sun-bronzed from the sea. Her eyes raced over the ridge of muscle that stretched across his upper chest and shoulders, down his arms. The stab wound he had received from her knife was a short, dark line below his collarbone now.

Down, carefully down, her eyes followed his flat, furred stomach to the inward curve of his abdomen, along his flank to the hard, muscled length of his thighs and—

She froze and slowly turned away. Her cool courage had fled at the sight of his nakedness, his certain longing.

He moved closer to her.

She controlled her urge to run.

His hands slipped the chemise down her arms. Then he turned her gently to face him and cupped her chin in his hand. His kiss was a slow, probing one, one that she had to answer.

Low in the laurel brush Jenna heard a meadowlark trill a sharp note on the cool midafternoon breeze.

Ian sank to one knee before her and peeled the filmy pantalets to the ground. His hands ringed her waist then, thumbs gliding across the sweet softness of her belly.

The lark's mate answered from a tree above them, and Jenna looked upward for the song. She should feel shame, she thought, as his cheek pressed to her abdomen. Then she felt the moist search of his tongue at her navel exploring the fragile inset, the faint kiss of his breath as he inhaled the rose-scented silkiness above her groin.

The throbbing inside her was so fertile and rich and forbidden. Seeds of disgrace should be growing there, she thought. Her hands framed his jaw and tilted it skyward, her face uncertain and bidding him—what? To stop?

Her eyes closed at the certainty she saw in his.

He gripped tighter around her waist and pulled her down, catching her atop him as he stretched prone on the royal-blue weave of her skirt, their bed.

Fright sealed her throat and she stiffened as her torso felt the swirl of soft hair along her leg and the insistent maleness that molded like warm iron to the inside of her thigh.

He rolled quickly to his side and gathered her in his arms, careful, less threatening.

"You are so very beautiful, love," he whispered. He kissed her deeply with a passion that told her his hunger was growing less controlled.

Yet Jenna felt less vulnerable here in his embrace, less separate, more understanding of his need, because hers grew, too, as his hands roamed her body, her back, her thighs, her buttocks.

How good his body felt against her. How natural to mold her skin to his. How lingering the trail of his fingers across her belly and breasts. Kisses began to burn with a frenzied hunger that left her moaning. Her own hands began to roam free, spreading the heat in her palms over his face and stomach.

Breathing ragged, Ian pushed her down on her back and

gazed at the length of her. His eyes seemed so dark, so glistening, so raw. As if her naked presence fed him, sated him, as if he wanted never to be full.

For a few seconds the cool breeze played lightly around the firm fullness of her breasts. Then Ian's warm hands stroked and the wind could no longer reach her. His fingers traveled the length of her, searching her, knowing her. Then his mouth followed. His tongue darted across her breasts and down her ribs. She felt his lips and his soft breath in the dark curls of her mound, but she pulled his head up to her lips. His kiss was hungry, demanding, filling her throat with its longing. She could do nothing but arch upward, lacking breath, lacking control.

His hand glided suddenly down her body, drawn to the warm, moist sweetness of her promise. There her desire rose tight and delicate to his touch.

Without warning he parted her legs and lowered himself atop her, probing shallow and gently.

The feeling was strange, not painful, but somehow not complete, she knew. His eyes caught hers. A warning. And a promise.

Still, his deep thrust caught her unaware. She uttered a small cry. He held her tightly, not moving, as her senses absorbed the alien tightness, the fullness of their joining together.

A kiss on her brow. A rain of kisses on her face, down her throat to her breasts. He shifted his weight to allow her to move in response, but did not lift the pressure where they were joined. His mouth caressed her breast until her senses began to soar again.

His thrusts slid deep, rhythmic and sure. But then his eyes claimed hers with an intensity that glistened, and she could feel his careful control giving way.

"Jenna," he breathed.

Each probe grew deeper, faster, the friction crystallized a knot of heat inside her. He was penetrating an entire private universe inside her, and she cried out against the trespass, a low, sharp cry strange to her ears, a hidden voice she had not loosed before.

The shuddering thrust of his release was a surprise to her. Her heart pounded tightly in its cage, trapped against Ian's heaving, solid chest.

The quiet.

She could again hear the soft wash of the river against its mud bank, the rustle of birds in the brush, the hum of a waterskeet on its way to still pools. She breathed carefully, not wanting to disturb the quiet.

Then the meadowlark trilled a song to its mate. They were loud, unabashed. She opened her eyes and found Ian watching.

"Ian—"

"No words," he said, his hand smoothing back the hair at her temple.

He kissed her open mouth with a searching tongue. The rest of him probed her, too, with a sure and constant rhythm.

It was too much. Her hands gripped his shoulders and she shook her head. No more, she breathed. Her nails bit into the hard muscle of his upper arm. She felt control slipping away, beyond the edge of a dark precipice somewhere behind her eyes.

Ian moved faster, harder, unrelenting.

At last she threw herself, groaning, into a sweet, sweet darkness that she had never known before.

"Jenna," he whispered.

Two slim fingers pressed against his lips to shush them.

He kissed her forehead tenderly. Then he rolled onto his

side, still within her warmth, still embracing her. They lay a long time together, until the larks flew nestward.

Finally he pulled away from her. She felt a sharp ache. Surely a part of her was rent loose.

"Stay here," he said with a kiss. He got up and removed a kerchief from his small pile of clothes. Unmindful of his nakedness, he stepped around the protective laurel brush. She heard water splash at the river's edge. He came back and knelt beside her, the dampened rag in his hand.

It was then that she looked down at the still-slick smear of blood on the inside of her thigh. Shame rose to her cheeks, shame that he should see how much he had cost her.

She turned her head away, guilt and fear nearly choking her. Then she felt him stretch his entire length alongside her, his body a protective wall molded to hers. His warm breath skimmed the soft creases of her neck. Then she felt the cloth. Icy and wet.

Gently, carefully, he wiped away the mark of her innocence. She stiffened and reached down to grab his hand.

Ian stopped and breathed a kiss into her neck. Then, silent, he rose to get his clothes and left the clearing.

Jenna sat up, resting her head on her knees, waiting for remorse. But, strangely, she felt only emptiness and a bursting fullness, both at the same time. A very strange peace.

What was it he had given her?

Proof that you are a woman, said a voice inside.

That is enough, she thought wearily. One tryst is enough. He cannot love me. I cannot love him. He has belonged to too many.

Jenna began to dress. The strange feeling inside her was not a painful one. She felt a tenderness, not only where he had pressed to her. Her whole body exuded a tenderness, an awareness that radiated far below her heart.

She donned the riding skirt last. The grass lay bent with the weight of their lovemaking.

As she hooked the waistband, Ian returned. He told her she would ride back to the inn alone. "I will follow at a distance and make sure you arrive safely." He was going on to Stonebridge Hall. His crewmen would arrive at staggered times, singly and in pairs, over the next twenty-four hours. They would be admitted to a hidden passageway beneath a hillside cottage at the edge of the estate. "I'm afraid Parrish will move his bribe box sooner than we think," Ian said.

She nodded, not meeting his eyes.

He helped her up the steep embankment, his large hands on her waist, hefting her upward as if she were weightless. They walked to the shady spot where her horse still nibbled contentedly on spring blades.

She put her foot in the stirrup, but Ian pulled her to him before she could mount.

"Have I struck you mute? You do not speak," he said.

She looked up at him. His confidence and stature belied his poor clothes, yet the rough cut fit him strangely well. Better than the button-down coat he had worn to tea two days ago. He would be meeting his "peers" soon, a coarse band of road pirates. She had given herself to a man who dispensed with manners when it suited him. As she did. She did not know how to control a person as willful as herself. A person as tormented by the past as she was. Yet she had given herself freely, at a price she was not sure she could afford.

"I owe you no words—" She hesitated, cheeks warm.

"And no more moments?" he smiled.

"You are still a stranger to me," she said.

She looked up at him then, as if to say he had not reached

her, as if he had not held her trembling in his arms with her first spasms.

His smile grew thin, a tight press of lips that did not reach upward to crease the sun-weathered lines at the corner of his eyes. "I think you do know me, Jenna." His voice was strangely angry. "We have become quite close. Joined, actually. For how long, I do not know."

"For as long as we lay on the grass. No more," she said quietly.

He sounded amused. "You think your curiosity is quenched? Your burden of virginity relieved? My dear thief"—he pulled her roughly to him—"you are only at the beginning of a long road. I did not accept your gift without responsibility for its good keeping." He kissed her then, a possessive tasting that demanded her response. She arched against him, trying to push away, or to press closer, she no longer knew the difference when she was in his arms.

He stopped. And slowly released her. "I will be with you tonight." The words were warm with anger—and anticipation.

"You said you would never take me against my will." Her voice had a desperate edge.

"I won't," he said, and walked away among the trees.

She mounted and rode as fast as she could up the grassy rise of the hill, past rocky crags and granite boulders that had shouldered the weight of the overlook for centuries. She fled the cove, the "Cape Cod" of her childhood. It was gone.

When she reached the guidepost, her hat was undisturbed. Glancing back down the hill, at the edge of the treeline, she saw him watching her. A dark rider who would follow.

She gathered her hair and pinned it up as best she could. Hat in place, she felt presentable, like the Lady Jenna who had begun the outing.

But you are different now, said the nagging voice inside her.

I will not show it, Jenna replied. She swallowed hard and looked down the hill for him. Ian was gone.

She kneed the chestnut to a trot across the field.

Like warm milk, the last droplets of Ian's seed coursed down inside her thigh to a white fold of pantalet.

Home was an hour's lurching coach ride away. She was dead tired by the time Eaton opened the door and coolly welcomed her home.

"Did my father arrive safely?" she asked.

"Yes, my lady. But he is gone again."

Jenna was astonished.

"He left your ladyship a letter."

In the privacy of her room Jenna checked the wax seal to make sure the missive had not been tampered with. Then she opened it. Her father wrote obliquely, but between the lines she could sense his fear: "Before my health fails and our family plans go further, I am off to your Uncle Wilkes's to beg his support."

Dear God, Jenna thought. Her father was the primary message bearer for McBryde and the local miners involved in the plan. How could he leave? If he wasn't here, what did that mean for Ian and the "bandits"? Greater danger? Or an excuse to call it off.

No, she thought. The bastard baronet would not end the secret crusade for vengeance. He would do just what he said.

And that means, her heart pounded, he will be here to-night. She sank wearily into a chair by the fireplace. She would be ready.

Ellen burst in, overjoyed to have her mistress back. News

of the carriage assault had traveled the grapevine with incredible speed.

Jenna half listened to her chatter. She changed quickly, then stopped in the kitchen to visit Cook. The wiry Irishwoman was at the pastry table topping scones with homemade jam. "'Ad a feelin' ya might be back fer tea." Cook looked up and pursed her lips. "Doan they feed ya in them fancy houses in Liverpool? Ya look starved."

"I am." Jenna bit into a warm scone.

"I 'eard yer intended kicked the dung nuggets outta that Parrish bastard." Cook pursed her wrinkled lips. "He didn't 'urtcha, now, did he?"

"I'm fine," Jenna said quietly.

"Ya doan look fine ta me. Ya look tired. 'N' edgy as a hummin'bird stealin' nectar in a tree full a snakes."

"I just need some rest." Jenna went close to leave a light kiss on the woman's white frizz. Cook's bony hand shot out like an eagle's claw and held Jenna close to her ear.

"Bilpo Grawlin's children were here lookin' fer the earl or fer you. They're orphans now. Got no mother to keep 'em. They're bound for a cousin's 'ouse in Lancaster. But they said their father left somethin' for the Thorntons."

"Will they come back?"

"I told 'em tomorra mornin', early."

Cook released her arm and shooed her loudly off to bed.

How many more people in the plot? Jenna thought. How long before her father would come back to take control?

"Oops," said Connell as the splotch of red claret spread across his father's starched white cuff. "You didn't need that little bit anyway. My balance is a trifle off," he grinned, plopping the wine uncertainly into Hutton's outstretched glass.

"You're more than a 'trifle' drunk," Hutton said, making no attempt to hide his disgust as he dabbed at the stain. The dinner table was laid with aspics and side dishes and thin-skinned new potatoes. Containing his anger, he called for a joint of beef.

"If you hadn't been drunk," Phillip piped up, "you wouldn't have tried to mount my sister in the middle of the opera," Phillip said.

"It was in the middle of a carriage, you dolt," Connell said, downing his glass.

"A little joke, eh?" Phillip grinned.

"She didn't have a chance to find out whether it was little or not!" Connell burst out giggling.

Crash. A silver plate of gelatinous chicken landed at Connell's feet.

Connell jumped. "For Chrissake, Fath—"

"You juvenile wet-nose! Both of you!" Hutton yelled. His arm swept the table in front of him and plates and silver landed with a mountainous clatter on the fine Persian rug he had purchased last month.

"You have played right into their hands!" Hutton seethed.

"Whose hands, Hutton?" Phillip asked warily.

"I don't know." Hutton stood up. "But I can smell them." He paced to the fireplace mantel and leaned inward toward the fire.

"Too much is happening for coincidence," Hutton said. "I have reports from London. Alexander McBryde and the pro-union lords are pushing Persh and Thicking toward support of the mine act. Both lords are keys to the neutral faction. If they fall, more will follow."

"I thought you had paid them well, Father," Connell said, stepping over the pile of plates and potatoes on the floor.

"That was three years ago, when the inspection act first threatened. I thought they might retain some loyalty."

Connell laughed. "You may have pinched one too many pennies this time, Father."

Hutton whirled around and smacked a crystal wine cup out of Connell's hand. "You do not amuse me, Connell!"

Connell's eyes did not waver from his father's. "But you do amuse me, Father. I have never seen you so lacking control, so anxious. It is quite a show."

Hutton stepped back and slowly smoothed the tails of his dinner jacket.

"I'm sure the meeting last night with Sir Ian has nothing to do with this lack of finesse." He picked up his father's wineglass and poured himself a draught.

"What happened?" Phillip asked.

"Basically," Connell smiled, "it seemed to be a staring competition between mad dogs. And my father blinked."

The whelp has gone too far, Hutton thought. Blue eyes closed as he fought the impulse to strike his son. Gradually he unclenched his trembling hand.

"Actually, Connell," he said softly, slowly, "it was what happened afterward that has me—unnerved. My son's stupidity was laid bare for all to see. And within a day the gossip will reach London. You have put our social credibility in great jeopardy."

"Hah!" Connell shouted. But he backed away as he saw the steely calmness begin to return to his father's demeanor. "Jenna says you have no social credibility. She says you're an affront to the peerage, that we want her as a Parrish only to strengthen your precarious acceptance as a tasteful lord of the realm."

"My sister's sharp tongue—" Phillip began.

"Carves right to the point," Hutton said, turning to Phillip. "You had promised to deliver her as Connell's betrothed this year, did you not?"

Phillip shifted uneasily in his chair. Hutton had never taken such an angry line with him before. It gave Phillip a sudden chill. "I—I certainly tried. I kept away suitors who wanted to call. Only allowed those I knew she'd despise. God knows I want her shrewish ways plaguing someone else's house. And if you want it to be yours, I—"

"And you promised to deliver your father's signature on a merger agreement to mine our adjoining properties, did you not?"

"But he doesn't listen! You know that! He's as daft as a drumstick!"

"Then it should be easy to maneuver him into doing what is profitable for both houses, correct?" Hutton's voice was like ice.

"It should be," Phillip mumbled. "But it isn't. He doesn't care how much debt I total. Do you suppose he knows that what I owe you is paper debt only? That you wouldn't call it due?"

Hutton didn't answer.

"I guess he doesn't. I'm—I must leave now, Hutton. I'm sorry everyone's overreacting to Connell's—um—over-enthusiastic approach to Jenna last night. I'm sure it'll all die down soon. Then I'll see what I can do about that too hasty engagement to Stonebridge." Phillip left quickly.

Hutton tapped a fork lightly against a china plate. "That man is nearly useless, Connell. Even when he becomes the earl, I fear he will be useless."

"Do you see him assuming the title soon?" Connell asked.

"I think the old loon will meet with an accident shortly," Hutton said. "And that will eliminate one person who might be the cause of our recent misfortunes."

"Could be Stonebridge," Connell said quietly.

"Of course it could." Hutton toyed with the fork, pushing the flesh of his fingerpad into its tines. "He's anti-labor, which is good. But he is my rival for Jenna—"

"*My* rival, Father!" Connell exploded.

"Of course, of course." Hutton picked up a chicken wing from the sideboard and began to nibble delicately at the skin.

"It can't be the miners. They're barely organized now." Connell downed his cup.

"It's a shame that little mole Bilpo didn't give us more information before he died," Hutton said thoughtfully, pulling the wing socket apart with a pop. "He was a tenacious little soul, though. And he sure as hell had something to hide." The chicken bone stopped on its way to his mouth.

"Connell. Get Stiles to check the safe at the mine camp. There were copies of our tonnage reports for Shadow Glen in there. Tell Stiles to bring them to the main vault here. Just a precaution.

"And, Connell," Hutton added, "make arrangements to ship the strike payroll tomorrow night. It's time to move quickly. We must take no chances."

The clean bone landed in the smoldering grate with a sizzle.

Chapter 12

That night Jenna sat at a small writing table near the fire in her bedchamber, marking entries in the column for "Servants' Wages."

It was nearly eleven o'clock. Ellen, grumping and huffing, brought the last bucket of hot water up to Jenna's room. "A body oughten take a bath so late," the old maid grumbled. "You'll catch a chill."

"Go on to bed, Ellen. I still have work to finish," Jenna said. The oil lamp burned brightly, but her eyes were tired. The "10 pounds" beside Eaton's name began to blur onto the line marked "6 pounds" for Cook. She put down her pen and sat up straight in her chair.

There was just enough cash in the household account to pay the servants. She had given her Lancaster solicitor orders to put the account off limits to Phillip.

How much Phillip owed to Parrish and other debt holders, only God knew. Each time one of Phillip's notes came due, it was bought up by anonymous collectors. Jenna had no idea how much of a fee they were adding, nor when they would call the notes in.

The good news was that there were no expenses for the kitchen fire in the village shop. Ian had already sent workmen to repair the damage, keeping the promise he had made at teatime two days ago. Jenna had been eager to tally the books, in case there was extra money to begin the irrigation system for Squire Ames's fallow field. But there was nothing extra. If only she were twenty-one. Her mother's trust monies would fall to Jenna's control. And then, Jenna thought, then I will make some changes.

You have already changed, said her conscience. You lie with a man whose temper will lead him to steal. Perhaps to kill. And you lie with him willingly, with grass for your bed and his arm for a pillow.

The hearth broke the silence with the scratch of a red ember as it dropped through the iron bars at the bottom of the grate. Jenna's face grew warm at the memory of how their two bodies joined. How could two people, so separate, so strange to one another, share something so private? And share it so openly under God's blue sky?

It still seemed unreal to her. Yet the sensations remained. And the most amazing was the moan and heat in Ian's breath as he lay panting his release into the small hollow of her neck. The only moment since they'd met that he had lost control.

One moment.

She had to regain control of her family's destiny, and of her own emotions. She needed distance between herself and Ian Stonebridge.

Jenna opened the small drawer of her desk and pulled out her father's silver-handled pistol. She laid it atop the yellowed pages of her ledger book. Then she began to undress for her bath.

Ian rode his black stallion up to the outer edge of the wooded grove surrounding Glen Manor. Abruptly, he reined Pitch to a stop, then softly stroked the cords of muscle in the thoroughbred's neck. Dead tired and logy with brandy, he had just ridden eight miles from Marguerite's house with a very unfamiliar sensation: indecision. Thoughts of Jenna had preyed on his mind and tugged at his breeches since the moment he lost sight of her at the inn.

There had been little time to rest that afternoon at Stonebridge Hall after he had followed Robert's carriage home. Ian had just poured a basin of wash water when Ross announced Marguerite's servant. The young Jamaican girl had ridden the two miles to Stonebridge Hall with a coded message: Ian's crew had begun to arrive.

The cellar and passageway underneath the old gamekeeper's house was the temporary hideaway and meeting place for the Red Bow band.

Ross the Scotsman smiled as he laid out clean clothes for his master. "No rest for the weary nor the wicked, eh? An' which are you today?"

"Both, I warrant," Ian said absently. The scent in his soap had suddenly shifted his thoughts to the bank of the river and the sweet rosewater smell of Jenna's tangled hair.

"Ya look tired." The tall Scot put his arm on his friend's shoulder. "Rest a bit. There's more'n a week before the band rides. You'll have plenty o' time with your sailors."

Ian reached for the clean pressed trousers on the bed. "They'll be rowdy and in need of drink. I've got to be there to clamp a lid on them. They think it's a grand reunion. Last night they talked me into plunking down a purse for a ship they want to crew." And with Marguerite upstairs in the house, the crew would need the ground rules of propriety spelled out in four-letter words.

An uneasiness was growing in Ian's gut. He was patching together these alternate plans too quickly. But he had no other options. He would have to trust his crew. And trust that feisty Bilpo Grawlin had not been tortured into tipping the Red Bow's hand. The return of the Bandit would be an important moral victory against Parrish. The beleaguered miners needed a champion here in Lancashire, because London and back-room politics were a world away from the earthen floor and hard bread of life in the camps. Somehow, somewhere, Ian knew, the earl would find proof of Parrish's theft of his neighboring lord's property. That would begin the fatal rip in the old bastard's thin cloak of gentility. Public ostracism was the longest-lasting hell the earl could think of for his enemy.

Before Ian left for Marguerite's house, he reviewed his alibi plans with Ross. When the Red Bow Bandit struck, Ian's whereabouts had to be accounted for. From an alcove in his father's room, Ian retrieved the carefully made duplicate of the Stonebridge ring he wore. He handed it to Ross.

"Be ready at a moment's notice to don my clothes and ride my horse to Lancaster. Keep a scarf wrapped high and my hat pulled low. You are dark, nearly my build. If you keep the burr off your Highland tongue and swill some whiskey, you can pass for me."

Ross's destination would be a discreet brothel house on the outskirts of Lancaster. Ian handed him a key. "Look for a bricked walk edged in laurel. You'll let yourself in the side entrance. Ask for Sara. She will support the masquerade."

"You're sure?" Ross asked.

"I lent her my presence and some money years ago. She's more than willing to repay the favor."

"And should I—"

"Enjoy yourself? By all means." Ian handed Ross a roll of pound notes. "And pray to heaven I can make do without your help when we ride as the bandits."

The gamekeeper's house was an old Stonebridge property,

a two-story cut-stone building with scrolled oak gingerbread gables, nestled against a high, wooded foothill of the Pennines Mountains. Ian had made it Marguerite's home ever since his return with her to England from the Caribbean. The beautiful island girl did not seem to mind the isolated spot. She was five months gone with child. Though Ian had been an infrequent visitor of late, he knew that his brother Robert was a more conscientious guardian.

Marguerite, her dark eyes happy, her small lips always separated by a smile, was growing more voluptuous each month. She had always been amply rounded. Now, Ian thought wryly, she was beginning to burst with an embarrassment of riches. If the child were his, he would be wishing for a son, simply because a daughter as impish and clever as Marguerite would be sure to give him fits.

Strange how Marguerite was so different from her cousin Tania. Ian's Tania. The woman he had married. Too late.

Jerking himself upright in the saddle, Ian fought against the memory of his wife. It was long ago, so far away. On a rolling mountain shielded by the smoky blue haze that draped all Jamaica's peaks. His lovely Tania was buried there beside an infant's grave. They had named the baby Ariel, after Ian's mother. But the child had died, as spiritless to Ian as her namesake.

The sound began like an echo in his whiskey-dulled brain. A hollow, sparkling sound. Then louder and close. And Tania's full-throated laughter rang out from the past. The full, burnished lips of her dark olive face came next. And then the image of her running alongside a field of young, golden sugarcane grass. She had jumped from a carriage, gaily dropping her bright yellow parasol as if it were the starting flag of her race to get to his arms. She ran, encumbered by the European skirts and petticoats her mother made her wear, swearing as expressively at the inconvenience as a field worker in need of a machete. Exuberant Tania had little tolerance for obstacles in life. She was honey-haired and French-born of a Portuguese mother, both countries present in the curious rhythm of her accent. She had grown up on her father's plantation, unrestrained, wild as the water winds that rose in peace-shattering squalls over the lush tropical forests and coves. It was her unabashed freedom, unmasked honesty that drew Ian to her. Hot curiosity at first. Then, like a fool, he grew to love her.

It was a lesson, he thought, and a warning. Not to let lusty curiosity go beyond the bounds of a bed. Until he'd met the spirited firebrand dressed in boy's breeches in Shadow Glen, he'd had no problem treating loneliness with a few select, lively bedmates. Never a virgin. Not since Tania. His good judgment had failed him this afternoon. But Jenna had not. Christ, how sweet, how satisfying she was.

No matter. He took off his hat and ran a tired hand through the thick black hair at his temples. He was older now. Safe from the impetuousness that hovered, ever ready like a storm cloud, over his younger days. He allowed himself few moments of spontaneity now. No rash decisions, not even the strike against Hutton Parrish. He had been planning it, in many ways, for fifteen years. The earl's scheme had happened along like a lost puzzle piece he had been waiting for.

And Jenna? She was supposed to have been a tiny square quickly snapped into place somewhere at the edge of the picture. But her part had grown. He found himself trying to fit other things around her. As he was tonight.

After a boisterous reunion at the gamekeeper's house with old Hautel, his coxswain, and three other sailors, Ian had told them all to go to hell, he was going to sleep.

"But I reckon it's not hell ye'll be lookin' for a'bed, will ye now, Capt'n?" the white-bearded coxswain had grinned. "More like heaven, mebbe? At the least a sweet piece of purgatory."

The men all howled. "Damned if I'll be so predictable to a bunch of fishheads," Ian said, donning his cape. "I may have to deny myself just to prove you wrong."

"Don't bother, Capt'n," piped up Orrie, the bald, skinny deckhand who would rather be climbing rigging than riding a horse. "Fer yer temper's sake, I'd rather ye flay a comely lass than my arse!"

Ian could hear the others howl as he strode down the dark passageway to the cavelike entrance hidden in the forest. With one low whistle, Pitch ambled up beside him. And Ian was in the saddle, his thoughts as plodding and uneven as his horse's hooves picking a careful path through the woods.

Now he was in sight of the second-story window he knew was hers. Lamplight flickered against a closed pane. Was he going to sit all night stroking his horse's neck when it was Jenna's flesh he wanted to feel? Jenna, he knew, would not be so easy to gentle the second time. Lost virgin's guilt would wash over her, closing off her body, sharpening the scissor of her tongue. And she would fight him.

Christ, he was tired. And he had too many people waiting for the Red Bow to lead them into risky business. Did he really want her badly enough to fight tonight?

The horse bounded forward as Ian's heels answered with a sharp kick in the animal's side.

Jenna's hair was nearly dry. She sat shaking her head side to side, catching the heat currents that wafted from the grate. She had stoked it to a roar.

Suddenly a raw metallic scrape competed with the loud

pop of burning wood. Jenna turned toward the door in time to see Ian closing it.

For a moment neither moved. She perched on the edge of her chair, clad in the loose white folds of a simple night-dress.

Her eyes burned, he thought, like a lioness caught napping in her lair.

Slowly, so slowly, she stood. The firelight cast a golden shimmer through her thin nightgown. The fine lines of her thighs were outlined, a backlit sketch of the path his eyes wanted to follow. One beautiful upturned breast was caught in profile, a soft, hazy beacon to his memory of the afternoon. He watched her, but did not move. Her back was stiff, her stomach taut, her mouth half open, waiting.

The man in the shadows dropped his cape on the floor.

Jenna made her way cautiously to the writing table. The pistol was in full view. She picked it up and turned, leveling it at Ian's belt. He had not moved.

"You must leave." Her voice sounded strange, far away to her ears.

"I know." He stepped forward slowly, taking off his hat, then slipping one arm from his coat.

"Ian!" She cocked the hammer with a warning click.

He stopped, his eyes never leaving hers. "You may kill your fiancé, if you like, and wake up your father and the entire household in the bargain. I'm sure you'll find an explanation." Ian shrugged the coat off his other arm.

"Father is gone."

Ian stopped. "Where?"

The gun never wavered. "He went to seek help from my uncle. Either Father has a strategy or he is very frightened."

Ian breathed in deeply. The earl's secret leave-taking

meant Ian alone would be responsible for the robbery. "Damn him!" Ian said softly.

"I fear we have all been damned since you made your pact with Father," Jenna said bitterly.

"So I am the devil, Jenna? And that was the reason for your warm acquiescence this afternoon?"

Only the flush of her face responded to his taunt.

"I didn't think you relied on self-delusion. I thought you a rare find: a lady honest with herself." He began to loosen the collar of his shirt and unbutton his vest.

"I doubt that you find any woman unique. Especially curious virgins," she said, grasping the gun with both hands. Its weight made her arm ache.

Ian froze as the gun jerked up erratically, angled at his neck. "You're wrong," he said. "I avoid the uninitiated. They create trouble. They do not know the game."

"Put on your coat and leave."

The tall man smiled and walked closer to her. He knew, suddenly, why he had come. To witness her spirit. To feel her fire.

"The gun is not loaded. You would not be so stupid as to wake Eaton and the others. This is a personal matter between us."

Her voice was steady. "Grabbing a cocked pistol from an emotional woman would be a stupid way to test your theory. I would have no trouble explaining your bleeding presence on my bedroom rug. You have a convenient reputation for jealousy. You came to accuse me of enticing Connell Parrish in the carriage or of lusting after your wealth in order to save Glen Manor. Or you are a confused bachelor whose feet are feeling the chill the closer to the altar he walks."

Smiling, Ian slowly pulled his shirttail out of his trousers. "Very good. You can add that I've been drinking, also. That always lends credence to erratic behavior." The vest and shirt went up and over his head.

"Stop!" she warned, an edge to her voice.

He could see the pistol beginning to shake in her hands. It was heavy. She would be shooting low, assuming it was loaded. Still, if he was to call her bluff, instinct told him to do it carefully. She was mercurial, unmindful of risks.

"I ask only two things of you," he said quietly. "First, no gut wounds. They are excruciating. Second, a bath."

"You are daft," she said.

"No," he said, sounding suddenly tired and wistful. "I am grimy from travel and weary of games. I need a woman, not a frightened child. My mistake."

He walked to the tub in front of the fire and trailed his fingers in the water. "Still warm. I only want this small comfort."

"You lie," she said.

"True. But I promise to settle for this. The day has been a long one. I will take a tub of warm water and a roaring fire. And leave lovemaking to another time."

"And to another woman," she said warily.

His answer was to strip himself of boots and trousers. Her breath caught in her throat at the effrontery. Or at the sight of his body. The tightness of his buttocks. The soft curly hair that shadowed his thighs in a long, shallow furrow of taut muscle. The solid breadth of the chest she had lain against.

She turned away as he lowered himself into the tub, his back to her, unconcerned about what she thought. But, she knew, he was very aware of the sensations he rekindled. Stripped and weaponless, Ian Stonebridge was even more of a threat to her. She knew she must go.

One hand grasping the gun at her side, Jenna tore through her armoire for a dressing gown. She threw it over her arm and approached the tub where Ian sat, chest soaped, arms resting on the rim.

"Leaving?" he asked.

"My bedroom seems to be occupied," she said, anger in her voice. She raised the gun and, instinctively, the hair at the back of Ian's neck began to tingle, on guard.

Her blue eyes storming, she clicked open the barrel of the pistol and tipped it. A burnished cylinder dropped neatly into her hand.

"You take too many chances," she hissed, tipping her hand. The bullet rolled across her palm and plopped into the water beside him.

"Only when the prize is worth it." Ian rose, dripping, from the water and stepped out, his body glistening in the firelight. Jenna turned to run, but he caught her around the waist and swept her into his arms, his lips finding hers in a savage crush that said she had misjudged how the game would end.

She recoiled at the bruising passion of his kiss and struggled against him, her long nightgown soaking up the dampness.

He carried her to her bed and laid her down, immediately lowering himself atop her to hold her still. Fear widened her eyes, but he murmured softly as he began to trail light, soft kisses across her forehead. "I will not hurt you. . . ." Down her cheek. "I want you badly." Along her neck. "And I will not take you until you want me, too."

His eyes searched hers until he saw that she understood. "And if I do not want you—?" she whispered.

"Your body will tell me," he said, and kissed her with a tongue that searched for clues. Her hands reached up to clasp his back, still wet and slick with soap. Her palms pressed warmth against the cool, rippling cord of muscle that spanned his shoulders.

Ian shifted his weight so that his own hand could journey freely over her wet gown. He found the taut peak of her breast and tore his mouth from her lips in order to roam hungrily over the firm roundness, more revealed than hidden by her clinging-wet gown.

"Jenna," he whispered. Both hands cradled her face in a kiss of longing tenderness. Then he grasped the neck of her gown and ripped slowly downward until a pathway from shoulder to thigh was laid bare and open to the flickering firelight.

She lay very still, marveling at the distinct sensation of his warm, damp leg against hers, of his firm belly pressing against her own, of his hard and unyielding presence burning a path along her thigh.

But she soon began to move, responding to the smooth glide of his fingers over her belly, her hair, her thighs and buttocks. A blaze began to flicker in the back of her mind, the warmth of the afternoon tryst that had never really died. And she knew that soon it would be too late for her to call herself back from the intense rush of sensation he created inside her. She must bring herself back. Now.

With all her strength she pushed away from the man lying half on her. With him off balance and swearing, she was able to twist away and scramble to the edge of the bed.

Damn the little minx! Ian thought, but cooled his instinct to grab for her sweet, fleeing rump. Almost. He had almost had her under control. But she was no flighty boarding-school ingenue. Nor did she have the base nature of strumpets in lady's disguise. Jenna was different.

Ian remained propped on his side and stopped cursing Jenna's timing. The respite would cool them both.

Jenna had stopped her headlong rush when she sensed that Ian was not in pursuit. In front of the fireplace she whirled to face him, the tattered flaps of her gown leaving her body open to his calm perusal.

"Does your handiwork please you?" she snapped at him.

"No. But yours does."

She closed her eyes tight against the rage that rose to battle his arrogance. Then she made her shaking hands slowly, carefully pull the torn gown together to cover her nakedness.

"You mistake your rights, bastard high lord of the privateers," she said, anger so hot her voice nearly broke. "You cannot steal into my room and take me in my own bed."

"And why not?" he asked. "Because it is the bed of a child?"

"No." Her smile was brittle. "You are not here for a child's body. I am a woman. As you proved today."

"As *you* proved today," he echoed softly.

She could not hold his gaze. "Leave," she said, sitting down in a cushioned chair, feeling suddenly heavy, the anger spent.

Ian pushed the coverlet aside and got out of bed, moving slowly. As his tall, lean body moved closer to her, she seemed actually to ignore him.

"This afternoon was a mistake." Her voice was soft, pitched toward the fire where low flames edged toward the last grains of unspent wood.

"Tell me what part was wrong," he said.

He was in front of her now, his dark body a tower of sculptured planes and muscled curves. She kept her hands fastened on the closure of her garment. If not, her hands would reach out and fasten on his warmth like mindless spring flowers desperate for sun.

"It was wrong for our bodies to be so close when our hearts are not," she said.

He smiled. The Virgin's Lament.

"And it is wrong"—she looked up into his eyes—"for you to teach me love and at the same time refuse it to me."

Ian sighed. How quickly she learned the Woman's Song.

"And it was wrong"—she averted her eyes, her voice becoming a whisper—"for me to think one time with you would be enough."

The depth of her honesty made Ian's heart sink to the pit of his stomach. There it met a tight knot of ardor that began to throb with an intensity that startled him.

Leave, he thought.

Instead, he sank down and pulled her to him in an embrace that pressed her tight against him. He lifted her forward, out of the chair, and her legs encircled his waist as he stood.

He kissed her then, slowly probing her anew, as if it were their first kiss on that dark night in Leona's cottage. And he found a woman where a confused girl had been.

The long hem of her gown swung against his knees as he walked slowly to her bed, making the kiss last until her head sank back on her pillow.

He hovered above her, hesitating. Her eyes seemed so filled with emotion, with expectancy. He knew he could not be what she wanted. He knew he should not try. Yet he wanted to possess her more than anything in the world.

"I cannot be yours," he said, smoothing her tangled hair back from her soft cheeks.

"I know."

"Promise not to give me your love." His eyes were suddenly hard. "I do not want to hurt you."

"I promise," she said, her finger tracing the firm, warm flesh of his lips.

He grasped her finger as it tried to press his lips silent. "You lie, my thief," he said.

She smiled, with tenderness but without humor. "Never question the pledge of one thief to another. The words are meaningless."

"But actions—" he said, teasing one pale nipple more taut.

"Shhushhh," she said.

But he did not allow her to keep her silence for long.

Chapter 13

Morning sun streamed through a dusty pane and struck the white tufted coverlet near her bare arm. She was alone. But not asleep.

Jenna had been awake from the moment Ian's good-bye kiss whispered warm breath against her cheek. A hazy aura of moonlight allowed her to watch secretly as he dressed, quickly, efficiently tucking his long white shirt into the tight band of his trousers. Cook and the lower servants began their chores in the hour before dawn. He had to be away from the house, away from her.

He picked up his boots. She could see his bare feet step quietly across the white lilies woven into the wool nap rug that led to her door.

He turned suddenly at the end, as if he had forgotten something. He gazed at her still figure a moment. A long, quiet moment.

Then silently, he was gone.

It was as if some palpable void took the place where he stood, leaving a gaping crevice in the room. Jenna pulled the coverlet high around her and snuggled deep into the covers, trying to recreate the warmth his body had molded to hers. But the bed was empty of his weight, his beard-roughened cheek, his knowing hands. And she herself was empty.

Slowly, Jenna turned onto her stomach and pressed the heel of her hand against the dark, curly mound of hair he had rested on for so long. She felt sore, tingling. He had taken her twice more, his tenderness and rhythmic control pushing her, reeling, into a hot, breathless darkness beyond the boundaries of thought. Then urgency would command him, as if he were driven, desperate to reach inside her. Almost as if he were fighting to escape something inside himself. At last they would rest, complete.

It cannot be like this, Jenna thought as she stood at her window looking out at the harsh gray haze of a new day. Love cannot feel so right from the beginning. He is the wrong man. It is the wrong time.

She leaned her forehead against the glass, looking across the fields of Glen Manor to the north, beyond acres of oak, beech and fir, to an estate and a hall she had never seen. Stonebridge Hall, it was said, was a forbidding Elizabethan fortress that the new baronet was rebuilding from the inside out.

Keep trying, Ian, she thought. Tear away the past. And see if the present becomes less painful.

The kitchen was busy and full of noises. The young scullery maid was in the washroom alcove scrubbing bread pans still warm from the oven.

"The little beggars came knockin' at the crack o' dawn," Cook told Jenna. "I put 'em in the cellar. Stolley's with 'em." Jenna opened the heavy wood door by the huge kitchen hearth.

"'Ere, missy." Cook stopped her and handed over a small bundle wrapped in a clean rag. "Give 'em this. They've got a long road."

The three Grawlin children looked at ease in the dim light

of Stolley's basement room. They were miner's children, poor and dirty. And used to the cool darkness below the earth.

Stolley was showing the youngest, a boy about five, a boat he had carved, but the child ran to hide behind his sister's skirts as soon as Jenna appeared.

The oldest Grawlin orphan stepped forward. He was a tall, thin boy whose body looked twelve and whose tense, dirt-etched face made him look like a forty-year-old man.

Jenna greeted him. "I am Lady Jenna, the earl's daughter."

"Billy, mum." The boy doffed his crumpled cap. "Named after me dad. This 'ere's Connie, me sister." He gestured the girl forward.

Connie stumbled closer, her legs bound by the arms of the littlest Grawlin. "Teddy, stop it!" She pulled his hands away and dipped a quick curtsy before she was trapped again. "Sorry, mum. Teddy's scared." Her round hazel eyes rolled upward at the indignity little brothers could cause.

"That's all right." Jenna stooped down to the floor in front of Teddy, her new damask gown settling into a nest around her. "I'd be scared, too, Teddy. Cook sent these for you and Connie and Billy. Can you take two and save the others?" Jenna unwrapped the scones, warm and fragrant with blackberry jam escaping beneath their crowns.

Solemnly the boy took the gift and sat down on the floor at his sister's feet. Jenna reached out to help him, but the youngster scooted away from her hand.

"We've been on the run awhile, mum," Connie said. "'E's not sure o' anybody anymore."

"I was saddened by the death of your father," Jenna said, rising. "He was a brave man."

"'E's a dead man," the older boy said quietly. "Stiles and

Gault, they took 'im away one night. 'E came back a bloody mess. Then they took 'im ag'in three days ago. An' the next mornin', me dad was stretched out at 'is wake. An' all because o' this." The boy reached into the shadows and brought out a rough-woven sack. He pulled out a thin notebook and handed it to Jenna.

Jenna opened the book. A pounding began at her temple as she skimmed the pages. It was filled with dates and tonnage reports for coal dug from the new "S.G. Tunnel."

Shadow Glen. It was proof that Parrish was secretly mining Thornton property. Proof that Bilpo Grawlin had died for.

"How did your father come by this account book?" Jenna asked, trying to control the nervous edge in her voice.

Billy said his father had sneaked into the house of Stiles's "lady friend," a woman named Iris, and stole away with the notebook over a week ago.

"Stiles knew it was missing?" Jenna asked.

"Not till yesterday," Connie said, a strangely adult anger in her voice. "That's when he came ta wreck up our 'ouse. We were 'idin' in the woods."

"'E left us nothin'," Billy said. "And 'e's put another family in our place. We got no 'ome now. Can't stay in th' camp. Connie's gettin' to an age where she's gonna get jumped. I won't always be aroun' to knock off the blokes. But we got a cousin, Able Stinson, up north a day who might take us in."

Jenna put a hand on his shoulder. "Billy, do you know why this ledger is so important?"

"No, mum," he said, bending to pick up his small sack of goods. "I don't read. But Connie does. But I told 'er not ta tell me. If Stiles gets me, I won't know nothin'."

Jenna's stomach tightened. Could her father have foreseen

how high the stakes would rise in his desperate plot? Bilpo Grawlins had been murdered. And his children were walking targets.

"Wait, Billy," she said. Then she turned to Stolley and signed quickly for him to watch the children until she returned. She ran upstairs to her father's room. Under the rug near his bed, she lifted a loose floorboard and found the box she had hidden there. Inside were four gold guineas, some pound notes and a few shillings. She gathered the coins and some notes.

When Jenna returned, she handed the money to Billy. He refused it. "We didn't come fer 'andouts, mum." His hazel eyes didn't blink. "An' there's no coin on earth ta take the place o' me dad." For a moment a teary glaze reflected the lantern light. Then the film was gone.

Jenna was quiet a moment. "I cannot help your father, Billy. But I would like to help you and your family."

At that, Connie stepped forward, wrinkled her short pug nose at her brother and calmly plucked the notes and shillings from Jenna's outstretched hand. "Me brother's prideful sometimes. Lucky for 'im I'm not so stupid. Thank'e, mum."

Jenna reached out and smoothed a strand of greasy brown hair from the girl's forehead. The girl's eyes were bright, clever. She carried a stubborn, self-possessed attitude under the grime. Connie would be pretty someday. Already the nipples of budding breasts were apparent under the girlish, no-color linen dress she wore.

"Best we go now," Billy broke the silence.

"'Ere," Connie said, suddenly bending over to pull a folded square of paper from her black stockings. "I wasn't gonna give ya this. The only thing I got left from me dad. But you can use it."

Jenna slowly unfolded the dirty, yellowed square and found a crude map. The drawing was certainly not surveyor quality, but landmarks like Squire Ames's stone fence, the crane at the entrance shaft in the valley and the high knoll of Shadow Glen were instantly recognizable. Underneath the knoll Bilpo had drawn tunnels that snaked across Thornton property almost to the squire's fenced field. If Bilpo was right, the network of trespassing shafts was much more extensive than Jenna had suspected.

Scratched along the edge of the paper was a list of nine names, written in a careful, neat hand. "I wrote those," Connie pointed. "Me dad told me who to put down. 'E 'ad no schoolin', y'know."

The list could be miners who worked the Shadow Glen vein for Parrish, or miners who were part of Bilpo's original Red Bow band. Jenna sighed. The children, especially Connie, knew too much.

"Billy, listen carefully. I'm going to ask Stolley to drive you to Clitheroe," Jenna said. "Catch the train there."

Quickly, Jenna turned to Stolley, hands and fingers forming a complicated message that, she hoped, would see the youngsters safely to their cousin's house. Stolley was to hitch up the garden wagon and pile its bed with straw. The children would hide there until Stolley was on the open road to Clitheroe. On the outskirts of the town, the children would get out and make their way to the train station.

"As soon as you return," Jenna signed to Stolley, "meet me at your mother's house."

Jenna turned to Connie. "Stolley can read and write, if you need to talk to him. Stay safe. I will look for you after the strike, after all seems settled."

"Stay safe yerself, mum." Connie's curtsy was quick, her grin thoughtful. "We're used ta skulkin'. Yer not."

* * *

Twenty minutes later Jenna watched from the morning-room window as the garden cart rumbled down the back road of the manor and out of sight. She raised her blue Willow tea cup in a silent salute.

"Excuse me, my lady," said a voice behind her.

Jenna froze. It was Eaton.

She turned to face him. "Yes?" She hoped her voice sounded icily detached rather than tense and wary.

"There's a visitor from Lord Parrish's camps who wishes to see you. A Mr. Stiles."

Bilpo's bloody murderer was fast on the children's trail. To hide her shock and pull Eaton's attention away from the window, Jenna moved toward the marble serpentine mantelpiece, where she set down her cup and saucer with a distinct *plink*.

She tilted her head and mused: "Why would a colliery supervisor want to speak with me, Eaton?"

"He said Lord Parrish gave him leave to speak with heads of house. It's a matter of charity, he says. Since the earl and Lord Phillip are away, the request comes to your ladyship's attention." Eaton was smooth, his eyes respectfully focused somewhere beyond her shoulder, his manner impeccably stiff.

"Tell him to go round to the kitchen. I shall see him there."

Eaton's mouth tightened, but he said nothing. It was plainly a rebuff.

Jenna went upstairs and waited a full half hour before making her way to the kitchen. Stolley and the children would be nearly halfway to Clitheroe by now. She hoped.

When she quietly entered the cavernous kitchen, she discovered that the wait had apparently not been uncomfortable for Stiles. The man was whispering in the ear of the giggling young scullery maid, Peggy. Peggy, startled by Jenna's entry, jumped up, blushing.

"Excuse me, mum," she said, starting for the door.

"Continue your work, Peggy." Jenna's command stopped her. "I'm sure Mr. Stiles's message is a brief one."

"'Tis indeed." Stiles stepped closer to Jenna. He was average height with a thin, sinewy build that left his clothes loose and drooping at every seam. The black beard stubble on his chin and cheeks gave him a dirty cast. He had a thin, pointed nose jutting above the dark line of his lips. But in his eyes the human countenance stopped. There she saw the slanted, ferret gleam that bespoke a man of small mind. Raw, uncivilized. A perfect pet for Hutton Parrish.

"We're lookin' fer three orphans, a lad, a girl and a little tyke. Their father got 'imself drunk and fell down the main shaft. Left 'em nothin'. I've got a lady friend who wants to take 'em in."

"I don't understand why Lord Parrish would send you to Glen Manor looking for orphans," Jenna said. "Does the camp have a shortage of children to send to the pits?"

Stiles smiled. "Against the law to send anybody under thirteen down the shaft."

"I know that. I'm glad you do, too." The man's level, unperturbed stare was unsettling. Jenna locked her hands together to keep them calm.

"Lord Parrish knows what the law says. He knows you Thorntons give aid to the strikers, too."

"We are happy to give food to those less fortunate, Mr. Stiles. A charitable gesture. Which, apparently, is something you're familiar with. You want to clothe and feed three orphans yourself."

Stiles almost grinned. "Yeah. We thought they might

come 'ere for help. If they do, send a message to the camp. We'll come and get 'em." Stiles picked up his hat from the table. He gave a good-bye grin to the scullery girl.

Then he walked closer to Jenna, disrespectfully close. The flowery scent of cheap cologne hovered around his unwashed body, blanketing the stench of his body smell as securely as a rotting net bag.

Jenna subdued an urge to back away from the bittersweet cloud.

"M'lady." Stiles's smile started a chilly tingle at the base of Jenna's neck. Then he gave a cursory nod that passed as a bow, and as he left pulled the door to a quiet close behind him.

As Jenna cantered Dulcy across the ruts in Glencur Road, she felt good to be in control of something, even if it was only her horse.

The secret ledger book and map were in an old leather satchel tied to Dulcy's saddle. Jenna did not dare leave them in her room, where Eaton could find them.

It was afternoon, and a fog was misting the tops of the distant Pennines. The valley dipped before her in a serene haze. She could see all the way to the brown rooftops and chimney stacks of Glencur. She veered off the road and across the heather-covered field to Leona's cottage, giving Dulcy her head along an old cart path.

The trumpet-shaped crowns of daffodils marched like yellow gilt soldiers along the crumbling rock wall that marked Leona's plot. Things always bloomed for Leona. For a moment Jenna felt safe and free. And pretty. Her new maroon velvet riding habit hugged her with close-fitting, tailored lines. At the wrists was a delicate rim of Belgian lace. Would Ian like it? she wondered.

Fool, she said to herself. This is no time to think of pleasing a man whose love is gone by morning light.

True. But I did please him, Jenna thought. Her body warmed to the memory of the morning and to the image of his strong, sculptured body locked to hers in the silent moonlit room. He had made her lithe body such a willing, wanting partner. She moved and responded instinctively, but with a new awareness of her effect on him, until she was lost in a pounding vortex that forced sound up from where their abdomens joined as one. Small unintelligible cries escaped her throat. He had been silent, except for the message in his eyes. It glistened with an inextinguishable heat that lasted long after his last, urgent thrusts.

Jenna's cheeks warmed as she slid down Dulcy's saddle. He had pleased her and gentled her. Aroused and assaulted her with a physical honesty she wanted to match with all her being. Yet they were not lovers. They were two bodies flung together like flint and stone matched to start a fire.

She could not allow herself to be consumed. But she could bask in the glow, she thought, at least for the next week. Until the Red Bow robbery.

It was time to start acting the part she had trained for—and fought against. She was a nobleman's daughter. And the gowns, though she disdained them as trappings for a mannequin, had suddenly become important to her. She had not even had a chance to try on all the dresses Ian had sent. Shimmering silks and rustling folds of taffeta filled her closets. She and Ian had a week to masquerade as fiancés. Jenna smiled to herself. She would play the part to the hilt.

As Jenna tied Dulcy to the gate outside Leona's cottage, she heard pawing and snorting from an outbuilding. Dulcy's nostrils flared, snorting a response. "It's just the gray donkey," Jenna shushed the horse. Stolley often borrowed the animal from the manor stable to carry firewood to Leona.

Inside, Leona was at the sink wringing out the dish towel. A large pot simmered on the stove.

"Smells good, as always," Jenna said, walking up to the thin, white-haired woman and giving her a hug. Leona kissed Jenna's cheek.

"Sit down," Leona said, wiping her wet hands on her apron. "Tell me what's wrong."

"Lee, you know me too well," Jenna smiled, relieved that she was with someone from whom she did not have to hide the truth.

Leona set a kettle of water to boil for tea. Jenna watched her, aware as always of the woman's grace and economy of movement.

Leona was the eighth of ten daughters born to a rich, ambitious gentleman. One by one, her sisters were betrothed to aged, titled squires or pallid young merchants. Leona had decided to choose her own love. She ran away with a house carpenter, Ben Mills. And was promptly disowned. After three miscarriages, Leona and Ben were blessed with Stolley. His birth was early, troubled. But "without him, I would have died," Leona had said, for Ben was killed in a fall from a rooftop when Stolley was small.

"I sent Stolley to Clitheroe," Jenna said now. "With Bilpo Grawlin's children hidden in the wagon." She spoke as Leona sat down at the table. "The children gave me proof that Shadow Glen is being mined." Jenna pulled out the ledger and map to show to Leona.

The older woman scanned the pages. "What are you going to do with this?" she asked.

"I shall have to wait for Father's return."

"Or give it to the baronet," Leona said. "If you trust him."

A warm blush hued Jenna's cheeks. "We have grown closer," she said softly, "but not in trust."

Leona was silent.

A cloud of steam began to roll from the spout of the black teakettle on the stove. Leona got up with a sigh and readied the pot for tea. "He is a forceful man," she said quietly. "An unsettled one."

"I am not asking him for marriage," Jenna said softly.

A whole potato slipped from Leona's fingers into the center swirl of the frothing stew, and she stirred.

"Then he will give you what he can," Leona said. "And that may change," she smiled. "He is a man of contradictions."

"Tell me what you know of Ian," Jenna said.

Leona paused. "I know more about his mother, Ariel. We were good friends for a while." Leona set the small china teapot on the table and wrapped it in a faded towel. "Jenna" —Leona seemed to pale—"I am also friend to another of Lord Parrish's conquests."

"What do you mean?"

Leona exhaled deeply and began to pour the tea. She had set out three cups.

"It was I who provided your father with an informant at Parrish Hall."

"Father's hawk? A friend of yours? Why would you—?"

"She did it for me." The voice came softly out of the shadows in the far corner of the room.

A figure emerged from behind Leona's small dressing screen. Jenna recognized the woman: the painted mistress of Hutton Parrish.

Only she wore no face rouge now. And, Jenna saw as she walked closer, the woman was naturally beautiful.

"Jenna." Leona placed her hands on Jenna's shoulders. "This is Carolina Durrell. My niece."

Jenna stared at the striking young woman before her. "Carolina? You are Parrish's—"

"Ward," the woman said. "His mistress. His—"

"Prisoner," Leona said softly, her voice calm. But Jenna could feel the tension in the slim fingers gripping her shoulders.

Carolina's eyes never wavered from Jenna's. Jenna saw no shame there, no warmth either. "Aunt Leona has always blamed herself for my misfortune," Carolina said, her voice soft and modulated. "She thought I followed her example. But I was only following my heart. I married a writer, a dramatist. I carried his child. But he ran away with an actress. Aunt Leona was the only one in my family who would take me in."

Carolina's arrival in Glencur came when Jenna was finishing school in London, shortly before the death of Jenna's mother. Carolina had been visiting a month when Hutton Parrish, riding through Glencur, saw Carolina and her three-year-old son, Ethan. He reined up so sharply that his horse reared. Sorry, he said, he had mistaken her for someone he knew.

He called the next day at Leona's cottage, standing in the doorway, his black cape and white hair stark. He suggested Carolina apply for employment at Parrish Hall. She refused. "Reconsider," Parrish had said. "I will call again when I return. I have business in London."

Worried, Leona wrote to Jenna's father in London, asking for help in sheltering Carolina. She swallowed her pride and wrote, too, to her own sisters who had disowned her. No one responded in time. For in three weeks, Parrish was back at Parrish Hall. Countess Thornton had committed suicide on the eve of the Parliament debate, and a note arrived for Carolina, addressed in her maiden name. Parrish knew everything. His note implied he had important news of Carolina's wayward husband, information that had a bearing on the future of her young son.

She went to meet with Parrish. At the same time Stiles arrived and tore young Ethan from Leona's frantic grasp. It was the last time Leona saw Ethan.

But Carolina was allowed to see him. Twice a year. The boy was housed with an elderly caretaker in London.

Carolina, poised and erect in a forest-green riding gown, remained emotionless throughout the story. Leona turned a tear-stained cheek away from Jenna's inquiring gaze; how desperately she would have clung to the chance of raising another child, Jenna thought.

"The only reason I live," Carolina said simply, "is so that I may see him. If it would help him, I would die. But Hutton would hurt him if I tried to take my life. So I stay."

"How can a man wield such cruel control of others?" Jenna said.

Carolina's gaze said Jenna was young and ignorant indeed. "He is a puppeteer. He finds the weak points for each person he wishes to break. And he ties a string there. And then"—Carolina's voice had grown soft—"we dance."

Jenna stepped toward her, but the statuesque, auburn-haired woman turned away to face the cold fireplace. "Hutton knew which strings to attach to your mother, as well," Carolina said. "He raped Lady Charlotte for the shock he would see on her face."

Jenna stepped back.

"He knew no one would believe your mother had enticed him into an affair. So he played a joke. When he finished he told her he had planted a gift in her for the earl. Syphilis."

"No!" Jenna's scream pierced the air. Dulcy, outside, whinnied nervously.

"You are cruel, Carolina," Leona said.

Carolina turned to face her aunt. "I have learned the real bounds of cruelty." Her voice was hard. "Telling the truth is a simple kindness."

Jenna had sunk into a chair, unable to control the sobs that broke in hard, wretched bursts. How horrible for her mother. And how horrible it was to know.

At long last she rose, feeling as stone cold and colorless as the tea in her cup. Slowly Jenna pulled herself erect, while Carolina's stiff posture seemed to grow rounder at the shoulder, sloping forward, as if bowing under a burden. She spoke quietly to Jenna.

"Each day I am punished. And do you know my crime? I am guilty of looking like Ariel Stonebridge, Ian's mother." It was the reason Parrish stopped so suddenly in the village at the sight of her. The facial resemblance was slight. "But my body, he says, is full and rounded like hers. He has a chestnut wig for me. And I smile, enigmatic, like Ariel, and sweetly sad. He says it is my only talent. A gift for disguise. For acting."

"Enough, Carolina," Leona said.

"I even recreate the scene when she rejected him. But it ends differently, of course. She does not leave him. He"— she swallowed and licked her dry lips—"masters her."

"You must be very strong," Jenna said softly.

"No." Carolina shook her head. "I am dead. In so many parts of my body and my being, I am dead. Unconnected to what lives there, what hurts there."

"But you are the hawk," Jenna said. "The brave hawk who gives my father information he needs to free you some-day."

Carolina leaned against the mantel, her hands cradling her forehead. "I try." Her voice was suddenly young and full of emotion. "I'm afraid. I don't know if he can—"

"We are worried for your father's safety," Leona said. "It is a long way to London."

"No," Carolina put in softly. "Jenna must first worry about her own safety." She turned to her. "You are being used. By your brother as a promissory note for his debts. By your father as bait in his war with Parrish. And by Ian Stonebridge, a black knight who needs a pawn to draw the dragon's fire."

"I understand—"

"No, you don't. I no longer play Ariel Stonebridge in Hutton's fantasies. I play you, Jenna."

Jenna swallowed and her heart began to pump hard.

"You are the obsession now. And it is—not easy to be you." Carolina frowned. Her hands nervously smoothed her gown. "He is never satisfied. I wear hair of your color. I become fair-skinned. I pretend virginity. But the words that he wants from me, the cleverness, the unexpected—I cannot provide. He means to have you, Jenna. It is the only weakness we can find."

"Then you use me as freely as the others, Carolina," Jenna said.

A small cry escaped Carolina's throat, a strangled sound, like a sob erupting from an empty jar. "You safe and stupid fool!" Carolina exploded. "I have been made to suffer in your name! You must help to destroy the bastard who tortures me!"

She started toward Jenna, but halted, chin tight against her chest. Something let go inside her then. Slowly her whole body bowed forward, like an exquisite marionette who felt her strings being snipped, one by one. Carolina sank to her knees in front of the empty hearth. Her forearms crossed in front of her and she grasped her shoulders, hugging herself. She began to rock urgently back and forth, with small painful cries. Gradually she quieted and slowed. "You cannot know, you cannot know," she whispered. "I have no baby. I have no life. But I cannot leave. He will not let me leave."

Jenna ached to go to her, but she felt Leona's restraining hand on her arm.

Jenna whispered: "I will help you, Carolina. But you must be strong. You must be a shell, a many-chambered shell. Protected. Hard. Hide the soft parts inside you. The parts that Ethan needs."

Carolina shook her head. "There is nothing we can do," she whispered.

Gradually Jenna learned why. An armed coach was leaving Parrish Hall carrying the money to lure strikebreakers. Tonight.

"Tonight?" The information left Jenna stiff and cold. "Does Ian know?" she asked.

Carolina shook her head. She had discovered it just two hours before.

"Ian cannot be ready," Jenna said. "Not all of his men are here."

"He is always ahead of us," Carolina said, her eyes fixed peculiarly on the door. "We can never catch him."

"Yes, we can," Jenna said. "With a dead man's hand." She picked up the satchel containing Bilpo's map and the ledgers of the secret shaft and stooped low to show them to Carolina. "We will prosecute Parrish for theft of property, unlawful profiteering, any violation we can," Jenna said.

If the Red Bow band could not strike tonight, Parrish would have to be attacked on another front.

"I will go to London. To Uncle Ronstead," Jenna said.

"And pray that your father is already safely there," Leona said.

They talked then. Jenna would have to leave immediately. Parrish's money would reach the southern laborers by tomorrow. Strikebreakers could arrive by train that same day. That meant bitter fights in the mine camps by suppertime.

Quickly Leona packed a musty, flowered travel bag with a gown, her best day dress and the few toiletries she could spare.

There was just enough time to catch the common coach at the Glencur fork; it passed through at dusk. The coach usually carried packages, freight and farm wives on their way to city shopping. Tonight it would carry a lady to Manchester to catch the train for London.

Jenna began writing a note to Ian. She paused as if in thought, but she had closed her eyes to still the racing of her heart. She did not want to leave. Him.

Good God, was she a moon-eyed schoolgirl with no more sense than a twit in a penny novel? She dismissed the tight knot in her abdomen that contracted as she wrote his name.

The letter was short, for the baronet's eyes only. Stolley would deliver it. Just in case there was a chance Ian could be organized in time.

She kissed Leona good-bye then. Carolina, pale but composed, sat at the table sipping cold tea.

"Good-bye," Jenna said.

"You'll need money," Carolina said. She handed Jenna a small embroidered change purse. It was sweetly scented, like jasmine in bloom.

"Thank you," Jenna said, checking her impulse to refuse the gift. Carolina grabbed her arm before Jenna turned for the door.

"My child," Carolina whispered. "My Ethan. Here is the address." She pressed a piece of paper into Jenna's hand. "If there is any way to—"

Jenna placed her warm hand atop Carolina's. "I will try. Perhaps my uncle can help." Jenna tucked the note into the cuff of her sleeve. Then she stepped out into the dim light of late afternoon. The fog had moved groundward, its mist lapping at the distant road to Glencur.

She closed the door on the stiff, lonely figure of Carolina.

God help her, Jenna thought. God help us all.

Chapter 14

Less than an hour to nightfall. Ian lay flat on his belly in the bracken of a ridge overlooking the Parrish manor house. His ship telescope was trained on the portico of the dark gray, cut-stone mansion. There, a large black carriage was harnessed to four restless horses. Five other horses were saddled. Ian swung the scope to the stables beyond the mansion. Six men—five riders and a driver—made boisterous small talk outside the barn doors. They did not seem fidgety, apprehensive or anxious to leave. And they obviously were not guarding the coach. That meant that the money was not yet on board.

Ian's ship's rigger, Orrie, had first spotted the arrival of the thugs and carriage on the afternoon watch. "Capt'n!" Orrie had run through the underground cavern, his boots echoing on the flagstones. "Looks like we sail tanight!" the deckhand grinned.

Ian took stock. Only four of his crewmen had arrived. Counting himself, the total would be five against six. That was not counting Hutton and Parrish riding with the money in the coach. Those were odds Ian didn't care for. But he could not risk his brother Robert's involvement in the robbery. And he had sent his valet Ross on to the expensive

Lancashire brothel where the servant would impersonate a lusty baronet.

Ian's crewmen had agreed to speak only in a Portuguese dialect common to the islands; their rough sailors' English could be recognized. Ian's good-luck token had arrived in the person of Simon Oxmain—his former partner and a fox of a friend who knew Ian better than any man alive. It was a relief to have the clever, garrulous Simon as second in command.

Looking back, Ian had set in motion all he could control. Yet he knew something was missing. He kept squinting through the eye of the scope as if the answer were at the end. He focused on the carriage house, where the crested Parrish coach was being cleaned. It had come back empty from Glencur a half hour before. That meant Hutton and Connell were left in the village. Why, for God's sake, when they had such important business to attend to before nightfall? Perhaps the money coach wasn't making its run until midnight or early morning. Or Hutton had decided not to accompany his money to the train in Manchester. Unthinkable. Hutton Parrish, as pinchpenny as a Scot, was sure to nursemaid his horde. Uneasy, Ian had sent Robert to the village for some careful inquiry into the whereabouts of father and son.

In the meantime, he counted the rifles a servant was cleaning under the portico. God's eyes, he swore. It was too damned easy. Everything they needed to know was out in the open. Something had to be hidden. He hoped that Robert would return soon with some answers.

Slowly, Ian belly-crawled back down the slope to a cover of brush, then made his way toward the small encampment where his men waited. He flexed his shoulder blades, stiff from lying watch for an hour. At least he was rested. Not from last night, he smiled. Quiet rest didn't enter the picture when you had Jenna's sweet body curled into your own. But he had slept, exhausted, when he returned to the underground hideaway.

She nagged at his thoughts, the little thief. It wasn't just her body. Her voice. Her touch. Her yielding. The breathless non-words that escaped her throat when he——

Damn, he thought, stopping in his tracks. He sat, his back against a tree, waiting for his desire to fade. How long would she allow it? he wondered. How long before she called a halt to hard-won trysts that left them both gasping for an end, grasping for more? Would he have to skulk away in the night each time? Or could he hope for a civilized affair? He shook his head. It didn't matter. He would take assignations with Jenna as he found them. Until his score with Parrish was settled. And then? God knew. But he could not imagine himself tiring of this curious, quicksilver mistress.

He was glad she had no part to play in the robbery. The thought of returning to her bed tomorrow was like a beacon to safe harbor.

Get your rest tonight, sweet Jenna, he smiled.

He set off on the trail to the Red Bow camp.

From a high trail above the Glencur fork, Jenna looked down on the main road. The common transit coach to Manchester churned dust not a half mile from the tiny tavern at the crossroads. Alarmed, Jenna kneed Dulcy to a gallop down the forest trail.

She reached the crossroads just as the coach was pulling away in the dim light of late dusk. Racing to the front of the four-horse team, she shouted to the driver to stop.

The coach wobbled to a halt, its sallow-faced driver

seeming angry at the thought of another passenger. "M'lady, I got a special run ta make."

"I'll pay for any inconvenience," Jenna said, throwing coins from Carolina's purse to the tavernkeep, who had appeared in the doorway of the squat coach house. Still astride Dulcy, she handed her traveling bag up to the baggage handler. She felt uneasy having the ledger and map out of her hands, but there would be no room for the bag in the tight quarters of the coach.

Quickly she dismounted. "Home, Dulcy," she commanded, and slapped the horse's rump. She hurried around to the door of the coach. The tavern keeper opened it for her. She nodded to him in thanks, then stepped up on the footrest and bent her head to join the other passengers.

"What welcome company on our journey," said the smooth voice of Hutton Parrish.

The shock stopped Jenna half in, half out of the doorway. Hutton's hand reached confidently across the coach and found her own. He drew her in slowly, with a steady pull, at the same time pounding the roof twice with his cane. The signal to go. The impatient driver immediately whipped the team forward and Jenna was thrown forward against Parrish's chest.

He said nothing, only smiled, as her cheek momentarily pressed his silken shirt. He felt her soft hair brush his chin and he took in its scent. He did not help steady her. She floundered against him. Quickly she pushed away with an exasperated breath. He marked the little sound in his mind.

Sitting across from him, Jenna avoided Hutton's shadowed gaze as she slowly drew back her knees so they would not touch his long legs. She concentrated on carefully adjusting her riding cloak to cover her dress and quieting the pace of a heart flung unexpectedly against the warm shirt of an enemy. Fear gripped each short breath, for beside her, Carolina's small money purse lay on the seat, its distinctive scent wafting like a signal.

Jenna cast her eyes down, as if embarrassed, so that Hutton would not see the apprehension there.

It was then that Connell, grinning, reached across her to raise the window flap and let in the dim evening light. Quickly Jenna closed her hand over the small reticule and pulled it inside the lined pocket sewn inside her cape.

Connell regained his seat beside Hutton. "We meet again in close quarters, m'lady."

Jenna quietly addressed Hutton: "Your pouncing boor finds my discomfort amusing."

"Haughty bi—" Connell leaned toward her, but Hutton's cane darted in front of him.

"How easily the lady makes you lose control, Connell," Hutton tsked. "She knows you too well." He caught Jenna's eye. "But she doesn't know me. Do you, my dear?"

"You are a political enemy." Her voice was quiet, firm. "And you lead my brother into debauchery. And debt. I would say that makes you my personal enemy as well."

Hutton smiled and slowly removed his top hat. "And what should two enemies do when they meet unexpectedly in such a small arena?" His hand reached to the back of his neck and smoothed the long white curly hair at the nape.

"As the one outnumbered, I suggest we call this neutral ground."

"I see."

"And that we toss out the door any one of us who tries to violate the integrity of the other." She glanced at Connell.

"Oh, now, Jenna." He paused. "Jenna." He said the name again, as if it felt good in his mouth. "Integrity is a matter of subjectivity. Hard to judge. Right now you could be harboring vile thoughts that castigate my character. Should I throw you into the road for your opinion?"

"Thoughts do no harm," she said. "Actions do. As your son has discovered."

Connell cursed.

"An unfortunate incident from a lovesick suitor, nothing more," Hutton said.

"Oh, it was much more," she said softly. "And you are very fortunate to have the chance to redeem the Parrish reputation."

The light was fading fast, but she could see his amused smile broaden. "What do you imply?"

"When I arrive in Manchester unharmed, unruffled, your behavior will belie the torrent of gossip that says crudity is a Parrish family trait."

Hutton sighed, as if contented. He turned to Connell. "You see what can be done when you have only wit to defend you?"

Then he leaned forward toward Jenna, not improperly close, but near enough that she caught the scent of cologne in his pomade, the rasp of his starched shirt collar scraping softly against the point of his chin. "Tell me, my dear"—his voice grew liquid, slippery somehow—"why you thought you would be harmed?"

She smiled to cover the throb of her heart. "It is obvious," she said. "I ride with a man who assaulted me two nights ago. And with the father who, I assume, taught his son everything he knows."

Hutton breathed in deeply, then out, disturbed at the comparison. "I assure you my techniques are completely different, my dear. Pouncing lacks finesse. And you, of all people, deserve finesse, deserve to be carefully prepared for what comes."

Jenna's heart beat so hard that she thought he could surely hear it above the clamor of harnesses and horses' feet. Had her mother's heart grown wild, too?

Her words gained a new edge. "Your prowess and your word games do not interest me. Getting safely to Manchester does. And if I have been assaulted in any way—by word or deed—I guarantee that the house of Parrish will smell like a leper's sore in every hall in London this season."

Jenna could not discern the look on Parrish's face. But even Connell seemed to be holding himself in check.

"Why should I care what others think?" Hutton asked. In the glow of a brilliant crescent moon, she could see his thin lips part in a smile no longer amused.

"Because you need to assure a well-titled match for your son and heir," Jenna said. She shook her head and smiled. "You really must give your noble peers more credit. They understand your greed and lust. They have the same inclinations. But that doesn't mean they want their daughters married to an embarrassment."

"I am too rich to be censured," he said quietly.

She paused. "If you believe that, Lord Parrish, you are a fool. Birth, not guineas, grants respect. And you have broken the first rule of your class: if you must be common, be discreet."

Long fingers on one hand wrapped around the polished gold handle of the cane he had placed between them.

"You may find my good reference and public forgiveness invaluable to recoup Connell's social agenda this season," she continued.

"'Public' forgiveness?" he asked with a smile. His cane was upright between his knees as he tapped it on the floor.

"It could be arranged." She lied as smoothly as if her life depended on it.

Bitterly, Connell broke in, "Your proud fiancé would never agree to that."

At the mention of Ian, Jenna could feel Hutton study her face intently. She drew back into the shadows, pretending disinterest, straightening the drape of her skirt.

"We have an understanding," she said, her voice quiet, businesslike.

"Oh?" Hutton smiled. "That means he can still frequent his favorite brothel in Lancaster? Or take delight in that dark-skinned island girl who keeps house in the woods for him? I didn't realize you were so generous, my dear."

To his delight, he could see her face darken in a blush.

"Your insolence is unbearable," she said with cold hatred, "but understandable. Parrishes have always spoken with the tongue of street curs licking up everything that smells rotten."

The Ice Maiden's haughtiness was wearing on the nerves. Hutton's cane tapped the floor in an involuntary tic, and he tilted his head back against the seat in order to savor the rage that built inside him. Oh, she was good, this one. He had not been baited so well since the standoff with Stonebridge at the opera, when he had nearly misstepped all the way to a duel. Looking back, he should have used the opportunity to get rid of the bastard baronet. Hutton was losing interest in playing games with a rival. He wanted his prize. Seeing her, hearing her, testing her, he wanted her with an ache that swelled his groin tight as a drum skin. It was wonderful. He expelled a sigh. This lovely little cat sharpened her claws on the hackles he raised to defend himself. How sweet the victory would be when he turned the tables.

It was time to find out why she was here.

"Connell," he spoke to his son, keeping his gaze on Jenna, "I begin to understand why this lady incites you so.

She nearly engaged my anger. I'm sure she realized that our whole discussion is an academic exercise. We would not think of insulting an eccentric—but beloved—daughter of the aristocracy."

He could see Jenna's neck stiffen slightly, tense, waiting.

"You exude a lovely perfume, my dear. A jasmine import, I believe? A favorite of mine. For a woman who complains of limited means, it's an expensive scent."

Carolina's purse. "I wear it in remembrance of my mother," she lied softly. "It was her favorite."

"Oh?" he said, frowning, as if searching his memory.

"My one personal extravagance is not your concern," she said.

"Quite right," he smiled, and slowly reached into a leather pouch beside him and drew out an orange, its dimpled rind looking smooth and dark in the dim light. He smiled at Jenna as he hefted the fruit in one hand. "An extravagance of mine."

Connell, looking bored, crossed his arms and leaned his head back against the cracked damask of the coach wall. He took long draughts from a flask. "You will find that most of father's passions are costly and imported," Connell said, looking out his window.

"I have no interest in an old man's obsessions," she said testily.

Hutton's eyebrows raised. "Oh, Jenna, you wound me to the quick. You make me sound ancient, infirm," he said. "I'm not." His fingers slid farther down the handle of his cane. Jenna heard a click, a scrape of metal. A stiletto blade gleamed in his hand.

"And you, of all people, should understand peculiarities of personality. You are hardly a conventional example of nobility." Carefully, he sliced a circle of rind off the navel of the orange. Then he worked his nail under the skin and pulled a swatch free. "You must admit that a riding habit is not accepted traveling attire. A common coach is not proper transport. And traveling unescorted is an invitation to trouble."

Half the small globe was exposed now. The tender fruit looked pale, vulnerable in his hand.

"Your sudden presence as our traveling companion puts questions in my mind," he smiled. Rhythmically, he tore small snatches of rind free with thumb and forefinger until the orange was bare.

"I journey on a personal matter," she said warily.

"I see," he smiled and reached for her hand.

Jenna pulled away. "What are you doing?"

He held out the orange. "I peeled it for you."

"I do not want it," she said, uneasy.

"All right," he said smoothly. "Could you hold it while I find a napkin?" Before she could reply, he had plopped the sticky wet ball into her half-opened hand.

She nearly dropped it. "My God, you—"

"Here, here," he said placatingly, spreading a white napkin on her lap.

There was a bizarre domesticity in the act. She frowned, startled, and had no time to worry what would happen next. For he leaned close to her outstretched hand and curved his warm fingers in an intimate cup under hers. Even as she tried to pull away, his other hand had guided the stiletto to the surface of the orange, a bare inch from her index finger. He held the dagger poised there, like a question for which he knew the answer. And she stopped her withdrawal. He smiled as he felt her fingers relax the tension of pulling away.

He pressed down on the blade and it broke the skin. Her

wrist was showered with cool droplets of juice. "You must stay very still. The blade is sharp," he cautioned. Then he began to saw downward very slowly. "You were saying you had a personal reason for waylaying a common coach?" he asked.

She was watching the motion of the blade. So thin, so steely. So smooth. Like Parrish. "I am pursuing my father," she said, her tone quiet except for the tremor. "He left with our coach and I have not heard from him. My leave-taking was a sudden decision."

"I see. Over the years you have cultivated a reputation for impetuous behavior. It saves you from time-consuming defense of your actions, doesn't it?" He smiled and sawed deeper. "I understand completely. I do the same."

The abundant juice overflowed her fingers and rested in a sticky pool in the hand cupped under hers. "You are too slow," she murmured.

"No. Careful." He smiled, sliding his bent fingers forward so that they could grasp her wrist. Her hand was locked in his grip. "I would not want you to jerk away and cut yourself," he said. "I fear I must deliver the bad news about your father."

"What do you mean?" She swallowed hard.

"This afternoon your father's coach was found crashed in a ravine on the road to Turton Bottoms."

"You lie, you poxed bastard," she whispered.

"Gutter language from a lady is not becoming." He raised his brow. "And I never lie about things like this." He smiled and gripped her wrist harder.

"Let me go!" Her jaw clenched in anger; her mind fought the reality of his words. With a cry she pulled away from him.

She felt the orange halves give way and part, then the knife bit a shallow trail in her palm.

"My lady!" Hutton said. "Look what you've done."

Jenna could feel what "she" had done. The acid juice flowed inside the open gash and seared the fresh cut. Hutton had not let loose her trembling hand. He watched the tears of pain sting her angry eyes. It was like viewing fire through a shiny glass. He liked it very much.

"We'd better see what we can do," he said finally. "We will need a bandage. Your petticoat will do." He reached down to lift the bottom of her skirt. Jenna's uninjured hand caught his cheek with a sharp crack.

Instantly Hutton gathered both her hands, wrist to wrist, in one of his.

"The one thing you may never do," he said softly, "is slap my face." He raised the knife hand to the side of her head, resting his fist in her hair, the blade teasing wisps of it out of the pins that held it. Finally a long strand fell free and coiled soft on her shoulder.

His face, so pale, so lean, was close to hers. She closed her eyes. "You can only be hurt by your own actions. Remember that, Jenna. And when we reach Manchester, we will have your statement of 'public forgiveness' all drafted and etched in our memory. All right?"

"Father," Connell interjected, his tone edgy. "You're compromising everything."

"I disagree. I am merely offering the lady assistance. And letting her know exactly where she stands. And, unfortunately"—his fingers absently played with the strand of freed hair—"she stands very much alone right now." He untied her cape and pushed back its flaps. "True, her poor father's body was not found with the wreckage." He tugged the lock of long hair lower, his finger advancing slowly across her bosom. With a delicate touch he arranged the ebony strand in a soft curve tucked under her breast. She stiffened, but did not struggle. The gold hilt of the blade lay against her temple, a wordless warning. "But it would be impossible to survive such a fall."

"Don't touch me," she said, her voice as small, unconvincing as the hope she clung to.

He smiled sympathetically. "I already have, my dear. Nothing you do or say can stop me. Don't you see? Your words, your wits are worth nothing against a man's strength. It is a valuable lesson for you to learn."

"I see no man," she said through clenched teeth. "I see a puffed-up coward flashing his weapon."

He shrugged and smiled. "Perhaps you're right." He lowered the knife and stabbed the half of the orange that had fallen on the seat beside her. "It's certainly not fair. But it's effective."

He raised the wet flesh of the orange to his lips and bit into it. "An unworthy substitute, I assure you," he said, eyes warm.

Suddenly Connell knocked his father's hand away from his mouth. The orange went flying. "I'm sick and tired of your sodding games! You can scare her all you want, but she's mine!"

Slowly, Hutton put the knife on the seat beside him and dabbed a white napkin across his upper lip. His eyes flashed a warning at his son. "Go back to your flask. I have no intention of taking her here."

Jenna saw a trembling begin in Connell's jaw. "By God!" He threw his flask to the seat. "You will not take her at all!"

Suddenly Connell's right fist swung wild. Hutton dodged as well as he could in the small space and deflected the blow to his shoulder. Then he wrestled Connell into the opposite corner near Jenna, landing on top of his son.

"Stop, you idiot!" Hutton shouted, jabbing a hard right into Connell's cheek. Connell's head lolled and his hands came up to ward off more blows. Hutton grabbed his son by the throat collar and sat him upright.

"We cannot fight over her," Hutton said, withdrawing and tugging his coat sleeves back down to his wrists. "If we do, she will play us one against the other. We must share, Connell. We must."

Connell didn't answer, his face strangely closed.

Beside Connell, Jenna pressed herself as far back into the corner as she could. Eyes closed, she repeated Hutton's words in her mind like a litany: "I have no intention of taking her here. . . ."

Finally Connell spoke. "I want to see her."

Jenna's heart went cold. Hutton looked annoyed, then shrugged and turned to Jenna. "It is a reasonable request." He smiled almost apologetically. "I will help you with the buttons."

Her eyes, so bright, cast down. Then to his surprise, Jenna leaned stiffly forward. Obliging? She couldn't be. . . .

Then he saw her hand sweep upward with his own dagger in her grasp. Quickly he lunged back toward Connell, out of the way. But Jenna immediately twisted in her seat to follow his motion.

Connell's knee came up as Hutton landed on his belly and Jenna's arm was knocked backward. Quickly Hutton pressed his length against her, grasping her wrist and choking off any motion of her arm.

"Drop it, Jenna." His cheek pressed close to her ear, the words as husky and soft as a lover's.

She tried to turn her head away, but she was backed against the carriage wall and could not move.

"Father, here—"

"Stay back, Connell," Hutton commanded. "I have the situation in hand," he said more softly, drawing back to look into her face.

Angrily, her fist opened and the knife clattered to the floor. He smiled at the hatred in her eyes. Her lips were parted as she made shallow gasps for breath. And he knew what he wanted. She stiffened at his touch and cried inwardly when his thin, warm lips fell hungry and open on hers.

"You greedy bast—" Connell grabbed his father's coat collar and jerked back.

The thunder of two gunshots cracked the night air, and both men froze. Jenna heard the snap of the driver's whip as he urged the horses faster.

"Jesus Christ, the money!" Connell exclaimed, pulling a pistol from the leather pouch. "For God's sake, Father! The money!"

Connell rested his gun on the open window and fired as the dark shape of a rider sped by. The horseman shouted something in a strange language, and an approaching rider fired into the coach door, nicking the trousers of Hutton's leg.

Jenna felt Hutton stiffen at the near miss. His light blue eyes searched hers. "The money," he whispered, pushing his weight off her.

Chapter 15

Outside, gunfire punctuated the shouts of pursuing riders. The horses' pounding hooves churned dust that filtered in through the window flap beside Jenna.

"Get down!" Hutton grabbed Jenna's arm and pushed her roughly to the floor. He lifted her seat cushion and pulled out two rifles, immediately bracing one against the window and firing a shot as he handed off the other gun to Connell.

An answering bullet whizzed past Connell's ear and he ducked. Hutton fired again, then reached inside his waistcoat and drew out a cloth bag. He tossed it into Jenna's lap. It landed with a heavy clink. Rifle shells.

"Load it," he said, laying the rifle across Jenna's knees and grabbing the pistol Connell had discarded. "Unless, of course, you are one of them"—he angled the pistol barrel out the window and fired—"and not one of us."

Jenna didn't move. She was remembering how his lean lips probed hungrily for a space between hers. "Whoever they are, I welcome them. Or death. Either is preferable to you."

"Oh, I wouldn't want death to take you from me yet." He reached down into her lap to retrieve the shells and gave a small smile as she stiffened at his touch. His face, taut and certain, hovered close to hers.

She turned her head away.

The rifle barrel opened with a sharp crack, like the snapping apart of a sweet fowl's wishbone. "Another time, m'lady." Hutton straightened slowly.

He stopped.

An eerie stream of air kissed his cheek. The arrow shot past and landed in the coach wall behind him, on a line with his high, starched collar. A small arrow, meant for high speed and deep entry, shot from a crossbow. He stared a moment at the dark red shaft that vibrated with the rumble of the coach. If he had straightened sooner, he would be gargling his own blood.

Connell eased his finger off the trigger, his eyes wide.

"Let the grimy little bastards stage their fun," Hutton said, absently fingering a collar button. "They will bleed another time."

Just then, the carriage rocked to an abrupt standstill. The shooting stopped. Jenna could hear someone giving orders, then the coach dipped sharply as the driver and his seat mate climbed down.

"Passengers!" shouted a deep voice. "Throw out your guns!"

Hutton nodded and Connell kicked open the coach door. The rifles and the empty pistol clattered into the road.

"Step out slowly," the voice commanded.

Connell looked at his father. Hutton, face grim, put his top hat in place and stepped down into the clearing.

He found himself in a twilight arena facing a silent group of mounted executioners.

The black-hooded bandits waited across the clearing, dark figures whose winded horses pawed nervously in front of a thick, gnarled stand of yew trees. The riders wore short black shoulder capes that made them seem broad and half-bodied in the misting twilight. Behind them the shaggy yews squatted like a line of grizzled infantry guarding the edge of the woods.

Hutton frowned as his eyes roamed the bandits. Five? Six? Only six of them? Surely there had to be more.

Unseen cicadas grew impatient in the humans' uneasy silence and struck up an intense evening trill.

One tall bandit ambled his horse forward.

Jackpot, Ian thought to himself as he watched Hutton's every move. Ian's hunch—and Robert's early sighting of Connell at the Glencur station—had paid off. The money had to be here.

"Evening, Lord Parrish," Ian said in a deep, controlled tone. Then he gestured expectantly to the guns lying at Hutton's feet.

Barely in control of his disdain, Hutton kicked the weapons across the clearing.

The bandit moved his spirited roan closer then, and the light picked up the gleam of the red-barreled crossbow lying across his saddle.

"Marry me mother," the driver breathed to his friend. "It's the Red Bow."

Hutton glared the pair of coachmen into silence and then concentrated on relaxing the tension in his shoulders. He had been able to straighten his shirtfront and smooth his hair, but his cravat hung loose. It bothered him. Along with the bloody timing of this sideshow. With calm deliberation, Hutton reached up to fix his wrinkled tie.

The bandit leader, silent, slowly grasped the crossbow and drew it up across his leg to rest on his forearm.

What a bloody piece of melodrama, Hutton thought. The filthy, greedy moles—

The Bandit spoke roughly. "Your mincing toilette can wait. Empty the coach. Or we'll make a sieve of it."

Connell, flush-faced and angry, flung himself quickly down the coach steps. "Flippin' strikers!" he shouted. "I know who you are!"

Jenna fought the nausea that rose in her throat as she listened to the bandits' derisive laughter. She leaned against the coach wall, her cheek pressed to the rotting, cracked canvas. How close she had come. How close to what her mother had endured. She made herself swallow against the bile. The acrid taste was almost welcome, purging her mouth of the unnatural feel of Hutton's kiss. With trembling fingers, she drew her cape around her shoulders and curled her bloodied hand gingerly inside the folds.

The coach tipped down as her weight fell on the creaking wood step. A cool wind played a strand of her loosened hair across her cheek, and she raised her face to shake it back.

He saw her then. From across the clearing. The Bandit's roan neighed sharply as the bit jerked suddenly, painfully tight.

Jenna could feel Ian's eyes absorb her distraught stance: the trembling hand at her collar, the ashen cast of her face around frightened eyes.

The roan reared high at the sudden kick of its master and bounded forward, toward Jenna.

She could not meet the rider's eyes. They were dark, enraged, full of questions she was too drained to answer.

Ian swerved right at the last moment, reining in an inch shy of the polished boot on Hutton Parrish's foot.

Hutton, as rigid as a fencer on guard, did not move, even when the horse's wet nostrils grazed his chin.

The heavy bow was balanced effortlessly on the Bandit's

left arm. With a quick snap of the draw lever, Ian cocked the bow and aimed it.

The white-haired colliery lord found himself eye level with the red bow. He could smell the musk of old age on its wooden shaft. And the iron-metal scent of the gun oil that had recently greased its trigger.

"Take care, man!" Simon Oxmain trotted up beside the roan. His words were terse Portuguese and full of worry. "We are here to divert the money. Not fight for a pawed-over chit. You endanger us all."

The warning only caused Ian to tighten the tension of his finger on the trigger.

"I will see you greedy moles in hell!" Hutton said, teeth ground tight.

"And there you'll find the sodding Satan who spawned you!" Ian hissed.

"The miners will be blamed!" Simon whispered, urgent.

The forearm that steadied the bow began to tremble as Ian fought for control. He dared not look at Jenna. If the bastard had harmed her. Christ, if he had touched her—

Crack!

The trigger released and its sharp messenger tore through the crown of Hutton's tall hat. The hat tumbled to the ground and the arrow thudded home in the side of the coach, its razor-edged head buried hungrily in hard wood.

"I will cut away each part of you that so much as grazed her skin," Ian breathed, his eyes never wavering from Hutton's.

"My master says to tell you we are not miners who slave in your pits," Simon "translated" quickly. "We have come to relieve you of a burden."

Quickly Simon nodded to Orrie, who scrambled to the top of the coach and began throwing down baggage. A black-hooded rider on the ground began to open the bags and tear through the Parrishes' finery.

The modest travel bag Jenna had packed at Leona's landed in the dust near Hutton's feet.

My God. Jenna tensed with alarm, fighting the numbness she felt. The map! The coal ledger from Shadow Glen!

A bandit moved to pick up the satchel. "Wait!" she called. "That one is mine." Cautiously, Jenna walked past the flanks of the bandits' horses. Keeping her bloodied hand hidden in her cloak, she stooped quickly to retrieve her bag.

"Do you know Lady Jenna Thornton?" Hutton's outstretched arm gestured gracefully as Jenna cautiously backed away. Hutton's eyes fastened on the Red Bow Bandit. "Lady Jenna was an unexpected companion on our ride. But—very welcome, I assure you."

I will kill him. He knows I will kill him. Ian's head pounded with the heat of his anger. Quickly he reloaded the crossbow.

Out of the corner of his eye, he caught the movement of Hutton Parrish as the viscount bent to pick up something on the ground. A piece of parchment.

"Fell from her sleeve," Simon whispered to Ian.

Jenna stopped. Her bags dropped unnoticed from her hands. The note. The note telling her where in London Hutton kept Carolina's son. If he discovered that Carolina was the informer, he would—

"No!" Jenna shouted. Anger flooded her body like a cleansing bath. She rushed for the paper in Hutton's hand. As she did, Ian's chest constricted with an apprehension so strong he wanted to shout a warning.

The snub-nosed derringer appeared suddenly in Hutton's hand. Jenna halted her headlong rush a foot from him, her small boots scraping a sudden foothold in the dirt.

The white-haired lord held the gun offhandedly, casually on its side, its toylike barrel aimed at her bosom.

The bandits tensed, looking to Ian for orders. But Ian was silent, gauging the direction and finger tension on the gun in Hutton's hand. Surely Parrish would not shoot a woman he wanted so badly. Surely, pray God. . . .

"This must be an important missive," Hutton said softly. "A love note, perhaps. Expensive paper." He fingered the folded note carefully. "I have similar stock imported myself."

Jenna's breath caught in her throat, but her eyes smoldered with hatred of the cold, smiling face before her. "My fiancé's words are not meant for the eyes of a loveless beast. Return what is mine."

Parrish smiled and began to unfold the note. As he did, he saw Jenna pull her arm out of her cloak and slowly raise her hand to receive the note.

The congealed blood in Jenna's open palm came into full view of the mounted bandits. The gash had bled enough to wet the sleeve of her gown with a dark stain that crept toward her elbow.

"Madre de Dios," breathed one of the bandits.

The Red Bow had already jumped from his saddle. He shrugged his shoulder cape free of his right arm.

Hutton reacted calmly and shifted the small pistol in the direction of the slowly advancing Bandit. Jenna knew she must speak strongly, quickly, before Ian's wrath tore the flimsy cover off the Red Bow's disguise.

"Ironic," her voice carried across the clearing to the coachmen and the bandit guarding them, "that the nobleman holds a gun to my breast and the road thief comes to my aid."

The jerkin-clad driver looked uncomfortable. His friend in knee breeches spat forcefully in the dust.

"Do you demand this bloody price of every woman who shares your company, seignor?" Ian's voice was tight-edged, deadly. "Or was Lady Jenna especially resistant?" The Bandit's eyes never left Hutton's.

Jenna could see the blood rise to the viscount's pale, steely visage. He glanced at her.

"My compliments on your sense of drama, Jenna." His voice was soft. Scary. "If it were not designed to get me killed, I would be much more appreciative."

"My fiancé's note," she requested, palm still extended.

Ian's right hand flashed a "get ready" signal to Orrie, perched on the coach. Hutton heard the creak of new leather gloves as Orrie's fingers found a firmer grasp on the wood stock of the rifle.

"Take my advice," Ian said softly. "Shoot me instead of the lady. That way, you will die mercifully in a shower of bullets. And you will not live to see your money destroyed."

Hutton hesitated, his revolver still trained on the Bandit. Then he laid the note gently in Jenna's outstretched hand.

"I do not plan to die," Hutton said. "And I will see your privateering guts hang from a tree before this affair is finished."

The Red Bow shrugged. "What's one bandit killed? Nothing. But a colliery lord, a stinking-rich one. Now there's a loss to the shire."

"Your little drama bores me!" Hutton shouted. Enraged and red-faced, Hutton threw the revolver at the Red Bow's feet.

Cautious, Ian bent to pick it up. Hutton's steel-toed boot swung instantly for the Bandit's jaw. The kick connected, but Ian rolled with the force of it, grabbing the other man's leg as he fell. Hutton cried out as his knee was wrenched in its socket. He landed in the dust beside the Bandit.

Jenna swooped quickly to grab the derringer, then backed away as both men rose, adrenaline throbbing for a target.

Hutton struggled upright, holding one knee stiff, his black broadcloth coat veneered gray with road dust. The black-hooded Bandit stood tall before him. With an impatient yank of the collar cord, the red-lined cape slid free to the ground.

"I know you, bastard." Hutton's words were low, hate filled.

Ian stepped closer, fists clenched.

"And I will drive you out of Lancashire, back to the sour belly of the ship you escaped on. A charge of murder, wasn't it, Captain St—"

The gunshot stung the dirt neatly between them, startling the horses with its short, sharp crack.

The two adversaries looked at Jenna. "Stop," she said, "both of you."

Her voice was hard-edged, but Ian could see her eyes glisten with a frantic wish. The ordeal must end soon. Her gun hand began to tremble. The raw metal of the tiny pistol bit neatly into the bloody gash of her palm.

"You protect him!" Hutton hissed, then he lunged for Jenna and the gun. But Ian rushed forward and gripped his coat. The lapel ripped, then held, and Hutton was jerked around. Ian's fist landed like a hammer blow on Hutton's jaw. Parrish whirled and dropped.

"We have no more time for an old man's ramblings!" the Red Bow roared.

"The money box! It's here!" Orrie shouted.

The metal box thunked to the ground near the coach.

The Red Bow rammed the flat of his boot into Hutton's

side and rolled the groggy viscount to his back. Ian towered over him. "The key," he said quietly.

Hutton rubbed his jaw and fished slowly in his watch pocket.

Ian roughly grabbed the key and unlocked the box.

It was full. Stacks of pound notes. Some cloth bags of gold guineas.

The driver's gap-toothed mouth fell open. "But there's more there than—"

"Right, my friend," Ian said. "More there than a week's salary to recruit one hundred farmhands from Hertfordshire."

Hutton's eyes narrowed suspiciously on the driver. With a nod from the Red Bow, Orrie leaned over the box and picked out the heavy bags of guineas.

The voice under the Red Bow's mask sounded darkly amused. "Clever Lord Parrish. Everyone in the shire knew he was going to ferry in a trainload of strikebreakers. But we didn't know he would risk his precious sweat fund at the same time."

"Blathering bastard!" Hutton rose to his feet, aided by Connell.

"Each quarter for the past two years you've paid the miners short. And you used their bloody sweat to build a treasury of cash that our Queen does not know about."

"Lying thief," Hutton said.

"You are a better bandit than I. You taxed the miners who bought goods in the village. Penalized them if they would not pay outrageous prices at the camp store. You taxed them for the Parrish grass their goats ate, for God's sake! And week by week you sucked them deep into debt for the ale you rationed."

"My business affairs are my own. The workers chose their lot. They stayed with me."

"Because they had nowhere else to go. That is not a matter of choice, seignor." The Red Bow's voice was low. "It is a matter of exploiting the unfortunate. I'm sure the irony appealed to you. Tonight the miners' money was on its way to London to be used to buy votes against them. You have a cruel slant to your humor.

"But then"—the Red Bow grabbed a rag-topped torch from one of his mounted men—"so do I."

Connell, still quiet, as if he wanted to be forgotten, backed almost imperceptibly toward the coach.

Hutton stood frozen in defiance. His hand stopped massaging his swollen jaw. "I know it is you," Hutton said clearly. "I can feel it. Your eyes burn. Like a stallion whose brood mare has been mounted by another."

The Bandit grew ominously still. "You do not know me," the Red Bow said in a tone too controlled. The match in his hand scraped roughly along the shoe sole of his mounted comrade. The acrid burning scent wafted toward Hutton's face.

Slowly the Red Bow turned his head toward Hutton. The white-haired lord saw the black hood distend as the Bandit slowly, forcefully exhaled.

"I am only a legend," the Bandit whispered. "An unhappy spirit—" The match touched the kerosene-soaked rag and the tall torch grew orange with flame.

Jenna held her breath. Dear God, don't let Ian kill him.

"—the ghost of a nobleman who could not bear to see men, women and children abused in the mines and mills of Lancashire," Ian continued, walking closer to the viscount.

Suddenly the torch dipped close to Hutton's face, throwing a fevered brightness around his widened eyes.

"How is it," the Red Bow said, "you 'know' a nobleman's ghost, yet you cannot see the bloody leech you have become? It is the blindness of a devil's pawn, Lord Parrish. I cannot use the devil's money. And neither will you."

The Red Bow quickly tossed the heavy torch into the open money box, and the pound notes began to burn with frenzied, crisp sounds.

Hutton trembled. He swallowed three times hard, his Adam's apple bobbing upward like the husk of a chestnut caught on a suction pool. Yet he did not cry out.

"Your guineas will be given to the vicar, charitable Christian that you are," the Bandit said. "You may try to convince him to give them back. But God made that man ambitious and enterprising, just like you. So he can take advantage of fortuitous circumstances. Just like you."

The Red Bow turned his back and gave orders in his strange language. One of the bandits unhitched two coach horses from their harness, then mounted one bareback.

"Now there is a horse for the lady to ride," Ian said, "so that her other hand need not be graced with your bloody hospitality." He picked up Jenna's soft satchel and latched it on to the vacant horse's saddle.

Jenna, her spirit numb, gathered her cloak around her and walked slowly toward the saddled horse.

"She is a madwoman!" Connell shouted. "Mad like her father!"

Jenna turned to him. "My father is dead," she said, her words quiet, drained. "Or so Lord Parrish says. You—both of you—have killed my father. May God have mercy on your souls. But only as much mercy as you showed my father."

She turned away, suddenly aware of how much effort it

took to put one foot in front of the other. She moved toward the horse as if she were dream-walking.

The black-robed, faceless Red Bow cupped his hand by the stirrup, awaiting her foot. She placed her uninjured hand on his shoulder to steady her ascent, but she stopped then, unable to move. The vital, solid heat of his body was a shock to the icy stillness she felt inside her. She knew the secure warmth that lay under his cloak, waiting to comfort her, protect her. Ian.

She pushed away from him then, fearful that she would be drawn closer, ever closer, until her face was buried airless, timeless, against his chest.

Quickly she mounted. Jenna looked straight ahead, drained of fear, of anger. She felt only a bone-deep emptiness that made her feel lost in a black well.

"Jenna." Ian's voice was soft below her. "I must know what happened." His words were quiet, pained. "Because if he did"— he paused—"I cannot leave him here alive."

The silence was heavy, because words had to come from the bottom of the well. "You came in time," she said, unfeeling.

She could hear the release of his breath against his mask. "Go now. Take the road to Glencur. Simon will catch up with you and lead you home with us."

Woodenly she kicked the horse to a trot, not looking back. And she would not let her eyes fill with tears until the horses' hooves hit the safety of dew-slick grass near the foothills of her valley.

The Red Bow himself was the last to leave. His bandits were gone, each in a different direction. He kicked his roan to a gallop, but a shrill whistle from the coach made him pull the horse to a rearing turn.

It was the coach driver. The sallow little man on the perch doffed his greasy cap and waved.

The Red Bow Bandit returned his salute and galloped on.

The driver turned to his seat mate and grinned. "We'll tell it like it was, eh, Richie? No matter what that rich old lecher in the box pays us, right?"

His sharp-chinned friend leaned forward on his emptied rifle. "Don't know, Perce. He's got an awful lotta money."

"Yeah. But a big chunk of it just went up in smoke." He elbowed Richie in the ribs and they both chuckled.

They chattered all the way to Manchester. There Lord Parrish hurried to the constable's office and Richie and Perce hurried to the pub.

Their story was so grand they got all the free ale they asked for. The crowd grew large, and Richie and Perce were set up on stools at the bar just so everyone could hear their telling of the Red Bow robbery.

At the same time, miles from Manchester in an isolated wood in the Pennines foothills, the last of the bandits straggled home.

The Red Bow dropped from the saddle with a grunt. The decoy trails were set. The rest of the band should be back.

And Jenna. He shook his head with weariness and wonder. Always the complication of Jenna.

Chapter 16

Beneath the gamekeeper's cottage Ian strode into the great hall of an underground chamber, discarding the Red Bow's hood and hat on a long table in front of the huge fireplace.

His brother Robert leaned on the rough granite mantelpiece, his posture tense. Simon Oxmain, free of his bandit disguise and seated comfortably in an old twine-bottomed rocker, did not even look up at Ian's arrival.

"Where is she?" he demanded.

"Upstairs," Robert said. "Betts is tending her."

Betts was Marguerite's maid, a good nurse. Ian relaxed the stiffness in his neck and reached for the brandy bottle on the table.

"Why in hell was she in that coach?" Ian asked, downing a tall shot of whiskey.

The question was straightforward, but Robert could sense the black rage underneath. Robert eased away from the mantel and stared at Ian's intense profile. He had seen jealous anger in his brother before. Yet never so focused and controlled. The masquerade had turned real then. They were lovers.

Slowly, Robert poured brandy for himself. "She was shaken, but she answered some questions." He repeated Jenna's quiet story—how Bilpo Grawlin's children secreted the Shadow Glen accounts and map to her. How Carolina revealed tonight's plans. How she feared the band would not be assembled to stop the money. "So she sped to the first coach for Manchester and—"

"And right into Parrish's arms!" The brandy glass shattered against the charred floor of the grate. "Why couldn't she wait? Why not trust me?"

"She's trouble, I grant you that, Capt'n." Simon Oxmain cupped the bowl of his curved pipe in his hand and pursed his whiskered lips. "She was nearly the death of us all tonight." The old seaman leaned over to tap the pipe gently on the ash-flecked floor of the hearth.

Ian's boots appeared before his face. Simon straightened in his chair, his bushy white eyebrows raised to a straight line across his forehead. "Bad sign when you get huffy at an old friend for tellin' the truth."

Ian exhaled the breath he was holding. "Simon—"

The stocky older man stood up and poked the lip of his pipe at Ian's heart. "You would've murdered a high and mighty bastard tonight. And there would've been hell to pay. With our hides. Strung up like a bunch of halibut twitchin' on a rusty line."

"You knew the risks. You knew they'd be armed." Ian was terse, annoyed.

"But I didn't know you'd be a ruttin' hothead!"

"The bastard lives. We all live. No blood was shed." Ian turned his back, the conversation ended.

"None except Jenna's," Robert mused softly.

The old seaman was quiet. A muscle in Ian's jaw twitched. The blow from Hutton's boot had left a small, angry mark.

"What next, Capt'n?" Simon sat down with a weary

grunt. "Shall we take her to the islands? Keep her safe until this eel of yours gets skinned?"

"He may skin me first," Ian said, pouring a whiskey. "He knows it was me tonight."

"But Ross is impersonating you at the game room," Robert said. "You'll have a good alibi."

"Only if he puts in a good performance, and I don't mean on his feet." Simon puffed on his pipe and smiled.

"Enough," Ian said wearily. "You cannot take Jenna."

"Why not? She's trouble for you here. And I'd hate to see you killed. You got two more big payments to make on our rig."

Ian shook his head. "She's not the kind to hide. From anything. Besides, she's too sharp-tongued a hellcat for an old man like you. Take her aboard and I'd have no ship left to pay for. She'd talk you out of your left testicle and into a dinghy."

Simon raised his eyebrows and exhaled a slow stream of smoke. "She weren't raisin' much hell when she came in."

Ian threw a chunk of oak on the coals. "She needed no more tonight," he said softly.

In a small bedroom on the second floor, a fire crackled merrily in the hearth. Betts, the dark young serving maid, talked soothingly in a voice that had the rhythm of a song.

"Was a bad man who done dis." She dabbed delicately at the dried blood on Jenna's palm. "Why? What do you do to him?"

"I wouldn't tell him the truth," Jenna said absently, not ready for the comforting numbness to end.

"Evil man. He doan deserve de truth. Where else he hurt you?"

Something stung behind Jenna's eyes. She didn't answer. She couldn't.

The girl dipped the soft rag in warm water and arched her eyebrows. "He hurt you where it cannot show. Smart som'bitch, him. Take off dese tings he touch. Dey dirty now."

Carefully Betts helped Jenna remove her wrinkled riding skirt, bodice and shirtwaist blouse, then the petticoat, until only the simple white chemise and pantalets were left.

"You are poor lady?" Betts asked, sponging Jenna's arms and neck, always returning gently to Jenna's right hand, where the gash began to show red and clean.

The question brought a puzzled smile to Jenna's lips.

"Dis." Betts picked at the plain material of Jenna's undergarment. "You have no lace. No ribbon. No fancy. You are poor lady."

Jenna nodded thoughtfully. "I guess so."

"Is all right. The captain will give you money. He so reech. He bring us here. He leave de islands to be with his father. But his father die. Den the captain get more money 'cause his father die! Den he have to make revenge on de rock seller. De rock seller make bad trouble for captain."

"The rock seller? Lord Parrish?"

"De man who put people in de ground to pick rocks. In my home we pick food from de ground. Yams and pineapple. Food from de trees. Banana. Coffee. Sweet oranges. Here you pick de rocks to keep you warm. Is a bad business for people. De rock seller is evil man."

"I know," Jenna said softly.

"He de one who hurt you?"

"It doesn't matter."

The girl took Jenna's face in two dark hands. Betts's eyes were beautiful pools of brown, churning with concern. "Yes!

It matter! If you do not get mad, you get scared. And den you shrink inside. And your heart cannot grow big enough to make room for a man. And you be cold there, just because one evil man make you scared."

Jenna shook her head, pulling Betts's slender fingers away from her face. "I want to be alone now."

"No, you doan," Betts said matter-of-factly, smearing a light film of ointment on Jenna's outstretched hand. "You need to make tears. No lady tears. A big sound to push de devil breath out of here." The back of her hand patted Jenna's chest. Then Betts began to wind a strip of bandage around the cut.

The door to the small room opened then. Ian walked in.

No longer the dark, hooded bandit, Ian's face was open to her. The lean line of his jaw was unshaven, and the shadows played around the dark handsomeness, highlighting the brow and hollow of his guarded eyes, softening the sharp ridge of his upper lip.

Involuntarily, her lips parted at the sight of him. But she turned her head. A wary tension and uncertainty stiffened her body.

"I am not dressed to receive visitors," Jenna said.

"I'm not visiting. This is my house. I came to check your wound."

Ian held her hand gently and unwound the bandage Betts had begun. "It is not deep. Good. I will finish, Betts."

Betts gathered up Jenna's clothes and was about to pull the door closed behind her when she popped back in. "I will be close." Betts frowned a warning and left.

There were no words as Ian finished bandaging her hand. She looked away from him, to the light chintz curtains at the small window of the room.

"I need a dressing robe," she said when he was done.

"Betts will find one for you."

"Now," she said.

"An attack of modesty?"

"No." She pulled her hand away and stood up. "An attack by your father." The words had come out cold and simple.

"I have no father." His voice was a harsh whisper. His eyes glared at her, a single question haunting them.

She backed away. "I gave him nothing." Her eyes closed suddenly, mouth tight as she felt Parrish's breath on her lips. Her hand strayed to the side of her head where he had loosened tendrils of hair with the dagger. Then she heard Connell's petulant request: "I want to see her."

"I need a robe!" she said, more urgent now.

"Jenna." Ian grabbed her by the shoulders.

She struggled and backed farther toward the fire. Her voice grew frantic. "No!"

"Wait." His voice softened. "Wait." Slowly, Ian removed his coat. "Take this. To cover you."

Jenna concentrated on breathing deeply, in and out. Cautious, she reached out for the jacket. Panic was a new feeling for the Ice Maiden. It had gripped her whole being when Ian grabbed her arms. Hysteria, she suddenly realized, was clearly not far behind. What a relief it would be—

But Ian did not move toward her. A minute passed. A piece of kindling snapped sharply in the coals. Slowly she began to don the coat. Then she crossed her arms across her chest as if chilled. She was, in fact, quivering. And Jenna knew that Betts was right. She had grown cold inside.

She looked to the fire. "Did you know he keeps Carolina's son prisoner in London?" she said softly. "So that he can keep her hostage at Parrish Hall?"

"Yes." He spoke quietly, tensed, waiting.

"And he said Father's carriage crashed. But they could not find his body. I do not believe he is dead. Do you?"

"No. I will send someone to find out."

"He was too strong, Ian," she whispered. "I could not fight him. If you had not come, I would have been stripped"—she paused, choking on the breath trapped in her throat when Hutton's lean, hard weight pressed against her chest—"of everything."

She sensed his nearness directly behind her. He had slowly moved closer.

A door slammed somewhere downstairs. And she heard a clock in the hallway sweetly chiming the hour. Eight? Nine? She lost count.

"What time is it? I must go—"

"It is time to forget," he said quietly.

She felt his hand on her shoulder and she turned to face him. His chest was there. Inviting her touch. She raised her hand to sweep the breadth of his shoulders. But her hand was bandaged.

"I thought"—she licked her lips, staring at her hand—"as I rode here in the dark—I worried that the monster might be in you, too," she said, staring at her hand.

His own hand stopped in midair on its way to stroke her hair, caress her cheek. "It is for you to say," he said, guarded, tight. "You know us both now."

She stepped back with a start, as if he had touched her. "That's not true."

Firelight caught his taut neck, playing on the sweat-glistening pulse point in his throat. It throbbed slowly, as if his breath were stilled, waiting.

"I know only that his heart is empty," she said softly. "And yours is full." She walked away, hugging herself. "Full of the past. Some dreams must die, Ian, because they are so dark. They hurt so many people." Jenna shook her head and narrowed her eyes to control the tears that threatened.

"Jenna." Her name escaped his lips like a mourning song for something he feared was dying.

"I know," she whispered, her eyes wide and glistening as she gazed into the fire. "You are not the cause. You are not him. Yet if you had not come here, Father's plan would have no champion. There would be no sacrifices"—she stopped and took a deep breath—"no madmen in dark coaches. No desire to—" She stopped, her face flushed.

"You're wrong," he said softly. "You would still desire to lie with a man. If not me, then—"

"Stop it!" She covered her ears.

He moved closer. "I want to help," he said.

She felt his warmth at her shoulder, but she resisted the urge to turn around. "How? With a persuasive technique like your father's?" Her voice was rising. "Does it run in the family, Ian? This love of watching people in pain?"

He felt glad to see her anger, yet he was sad beyond measure. Firmly he turned her around and folded his arms around her.

His white cotton shirt smelled of the night. The sweat of his fight. The smoky scent of the pound notes set ablaze. She stiffened, not knowing whether to fight or flee.

From somewhere came an incongruent clean fragrance of spring grass. Her eyes closed and she lay her cheek lightly along the folds of his shirt, barely pressing the material to his hard chest underneath. The green stain of meadow grass was buried somewhere in the fiber of his shirt. Her cheek skimmed the surface, searching. Then slowly, like a chrysalis softening, she melted into the warmth of his chest.

The sobs began silently. He felt them dampen the thin

material of his shirt. Then a sound wrenched free and she bent double. He sank with her to the floor, gathering her in his arms, each of her sobs hammering against his heart.

She was crying, he knew, at the injustice of it. Of being forced to see the black monsters that inhabit a man's soul. She would be older and wiser after this night.

And so will I, he thought. Never again would he hesitate to pull a trigger on Hutton Parrish.

Betts tiptoed through the door, but straightened up when she saw Jenna sitting alone by the fire.

"You feel better now?" she said, placing a clean dress on the bed.

"Yes," Jenna said, eyes closed. "Tired." Ian had left her quietly. His warmth remained. She felt drowsy and, finally, safe.

"My lady, she feel tired all de time. She is gettin' big now. De baby, he grow an' grow. An' soon she will not see her toes 'til dat baby come out."

A sharp voice from the night cut through Betts's singsong rhythm. It was Hutton's taunt: "And you don't mind the island girl he keeps in the woods?"

"Your mistress," Jenna said. "Who is she?"

"On de island, my lady was Marguerite Maria de Brochmère. Third daughter, you should know, of de biggest plantation master of all. But here she is Marguerite Stonebridge. Such a plain name for my beautiful lady." Betts plumped up the pillows on the high four-poster bed.

"She is married?" Jenna's heart grew still.

"Of course! She would not come all dis way to his cold home unless her heart and her hand were his, eh?"

"And the baby—"

"Will come at de end of summer. De captain tease her an'

say de baby hate de cole as much as my lady! He say we cannot go back 'til de spring. But de devil winds blow in de spring, I tell heem! We—"

Her voice sang on. Jenna could not hear.

Married. At least the foreigner Marguerite had the honor to demand marriage from the man who bedded her.

"Why is their marriage kept secret? And why does he hide her here?" Jenna interrupted.

Betts looked suddenly uncomfortable. "Because de English are stupid. They do not like a dark lady to go to their parties and fancy tings," Betts said huffily. "When we get back to de islands, then—"

"We'll have a party every day!" a voice interrupted.

Marguerite Stonebridge, pert and pretty and the color of tea and cream, stepped into the room. "I am so glad to meet you," she smiled. "My husband has told me so much about you." Marguerite extended her hand and Jenna, in shock, barely regained enough control to clasp the pregnant woman's warm fingers.

"Ian says you have the courage of a tiger. And Robert calls you a raven beauty. They are both right, no?"

Her accent was not like Betts's. It was more European.

"They both exaggerate," Jenna demurred, finding it difficult to talk.

"I am sorry," Marguerite said quickly. "You are tired. You have had a terrible assault. And I stand here wanting to chat. As if Betts and I do nothing else all day!"

"I do other tings! You jus' grow de baby!" Betts said with a smile.

Marguerite tsked, gave Jenna a warm smile, then took her leave.

"De Captain have dis dress sent from de big house. I will

come to help you in de morning." Betts said good night and closed the door.

It took only ten minutes for Jenna to dress and pack the bag Leona had loaned her. The secret passage at the end of the hallway was easy to find. It was still open. She swept down the musty, kerosene-lit stairwell as quietly as she could, emerging in an empty corridor. She recognized the passage Simon had led her through, and she could see the flames of the lanterns bend toward her. A draft. From the outside.

She took the first saddled horse she saw. The Red Bow's roan.

He would not need it any longer, she thought. The masquerade was over.

On the following afternoon in London, horse hooves clopped soothingly down Piccadilly Circus, past the park, turning right, across the park lawn, onto a dogleg path that led to Curzon Street.

Inside the hansom cab Jenna nearly fell asleep with the motion of the ride. She had not slept well on the train, even though she had used Carolina's generous purse to buy some privacy.

The carriage rumbled past number 19 Curzon Street, a five-story redbrick house with neat, white-paned windows. Jenna recognized the home of former Prime Minister Benjamin Disraeli, feisty orator and favorite of the Queen.

Three houses away the coach stopped at the curb before a four-story whitestone with a large colonnade.

Baron Ronstead Wilkes was stepping quickly down the stairs on his way out to an early hand of whist when he saw the cloaked figure standing in his foyer.

Hiram, the butler, took a threadbare satchel from her hand

and was about to present her. But the baron hurried to her side, his hand extended.

Jenna placed her bandaged palm in his. "I need your help, Uncle."

"So it appears," he frowned.

"Was she not magnificent, Connell?" Hutton energetically sponged a soap trail down his arm and across his chest. "Did she not give good sport in the carriage?"

Connell smeared jam on a honeyed tea biscuit and popped it into his mouth. He shook his head. "You ruined everything. Slicing her hand like that. Why'd you do it?"

"I don't know. Serendipity, I suppose."

"Unlike other 'great notions,' Father, this one will haunt you. It gives the lady damning evidence of your intentions."

"Perhaps."

"Are you not worried?"

"No."

"Why not?"

"People know she is strange. Like her father. We will call her mad and show pity for her condition."

Connell frowned. "Surely you don't believe that's enough."

"No, actually. Not with your clumsy attempt to steal a kiss in Liverpool. I'm not worried because I know who the Red Bow is. And I know she will keep quiet to protect him."

"Stonebridge has an alibi. The whoremonger was busy making a scene at Madam Lily's Game Room on the forked road."

"An impostor. I will prove it. All it will cost is a tidy sum for the lady who's lying for him."

"More than a whore caught sight of him. He carried her up the stairs with a bottle of wine balanced on her flippin' navel. Then he yelled, 'Drinks for all!' and threw the Stonebridge ring down the stairs to seal the bill."

"Mmmmmm," Hutton murmured, signaling Carolina to hand him a thick towel as large as a blanket. "You've got to admire the bastard." Hutton sat down in an ebony straightbacked chair.

"What the bloody hell do you mean?" Connell snapped his silver cigarette case closed.

"Oh, Connell," Hutton sighed and reached past Connell to the stand where his glass of claret sat. "His attention to detail. His quick planning. We upped our schedule and he one-upped it." Hutton nodded over his shoulder. Behind him, Carolina poured perfumed oil into her palm and began to massage it slowly into his shoulders and neck.

"You 'admire' him? When he destroyed our cache? I can't believe you're taking this so—philosophically." Connell spat the word.

"I'm furious, of course," Hutton said, his neck rolling with the rhythm of Carolina's pressing hands. "But it feels so good to have a worthy, unpredictable adversary."

"Perhaps he is more worthy of you than I." Connell stepped solidly in front of his father, a strange smile on his face.

Hutton craned his neck upward. "Nonsense. You're my ally, not an enemy. Where I shall relish his destruction, I would not enjoy yours."

The tone hit Connell strangely. A cold weakness washed over his knees, like a meat gelatin about to collapse. He stepped away toward the fire to disguise the tremor. "Is that a warning, Father?"

Hutton smiled. "A whim, Connell. I want her. For myself. For what time I have left on this spiritless earth."

A deal, Connell thought. And his posture straightened a

little as he sensed he had something his father wanted. "And if I agreed to withdraw my half-hearted pursuit?"

"Your inheritance would be hastened. A part of it, at least. I would eliminate Phillip Thornton. And the estate would fall to Jenna, thus to me. I would give it to you. Immediately. As a young man, you could control the richest vein of coal Lancashire has known."

"You have coveted Shadow Glen for years. Why is one maidenhead worth so much?"

"It isn't. She hasn't one left to give." Hutton pulled away suddenly from his soothing massage and stood up to grab the neck of the wine cruet. "I felt it. His possession of her." Hutton breathed deeply and sat down. "Curiously, I want her no less." He signaled Carolina to resume. "Perhaps it is love, after all." He sipped thoughtfully at the glass in his hand. "I must still think of a punishment, of course."

Hutton smiled up at his son. "Leave us now."

Connell gave a hesitant nod, then walked away, silent.

"I think you will need more oil, my dear."

The words were a sinuous murmur. Connell closed the door quickly.

Chapter 17

Lord, what a week!

Baron Ronstead Wilkes angrily chewed the end off a fresh, fat cigar and spat the tip into the shiny brass coal scuttle. "More whiskey!" he yelled to the butler Hiram, who left to fill the decanter again.

Politics. How he hated politics. It had taken over his life ever since his bedraggled niece stepped over his threshold.

The baron ran a hand through the thick salt-and-pepper thatch of hair on his crown and tried to calm his trepidation.

Tonight's meeting was something Jenna had demanded from the first hour she spent under his protection.

"Impossible." He had shaken his head.

"Quite necessary," she had nodded. And he had listened to her story, the whist game at Lord Howatch's forgotten, replaced by a dark matter of family honor.

At the story's end, the outraged baron agreed that Hutton Parrish should be censured. "But privately, my dear. Carefully." Hutton had the keys to too many closets in both the House of Lords and the Commons. And God only knew what skeleton he would pull from the Thorntons' past to fight the scandal.

"Poor Jenna. Poor us," he sighed.

They had received confirmation four days ago. The authorities found only one body in the wreckage of the earl's coach in Lancashire. A lad named Nivett, the gardener's boy who had driven the carriage.

A tragedy. A mystery, too: where in the hell was Arthur Thornton? Damned peculiar that Parrish should announce the accident to Jenna before anyone knew of it.

That's assuming she was telling the truth about what happened. And for all the faults he found in his strong-willed niece, lying was not one of them.

The baron shook his head and blew an odoriferous ring of cigar smoke close to the flue. It was unnerving to him, all that strength and purpose in one young woman's body. And she wasn't always subtle about displaying it, either. Wearing the gauze strips about her hand like a badge of honor each time she was invited to tea. And those times were many. In one week she had become the most sought after guest on the Piccadilly circuit, much to the delight of the baron's wife, Enid, who escorted the notorious girl around like a mother hen nursing an injured chick.

Hiram brought the decanter on a tray and poured his master a tall draught. The baron sank gratefully into the chintzed and billowed folds of his favorite stuffed armchair, rubbing his temples.

He could hardly believe he had arranged this. A secret meeting. Five of London's most influential Liberal lords. Plus a union leader. Plotting in his own house. Despite his vow, upon the death of his beloved sister, never to be involved in Thornton's politics again. It had killed her, he knew. In some deep, dark way politics killed Lady Charlotte. And none of it would have happened if she had not fallen in love with that orating fool, Arthur Thornton.

The baron downed the last swallow of his second glass

and set it on the inlaid marble top of the expensive loo table Enid had bought for the library.

Quickly Hiram removed the glass from the cover of the fox-hunter's quarterly the mistress had ordered for the baron. A dozen magazines, reviews and periodicals in three languages were carefully arranged like overlapping layers of limp toast. The master never read them, except for the Dickens serials. But Lady Wilkes insisted they be there in case the urge for culture struck.

At the center of the table, an oversized limewood carving of a dead pigeon lay encased under glass. The baron frowned at it. Damn if he didn't feel as bloody stiff as the bird. This whole affair was draining him. His whiskey paunch was coming back. And the bags under his eyes made him look like a sixty-two-year-old insomniac. Which he was. The sordid affair faced him at every social engagement —from drinks at the club to a chamber recital with the Duke of Gloucester, where the baron returned grim smiles to noblemen wearing arched monocles and curious looks.

He had heard Jenna called a mad fool like her father. A conniving young woman with an endangered inheritance and a plan to lure Parrish into a compromising position.

"Hogwash!" the baron grunted aloud. Hutton Parrish was never prey. He hunted. And not with honorable intentions, either!

Only one day after Jenna's sudden arrival, public knowledge of the assault had been rampant. The penny newspapers reported snidely, mocking "the amorous fits that grip coal lords when they're in dark confines."

The items were obviously planted. And very effective. By contrast, the stilted after-dinner defenses advanced by Parrish's puppets in the Conservative camp rang a little too virtuous for those who knew the viscount.

A sudden flare outside the window of the baron's den told him the gaslights of Curzon Street were being fired for the evening. Only an hour to go. Where was Jenna?

She, not he, was the real organizer of the meeting. From that first day she had pressed him with a calm rationale unnatural to a frail, traumatized female. She insisted she had evidence vital to the fight for the mine act. "And proof of a high lord's thievery," she had.

"I don't give a damn about coal miners!" he had exploded, beyond patience. "And I surely don't care to castigate the business practices of my esteemed peers!"

"Do you care to remember your sister?"

The question made him stop his pacing and look her fully in the face, his anger mounting with each word. "You are an impertinent young wo—!"

"I am her daughter," Jenna said. "And this is the closest semblance of justice she will ever have."

Dear Christ. That tranquil voice. It was so like Charlotte's. He turned from Jenna and walked to the open window of the sitting room, breathing in cool air to still his heart.

"What are you implying?" he asked finally.

"That if you care, you will help us."

"And who is 'us'?"

She paused. "The survivors," she said wearily. Slowly Jenna stood and walked toward the door. As she passed by her uncle, his arm descended in front of her like a gentle barricade.

She had hesitated, looking up at his tired visage a moment. Then she had leaned into his embrace, grateful.

Her mother would have been proud of her, the baron sighed. Jenna had sensitivity, intelligence and a subtly sensuous beauty that she had the grace not to flaunt.

But the girl was headstrong to a fault. Alone in his den, the meeting nearly upon him, the baron leaned against the mantelpiece, his fingers squeezing his eyelids tight. "Oh, Charlotte. Why? She won't tell me why."

The grandfather clock chimed three as the baron trudged down the hall to his bedroom.

Hiram had left a lamp burning, but the fire had gone cold. And Enid had gone to sleep, curled on a fringed paisley lounge chair.

He tiptoed quietly to her, smiling as he watched her. She had the softest snore, like a well-mannered motor. He had missed it when they began sleeping in separate chambers. If the truth be told, he missed more than her snore. But, Lord, one didn't think about that at his age.

"Enid. Enid." He shook her gently.

She awoke with a start. "What did you decide?" she asked immediately.

"About what?"

"About Hutton. Will you blackball him at the club or something?" She sat up, straightening her gown.

"This was not a meeting of the club," he said, jerking his cravat out of his vest and discarding his jacket.

"I know that," she said, carefully buttoning her organdy brocade gown to the throat. "Jenna told me. In confidence, of course. I can only hope he gets his comeuppance quickly."

"You're a little prejudiced in this affair, you know." The baron sat down in a chair and leaned over to unbutton his boots.

"Let me, dear," Enid said, and bent to the task, talking all the while. "Of course I'm prejudiced. She's family. But she's also a well-connected woman of noble house. And we can't have randy old moneybags being peculiar with our young ladies."

"Enid! One week with her and you're becoming frightfully direct!" One boot slipped off and he gave an "Ah" of relief.

"Not as direct as that beast was with her," Enid said, unfazed. And she jerked the second boot off with such emphasis that the baron was pulled to the edge of his seat.

"She wouldn't tell us everything, of course," his wife went on, shaking out his jacket. "But what she didn't say said everything. If you know what I mean." She arched an eyebrow at her husband and deftly draped the coat over the valet rack beside his bed.

The baron expelled a sigh. Enid's comments were confirming the speculations of the six men who had just taken their leave through the slatted door of his walled garden. They had met in the cigar-musty confines of the baron's smoking room. The Liberal lords said outraged mavens everywhere were spewing epithets against Parrish in nightly pillow talk. It was good news for the Labor activists of Parliament, who needed anit-Parrish sentiments to aid their cause. The night's most damning news, though, came from Jenna. She had calmly handed a cracked leather satchel to one of the union's most staunch supporters, Lord Shraftmon. He drew out a scuffed, torn ledger book and a yellowed parchment. He smiled as he examined them, then passed the satchel to the burr-tongued union president Alexander McBryde. It was a map of the Shadow Glen coal vein Parrish was pirating and a careful accounting of the tonnage mined.

"Will it be enough to lobby more votes for the mine act?" Jenna asked.

McBryde had pursed his lips and smiled. "We'd be pretty

poor cooks if we couldn't roast a goose in his own drippin's."

"—and did you realize that Lady Whitston came back early from her retreat in Liverpool just to see Jenna?" Enid's sharp tone brought the baron's mind back to the bedroom. "She's livid, Ronnie, just livid!"

"Of course," the baron murmured. Feeling muddled, he poured himself a nightcap from the wine stand and sat down across from his wife. "You've obviously changed your feelings about Jenna," he said. "Just last season you found her strange of habit and much too arrogant."

"That was *not* last season, that was more than three years ago, before her mother died!" Enid's small, round face was indignant. "And I have forgiven her the improprieties of youth. She's done the best she can, what with having a grandfather who treated her like a woodland gypsy instead of a young lady."

Enid walked behind her husband's chair. "Oh, I wish you could have seen her at Lady Howatch's tea." Enid reached over the chair back and began to gently massage her husband's stiff neck. "Jenna was so lovely. So poised. And so sad. Even though she outright laughed once. Lady Pierce was telling us how her husband found four torrid Ouida books under her lingerie last week. And they were, she assured us, well hidden."

"Enid," the baron groaned. "No gossip."

"Well," Enid sniffed, "most of the time we discussed the nature of men, prompted by the beastly example set by the viscount. And, in due course, we began to ask about that Lancashire baronet Jenna's engaged to. And I cannot tell you how agitated she became. She blushed, Ronnie. Actually blushed at the mention of his name."

"What do you make of that?" the baron asked, interested.

When Jenna had left the meeting, the lords had questioned him about the absent fiancé.

"Well"—Enid gave a last, pummeling flourish across his shoulder blades—"either she's in love or she's embarrassed by his reputation. Lady Howatch says Lady Whitston says he's a dashing womanizer, but that he's been absolutely smitten by Jenna. And he has money to burn, of course."

The baron sat up straight. "What do you mean?"

"He's filthy rich, Ronnie. Being landed gentry wasn't enough for him. He dealt in the mercantile as a trader, you know."

"Oh, yes," the baron hurried to the wine stand. At least Hutton's latest charge hadn't hit the Piccadilly gossips yet. Preposterous. That Jenna's fiancé was—

"And you know that Hutton is saying Sir Ian dressed up like the Red Robin," Enid went on.

"Oh?" The baron dabbed his shirtfront. The wine had somehow missed his mouth.

"Yes. What piddlewits he must think we are. To believe such rot. When Sir Ian has a perfectly good explanation of his whereabouts, and at least a dozen witnesses who saw him carry the naked woman up the—"

"Enid! I will hear no more of this whole pestilent affair!"

"Of course, Ronnie," Enid nodded. "I know you're tired. Just one more thing. Did Lord Shraftmon talk about that bank rumor tonight?"

"Damn it, woman!" His foot stomped the Persian rug by the hearth. The newest, choicest information of the whole scandal! His wineglass went bottom up and he downed the rest.

"The story, Ronnie. What did the lords say?"

So he told her. A respected Midlands bank, Lambeth's of York, had indeed turned down a loan request from Parrish.

Incredible that the richest coal baron of the Midlands would be deprived of financing. Unless, of course, the bank knew something other investors didn't. Perhaps the project itself —modernization of the tipple and new tracks at Parrish's mine—was a losing proposition. Whatever Lambeth's knew, it was keeping quiet.

Enid, of course, was not.

"Well, for Jenna's sake, I hope he doesn't show up at the Howatch's spring ball tomorrow night." Enid began to unbutton her organdy dressing gown.

"Hutton is invited?" The baron was aghast. Enid was not leaving for her private chambers.

"Oh, ages ago. But we'll see if he has the effrontry to come."

The baron shook his head in wonder. "You ladies don't talk much about needlework and charity dinners and the like, do you?"

Enid smiled sympathetically. "You need to relax. Come to bed, dear. I'll rub your temples."

With a too eager smile the baron crawled under the coverlet with his wife, a snug and comforting armful.

Lord, what a week!

Jenna was finished. The quiet maid who had helped her dress for tonight's grand dinner dance curtsied and left.

Jenna dared not sit. The satin flounces in her exquisite skirt would be crushed. She felt annoyed, like a fancy toy doll no one could play with.

Part of the irritation was the dress itself. Ian had sent it, along with most of her wardrobe from home. And it had appeared in the crested Stonebridge coach within two days of her arrival here. That meant he had found out immediately where she'd gone.

He had also sent a ladies' maid and the jeweled necklaces he had given her in Lancashire.

Ian Stonebridge did not act like a married man. Perhaps Marguerite knew this. Maybe she expected nothing different from him.

I would have, Jenna thought angrily. I would never have allowed him to become publicly engaged to another woman just to satisfy his lust for revenge.

Because, just maybe, he would want to satisfy other lusts. And he could not be trusted.

Neither could the other woman, taunted the little voice inside her. And from the voice of her conscience grew a pounding of her heart. A painful prelude that would grow into a chorus of epithets against Ian, against her father, against Hutton Parrish, whose very existence was the cause of everything wrong with her life.

And then the tears would start, Jenna knew. And she would not allow them this night. As she had so many others.

She had excused her moodiness this week as a natural response to the assault. To her feeling of helplessness. But the tears did not heal, as the islander Betts had promised. They left her lonelier, more empty than ever before.

She was especially vulnerable in the cold hours before dawn. Alone in her bed. When she wished she were home. Where Ian's strong, hard body had once lain next to her, protecting her. Absorbing the heat of the fire inside her until it belonged to both of them.

How secret, this ache of wanting him, she thought. Hidden beneath heavy satin, underskirts and petticoats, barricaded by a corset of bone, throbbing softly, secretly against a whisper of lace-edged pantalets. The feeling was hers and hers alone. Unknown to anyone.

Except him.

"Jenna?" Her aunt Enid's knock came abruptly. The older woman entered hurriedly, skirt billowing over the carpet nap like a yacht in full sail. "We're ready, my dear. How stunning you look! The young bachelors will certainly envy that fortunate baronet of yours tonight. A pity he could not be reached. I'm rather worried. . . ." Her aunt frowned. "I'm afraid Hutton does love his social fun. And I don't know what we will do if he has the nerve to appear."

"I hope he does," Jenna said, gathering her reticule.

"Jenna!" Enid admonished, tsking as she bent to the mirror to check her lip rouge. "Surely you jest."

"I have something to return to him," Jenna said softly.

She dropped the pearl-handled derringer into her bag and drew the drawstring snug.

In an elegant second-story bedroom in the prosperous West End, Hutton Parrish tugged his tailcoat snug around his trim middle. He checked the mirror. Carefully he hooked the chain of his pocket watch inside his vest and draped the loop of sparkling gold across to his watch pocket.

The door opened. Connell walked in, his shirt undone, claret in hand. "I'm not going," he said. "She's going to be there."

"Which is the very reason we must go, Connell. Staying away is an admission of guilt." Hutton stood before his dressing-table mirror, frowning critically as his hairbrush smoothed over a strand of wavy white hair.

"Things are not going as well as you pretend," Connell blurted. "You will have to face them alone."

"I will admit the loan refusal was a surprise." Hutton picked up an atomizer of cologne and spritzed his neck lightly. "It appears Stonebridge has friends I didn't know about. Using his father's old connections, I would guess. But I have a few surprises, too."

"Faugh! Phillip's no surprise."

Hutton smiled. "True. But the poor boy seemed so when I explained the situation to him today. I have all of his debt notes. All. And he has nothing but a due date. Soon."

"Phillip won't help you defeat the mine act."

"No." Hutton picked a piece of lint from his sleeve. "But I thought a bloody riot by the Glencur miners on the eve of Parliament's debate would be appropriate."

"What do you mean? The miners have been sticking together like boys at a Sunday school picnic—"

"And they're just waiting for the parson to turn his back," Hutton smiled. "The union leaders policing them are about to be called back to London."

"By whom?"

"By their president, McBryde himself."

"I don't believe it."

"I've been talking with him. He's a man of great understanding."

"Is this understanding fraught with gold guineas, by any chance?" Connell asked.

"Of course. He's got good sense. I can boost him to a seat in the House of Commons."

Connell laughed. "He can get there by himself if the safety act passes!"

Hutton did not smile. There was silence in the room. Connell glanced at his father. "Is something wrong?"

His father stepped near. The scent of his cologne hovered between them. Hutton smiled and raised one hand companionably to Connell's shoulder. But the thumb and fingers suddenly encircled Connell's neck, pinching tight against his larynx. An intense, smothering pain pressed against the knobby bone in Connell's neck. He writhed out of his father's grasp and stumbled, gasping, over an ottoman.

"Do not laugh at my arrangements," Hutton said, teeth tight, "unless you've got damn better ones to offer." Hutton straightened his cuff. "Pack up. You're returning to Lancashire. Stiles will need help to prod the miners to riot." Hutton turned away and picked up his brushed-velvet top hat.

Hutton stopped at the door, his back to Connell. "I know what you're thinking," he said, his eyes blankly focused ahead. "It's a bad sign when I get touchy." Hutton's chin tucked to his chest and he heaved a sigh. Then he raised his head with a smile. "I love it, though. It means the run is challenging. And it will make the kill that much sweeter."

On the country edge of London, where grassy meadows rolled to a fringe of forest across the River Thames, a cab drew up at the door of a secluded three-story house.

A tall man emerged quickly, flipped the driver a shilling and hurried to the door, his shoulder cape rustling in the breezy night air.

The double door opened before he could knock.

"Evenin', sir. You've not got much time."

"Time for a bath?" He slipped off the cape and frock coat in one motion.

"It's waitin'. A mite cold by now."

"You're a mind reader, Ross."

"Not completely. Were ya successful this trip?"

"Yes."

"That means yer also a lot poorer, right?"

Ian Stonebridge nodded grimly. This pretend betrothal had, to date, cost him all the profit he had made selling his two largest ships.

And yet, he thought as he ran the soaped sponge around his neck and across his shoulders, I would gladly pay more.

To insure the destruction of Hutton Parrish. To acquire the appreciation of a rare woman.

He smiled. Either could cost him his life.

Chapter 18

The ballroom glowed. Cool white light reflected from shiny marble floors and high polished colonnades. And the sparkle of jewels and silk from society's elite added a rich luminescence to the dance floor.

Wide, terraced steps fed a constant stream of guests into the high, coffered room.

The baron, stiff with tension, escorted Jenna along the entrance hall. Behind them, Enid chatted with Lady Howatch, a fringed Oriental fan hiding the baroness's small rouged mouth.

The gilt-stenciled wall borders and molded plasterwork of the lighted passage seemed endless, broken only by the fiery red and blue of Chinese dragons glaring, eye level, from tall porcelain plant stands. Lush, giant ferns reached out with welcoming fronds. But, to Jenna, their touch seemed as dry as the polite words she uttered in conversation after a uniformed servant announced their arrival. She descended the black-veined marble steps carefully, knowing every eye was on her.

After twenty minutes of strained conversation, Jenna excused herself and escaped to a hall gallery to sip her punch and study paintings. Her main goal was to hide from curious stares. What must she look like to them? she wondered. An eccentric daughter of the aristocracy saved from degradation by a folk bandit. The notoriety was not easy to bear. Neither was the thought that Hutton Parrish might appear any minute.

She was studying the brilliant colors in an Arthur Hughes oil when a hand touched her shoulder. She started.

"I'm sorry, Jenna," her brother Phillip said.

Jenna stepped back, silent, wary. Phillip had never apologized for anything.

"It's been so long since we last—"

"Fought?" she interrupted.

He managed a smile, a weary, perfunctory one. There was a deep fatigue in his bearing, as if the act of holding himself erect was an effort. Yet Jenna was afraid to give him a chance to take the offensive.

"I will not retract the truth of what happened in the carriage, Phillip. No matter—"

"I know." He held up his hand to fend off her argument. His other hand held the crystal stem of a half-empty wineglass. "Hutton sent me here to mingle and tell everyone what a madwoman you are. Subject to delusions, like Father is—or was. We don't know if he's still alive, do we?" Phillip leaned heavily against the wall and stared upward into the vibrant green grass of the painting. A cloaked girl knelt beside a tired boy in uniform.

"I believe he lives," Jenna said quietly. "I would feel it if he died."

Phillip smiled. "That is the difference between us. I would feel nothing." He downed the last half of his drink.

"How can you not care?"

"Good question." He pursed his lips. "I thought about that today. Tried to remember just when I lost respect for the old man. It was long ago. When he married your mother."

"Phillip—"

"I was furious. He was wildly in love with Charlotte Ashley. He did not care half so much for my own mother. Nor for me."

"That's ridiculous," Jenna said.

"No, it's not. I am wiser about these things than you know." Phillip tipped his glass to his lips, but found it empty.

"Phillip," Jenna rubbed a finger to temples that threatened to throb.

"You've always underestimated me," he said with a strange smile. "You think you're such a good manager. Well, I know more about estate building than you think. In my own way I was expanding our properties. Hutton promised to help me. He said I would be president of the merged company as soon as Shadow Glen—and you—were his."

"How could you take the word of a liar?"

"He believed in me! More than Father or any member of my own family ever did! But I let him down, dammit. I couldn't get Father to be his partner. I couldn't get you to be Connell's wife. And now he doesn't believe anymore. . . ." His voice trailed away.

She shook her head and swallowed hard, knowing it was no use to argue.

Suddenly his dull eyes grew clear as sweet gin, and he grabbed her arm roughly. "Don't feel sorry for me! Save some pity for yourself. Hutton has my notes, Jenna. They're all due tomorrow."

She opened her mouth to speak, but Phillip pushed her away with a gentle shove, as if she were a hare set loose to run the dogs.

"Unless," Phillip said, "you recant your story and reveal

your 'real' desire. To marry him." He paused and smiled, taking a handkerchief from his pocket.

"But that's impossible, of course." He wiped sweat from his upper lip. "How in keeping with my game. That I hold no trump card to get me away from the table." He took her hand, and she was alarmed at how it trembled. "You will think of something, Jenna. You must." Then he turned and started down the hallway.

As if in answer to a hellish prayer, she heard the butler announce a new guest.

"Lord Hutton Parrish, Viscount of Tyne."

The name caught the attention of standing groups and gliding dancers. Stiff-backed men leaned forward over half-amber glasses to catch the whispers of the ladies. Dancers slowed their pace to see the handsome white-haired lord descend the wide terraced steps to the grand ballroom.

He seemed to accept the conspicuous, silent stares as a natural part of his entrance. And he smiled engagingly at acquaintances as he crossed the floor toward the bar.

He was intercepted, though, by a sea of people backing away, parting before the advance of someone else. Looking over the freckled shoulder of a dowager, he saw her.

Jenna. Moving slowly toward him. As if a line had been drawn from his viscera to hers, he thought. The anger in her eyes was magnificent. The set of her jaw. Her shoulders square and erect, pulling the creamy curves of her breasts taut against the pale rose satin of her gown, the dark ringlets of her hair dipping into the succulent hollow of one white shoulder. Hutton's eyes actually closed a moment. To think she would be his. That he would have her sweet body and high spirit to delight him in the evening of his life. Surely he would live longer because of her. He opened his eyes and smiled.

She stopped not six feet away from him. "It is good that you came," she said.

He bowed. And noticed in the wake behind her that some-one had dropped a cranberry-colored evening purse. "I agree, my dear," he smiled. "There are misconceptions that must be corrected."

"And gestures that must be returned," she said, drawing the derringer from a fold of her skirt.

The crowd gasped and a rumble of fright began. But Hutton raised his hand to assure them he had control.

The gun barrel was level with his chest, her finger caressing the trigger. But the weapon lay on its side in the palm of her upraised hand. Casually posed. Ready to fire.

"An unfriendly gesture, Lady Jenna," he said, noticing how neatly her slim finger curled around the silver trigger.

"Yes. But very clear. As you were with me." Her voice was not loud. Yet her words carried everywhere, kept aloft by the anxious, shallow breathing of the bystanders.

"I fear you have overreacted, irrationally, to a small accident with a kitchen knife." He smiled sympathetically.

"Then you must be comfitted indeed"—she slowly turned the gun upright—"knowing that I'm in complete control now."

She cocked the hammer.

Hutton narrowed his eyes. My God—the thought hit him with frightening speed—she's going to fire.

In her eyes he saw the cold intensity of a hunter with a sure shot. She wanted him dead.

He took one step backward.

Her gun arm straightened.

"My lady—" he warned, his words beginning to rasp.

The crowd edged backward.

"Am I late?" A strong voice sounded from the reception entrance deep in the marbled hallway.

Jenna's heart quickened.

Footsteps echoed as the new arrival talked with a servant. "My fiancée has already joined the party."

If only she could fire quickly enough, hold on to her courage before—

A servant took his stance at the arched collonnade. Before the bewigged man could open his mouth to announce the belated guest, Sir Ian Stonebridge appeared at the top of the ballroom steps.

He took in the scene at a glance. "Jenna!" he called instantly, his voice loud, delighted, playing to the crowd. He came down the steps quickly, adroitly skirting the crushed throng of satin and taffeta.

"My love"—his voice turned mock serious as he neared —"you have no license to shoot wild boars."

The younger spectators laughed. But those who were close enough to see the beautiful young woman still concentrating on her target dismissed the levity.

Jenna swallowed, nervous, her eyes never wavering from the black broadcloth covering Hutton's heart. It would be an act of charity to rid the world of him. He had raped her mother. Abused Carolina. Threatened Jenna. Touched her. And it was only a tiny taste of the cruelty he would plan if he ever—

"Jenna." Ian's low, sure tone interrupted.

She felt his warmth on her back. A palpable heat he seemed to radiate to her. Did others feel it? she wondered. Did Marguerite? Her eyes closed at the thought.

He stepped in front of her then. An imposing figure in correct formal dress. Carelessly handsome. As if he had dressed quickly, unmindful of the effect.

He reached for her hand. The hand with the gun. She felt the eyes of everyone on the two of them.

"You're making a mistake," she told him quietly.

"I know. But yours would be a criminal one. Do not give him the satisfaction."

He waited, not pressing her.

Slowly her thumb closed the cocked hammer. Her heart, so still, began to throb painfully and deeply, as if gasping for air.

He took the gun from her and raised her empty hand to his lips. Slowly he tilted her hand palm up. Hutton's knife wound was a dark, clean line of red. He kissed it tenderly, his lips lingering. Until she grew flush.

At that the crowd began to breathe freely again. The pent-up excitement became a rumble as spectators related details to the unfortunates farther back.

And Hutton Parrish, alone on the small center stage with the woman he wanted and the man who had claimed her first, felt a tremendous rage fire his insides.

But he did not speak, for Jenna was walking toward him, cheeks still flushed from his enemy's touch. She handed the small gun over to him, dropping it in his outstretched hand.

Ian was behind her. "In all fairness, my fiancée should have the right to spill your blood. As you did hers. But I cannot allow her to assume my responsibility. A duel is in order, Lord Parrish."

"Duels are no longer a legal way to settle a matter of honor," Hutton said gruffly, a black madness tearing at him as he watched Ian tuck Jenna's arm firmly in his.

"You have no honor to defend. But if you did, and if we were able to duel with weapons of your choosing, where and when do you think we might meet?"

"At the meadow of Sitwell's Corner. In three days. Dawn.

So that the rest of my day will be free." Hutton smiled grimly.

"Accepted. Hypothetically, of course." Ian's voice was hard-edged. He turned his back then and began to lead Jenna away.

"Stonebridge!" Hutton called.

Ian turned.

"I guarantee this meeting will end differently than your Red Bow melodrama," Hutton said loudly. "Your bandits will not save you this time."

Ian smiled. "I have heard your desperate theory. And I find it entertaining. Up to a point." Ian's voice turned hard. "But nothing about you entertains me very long, Lord Parrish." Ian turned in dismissal and walked toward the dance floor, Jenna on his arm.

Hutton's pale face flushed with anger. He watched the backs of the tall privateer and the graceful Jenna recede to the dance floor. Each step gave him a taste of gall. For the worst part to bear was the fact that Stonebridge had saved him a bullet in the heart. And the bastard knew it.

Each step forward took exquisite control. For there was only one thing on Jenna's mind. To run away. From the room. The conflict. From the man who grasped her arm so tightly in warning.

He bent to whisper in her ear. "I have never danced with a would-be assassin. Can you follow my lead?" He stopped in the center of the dance floor and placed his arm firmly around her waist.

Ian nodded expectantly to the orchestra. The musicians rushed to poise bows to strings and reeds to lips, as if they had somehow missed a cue. With soft fanfare, they restarted the waltz that had died when the excitement began.

The music filled the hall tentatively. All eyes were on the

striking couple, frozen in a ballroom tableau. Jenna's head was thrown back, her gaze intent on her fiancé, the long ringlets of her hair cascading to the hand that rested possessively above the small of her back. The darkly handsome baronet held her close, oblivious to the spectators.

"I cannot," she whispered, sure that she could not move.

"Forget about them." He pulled her closer then and smiled as she resisted. The hand on her back suddenly pressed her hard toward him. At the same moment he stepped back and whirled her clean around on a count of three. The surprise of the movement brought an unbidden smile to her face. Quickly he led her off in a slow, graceful whirl across the floor.

"You should smile more often," he said.

"I rarely have reason to," she said guardedly, but oddly content in the dip and sway of the dance. She stayed stiffly correct in his arms, refusing to melt closer to his length. He was a man with a pregnant wife. And she would be damned before she gave in to him and risked becoming a pregnant mistress.

"I saved you a trip to the gallows. That's not enough to make you smile?" he asked.

"No. I would have killed him. And you would not have to continue this charade with a duel to the death on Monday." She looked up at him. "What makes you think you can survive? He has killed three men with a dueling pistol."

Ian shrugged, then smiled, his eyes searching hers lightly. "At least I will have you to grieve for me. Would I not?"

She fastened her eyes on the satin edge of his lapel. "Of course. I mourn the death of all lesser beasts."

Ian's laughter rang out. More couples streamed to the dance floor.

But Ian and Jenna were given a wide berth, as if sharing

their spotlight was too risky. Ian welcomed the isolation. There was much to talk about. And recapture. He had spent a week with only memories of how it felt to hold Jenna in his arms. The stiffness of the dance—and her cool reserve —were frustrating. Conversation, he knew, would have to be kept at a businesslike clip.

He asked if she still had the ledger. Jenna told him briefly of the secret meeting with Parliament's Liberals and the union leader Alexander McBryde.

"McBryde has the ledger and map. He's hopeful, but worried, too. There's not enough time to amass a majority vote for the mine act."

"Were the politicians as pessimistic?" Ian asked.

"No. They said they might be able to postpone the vote. And that, in itself, would be a victory."

She held her breath as he suddenly pressed her closer.

"I look forward to any victory." His voice was warm.

"Triumphs await you at home. Not here," she said, her tone so cold that they slowed to a stop, Jenna's dress trailing a soft swish of protest. "I would like something to drink," she said.

"Of course," he echoed her cool, correct tone. Inwardly he cursed the mercury of her mood. Too damn chilly for comfort. And a certain comfort had been uppermost in his thoughts for a long time. Along with a haunting worry: Parrish's attack could easily have stunted the passion that bloomed so naturally in her.

Jenna and Ian spent the next half hour arm in arm, chatting with acquaintances and curiosity seekers. Young couples especially gathered in timid awe, the dash and panache of the confrontation holding too much magnetism for them to disapprove of such shocking behavior.

The earl's daughter and the rich baronet wandered, finally, alone onto an outside balcony.

"We do better than I thought. Socially, I mean," he murmured.

She remained quiet, thinking about the warm, thick timbre of his voice. She wanted to reach up and shush his words. Put her fingers gently against his lips. Catch his breath softly in her palm.

Instead she closed her eyes and looked away.

"What a troubled little thief you are," he said, low.

"I do not steal that which belongs to someone else," she said softly.

Ian frowned. "What do you mean?"

"You're not an honest man."

"God never created such a being. Except in an ingenue's imagination," he said.

"Perhaps," she said. "But there are things about you I have a right to know."

"And where did you gain such a right?"

She looked at him in silence, then turned away toward the sculpted, flowering gardens below them.

It was on a riverbank, he said to himself, where you yielded so completely you made my head spin. The memory of her giving, trusting body triggered the fullness of his desire. He moved physically away, down a marble step, painfully aware of how much he wanted her.

He shook his head. "You are like all women. Craving deep truths where there is only one man's shallow, pitifully human reaction." He took a drink of wine.

She turned quickly. "What's pitiable is your treatment of Mar—"

"Aren't you feeling well?" Lady Whitston's voice suddenly pierced the air behind them. "You've been out here long enough. People will talk."

"They're already talking," Jenna said.

"Well, you gave them quite a conversation starter, my dear," the dowager grinned. "Come now"—she tucked Jenna's arm in hers—"I want you to meet my friend the countess."

Jenna sent Ian a pleading glance.

"I'm afraid we must go," he said quickly. "It's been a trying evening for Jenna. I'm escorting her to the baron's house."

Being alone in a coach with Ian was not the escape Jenna had been pleading for. "Perhaps—" she began.

"Of course," Lady Whitston agreed. "Quite understandable. Let us make your good-byes." She pulled Jenna away.

Jenna waited for him in the high-ceilinged foyer, evening wrap already on, coach called for.

What a rake, she thought as he donned his long black evening coat and high silk hat. Dark sideburns framed his hard, strong jaw. His nose was straight, arrogant. His dark eyes roved over her much too personally.

They settled into the carriage, sitting across from one another.

He took off his hat and loosened his coat.

She drew her wrap tighter under her neck.

He smiled.

She looked away.

"Are you frightened of me?" he asked.

"Of course not."

"Then why do you play the Ice Maiden with one who knows you as quite the opposite?"

"Why do you not tell me the truth?" she said, angry that he would not admit he was married.

"What truth?"

"I have met Marguerite."

"You disapprove?"

"Of course, you idiot!"

"I did not know you were so narrow-minded."

If her hands had not been safely encased in a fur muff, she would surely have slapped his arrogant face. "Narrow-minded—!"

"You disappoint me." A cool disdain shaded his eyes. "I had not thought you biased against a person simply because her skin is darker than your own."

"Don't toy with me! I couldn't care less if she were indigo blue! She is your wife, Ian. And she carries your child!"

At that, he sat back and smiled. "Thank God."

"For what?" She eyed him coldly. "God grants no favors to an adulterer."

"He granted me a beautiful poacher with high-flying morals."

"Since you have none, I'm surprised you recognize the virtues when you see them." Oddly, she felt close to tears.

"Jenna"—his voice was soft—"she is not my wife."

"You faithless puddle of pig swill! How could you make your child a bastard?"

"It is not my child." He reached over to grab both her arms.

She did not struggle.

"Marguerite is Robert's wife."

Jenna was wide-eyed.

"They fell madly in love when Robert came looking for me. They married in the islands. And they'll return there when the baby is born."

Jenna could feel a strange sinking sensation palpitate in her stomach. "But Betts said—" Then she remembered the pieces of the conversation that had led her to the false conclusion. "I see."

"Do you?" he asked, pulling her across the space that divided them. "It means we begin again. As we were. Before the robbery."

"Things have changed," she whispered. "I have changed."

He cupped her chin gently and guided her lips to his. His kiss was tentative, soft, his breath hot. She drew back quickly, as if burned.

"Not so much has changed," he said quietly.

She looked down, curbing an impulse to lick away the tingling wetness he had left on her lips. Slowly she reached up with her fingertips and trailed them lightly down the skin of his cheek. Two fingertips came to rest in the moist parting of his dark lips. He kissed her fingers. Then the palm of her hand. The soft fold of her wrist. Her arm went up and around his neck and she threw her head back as his mouth pressed warm against her neck.

"Nothing has changed," he whispered.

Chapter 19

Too soon, Jenna thought, her head spinning, her mouth crushed against his. It is ending too soon.

The coach stopped in front of her uncle's Curzon Street home.

With eyes closed against Ian's searching look, she pushed away from him. Slowly Jenna took the seat opposite him. She kept her face turned to the half-open window. A gas lantern beckoned outside on the balustrade of the steps. But it receded quickly. Ian had ordered the driver to drive through Regent's Park.

Inside the carriage the air grew warm, the darkness heavy with silence.

Jenna did not move. She wished the throbbing deep in her abdomen would subside. Her breathing was uneven, shallow, as if she were afraid to reach down too deeply inside. Instinct waited impatiently there.

She answered, finally, what he had not asked. "We cannot be together. Find someone else."

"I want no one else."

She was silent, not daring to look at him. "You may be dead in two days." She said it calmly, her hands cold as ice. "I will have lost something I invested dearly in."

"Honest, but mercenarily put." The words were not harsh.

"Even if you survive"—she leaned her head back against the seat, frowning—"you would not stay here."

The statement struck him like a blow. How could she know? He stayed quiet, wary, watching the moist fullness of her lips move in the shadows.

"You would be bored as a country squire," she said. "And you despise the social life of London. You will leave as soon as your land is safe from Parrish and your house rebuilt for another Stonebridge generation."

His mouth felt dry. Uneasy, he shifted in his seat, the musty, aged leather creaking under his frame. "Either you are extraordinarily perceptive or I have become transparent."

"Will you go back to your islands?" she asked.

"No. To America." He began to smile. "Industry is booming from the foundries of Philadelphia to tradeships in the Pacific. Endless possibilities."

"All your possibilities may end at dawn Monday," she said.

"True."

"So I will need your help now. I want to free Carolina's son and take him back to Glencur."

"Good God. We have enough trouble. We can't afford—"

"Ian." She was close, two fingers stilling his lips. "The only thing I can't afford is you for a lover." Her fingers strayed down and around his neck to the thick length of hair along his collar.

He moved closer, pushing her full satin skirt aside. "And what if I become more valuable to you?"

Her heart quickened.

His thumb roamed softly, caressing the smoothness of her cheek. "If I agreed to help you find the boy? Would that pay for a night with you?"

"No," she whispered as his mouth hovered within inches

of her ear, his breath hot on the soft skin of her neck. "But it would make up for my lack of good sense."

His house at Sarbin's Crown stood at the edge of London proper, where the city met the meadows of the rolling countryside. It was a small house on a winding lane, but with a country grandeur and arched facade that spoke of monied care.

Ross, Ian's valet, opened the door before she knocked, not surprised to see her standing unescorted, in satin gown and jewels, on the hazy, gaslit stoop at two in the morning. The dark-haired Scotsman smiled as he took her coat and left the hall.

Jenna had insisted she be returned to Curzon Street, as Ian had promised her uncle.

There Jenna ordered her maid to pack and send her things home to Glen Manor. The letter to her aunt and uncle said simply that she had to go away.

Apprehension returned as she stood alone at the bottom of Ian's oak-bannistered staircase. The same dread she had felt when she had sealed the letter to her uncle.

This is wrong, Jenna thought. So wrong.

Yet there was no other decision for her. She wanted him. She wanted to be safe with him. For a while. And for that time she would be intensely alive, like a flame fanned until her fuel—until he—was gone.

"Jenna." He stood in a doorway not far from her, staring. He was without a jacket or vest, his shirt loosened and opened at the neck.

He walked toward her slowly, painfully aware of how lovely she was, how much he wanted her, how afraid he'd been that she would not come.

He stopped close to her, not touching her. Uneasiness

hovered between them. A volatile, frightening understanding that whatever they began, they would finish.

As calmly as she could, Jenna lifted her skirt and mounted the stairs. Halfway up she looked back at him, her face composed and certain.

Dear God, I could love her, he thought, his senses alive. To feel her beside him, to hear her muffled cries, to see her dark hair loose against the pillows of his bed. It was, he suddenly realized, what she had wanted all along. This woman. In his house. In his world.

He followed her. At the landing he swept her against him, his mouth buried in her hair. He picked her up and she arched her neck back to receive his kiss. But he did not take her mouth. His lips trailed a fevered path to the hollow at the base of her throat. It was there he felt life pulsing underneath, a flowing, powerful force he would join. Very soon.

He climbed the remaining steps slowly. Sounds assaulted him. The rasp of her gown as the skirt swayed against him with each step. The scuff of his sole on the carpet. The disembodied ticking of a clock somewhere deep in the darkened hallway. The soft, sweet noise she made when he set her down near the glowing hearth in his bedroom.

He kissed her then, a kiss he tried to control, but his tongue went deep without warning, and her hands raked his hair, groping for equilibrium.

He pulled away from her roughly, his eyes warm with warning.

She understood. There would be no delay.

She said nothing as she watched him jerk away each piece of his clothing in the flickering light. She did not move to undress. She knew he would do it for her.

His body was as she remembered. Muscled and lean, his thighs tight, covered lightly with soft, dark hair.

She found herself walking toward him, aware of his readiness, impatient with her own. In one quick motion the neckline of her gown had slid to her waist. She felt the buttons down her back pulled roughly from their loops, the waistband of her voluminous skirt jerked away so that it fell, petticoats and all, folding in on itself as it met the woven rug.

Her corset was thrown down, stays broken like skeletal soldiers. The flat of his hand reached low into the thin material of her pantalets. She gasped and he pulled the garment away and then stood back to look at her.

She quivered with a readiness and a fear of him that caused him to slow his pace, to pull her gently down onto his bed.

But once there, they both lost all grasp of time and temperance. She screamed when he entered her, and he could not apologize, could not pull away, only be with her, kiss her parted lips and hear the frantic, primitive cries that echoed in his mind long after his rhythm stopped.

She awoke slowly, with a sure and savored awareness of where she was, her skin noting each warm place of contact with his flesh. The contour of her back fit snugly against his chest, her shoulders nearly lost under the breadth of muscle behind them. Against her soft cheek lay the rough cord of his arm, a hard and natural pillow she had drowsed against, exhausted. How many hours ago?

Her eyes blinked open, assaulted by a room full of midmorning light. Then she felt him stir behind her, the warm length of his thigh coming to rest against hers. A hand enclosed the tangled mass of her hair, lifted it up, and she felt his lips warm against the nape of her neck. She shivered involuntarily and arched away.

"A sensitive spot?" he asked.

She nodded and turned onto her back so she could see his face, her pale nipples constricted, upraised, unashamed. His hand reached over to caress the soft underside of her breast. There was an aching tenderness in his touch, a strange controlled intensity that caused them both to quiver. Instinctively, she reached upward to pull his head close to her. His mouth tasted lightly of liquor and the long night. As they kissed she was aware of a fragrance that sent a line of heat surging to her groin. The unmistakable scent of her own longing for him. Lingering. Reminding her of how he—

She wrenched away, her cheeks flooding red as she turned from him. She sat, hands pressed against her temples, with her back to him, replaying the sensations he had caused, the responses she could not control. Dear God, how much he knew of her, this uncommitted lover. Each fold of her body had been mapped. And marked. And explored.

Her long, tangled hair was a scented curtain covering her back. He waited behind it, not pressing her. Inwardly he cursed at her need to feel shame. She was so young, so unsure of what was right. Thank God, she would not be satisfied with a proper coupling—the emotionless discharge a gentlewoman would allow. At least he would leave her with that much—trust for her instincts. She would enjoy her marriage bed. As Tania had.

Something hot and tight gripped his heart. He didn't know whether it was the memory of his passionate wife or the thought that Jenna would someday respond to someone else. His senses rankled. He was confused and he rose quickly to his knees to reach out for the solace he did not want to give up.

Ian's arms encircled her and pulled Jenna back against

him. He brushed aside the hair covering her ear and pressed his cheek to hers, speaking softly.

In her confusion, in the warmth of the passion he began to arouse in her, Jenna understood few of the words he whispered. But these were seared in her mind: "Don't leave . . . my love."

How dare he, she thought, shuddering as his mouth released her nipple and traveled downward. How dare he say he loves me. She cried out and reached down to place her hands on each side of his head, guiding it upward, his beard-roughened cheek marking a path on the pale, soft skin of her belly.

She was going to tell him, when she met his eyes, that he could not, must not, lie to her. But when their eyes met, he slid deep past her defenses into the heart-quickening warmth that waited for him. And tenderly, so tenderly, he moved her to forget, for a time, the words that separated them.

It was midday. The French doors at the far end of the bedroom were open wide. The warm sun filtered across the wrought-iron rail of the second-floor balcony.

Jenna was alone. She washed. And could not find a shred of her clothing. Unconcerned, she donned Ian's white linen shirt. It fell below her knees.

She leaned against the rail outside, hugging herself as the cool spring breeze blew through the loose folds, welcoming the solid chill of the cut-stone floor under her bare feet. It was odd, she thought. How peaceful she felt when so much of her life was in turmoil.

She turned her back to the sun's rays and, with an effort, thought about the uncertain future awaiting her. Today Parrish would call Phillip's notes due for payment. She would require help from her father's solicitor to see if Parrish could be fended off, at least temporarily. She needed to make plans to rescue Carolina's son from Parrish's keepers. And, more immediately, she had to find her clothes and overnight bag, the battered piece of luggage Leona had sent her off with when she'd left the cottage less than two weeks ago. Such a short time. Yet she had traveled a long, long way. Parrish had seen to that.

And Ian. She had no words for the way she had given herself to him. She knew only that the hunger that had raged inside her was cooled, resting. And that, for the moment, she was where she wanted to be.

Ian opened the door on a scene of pastoral beauty. Beyond Jenna a line of rich-leaved oak and London plain undulated over the grassland at the edge of the meadow. And the river cut a muddy green swath to her right. The neck bells of a flock of shorn sheep clanked in counterpoint as they went across the pasture for water. And a glorious wind wafted through the room, molding his shirt into every crevice of her body as she leaned over the railing.

He pulled his eyes away and set down the breakfast tray he carried, annoyed. She would be seen. And her reputation, only recently gaining in sympathy, would be gone because of him.

"I think you should come away from the window. Someone will see."

She turned with a small smile on her lips and gave a shrug. "It wouldn't matter. They would just mistake me for one of your 'loves.'"

He turned his back on her and began to pour tea into two large china cups. "Love is rare." His voice was quiet, a gentle reprimand. "I am careful not to use the word. It only creates misunderstanding."

"Then you never pledge love to a woman!" The question

was lightly phrased, but it hung uncomfortably between them and it demanded a serious answer.

"Once," he said, arranging a chair near the teakwood breakfast tray. "I had a wife. Her name was Tania."

The strained civility in his voice warned Jenna she could not trespass further into the past. She kept silent, watching a cool guardedness appear in his eyes.

"Here," he said, handing her a steaming cup of tea. "Take care not to get burned."

Hutton Parrish stepped down to the sidewalk and threw a shilling to the river. He walked energetically under the portico, past the marble statuary, up the fern-draped steps. The tall front door opened for him as he approached.

"Lord Parrish," nodded the maître d', taking Hutton's tall silk hat, coat and brass-trimmed walking cane.

Hutton tugged his vest straight at the waist and walked down the hallway to the wide, polished staircase that led to the sanctuary of the club. He paused to light a slim brown cigarette, giving an absent smile to an acquaintance passing by.

He frowned, trying to remember the name. Oh, yes. He inhaled deeply. Simpering little snip of a codfish he met over cards. Cousin to a lazy count who had wanted Hutton to invest in farm implements. Hand plows in the age of machines.

Dolts. The viscount exhaled slowly, shaking his head. He was surrounded by them. Men who didn't know how to make things happen. He started up the stairs. Christ. Even in Parliament. His Conservative allies were suddenly choking on the dust of the Liberals who had latched on to the explosion at the Bolton Colliery as a cause célèbre.

The cave-in was a month old now. Suddenly it was a tragedy. One hundred moles die a quick, suffocating death and, bang! the mine act becomes an issue for everyone.

Hutton pursed his lips and gave a short sigh. Things were getting a bit more messy than he had anticipated. It was all these peripheral matters.

Having to meet with McBryde to make sure he recalled those union leaders from Glencur. Agitators were set to spark a riot Tuesday at the miners' monthly rally.

And what else? Oh, yes. Carolina.

Poor, dear Carolina. Such a gifted actress. He was sorry to lose her. He exhaled slowly. I wish I'd known she had spunk enough to defy me, he thought. The games could have used a little more resistance on her part.

He reached the second landing and heaved a sigh. His foreman, Stiles, had seen Carolina leave Leona's cottage the night of the robbery. Right after Jenna Thornton took off at a gallop to make the transit coach to Manchester. He had taken his time to deal with Carolina. She had deserved at least that.

And of course there was the matter of the coach incident itself. The tabloids were positively giddy after last night's ballroom drama.

Hutton smiled in spite of his pique. A wonderful stroke on Jenna's part. To bluff her way back into society's good graces. And then, when she could hold the facade no more, to face him honestly, squarely, with the message of death in her eyes.

Oh, he exhaled a breath drawn from deep below his diaphragm. He was so tired of being without her. So angry that he hadn't tried to possess her sooner. Before the schoolboy he had tormented arrived home from the sea, a full-grown thief, armed with spite and vengeance.

Hutton passed by a spittoon and flicked the dark butt inside. The bastard would get his due. Lindstrom was on his way to London. The hulking Swede had a surprise part in Monday's duel, Hutton smiled. He had no doubt Stone-bridge would remember his cellmate of long ago.

Hutton stopped for a moment before the huge double oak doors of the barroom. He took a deep breath, bracing for the stares from compatriots and the curious. The attention he received was actually quite flattering.

But the game—he set his jaw tight against the twitch he felt beginning under his eye—the game was no longer amusing. Phillip's notes had disappeared. And with them, Hutton's hold on Phillip, Jenna and Shadow Glen.

How carefully, methodically, he had stockpiled Phillip's losses, buying the notes in others' names, until he had them all.

But the bastard had located the holding company. All he had to do was promise that sniveling accounts clerk a higher percentage and, voilá! the clever baronet had everything. Thornton family debts in one hand and Jenna in the other.

Hutton's hand began to tremble on the huge brass handle of the door. He calmed the tremor. He need not worry. Come Monday, the young squire of Stonebridge would find all earthly possessions quite useless.

Jenna wandered impatiently in the library that afternoon, feeling like a prisoner waiting for reprieve. She could not go out because she would be seen. She did not need to contact the solicitor because Ian—God love him and damn him!—had bought up the notes at exorbitant interest and paid for Phillip's excesses.

"How much?" she had whispered, hardly daring to believe her home was safe.

"Twenty thousand pounds."

"Dear God. Parrish means that much to you."

"Yes," he said hotly, angry that she knew instinctively he had not done it for her. "The money is nothing."

"Ian—" She had placed her hand on his arm, a worried touch. "Are you sure you're going to be in a position to collect 'payment' from me after Monday?" she asked.

His arm slipped away from her grasp and he moved toward the door. "I think I'll survive." His back was to her. "But I shall not win."

In the cozy quiet of the library her heart pounded with as much fear as when Ian closed the bedroom door with that soft, regretful click.

Jenna stopped her useless wandering in the tall, musty cases of leather-bound books. She was too on edge to be caged. Here in the house her fears collected like a suffocating vapor that washed over her at unexpected moments. Everywhere she wandered was a reminder of his world. He had a penchant for clean lines and solid, functional furniture. No clutter. Just enough bric-a-brac for show. Strange teak carvings. Paintings. A black-skinned man in a sea of tall green stalks. A multicolored marketplace bustling at dockside.

Ian's world. So different. Its wild, unsettled nature called to her. And frightened her.

Long past teatime, on the edge of evening, Ian returned with Ross. The business was done. Solicitors satisfied, his brother Robert alerted, Ross rehearsed in what to do to keep Jenna safe.

He had wanted it all done today. So that tomorrow would be his. And Jenna's.

When he stepped into the house, his uneasiness intensified. The fear he'd had all day that she would be gone. He walked past the downstairs rooms as calmly as he could, Ross's eyes on his back. His boots made a hollow, echoing sound in the foyer.

Then Ian climbed the stairs slowly and went to the bedroom.

She was gone. The room was cold. And the door to his wardrobe closet stood slightly ajar. He frowned. What had she been searching for?

His hand raked wearily through his hair. From the open balcony door he heard the faint call of the shepherd goading the slow-moving animals homeward. As Ian approached the railing he saw there were two shepherds. Only one was working. The other sat on a high peak at the river's edge, nearly lost in a tall thatch of grasses.

He could feel the heat of relief rise to his face. He bent his head, breathing deeply, alarmed and amazed that this woman could make his heart pound like a hammer breaking open a long-closed door.

She had seen him approaching far in the distance, swinging a cloth bag at his side. She waited, comforted by the soft washing sounds of the water.

"I find a thief in the woods." His voice blended low and naturally into the quiet moments before sunset.

"I have taken nothing," she said, rising.

"Nonsense," he said softly, pulling the broad-brimmed field hat from her head. "Those are my favorite breeches."

She pulled at the worn, loose-hanging material at her thighs. "They look as if they served you well. You keep a mixed class of clothing in your closet for a rich man." Her tone was light, but slipping close to breathiness.

"Were you going to leave?"

She swallowed and turned her back. She shrugged. "It doesn't matter."

"It would to me."

The riverbank filled the silence with the soft, wet slap of ripples against the bare mud bank.

From behind she heard him breathe deeply before he spoke. "I have had some success with pistols. I would not be so foolish to challenge him otherwise."

She smiled, shaking her head as the film began to blur her eyes. He knew her so well. It was not commitment she wanted. Just reassurance. For now.

"And I lied to you. Phillip's notes cost me dearly. Stonebridge Hall is mortgaged for the chance to pound a nail in Parrish's coffin."

"Ian—" She felt his powerful hands on her arms, and she was whirled round to face him.

"There is nothing to explain right now. It is time we had dinner like a civilized couple."

She looked doubtfully at the small bag lying in the grass.

He shrugged. "A bottle of wine, a loaf and some sausage."

She smiled. "A feast. If I were a starving woman."

"I was rather hoping you were." His fingers reached down to loosen the cord that cinched his pants at her waist.

Her hand reached out to steady herself, grasping his shoulder, then moving slowly, palm flat and exploring, across his chest. He pulled her palm away from his chest and kissed it.

They sat down and he held her close as the dew settled on the grass around the unopened bottle of wine.

Chapter 20

That night they lay side by side in bed, listening. Downstairs Ross was closing up. Through their open bedroom window, they heard the bolt on the front door grate sharply into its slot. The den windows clicked shut. The kitchen door creaked open and a metal pan scraped against the stone stoop. Ross was setting out a basin of dinner scraps for the stray dog he had chased away earlier in the day.

Jenna smiled, aware of how small moments seemed larger, more defined, when she lay next to Ian. Tentatively, Jenna stroked the length of Ian's body, her hand gliding slowly over the strong planes of his back, the tight cord of muscle that connected the small of his back to firm buttocks. Her hand smoothed farther downward to his thighs, then stopped. She bent over him to press her kiss moist and low on his back, her hair falling forward to clothe his pelvis in soft, tickling tresses.

He could sense her hesitation, and he rolled over onto his back to guide her hand upward. Lightly, curiously, she explored at first, aware of his breathing, aware of his watching her. Then her hands moved with more serious intent, trailing a warm path deep into the dark folds between his thighs. Her slim fingers curled round him in an intricate flutter at first, unsettled, unsure. Then they grew bold and solid in their grasp, absorbing his heat, containing it.

She marveled at the power of her touch, the careful, measured contact that would take him to the brink of conscious control and back.

"Jenna—" he breathed at last, an apology or a plea, she did not know which. But he pulled her up to lie astride him. And she found her power lost, freely relinquished, as he probed for her reply. She smiled and would not answer. Eyes closed, she kept it from him. Again and again. Until it took both of them in unison to wrench it free.

They were left breathless and spent, cradling each other in the quiet. For a very long time they lay awake and aware of one another.

Finally Jenna got up and went to the hearth to prod the fire to life. Then she wrapped her body in a comforter and sat in a chair to stare at the crackling blaze.

She heard the bed creak behind her as the wooden slats were relieved of Ian's weight. He knelt beside her, most of him cast in darkness. Her face was highlighted by the fire.

"Is something wrong?" he asked.

"Is it like that for everyone?" she asked.

"No, I think not," he smiled.

"Is it right?" she asked.

"Dear God. I have not had anything so right in my life. What makes you ask that?"

She shook her head, the sensations they had shared sending a spasm of remembrance through her body. "Would I have the same feeling with another man?"

The question shocked him. Because he sincerely hoped not. Instead he answered: "Of course."

"Have you had the same feeling with another woman?" she asked.

He leaned his head back and looked up. God have mercy on a blind dumb fool who should have looked where she was going.

"Jenna," he smiled, sitting down on the rug in front of her. "You're not as innocent and impressionable as you seem."

She smiled. "Perhaps you're just a remarkable teacher."

"Trapped by my own blind arrogance once, I will not stumble again."

"I can only tell you what I feel," she said softly. "And I am not comfortable with the—intensity of the feelings you arouse."

"You think that is wrong?"

"No. I think it is not as you said. I would not feel the same with another man. I don't understand why I should look elsewhere for love."

"People change. Emotions die—"

"Or they grow. And deepen."

He studied her a moment. "Jenna. I am your first love. Your life will be filled with others."

"For a man of experience, what you know of love wouldn't fit on a flyspeck!" Large, angry tears spilled over her cheeks, unannounced, like a sudden summer downpour.

What a quicksilver creature he had. Decisive and wise, yet so vulnerable and scared. He used to think she reminded him of Tania. But Tania's main attribute was a wild and reckless honesty. She had suited him so well during their time together.

Jenna was harder for him to understand. A wise child temptress and a strong, lovely woman lived inside her. If he got skillful, he could prompt the reaction he wanted.

But the risk was great, he thought wryly. At the same time

she could grow more adept in getting the response she wanted from him.

His voice was firm. "Then you must enlighten me about love. As soon as you stop acting the ingenue."

He was not prepared for the look of utter scorn she directed at him. He grew uncomfortable. Each moment that passed seemed to separate them further.

Finally she spoke, her eyes on the hearth. "If experience taught you anything at all, you would not make a woman feel small and mean."

"Your coy reference to marriage was not small," he said softly.

She shook her head. "I talked of love. Not marriage. You are not a marriageable man."

"Oh. But I am a lovable one?"

"Sometimes. Her expression was a pensive one. "Most of the time you are simply hungry."

He smiled. "I don't mean to be so obvious." He raised himself to his knees and bent over her lap. "But I have never known anyone like you."

"Not even Tania?" She kept her eyes on the fire.

"Not even Tania," he said softly.

"You must miss her."

The palm of his hand closed under her chin and she felt his gentle turn of her head, forcing her eyes to settle on his. "You do not remind me of Tania," he said. "But the closeness does." He said it carefully. As if he would not want to say it again.

"How long will we feel it?" she asked.

His stomach tightened and he pushed himself away from her. For he wanted to feel close to her as long as he had breath to answer. "As long as we can."

She stood up, letting the comforter fall back in the chair

like a cocoon, shed. The firelight danced on her body, dappling her skin with burnished shadows.

A stillness rose around them, encircling her with an oppressive silence, compressing his shallow breaths until motion stopped.

She spoke softly. "When you are gone from me, I will mourn you as a husband. But if I were to leave you, I don't know what you would feel."

"Broken," he said, grasping her two hands in his. "Empty." He pulled her slowly down on top of him. "So angry." He pressed her head gently to his chest and breathed a kiss into her hair.

"Angry?"

He closed his eyes tight. "To think that I had lost you. Before I said I loved you. As I've never loved anyone in my life."

He would remember that night for its peace. She would mark it as the first time she was no longer alone. Words were few. They spoke more honestly by touch, lying close, not fearing that morning light would break the spell.

They had learned the incantation.

One more day together. They rose late, reluctant, to a day more filled with business than pleasure. The morning was spent at target practice. The afternoon at plans Ian wanted no part of.

"Parrish has probably made Ethan his legal ward, as Carolina is. We would be charged with kidnapping, not lauded for rescuing him," Ian said emphatically, laying a knife across his plate, his half-eaten dinner a sign of his concern.

Even if, God forbid, he was killed tomorrow, he knew Jenna would go ahead with her plan to reunite the mother and child. And if he survived the duel, he would have to escort her that afternoon to a dingy, lower-class borough and steal a child he did not care about.

He stood and threw his napkin to the table. "Why are you so adamant?"

Jenna pushed herself away from the table and stood slowly. "He has made motherless children of two people I know. My mother cannot be brought back. For young Ethan, it will be different."

Wearily, Ian clasped the back of his neck with one hand, pressed deeply to ease the tension, then abruptly left the clutter of the drop-leaf dining table behind. He strode out of the room and across the hall to the library.

She came in quietly, carrying a silver service of coffee. She set the tray on a mahogany claw-foot table next to a pair of carved white sandstone lions. They were fierce, singular mementos, like many in the den, bespeaking the wanderlust in their owner.

"Here." She walked over to the wide expanse of paned glass that made his library the antithesis of every dark, masculine den she had ever encountered.

He took the cup without acknowledging her. His eyes were on the pasture, where a speckled hunting dog nosed through knee-high grass to flush a nest of quail.

"We have become no better than he," he said finally. "Stealing and spreading scandal and using loved ones as a cloak of respectability. You use your uncle as I use my brother. To achieve a measure of revenge."

She shrugged and picked a spot at the far end of the window seat. She sat, drawing her knees up so that her chin could rest there, studying his face. He was troubled. And tense.

"We all use one another," she said softly. "That's what a society is for, my father says."

"Your father. I'm beginning to feel used by him most of all. He knew he need only wave Parrish under my nose and I'd take off like a hound. Then he disappeared and left me to—"

"—do all the things you are good at and he isn't. Organizing men. Leading them. Confronting an enemy. He has left you the chance you have wanted for many years."

He did not answer. Then, softly, as if to himself: "And he left me you."

She stood up on the window seat, fingertips braced lightly against the glass for balance as she walked toward him. "It is I who give myself away," she said.

He had to look up at her as she approached. She placed a hand to each side of his face.

"I must be careful with such a gift," he said.

"It cannot be lost," she said softly. Her thumbs ran slowly down the curve of his jaw, then up around his eyes, tracing the arc of his brow.

He buried his face against her, then embraced her fully. They stood for a long time. Until the gunshot.

The sudden crack from the meadow behind them made Jenna's heart jump painfully in her chest. It was the quail hunter landing his dinner.

A trembling began in Jenna's hands. She clenched her fingers in his ebony hair and pulled his head sharply away from her midriff so she could see his face.

She saw a serious man, preoccupied with the future—but intensely aware of the present he held in his arms. "Do not worry," he said softly, with a small, wise smile, as if he somehow had control of their fate.

Gently, he pulled Jenna toward him and swept her warm, lithe body into his arms, cradling her tightly.

His lips pressed full on hers, tenderly, carefully quelling the tremor that was beginning there.

Carriage wheels crunched unevenly in the rocky troughs of a wagon road that wound through the meadow at Sitwell's Corner. Footmen with oil lanterns rode atop the coaches, holding the swaying lights aloft like beacons for the horses of the coaches behind. In the black predawn darkness, it was a somber procession.

A hundred feet from where Ian stood, two dozen gentlemen chatted sociably under a tented awning their servants had erected. The air inside crackled with sounds: sausages sizzling in an iron skillet, teacups clinking on saucers, loud words and soft rumbles of men in conversation. All around was the tension, the anticipation of damn good sport.

Ian steeled himself against the noise, turning his back to it, his long, tailored greatcoat creating a gray-black wall against the commotion. The scent of blackened sausage wafted by as a reminder, though. His personal vendetta had become a spectator sport. If he were in better humor, he would smile at the irony. He was sure Parrish would.

Wearily he walked on, stopping to lean a shoulder into the rough-ribbed bark of a black oak. He had come early hoping for solitude, a chance to focus on the task at hand.

But his mind was fixed on something else.

Gently, carefully, he had pulled away from her this morning, leaving her curled body alone in his bed. Fortune was with him, for she did not wake. He did not want to tell her good-bye. The thought—let alone the word—did not exist in relation to this woman. She was changing his reason for living. And in the test of will he would face this morning, it meant she had weakened him.

Destroying Parrish had always been his goal, a cleansing act that would purge his past. And he had always been willing to die for it. Until now.

Ian frowned and sipped the hot tea he had bought from the roadside beggar. The scruffy man, like other street merchants, sniffing the possibility of gathered customers, had camped at the edge of the meadow arena, setting up his cooking fire. A red kerchief was tied to his cook pole and he used it to dry the tin cups he washed.

Ian could see that the tall beggar was watching him. Indeed, many eyes were on him. He must look like a worried man, he thought. The gentleman bettors under the tent were gambling that his more youthful reflexes might triumph against the older man's.

Ian smiled bitterly. Perhaps now they would hedge their bets, sensing that the odds had indelibly changed.

Footsteps sounded behind him. He turned.

His brother Robert smiled and put a hand on Ian's shoulder. "Intimate little gathering you have here. You should have thought to sell tickets."

Ian looked at the fair-haired younger man whose easy humor and strong instincts he had only recently come to appreciate. Robert's loyalty was unquestioning. The fact hit Ian with a pang. He hid the moment with a flip of his hand, tossing the last drops of tea into the weeds behind him. "Thank you for agreeing to be my second," Ian said.

"Wouldn't miss the show," Robert said. "I trust I won't be dismayed at the finale."

Ian laughed outright at his brother's directness. "I'll try not to disappoint you. Is Marguerite well?"

"Yes. The child grows bigger and she grows impatient.

And nervous. The earl is there, you know, using the bandit passageway as his hiding place. Physically, he seems to have escaped the crash without a scratch, she says. His mind, though, wanders away from his words sometimes. I must tell Jenna that he is safe. Has she really returned to Glen Manor, as her uncle says?" Robert asked with a smile.

Ian hesitated.

"She is with you, then?" Robert said.

"Yes. In the house at Sarbin's Crown." Ian paused. "And she will need your help if I am unable to protect her."

Robert was silent a moment. "Of course." ·

Ian nodded for Robert to walk with him then. He gave Robert the news of the mortgage against Stonebridge Hall. "My personal holdings will go immediately to you in the event of my death," Ian said. That meant his property in Brightlingsea and the London home could be sold to pay the lien against Stonebridge Hall. And Robert could still hold on to Phillip's notes.

Ian handed over an envelope, stuffed and sealed. "These mean everything to the future of the earl's estate. Do not let them fall into Hutton's hands.'·

Robert carefully slipped the envelope of debt notes inside his breast coat. "I brought the horse, saddled and ready." Robert motioned to the gray gelding tied to the Stonebridge coach a few yards away. "You must feel you'll be able to ride away upright."

Ian shrugged and smiled absently, looking beyond Robert to the pink edge of dawn on the horizon. "Habit. I like more than one exit."

The brilliant spring sun had streaked half the sky pink when Hutton's four matched bays drew his carriage to a halt near the tent. He descended, unhurried, and walked straight to well-wishers, smiling as if this were a novel site for a party.

Ian, who stood in the open with a small group of men, made note of Hutton's arrival. Inwardly Ian found himself smiling at the man's correct bearing and showy style. But the amusement fled as Ian looked beyond Hutton to the companion who descended the coach steps.

Lindstrom.

A vein at Ian's temple began to throb as his jaw tightened.

"What's wrong?" Robert saw the sudden tension.

Ian's voice was even. And cold as ice. Parrish has brought an old acquaintance of mine to be his second."

Clad in an ill-fitting suit, the man was taller than most, but his height was misleading, Ian knew. It was the breadth of his massive chest that made him look like a hulking giant. And his hands, Ian's eyes closed a moment, then opened. Lindstrom's hands were the size of cast-iron skillets. Or at least they felt that way. Ian took a deep breath and turned his head toward Parrish's group. There, over the shoulder of a talkative supporter, Ian's eyes met the vicount's amused gaze.

Slowly, Ian arched a brow and raised his battered tin tea-cup in a mocking salute.

Lindstrom was the man who had beaten Ian to the brink of death thirteen years ago in a dark jail cell. The man who so carefully, effortlessly, lifted Ian's middle finger out of its socket before bending it back, far back—

The memory caused a gut-tightening twist. Oh, yes, he smiled grudgingly. What a cunning stroke it was to bring Lindstrom. An unnerving man from his unsettled past. A signal that the murder of Ian's boyhood tormentor, Hasting Wills, had never been solved. And Ian had been the one and only suspect in the case, arrested by uniformed officers who were paid lackeys of Parrish.

"Are you all right?" Robert asked, seeing the strange smile twist Ian's lips.

"Yes," Ian said. "Yes, I am." The voice was firm. For instead of upsetting Ian, Lindstrom's appearance had helped him. He now knew part of Parrish's plan.

And he also knew, as surely as blood runs red in a black barred jail, that he would not let himself be taken alive.

Ian began to unbutton his jacket. He slipped it from his shoulders and flung it to Robert. The men around him had opened up the semicircle so that Ian could walk out.

Ian went slowly into the grassy clear space. Far to his left was a small abandoned barn, to his right nothing but hay mounds and rock beds. He unhooked his neck cloth, removed his vest and loosened the cuffs of his white shirt.

It felt good to stand alone, the breeze flinging strands of dark hair back from his forehead, ruffling his shirt front.

"It is past dawn!" he called.

"Excuse me, gentlemen," said Parrish to his group. "The rooster crows." Hutton left their laughter behind as he walked toward the open space opposite Ian. He stopped six feet away from the young baronet and nodded a slight bow. He waited for Ian to return the gesture.

Ian did not move. "That is the problem between us," Ian said. "Neither truly bows to the other."

"I promise to remedy that," Hutton said, his white wavy hair buffeted suddenly by a rising wind. With a gloved hand he motioned to the rough-looking Swede waiting at the edge of the crowd.

Lindstrom lumbered forward, carrying a long rectangular

case. Robert followed at a thoughtful distance, puzzled at the grand size of the pistol box.

Ian nodded once in Lindstrom's direction, his smile grim, his voice soft. "And what other surprises have you for me?"

Hutton smiled and reached down for the gun case.

Chapter 21

Sabers.

Inside the case two swords lay side by side.

"Guns have been my sole weapon of choice for so long. I was ready for a sporting change," Hutton smiled. "My father was a captain in the cavalry."

"I'm sure he taught you well," Ian said thoughtfully, studying weapons he had held only once before. In sport. The long beveled blades curved to thin, angled points, very different from the short-bladed knife Ian used in close combat at sea.

"Absurd," Robert said. "Gentlemen do not go hacking at one another. Ian—"

One sharp look from his brother stopped the protest.

"This more primitive means is really quite apropos," Hutton said, extending the case toward Ian. "We're dealing with base passions, are we not?"

Ian glanced once at his enemy before grasping the hilt of the sword closest to Parrish. The grip was black and ridged, the crosspiece inlaid with the Parrish crest.

"It is nature's way," Hutton smiled as he picked up the remaining saber. "Males have always fought for the most desirable female. You may have had her first. But you will not be the last."

Ian had to close his eyes to quell the pounding in his head. "Get on with it," Ian could hardly whisper.

"Gentlemen," Robert interjected, fear for his brother almost palpable in his voice. "This 'affair of honor' will end with surrender of one to the other and a full apology."

"No," Ian said shortly, his eyes never leaving Parrish.

"Agreed," Parrish said, flinging his vest coat to the Swede. "To the death."

The two men backed away from each other then. Their boots ground pebbles under their soles as they found their stance, right arms outstretched, blades extended high.

The spectators near the road stopped all conversation.

Parrish moved a step closer so that the flat of his blade grated lightly along the edge of Ian's weapon. A chill rose the hackles on the back of Ian's neck. A salute. And a warning. He heard a teacup settle into a saucer with a final clink. And the meadow was quiet.

Then Parrish lunged hard. Ian caught the thrust on his cross guard and circled it away. But Parrish quickly shifted position, arcing the point of the saber up and across Ian's chest.

The blade was so sharp the cloth gave no whisper of protest as its edges parted and grew dark with Ian's blood.

It was a shallow wound, but the sting shocked Ian.

Suddenly more wary than angry, Ian curbed his instinct to charge. This man, more than twenty years his senior, was quicker, more agile than he thoug—

Damn! Parrish nearly caught Ian's rib with a swinging crosscut. Ian blocked it with a massive clang that left both their hands jangling painfully at the collision. The force knocked Parrish off balance for a moment, and Ian swung quickly, nipping the shoulder of Parrish's left sleeve. A circle of blood, stained the fine white cotton of Parrish's shirt.

But there was no time to savor small victories. Instantly the viscount's right arm swung forward, a trajectory high and fast, its target Ian's exposed neck.

Ian dove groundward and watched Parrish's blow slice the air where his collarbone had been. Ian rolled once, feeling the rocks tear at the gash in his chest. He rose quickly to his feet, the panic of the close escape burning brightly in his eyes.

"You fight like a butcher," Ian breathed, warily taking his stance.

"What did you expect?" Parrish exhaled a deep breath. "A gentlemanly end? You have gone too far for that." Parrish teased the end of Ian's sword with small slaps, then suddenly thrust over and down, catching Ian's blade with his crosspiece. The motion jerked Ian forward, within range of Parrish's upward thrust, but Ian recovered and with a twist of his hand bounced Parrish's sword away.

Parrish backed up and eyed his opponent. "You are a quick study. But you did not learn swordplay at school."

"I was fighting the mongrel you set at my heels!" Ian lunged forward, but his opponent had dodged, stepped left and turned full circle and caught Ian's leg neatly on an upward pass.

On the sidelines by the tea tent, Parrish's audience grunted their admiration.

The gash ran deeper this time. And the pain crystallized a warning for Ian. He could not afford to lose his temper.

He took a deep breath and feinted forward. Parrish stepped toward him to parry the blow, but Ian shifted back and withdrew his sword, leaving Parrish's blade frozen in thin air for one vulnerable second. The vital point under Parrish's arm was momentarily exposed, within range.

A lunge to Parrish's lungs would end the show. Ian hesitated.

Quickly Parrish crouched to shield his exposed side. "Where's your appetite, bastard? You missed your chance," Parrish spat, chest heaving, both hands gripping the hilt of his sword. Then he swung down hard with a velocity that left Ian staggering as he locked his sword to Parrish's. For a rigid moment they pressed against one another, close enough to catch the stench of acrid sweat. Ian stared once into the ice-blue eyes that had the shape and countenance of his own black-brown ones. With a rough cry he pushed his enemy away with a force that surprised both of them.

Parrish paused but only a moment. He rushed Ian again, this time hacking downward at odd angles, sharp chops meant to back him into retreat. But Ian stood his ground, feinting and blocking until his hand ached with the reverberations of colliding metal.

Parrish backed away, breathing hard, his white hair a mat of dark, wet gray.

"Tired?" Ian asked, his own breath coming in gasps, his ears ringing and his shirt hanging completely off the shoulder where Parrish had shorn it on an upstroke.

"Not of seeing you sweat and bleed." Parrish lunged forward. Ian threw himself right, away from the swing, but the saber point followed him like a snake, leaving a shallow bite under his left jaw.

"That's what I want," Parrish smiled as Ian, out of range, staunched the blood with his torn shirt. "A face she cannot love."

"That face is yours," Ian hissed as the sting of salty sweat mingled with the open wound. He walked forward and took his stance.

"Love—is not something—I require from a woman." The

words came out in broken syllables as Parrish panted, bent at the waist, hands on his knees.

"She is free," Ian said. "You have no debt notes to bargain against Shadow Glen."

Parrish straightened upright, glaring. "Triumphant thief. Someone will pay for your cleverness." His voice grew soft. "A black-haired beauty. With lips that part with a sigh. And breasts so firm and full they—"

"Enough!" With a furious cry Ian slapped Parrish's sword on guard and immediately drove the viscount back with three savage thrusts. Parrish caught the last one and they locked swords, nose to nose, at the crosspiece.

"If you ever touch her—" Ian hissed.

"You know I will," Parrish whispered.

A black anger ballooned in his chest and Ian thrust Parrish back and watched him stumble. Boldly Ian took the offensive, his sword arm aching, the wound on his leg swelling, threatening to stiffen his knee. But he did not notice. The image of Jenna in Parrish's arms was suffocating him. He slashed downward again and again, fighting for air.

Parrish had to use both hands on the hilt to deflect Ian's powerful swings. Each ringing clash of the swords grew lower as Ian swung faster, giving Parrish no time to stand upright in a position to attack. Parrish felt the whisper cuts of the saber licking at his shirt. Seeing a chance, he jabbed upward, catching Ian's sword midway along the blade. Parrish rose up, pushing high, twisting the arc away from his chest and back toward Ian.

Ian whirled and ducked as Parrish's swing rent nothing but air. Then Ian jumped quickly forward, thrusting straight, then angling outward. The saber point licked a neat trail from midcheek to chin, and Parrish backed away with a hissing cry.

."My face! You wet whore's bastard!" Parrish pressed his palm to the gash and looked at the blood there.

Ian backed away, his chest heaving painfully for air, his sword point dragging the ground.

"Now," Parrish whispered. "I will save Lindstrom the pleasure." Rigid, sword thrust high and forward, he positioned himself close to Ian.

"When will your pack of officers come to save you, old man?" Ian taunted, grating his sword roughly across the blunt edge of Parrish's.

"Soon, bastard. But you will not see them." The upward slash of Parrish's sword knocked Ian's out of the way and Parrish advanced quickly with a deep thrust at Ian's shoulder. Ian twisted to the side and the blade caught a piece of tattered shirt. Ian crouched, put two hands to the hilt and swung hard right, jarring Parrish off balance. His sword tilted out of control and Parrish crashed to the ground, landing on his wounded shoulder. Parrish gave a sharp gasp and then lay still, breathing deeply. Ian advanced cautiously, hoping he would call surrender. Maybe it was finish—

Like lightning the saber sliced upward and Parrish rose with it, the blade riding a shallow red trail across the dirt-darkened cuff of Ian's sword hand.

And Ian whirled and came into position at Parrish's side. With a cry he brought the protruding crosspiece down across Parrish's wrist in a paralyzing blow.

And the sword clattered to the ground.

Grimacing in pain, Parrish dove with his other hand for the dark leather grip that lay at his feet, but Ian threw himself forward and knocked the viscount to the ground.

Ian rose first, with Parrish's sword in hand, his face streaked with hot rivulets of sweat and blood. He walked slowly toward the fallen viscount, the glimmer of his victory just beginning to cool his heartbeat.

Then he heard the horse hooves.

Pounding. Racing. A carriage on its way.

Parrish, one hand covering his wounded cheek, gave a small, terrible smile. "Lindstrom will have the pleasure after all."

Like a man facing hell's hounds, Ian turned and ran toward the spectators, swords flat against his side. The beggar. He had to reach the tea-selling beggar before the police reached him.

"Ian!" It was his brother's puzzled cry.

To his left he heard horses neigh as their bits were wrenched backward. The constable's coach drew to an abrupt standstill. Uniformed officers poured out. Baffled gentlemen who had come for a bloody good show found themselves rudely pushed aside as the policemen wrestled through the line. "They're arresting him!" said one dandy, overjoyed at the excitement.

They were not the same brutish lot Parrish had sent to apprehend him thirteen years ago. But they were similar thick-headed stock, Ian knew. Carrying out the orders of one of Parrish's high-placed cronies. Ordered to roust him into a crowded carriage so he could be dumped, bruised and bleeding, into a holding cell. With Lindstrom.

Ian increased his stride and pulled closer to the cookfire the disguised beggar—Ross—had erected. The remains of his tattered shirt had slipped off his shoulders and flapped behind him now, held to his body by the waistband of his trousers.

Ian rushed past the street beggar, appearing to bump the man out of his way. As planned, Ross snapped the handle of a loaded pistol snugly into Ian's palm.

The fastest officer, the leanest of the lot, was close. The man stopped and fired a warning shot that went wild. Ian's return shot did not. It stung the dirt at the officer's feet and the man danced backward.

Ian whirled and ran for the gelding tied to Robert's coach. He threw down his own saber and jerked the bridle free. Then he swung into the saddle, the muscles in his wounded leg protesting.

Nearby spectators shouted his whereabouts and Ian stole time to study the commotion. From the corner of his eye he saw Robert gesturing angrily in conversation with the constable. In the meadow a small group of men had gathered around Parrish, who was standing and gazing hard at the bloodied, bare-chested man on horseback.

Ian, exhausted, struggled to fit his right foot into the dangling stirrup. He did not see the broad shape that lumbered up silently behind his horse.

Thwack! Lindstrom's hand landed flat and hard against the gelding's rump, and the horse reared with a frightened snort.

Ian, tilting wildly in the saddle, made a grab for the horse's mane and tried to hold on to his pistol with the other hand. As he grappled to keep his seat, he felt Lindstrom's monstrous hand encircle his thigh.

Quickly he rose up in the saddle and grasped the gelding's ear, wrenching it hard right. With a squeal of anger, the horse pawed groundward with a twisting, bucking turn that hit Lindstrom broadside.

The blow knocked the giant away, but Ian was dragged from his seat by Lindstrom's stubborn grip. Ian hung there, one hand in the horse's mane, one leg hooked on the ridge of the saddle, his wounded leg dangling straight. If he dismounted, he would never regain his seat. The horse would be gone. And his chance of escape with it.

He saw Lindstrom rise up slowly from the grass not three feet away, with the saber Ian had discarded in his giant paw.

Grimacing with effort, he pulled upward with all the leverage his left leg could afford. The pistol in Ian's free hand instantly drew a bead on the advancing man and Ian fired fast, aiming low.

Lindstrom blinked and stopped for only a second. Then he rushed forward, the sword raised, the hand that gripped its black hilt dripping red.

Ian's heels jabbed the horse's side twice with a fierce demand for speed. The panicked animal was only too happy to oblige. His legs pumped quickly to a gallop as, behind them, uniformed police caught up with Lindstrom.

Ian ducked flat against the crown of the saddle, his face pressed low against the horse's neck. The carriage would be easy to outrun, but the guns were another matter.

Lead beads whipped by in a haphazard shower, and Ian prayed that he, not the horse, would be hit.

Because the horse still had energy to run. And he, numb and bleeding, had none.

The library clock chimed ten o'clock in the morning. And as Jenna listened to Robert's description of the duel, her mind focused on a single phrase: "He is alive."

Her heart pounding, she slowly escorted Robert from the library to the front door. Their footsteps seemed loud, too heavy for the silence of the hallway.

"Thank you for the news of my father." Robert had told her the earl was in hiding at Marguerite's house. "You are certain Ian's solicitor can quash the murder charge?" Jenna asked as Robert retrieved his top hat and coat from Ross.

"Yes. But not soon. It will take days to research and compile evidence."

"And until then?"

"Ian will run." Robert shrugged.

"Where?"

"Nowhere you or I should know. We would be followed. And Parrish would have him." Robert's words carried a warning. Did he know she planned to confront young Ethan's guardians on Redding Street tonight?

"I am sure he is on his way back to Lancashire," Robert added.

"I hope so," Jenna said softly. "I leave for home also this afternoon."

"Good." Robert was relieved. "Ross will see you aboard the train. Please visit Marguerite when you get there. Tell her I'll be home soon."

Jenna smiled. "She's a lovely woman, Robert."

The fair-haired man nodded and donned his hat, his lips pressed in a firm line of concern. "And a worried one. We shall all sleep easier when this affair is over."

"The mine act comes to a vote in two days," Jenna said. "If we win, it will end Parrish's influence. He has no coal except for what he steals from Shadow Glen. Government inspectors will protect that. He will be finished."

"Well, someone must tell him that. Because he does not fight like a dead man, my sister-to-be."

Jenna opened the door for him. "I am still just your neighbor, Robert. Ian and I have no plans to marry."

Robert paused on his way out the door. "Go home, Jenna. So that Ian can find you when this horrible business is done."

It would have been the sensible thing to do. But the sensible Jenna was lost. She had fled long ago so that there would be mornings of waking next to him. She had needed to feel his breath warm against her hair, and his firm length molding itself to her so tightly that they awakened as one.

Jenna's eyes closed tightly. She had almost cried out when he pulled away this morning. But she lay still, pretending sleep.

She shook her head to clear the burning in her eyes. Robert was wrong, she knew. Wounded and hunted, Ian would not leave London. His recklessness matched her own. He would find no better place to hide than the eye of the storm.

And she would have no better chance to see him than tonight at the house where Carolina's son was kept.

Late that afternoon Jenna boarded the London train to Manchester with Ross. He helped her find her seat. Then he stood rigidly on the platform near her window until the train whistled all aboard! Sluggishly, it began to pull away from the station.

She looked back and waved once. She thought she could see the tall Scot's shoulders relax with relief as the distance between her car and the boarding platform widened.

For thirty minutes she listened to the soothing rattle and roll of the tracks. Then she debarked at the first stop and waited calmly for the train back.

By the time she stepped down from the hackney coach in front of 214 Redding, it was twilight. A ragged man with a stepladder was lighting a street lamp halfway down the litter-strewn block. Two long-haired boys in knickers careened past her, chasing a leather ball. Pedestrians were few.

She paused on the sidewalk, aware that she might have been followed. But she had been careful and had taken two cabs. Yet a woman alone was always suspect. She wanted to stay and wait for Ian, but intuition told her to keep moving through the dimming light. A disembodied guffaw echoed from the corner pub down the street.

She walked purposefully up the stoop to the paint-peeling door of 214 and knocked. A tired-looking housemaid answered.

"I've come for the child," Jenna said.

Instantly the woman frowned. "Sorry, mum?"

"Surely Mr. Northrup, the solicitor, contacted your mistress to tell her that I would be coming for Ethan."

"She got no such word as I'm aware of." The woman shook her head, and a lank strand of hair fell from behind her ear.

"May I speak with her, then?"

The maid shrugged and let Jenna step onto the welcome mat inside the tiny foyer. "You'll have to wait in the parlor. There's a gentleman there, too. A strange night for visitors," the squat woman muttered.

Jenna's heart leaped.

Quickly she followed the maid down the corridor, past a narrow staircase and across the threshold of a small, chilly room that smelled of leather cream.

"Hello," said Hutton Parrish.

Behind her the door creaked closed.

He rose elegantly from a chair by the fire, a buffing rag in one hand. He was polishing the brass bit on a new bridle.

"So you have come to kidnap my young ward?" he said quietly, slinging the leather straps across one arm and approaching her slowly.

She did not move. She could not.

Smiling, he took her hand and raised it to his lips, watching the bosom of her gown for a fearful intake of breath.

But she pulled her hand away slowly with a control he didn't expect.

Good, he thought. Not even the angry red line across his cheek could frighten her for long.

"Where is Ian?" she asked, heart pounding.

Hutton smiled and turned away from her to reach his cigarette case on a nearby table. "I don't know. But I suspect that wherever you are, he will turn up soon."

Her eyes closed.

"Now, now." He bent to the fire. "Don't blame yourself. I didn't know for sure you would be here tonight. I had a feeling. Backed by Carolina's confession that you would try to find Ethan." He inhaled deeply on the dark, slim tobacco. "I realized time was running out, and I thought you might try a last noble gesture before returning home."

Jenna's fingers managed to open the drawstring of her small cloth bag. She drew out an envelope. "We have a solicitor. And Carolina's permission to fight for custody of the boy."

"Carolina is dead. Unfortunate accident," Hutton said softly. "She left me legal guardian of the child."

The envelope began to slip. She tightened her grip.

"My aging cousin adores him. He is her reason for living," he smiled. Then softer, "We all need a reason to live, Jenna."

The words had an intimacy that left her queasy.

Jenna turned woodenly and opened the door.

"Not yet," he said, coming closer behind her, the brass on the bridle jingling with each step. "You cannot leave yet."

Suddenly she flung herself headlong through the corridor. She rushed toward the front door, but he caught her easily as she rounded the bottom of the staircase. His arm encircled her and he whirled her around to face him.

With a rough jerk, Hutton grasped her wrists behind her and crushed her against him. The sudden embrace forced a cry from her parted lips, and Hutton's mouth was there to catch it and press it back to her with an insistence that left her close to tears. One hand imprisoned her chin, the oily metal scent of acrid polish dominating the air she fought to inhale.

Then Jenna heard the wooden floor above them creaking under the weight of steady footsteps.

Jenna struggled wildly. At the feel of her, Hutton felt his groin tightening. Finally her mouth wrenched free from his. But as she caught her breath to scream, his hand clamped over her mouth, thumb and forefinger expertly pinching her nostrils closed.

She could not breathe.

"Sorry, love. You must remain quiet. My cousin is not to be alarmed."

Nearly in a swoon, she gave a weak nod. She would not scream.

With a soft, sad look in his eyes, he released her.

Jenna stumbled back toward the front door, beyond his reach. "How easy it was for you to kill her," she whispered.

"Dead bodies hold no interest for me," he said. "I think you sense that. Carolina took her own life."

"With your help," Jenna said bitterly. "Just as you helped —" She swallowed. "As you made my mother—" Dear God, the words would not come.

"You must understand that men go to extremes in a time of war. Your father was close to pressing through the inspection law. I had to do something."

"And you," Jenna seethed, "with your great 'intellect,' your disdain of all that's common—all you could muster was rape?" Her voice had risen. "What a disappointment you are, almighty Hutton!"

He could not control the stiffening of his upper back, the painful clamp of his jaw against his teeth.

Her hand rushed to find the door latch.

But he was there to stop her, his arm outstretched above her head, holding the door shut.

She did not release her grasp on the door handle. She glanced at the large, fine-boned hand that barred her way. "You've always lacked creativity." She avoided his eyes.

"Brute force is too effective," he said.

"But never fully satisfying, is it?" Her voice was soft.

The muscles below his abdomen began to tighten with an intensity he hadn't felt in years. Not since Ariel Stonebridge had graced his bed that once. That very special once. His eyes closed a moment. Then he reached out to her slowly. The ash scent of sweet, strong tobacco hovered in his sigh. His thumb gently smoothed a strand of her dark, fine hair away from her cheek. "Just a few hours more," he whispered. His hand trailed away from her. Then he stepped back from the door.

Suspicious, she opened it.

He did not move.

Then she stood on the threshold and turned to him. "I am allowed to leave?" she asked, her heart beating faster.

"I'm afraid you must."

"Then I am the trap for Ian," she said softly.

Hutton's heart made a jealous leap when she sounded the bastard's name. "As long as he lives, he stands between us."

"You realize you are truly mad," she said.

"That's not what makes me dangerous," he smiled, slowly closing the door between them. "I'm a dreamer." He paused, voice soft. "My dream is you."

Chapter 22

The weather-beaten door shut with a sure thud. And she was left alone outside the dreary brick house, looking down at her fist, clenched and ready to pound.

She whirled to face the darkened street. She had to leave quickly before Ian came to meet her. She hurried out to the narrow road. There were gas lanterns halfway down the block to each side. But no vehicles rolled along the uneven seams of the filthy bricks.

A long neigh sounded somewhere to her right. In the darkness down the block, she saw the shape of a parked hansom cab. Heart pounding, she walked as quickly as she could toward the black carriage.

"Driver! Wait!" she called to the man standing in the metal seat at the back of the cab. The driver turned and tipped his hat.

She finished her stride, then froze.

It was Gault, the stocky hothead who took orders from Parrish's foreman, Stiles. She backed away slowly, her senses on guard, taking in the street scene more clearly. Across the street from Gault's cab, two men in uniform leaned silently against the side of a house. A hundred yards to her right, where Redding intersected a cross street in a haze of corner lanterns, she saw a man run across the open space. His tall rounded hat marked him as a policeman.

To her left, near the house where Hutton waited, she noticed a slim figure in the shadows. A slouching shape she had hurriedly passed. Stiles. The sharp-faced ferret who had come looking for the Grawlin children at Glen Manor.

Jenna felt chilled. Unconsciously she rubbed her upper arms to stop the shudder. Beyond Stiles, on the other side of the street, a huge man in a tight-fitting jacket sat on the step of a house, scrutinizing each pedestrian that passed.

She could see no farther than the hulking shape, but she knew police would be waiting at the other end of the street.

Around her, the sounds of normal evening life were everywhere: a spoon clanging against a pot, a baby's cranky wail, a man yelling for quiet from a second-floor window. On the street scattered couples made raucous jokes on their way to and from the corner pub.

As calmly as possible, her mind racing, Jenna adjusted the bonnet that had come loose in her struggle with Hutton. She tied its ribbons securely under her chin and placed her cold hands inside her muff.

She began to walk slowly then, back the way she had come. She concentrated on the random passersby, afraid she would find a tall figure, a powerfully built man who, from what Robert said, would be walking painfully with a stiff right leg. Surely, she prayed, Ian would see the police and stay away.

She passed Stiles, leaning in the shadows. He eyed her casually. He found no need to follow her. That meant the police blocking the street would hold her securely until Ian —or Parrish—came for her.

She stepped out of the way as a tipsy man wearing odorous rags and a dirty cap walked by. He gave her a friendly grin. "Wha' a neat 'n' tidy tumble you'd be," she heard him mumble.

Jenna turned and walked on, realizing she was completely alone. Even if she found a sober stranger and convinced him to help her, where would he take her? They could not go beyond this street.

A shrill drunken laugh broke from the darkness ahead like a mocking salute. Jenna stopped, numbed. There was nowhere to go.

Suddenly she felt her foot give way and she grabbed at a street lamp to stay upright. She had slipped on a pile of rotting peels left at the edge of the road. This was a London she had never experienced. A London without servants to carry away the refuse of life, where the street was the slop jar shared by all.

In front of her a man and woman stepped into the half-light at the edge of the lantern's glow. Their shoes scraped loudly in the grit of the nearly vacant street. They walked arm in arm, the woman dressed in a gown that exposed cleavage to gravity's grip. And she erupted often with a low, throaty chuckle that said she was enjoying the ribald comments of her companion.

As they drew close to the lamp pole, Jenna smelled the advancing cloud of the redheaded woman's heavy perfume.

"Evenin'." The man stopped and doffed his cap at Jenna.

"Benny, ya bloomin' biscuit!" The woman punched the man's shoulder playfully. "Doan tell me ya'd like ta'ave a nibble like that instead of a real feast," the woman smiled, watching Jenna intently.

"Course not, Tess."

The woman turned a sly eye to Jenna. "You'd bet'er move on a'ead, missy. Else you'll be gobbled up like a lit'le sweetmeat, eh, Benny?" The woman fell chuckling against her companion. Then, gesturing while she laughed, the woman's fist tapped her heart once. Her hand opened to a flat, extended palm.

The gesture was quick. And not quite natural. Jenna frowned, confused. The woman named Tess smiled once more, arching her brow wickedly, then walked on in definite possession of her bloke.

All at once Jenna's breath quickened and a warmth began to spread over her, nearly weakening her legs. The sign: "My heart hurts." It was Stolley's gesture of apology, part of the language Jenna and her mute friend had created. How in God's name had a prostitute—?

Jenna was suddenly aware of the bright lamplight on her face, and she made her countenance a blank mask. "Move on ahead," Tess had said. Jenna stiffened her posture and walked on, hoping her face showed nothing more than annoyance. But her heart was beating wildly in her chest. It was a message sent by a man who had seen the gesture only once. One rainy night in Leona's cottage after he had been attacked by Stolley.

Somewhere Ian waited for her.

Jenna concentrated on keeping her pace slow and even. But the sounds of footsteps behind her began immediately. Stiles's hard-soled shoes echoed on the bricks. The giant was slower, with a flat-footed, dirt-grinding step.

She passed two other men. They made no sign, only leered. She walked on, nearing the tavern at the end of the street. Two buildings beyond the pub, policemen were hiding in the shadows of the cross street. How could she get through?

More people passed by her now, locals entering and leaving the pub. Two hundred feet ahead, in the dim light thrown by the pub door, a tall man slouched against the building.

As Jenna drew nearer, her hopes sank. The man was too thin and sinewy to be Ian. He was a chimney sweep, covered with soot, talking heatedly with a shorter man.

Suddenly his fist hit his heart and he opened his hand as if in a shrug and went immediately inside.

Jenna stopped. The end of the street was near. Stiles and the giant were less than a hundred feet behind her. There would be no other chance to reach the pub. Jenna dropped her muff, lifted her skirt and began to run.

She heard Stiles's quick "Bloody hell!" and then nothing but the rapid taps of his heels on the bricks.

Jenna's boot slipped on street filth and she nearly lost her footing. As quickly as she could, she recovered her balance and ran on.

Stiles's shoes clacked faster, closer.

Breathless, she pushed past a couple who had just left the pub. She tore through the door—and was stopped instantly by the crush of the crowd. The tiny tavern was packed.

Then she caught a movement in the corner of her eye. The chimney sweep. To her left. She dashed for him. Outside, the running footsteps of Stiles slowed and she heard his curses as he pushed through the departing customers.

By the time he yanked open the door and rushed in, she was nowhere in sight.

"Where'd she go?" Jenna heard him yelling questions and curses. But she had no idea how people answered.

She had been pulled behind a false wall into a card room full of patrons. And the chimney sweep had her by the arm and was pulling her through at a breakneck pace. She followed without question. They had few precious minutes before Stiles learned her whereabouts.

The sweep stooped down to open a small door and they rushed through to a narrow corridor that led between two buildings. The tight space was damp with rough walls that caught at her shoulders as they bumped and lunged through.

"Faster," the sweep said as they broke into a tiny courtyard, his large hand encircling her wrist.

She could not reply, only gather her skirts higher with one arm and run two strides for one of his past hanging clotheslines, broken furniture, washboards and huge wooden tubs.

They went diagonally across the open space, dashing into a foul-smelling alley, then the sweep stopped so suddenly she collided with his back as he wrenched open a rickety wooden door in the side of the building.

He pulled her through and slipped the bolt on the door. Jenna fell back against a wall, gasping for breath. But the sweep yanked her forward like a doll. "Canna rest yet," he said, the soft Scottish burr vaguely familiar to her. But she had no time to try to recall where she had heard it.

He pulled her along as they careened through small rooms, past a family eating dinner, a cradle with a crying baby, an old man whittling by a lantern. No one stirred except small children whose giggles echoed in Jenna's ears as they tried to join two grown-ups in a game of chase. A woman in a kerchief cap shushed them. " 'Bye, Uncle!" the children called as the sweep and Jenna clattered down narrow stairs to a landing.

They twisted through a small kitchen and the sweep grabbed a flickering lantern before they descended cautiously into the damp blackness of a basement. Their footsteps slowed as they picked their way across the dirt floor, the pungent smell of earth and offal barely noticed as Jenna's cheek caught a thick, sticky mass of spider's web.

A long way into the darkness, the man found the space he

was looking for. Quickly he ducked into an arched stone passageway. He let her hand drop as he bent double so he could move quickly. Jenna stifled a cry. For in the shadows thrown by his lantern dozens of black shapes fanned out ahead of them. Rats. Their frantic scratching echoing in the passageway.

Jenna stopped a moment, paralyzed, as the sweep and the lantern light moved steadily ahead. "Wait," she whispered, but the word was swallowed up by the blackness. She moved one more step but could not breathe.

Thank God, the lantern turned. The sweep's face loomed suddenly in its brightness, startling her, its sooty cover like the suffocating blackness around her. But her eyes, wide and frightened, locked on his. And she recognized him.

"Take ma hand, lass," said Alexander McBryde, the leader of Britain's coal miners. "Ya'll get used t'it."

Her fingers clamped on to his wrist. "If you say so," she choked. Then she bent down to follow on his heels, the quick parting of his smiling lips a sign that there was hope they would emerge soon.

They didn't. The passageway was long. Her back ached. She could only imagine the pain tall McBryde must feel. They passed three forks in the cold stone corridor. "How much further?" she breathed.

He never slowed. "Not far. We've gone a good half block."

At the fourth fork McBryde veered right, scattered the rats and opened a wooden door.

"There's a ladder inside. I'll be right behin' ya."

Jenna went in and nearly bumped into the steep wood steps. Breathless and exasperated by her heavy skirt and layers of petticoat, Jenna quickly reached down and rolled the whole front of her dress, underskirts and all, to her waist.

McBryde's eyes flicked away to protect her modesty.

"You can't climb a ladder looking sideways," Jenna said, short of breath. "And I can't climb it with a sack around my legs."

McBryde smiled as he panted for breath. "I never stop a woman when she's improvisin'."

Jenna stopped after three steps up the ladder, the question preying on her mind. "Is Ian—?

"This is na th' place ta chat, lass. They'll be searchin' the block, house by house. Our only chance is speed."

Jenna climbed higher and higher until her head bumped the ceiling.

"Pound twice," McBryde said.

A trapdoor opened and Jenna welcomed the light and fresh air. But as she was helped up through the little door, the fresh air became a cloud of competing perfumes. And the lantern light showed through the flimsy lingerie of Jenna's two well-endowed helpers.

"Been waitin' for ya," tsked the heavier woman. It was the redheaded Tess, who had relayed Ian's sign language on the street.

"Thank you," Jenna panted to Tess as McBryde hoisted himself up through the floor.

"Don't have ta thank me. Yer fella's payin' so's me and Millie kin start our own business an' get us out o' this bed-bug heaven. C'mon, Alex," she said briskly. "Yer takin' too long to enjoy the view." She adjusted the bodice of her thin gown and started for the door. "Yer clean clothes are over there," she pointed as she rounded the corner. "The young lady comes wi' me."

Jenna hurried to loose her skirt and catch up.

The unadorned hallways of the brothel were thick with smells of cigars, spilled liquor and cheap perfume.

They made their way slowly up narrow stairs. "Where are we?" Jenna asked.

"More'n a block cattycorner from the tavern. On Chilton Circle. Police whistles are blowin' 'ere an' everywhere."

Tess stopped at a dingy door. "Get dressed an' be quick."

She opened the door and both women froze.

A policeman, round hat strapped to his chin, got up slowly from a chair by the open window.

He stood off balance, one leg bent. Jenna nearly cried out with relief. She could not see his eyes under the low brow of the hat, but she knew they were brown. Intense. And on guard even now.

Jenna rushed into Ian's arms.

"Jesus Christ, me bowels sunk 'alfway to me knees," Tess said, palm flat against her bosom. "Next time tell me 'ow in the 'ell yer gettin' past the bobbies."

Jenna heard the door close, a sign that, for the moment, the world was outside. And they were safe.

"You should have gone home," he said, his voice low and soft against her ear.

"I couldn't."

"We have no time," he said quietly, not letting her go, folding himself more tightly around her. "No time."

Finally she pulled away. "You saw a surgeon?"

He shook his head. "No. You must get dressed."

"In what?"

"Your maternity clothes."

The incredulous look on her face would have made him smile if they weren't preparing for a masquerade on which his life depended.

She looked at the clothes laid out on the bed: a large

shapeless dress, a garish hat with long red feathers and a large bustle.

As she undressed, Ian picked up the bustle. "The child." He explained, fitting the rounded bustle low on her stomach and tying it at her waist in the back.

"We're lucky you didn't get the boy," Ian said.

Jenna paused as she was drawing on the shift. "Hutton was there." Her head came through the top and she looked down to button the dress, avoiding Ian's eyes. His hand caught her chin gently and tipped it upward to see the unspoken question on his face.

"He let me go. To bait the trap for you," she said softly.

He released her. There was more to her encounter with Parrish, he knew. There always was. But they had a chance to escape. That was enough to expect for one night. He stepped back from her and donned the policeman's hat.

Tess returned. "Good God, ain't ya ready?"

"I just need the hat—" Jenna began.

"Ya got no rouge, no powder, no color round yer eyes. No good-time girl worth a bob looks like a nun!" Hurriedly Tess applied gaudy enhancements to Jenna's face. "Wouldn't hurt to have a little maternal instinct showin' at the top 'ere, either," Tess said, pulling at the bodice of the shift. "But we're outta time. Alex is waitin'. And fer God sakes"—she flicked the padded bustle—"lean back like ya got a little bastard growin' there."

They went down the backstairs, very slowly, Jenna suddenly aware of how difficult it was for Ian to walk. His limp would be noticed. Unless she and the rest could cover for him.

They met McBryde in a small hallway. He was nattily dressed in an evening coat and top hat. "Congratulations, lassie," he said, nervously patting the bustle. "This'll be a great lark."

"Or a flippin' lynchin'," Tess retorted, hoisting a piece of luggage. "Get on with it."

They went out the back way and around the side of the brothel to the street. As soon as they reached the glare of lamplight, Tess began the commotion.

"Get 'er outta 'ere! 'Er figure's drivin' away me business!" Tess ranted.

Jenna, escorted by Ian, protested tearfully into her handkerchief. McBryde tried to placate both ladies, and Ian in his uniform remained quiet, surveying the street to see how many officers were posted.

One policeman came running up quickly. "You found Stonebridge?" he asked Ian, eyeing McBryde expectantly.

"Hell, no," Ian said roughly. "I found Judge Harcourt's chippie."

"Rude bastard," Jenna said in a common dialect. "The judge loves me. And me babe." Jenna placed a hand protectively over the bustle.

"Then the judge kin 'ave 'er!" Tess cried, throwing the luggage at Jenna's feet. "She can't work! All she does is sit moonie-eyed. Bad for me girls' morale, 'tis. Surely ya understand, officer," Tess walked close to him, the lantern light illuminating the full extent of her own maternal instinct.

Before the young policeman could get his fill of looking, McBryde pushed forward and put a hand on his shoulder. "Officer, I'm Willard Eckmar, solicitor. The good judge called me in to handle this, uh, potentially embarrassing affair." McBryde cleared his throat. "If you know the judge, you'll know he wants this disposed of quickly and, well, sensitively."

The officer nodded. Judge Harcourt was an enterprising jurist who had his fat, rich fingers in quite a few political pies. As a matter of fact, he had signed the warrant for the dueling baronet's arrest. But that didn't matter. What mattered to the officer was to get this matter out of his jurisdiction.

"If you could just call a hackney, we'll take the young lady to my chambers and settle this," McBryde said.

The policeman glanced at Ian. "What division are you with?" he asked.

"Hampton Court, on detached duty for tonight," Ian said quietly, glancing at the pregnant chippie so ominously that the young officer shivered.

"Of course," he said. Then blew his whistle three short blasts and waved a carriage through the police blockade up the street.

The coach pulled up quickly. Tess drew the officer's attention just as Ian prepared to maneuver up the vehicle's steps.

But another policeman, curious, came around the side of the coach and held the door.

"Evening." McBryde tried to catch his eye.

The policeman's gaze was on Ian and the nice little piece of used goods he had inside the coach. Without hesitating, Ian nodded curtly, then entered the coach, balancing his step as normally as he could.

The pressure forced the gash open and new bleeding began at the edges of the badly swollen flesh. Ian held back a gasp and took his seat.

McBryde jumped in, signaled the driver and began chatting loudly to calm the pregnant woman. He kept up a nervous, one-sided conversation until they were well past the blockade.

Jenna, exhausted, was oblivious. She sat silently, watching the intermittent light of the street lanterns play on Ian's strained, pale face.

" 'Tis safe to change now," McBryde said softly.

Grimly Ian began to unbutton the jacket of the uniform. McBryde opened the bag and drew out a common coat, vest, a shirt and trousers. Ian shook his head. "Just coat and shirt," he said, grimacing as he pulled his arms out of the jacket sleeves.

Jenna bit back a cry as lamplight slanted across Ian's shirtfront. It was dark with dried blood.

"Ian, ya bloody fool! I thought ya saw the doctor," McBryde said.

"No time." Ian unbuttoned the shirt to check the thin wad of bandages he had applied to his chest after the Haymarket barber quickly stitched his leg. "I'm just lucky you were home and had your wits about you."

"And fortunate that Parrish thinks I'm still in his pocket," McBryde said grimly, wincing in sympathy as Ian tugged the dried shirtfront away from his bloody bandages.

"He's countin' on me to help him stage a riot of Glencur unionists tomorra' night. But the bastard's gonna be surprised. My boys'll be there to set things straight." McBryde helped Ian pull off the shirt.

"I only hope we can keep the lid on the rally. One more day. We've got the votes. Just have to hold on to 'em," the union leader sighed, slipping Ian's arm through the clean shirt. "Yer awful quiet, lass." McBryde smiled suddenly at Jenna.

"Being with child is tiresome." She looked at Ian.

"You'll need the disguise only till we board the boat at the docks," Ian said, slowly settling sideways on the seat and gingerly placing his leg up. "We'll steam upriver till dawn. They won't alert the train stations outside London. I hope."

Jenna's eyes closed with relief. They were going home.

"Damn but yer a lucky devil." McBryde leaned his head back against the seat and relaxed. "Survive a flippin' sword fight, slip out and thumb yer the nose at half the police force and take yer leave with the prettiest little quick-wit I ever escorted through the sewers."

He looked across at Ian and Jenna. Neither was smiling.

Ian was concentrating on the fire that burned along the length of his leg. Infection would set in tonight. After Jenna was home safe, he would get Betts to put her island medicines to work.

Jenna was gazing intently at Ian's profile, aware of the sweat beads forming at his temple. Absently she rubbed her clammy palm across the empty cage that covered her abdomen.

McBryde debarked on a Piccadilly corner. The coach pulled away and Ian reached down into the bag and pulled out a thonged leather belt. She watched him sling it over his right shoulder and secure it under his left arm. Puzzled, she looked deeper into the bag. Slowly she pulled out the pistol.

He took it from her without a word and slipped its nose snugly into the thongs.

"I could have killed him this morning," Ian said, not looking at her. "And I didn't."

"He's your father. The reason you were born."

"Blood is the only thing that links us," Ian said. "He drew a good taste of it today."

Chapter 23

The steamboat captain, Henry Hawks, was a shipmate from Ian's privateering days. He secreted them swiftly to a cabin belowdeck and then weighed anchor.

"Do you have a surgeon on board?" Jenna asked, shedding the bulky bustle.

"No." The lanky seaman watched Ian ease himself carefully onto the tiny bunk. "Could find you some food, though."

"And a basin of water," Jenna said. "That would help."

His fingers tapped his knit cap in deference and he left.

"So"—Ian gave a small smile—"you're going to remove my trousers whether I like it or not."

"You need new bandages," Jenna said, lifting her skirt and slipping a full petticoat down to her feet.

"If I were in better shape, I would ask you to donate more," he said, wincing as he used both hands to lift his leg upward. "As it is," he hissed a short breath, "I'll be satisfied with Henry."

"Ian—"

"Go topside," he said, unbuttoning his pants. "Get some air—"

Ian stopped and closed his eyes, then breathed out slowly as the spasm eased.

"I can help." Her voice was soft, nearly pleading.

"Not this time." He shook his head. "Not always."

She gave him a strange look, as if she were humoring a fool. Then she left the room.

He lay on the small, hard bunk, alone with his pain. The one in his chest was the worst. It was fear: fear that there would come a time when neither would be able to help the other.

Thank God, Leona's cottage was in view.

Jenna drew back from the coach window and glanced at Ian's ashen face. The pony-cart ride from Ribchester had taken its toll. Silent and sweating with fever, Ian gripped the cart's side and the edge of the narrow seat, steadying himself against the constant jerking.

They had not talked since getting off the train at Ribchester's small station.

"You should see the doctor here," Jenna had said, steadying Ian as he stepped down from the train.

"Betts can stitch it. She makes an ointment."

"But—"

Ian's warning hand on her arm cut off her words. Far down the row of train cars, a thin man in a broad hat was watching passengers crisscross the platform in front of him. He leaned against the wall of the station, the casual, slouching fold of his body still fresh in Jenna's memory.

Stiles.

Ian and Jenna stopped and turned to one another as if in a discussion. "Find someone to drive us," Ian said, reaching inside his coat. Jenna tensed, but instead of the pistol, he drew out a wad of bills.

They had turned then and joined a group of people heading in the direction opposite Stiles. The tightness in Ian's jaw was visible. His limp made him a marked man.

Jenna prevailed on a farmer to give them a lift. Fortunately he was not talkative, and Jenna and Ian were able to sit in silence. And long past teatime, close to dusk, the cart halted before Leona's cottage.

"We'll stop here. Stonebridge Hall is an hour further. I'll send Stolley to bring Betts," Jenna said.

She expected a protest. He was silent, as if the decision were a crucial one. Grimly he nodded, his eyes glossy with fever.

Stolley came running up to the cart. His smile at seeing Jenna needed no words. She hugged him tightly and then gently clasped his hands in front of him to keep them from flying in long-delayed conversation.

"Ian is hurt," she signed.

Stolley helped Ian out of the cart, but then was pushed away gently. Slowly Ian advanced to the door of the cottage. The farmer drove away quickly, his face a suspicious mask of unasked questions.

In the door frame, Leona waited, reading Jenna's hands as she signed to Stolley news of the duel and the mine act.

Jenna stepped up to face Leona, the grief of Carolina's death etched in taut lines around the older woman's eyes. Jenna had no words for her. She reached out to embrace her friend, and Jenna found herself clasped to Leona's firm, strong frame. That, at least, would never change. Leona was a rock on which they all depended.

"Have you heard from Father?" Jenna asked as Ian made his way to a straight-backed chair by the hearth.

"No. But the miners are saying the earl will attend their rally tonight." Leona set water to boil on the stove.

Jenna placed a footstool under Ian's injured leg. Slowly she eased his arms out of his coat and vest.

She began to slip off the leather sling that held the pistol, but his hand stopped her. "Leave it close," he said, his voice tight, his mind on the fire in his leg.

She lay it on a nearby chair behind him. Then she began to remove his shirt.

He welcomed each accidental brush of her fingers on his skin. For each small touch connected him with a world two days past, so far away from them now. Her hair, loosened by rough travel, swung cool against his cheek as she leaned over to pull away his shirt. His fevered awareness magnified her nearness, her careful ministrations, into hopes they could recreate the time at Sarbin's Crown. But his rational mind smiled on the fantasy. Fear and a new maturity had settled on them both. Nothing could ever be the same.

Ian's makeshift bandages were soaked through. With a basin of clean water Jenna sponged them away from the shallow chest wound that ran from navel to shoulder. He was so hot. She dabbed the cool water over his neck, his shoulders, smoothing the wetness across his chest and along his back.

Leona talked quietly as she readied fresh bandages, scissor and clean water. There were fears the miners would grow wild tonight, impatient with the hardships of the strike, she said. "The older ones say the Red Bow will come to stop the hotheads and give everyone money for food," Leona said.

"Not tonight," Jenna said softly, pausing as Leona knelt beside Ian's leg.

"The Grawlin children came back," Leona said, gently snipping along the calf of Ian's trousers. "They live in your basement at Glen Manor most of the time. I buy the coal they scavenge. Cook feeds them well." Carefully Leona peeled back the material, exposing the lower portion of the gash that started at his ankle. "Phillip never returned from London. And Mrs. Searle—" Leona could tear no farther than halfway up his calf. The material was stuck to the oozing wound. "Mrs. Searle has been more of a grand lady than a housekeeper since you've gone." She dipped a clean rag in the warm water and began to soften the packed mass.

Jenna was not listening to the low-toned monologue. She signed for Stolley to bring a lantern nearer. As Leona gently cleaned, Jenna bit back a gasp at the extent of the damage caused by Parrish's blade.

The gash ran deep along the side of Ian's leg, nicking close to the bone at the knee, exposing a large, protruding layer of muscle and flesh in Ian's lower thigh.

The edge of the wound was red, inflamed, wet with the fluid of severed tissue underneath.

"This will take a doctor's skill," Leona said.

"It cannot wait," Ian said. "Bathe it in a solution of warm water and salt."

"You can't be serious," Leona said. "Salt—"

"Will keep it clean. We don't have time to argue."

"Will you need whiskey?" Leona asked as she mixed the salt and water in a brown jar.

"No, goddammit. I'm groggy enough," Ian said. "I can't—"

There was a crunch of wheels outside, close to the door.

With a guttural cry Ian swung his leg off the chair, upsetting the basin with a clatter. He dived for the pistol that hung on the chair out of reach just as the door burst open.

The rifle blast was thunderous in the low-ceilinged cabin. Pottery shook in the cupboard and the jar of cleansing salt water fell from Leona's hands in a shatter of wet glass.

Ian slumped to the floor, his left arm beginning to stream with fresh blood.

"No!" Jenna cried as she saw Stiles in the doorway, rifle cocked to fire again, his mouth a gap-toothed smile. Jenna turned to rush to Ian, but she stopped. Stolley, standing closest to the pistol, was leaping to grab the gun and draw Stiles's fire. Jenna lunged in front of Stolley as another blast sounded, and they both fell to the floor.

Stolley got up slowly. He helped Jenna to her feet. Stunned and hardly breathing, she felt nothing more painful than the pounding of her heart. When she turned, she saw why.

Hutton Parrish had entered just after Stiles, pushing the rifle barrel toward the ceiling so that the shot went wild.

"For God's sake, save gallantry for the men," he said tersely, a pistol in one hand.

With his hand still on the rifle, Hutton turned to his foreman. "If you ever cause the slightest blemish to that woman, Lindstrom will stuff your bowels and your brains into wholly different places."

Stiles didn't move, but a strange, cautious look settled on his face.

Hutton stepped forward and grabbed Ian's pistol from the chair, tossing the weapon to Stiles. Then he shook his head and sat down, smiling as Ian slowly crawled to the cold stone hearth and leaned exhausted there, facing Hutton. The new wound dripped new paths of blood through his fingers and across his bared chest.

"You're looking the worse for wear, my friend." Hutton pursed his lips. "Drop by drop, piece by piece you're leaving her to me. It must be frustrating."

Ian was silent, dark hair on his forehead screening his fevered eyes against the older man's insight.

"This has all been quite educational. I find, in my maturity, that I don't need worthy foes. It has made me appreciate the safety of being surrounded by mediocrity," Hutton smiled. "But I do respect your abilities. And I will reward you with a quick death." He rose and walked toward Jenna.

"But first I require some small retribution." Hutton stopped before Jenna. "For I cannot forgive you for winning the prize so early in the game."

"Leave him here," Jenna said quietly. "Leave them all. And I will go with you."

Dear God, that voice, he thought. And the honest, anguished promise in it. The muscles high inside his thighs twitched in readiness for the tightening that would come. He moved away from her to control it.

"I wish it were that easy. But, you see, you have also played me for a fool. And I must teach you not to do that." His boots thumped hollowly as he walked back to Stiles.

"At this moment the miners are rallying, sickening in their unity. Because McBryde lied to me. He told me he could be bought. And he couldn't." Hutton reached into Stiles's pocket and withdrew a broad, sheathed knife.

"What's worse, I find that a copy of Shadow Glen's ledger has been ferried to McBryde. By you, my dear. Each ton of Thornton coal carefully documented. It makes for a damning case I hadn't counted on defending. That's not your fault, of course," he smiled, withdrawing the beveled blade of the hunting knife.

"It's Stiles's fault." He turned casually to his foreman, the knife angled up in his palm. "He neglected to tell me his copy was missing."

Stiles stepped back.

"Work well tonight, Stiles, and I may tolerate your stupidity. Lindstrom!" Hutton called.

The huge man appeared in the doorway.

"Build a fire for us."

The Swede went to the fireplace, reached down and grasped Ian by his wounded arm and pulled him up slowly. Nerve endings screaming, Ian grimaced and grabbed for the giant's face with his free hand, fingers pressing quickly, expertly into the eye sockets.

Lindstrom yelled and flung Ian away like a toy. Ian crashed against a chair, then tumbled to the floor, with the Swede lumbering toward him like an enraged bear.

With an unintelligible cry Stolley leaped atop the Swede as the huge man stomped his foot into Ian's belly. Stolley was shaken off, tearing the Swede's coat sleeve.

Just as Stolley was thrown free, a dull thwack sounded in the giant's skull. He turned in surprise. Jenna had swung a leg from the broken chair against the back of his neck. Lindstrom reached for her.

Then a pistol cracked in warning.

"Goddamn every one of you!" Hutton shouted.

"You!" He pointed to Leona. "Control this idiot pup or your precious Ethan goes to a poorhouse." Hutton nodded at Stiles and the foreman herded Leona and Stolley to the door.

Hutton stepped forward, poking the double-barreled pistol under Lindstrom's chin. "So help me God, if you kill this man before I give the word, the miners will be told who killed their plucky little Bilpo Grawlin. And your carcass won't be worth a slag heap in any mine in England."

Then Hutton advanced on Jenna. "And you"—he tilted her defiant chin higher to keep her eyes on his—"if you put your lovely skin in jeopardy one more time, I will burn your precious Leona alive," he promised softly.

"Don't bother," Jenna hissed. "It is hell enough for us all just to be in your presence."

Hutton smiled at her vehemence. "You'll find hate is as blind a force as passion, my love. I can guide it in any direction I choose." His hand grasped hers and pulled it up to his face, her fingers trembling to pull away at first, then acceding to the pressure. Slowly he pressed them to the angry red scar Ian's sword had left in his cheek. He guided her fingers lightly along the ridge of the shallow wound, down to his mouth.

She felt his lips grasp her fingertips, his tongue skim them lightly. She recoiled.

"We can all be hurt," he said softly. "But we recover." He forced the flat of her hand lower, across his chest, his stomach, to the source of his throbbing pain.

She immediately swung her hand to his face. But he intercepted her arm with his pistol.

"Lindstrom," he said. "Find our friend a seat so that he will have a clear view." Then he threw the pistol to the Swede and stepped back, loosening his tie, removing his coat. The sheathed knife lay snug in the waistband of his pants.

Ian lay doubled over on the floor. He had tried to roll with the kick to his midsection. But the bile in his throat told him his reflexes hadn't been fast enough.

Lindstrom yanked him upright. Ian struggled for footing as the Swede tied his hands behind his back and pushed him onto a chair.

"The fire," Hutton reminded. "The lady will be cold."

As Lindstrom broke kindling, Hutton drew the knife and approached Jenna.

Ian could not trust his voice to speak, nor his eyes to meet Jenna's.

Hutton placed the knife point at the neck of Jenna's gown.

Ian jerked forward, wiling his leg to take the weight. But

Lindstrom grabbed the rope that bound his wrists and pulled him back with a force that sent new lines of pain shooting down his arm and across his chest.

Slowly the blade descended, parting Jenna's gown to the waist, exposing the simple white chemise underneath.

"Parrish!" Ian choked.

"You'll disturb my concentration," Hutton said quietly as the knife continued downward, carefully, past her abdomen, down to the floor.

She had not moved.

Hutton stepped behind her then and with one hand slipped the gown off her arms like an evening coat.

The fire had caught hold and flames rose high, flickering across her bared skin, the hollows and folds of her white chemise and pantalets cast in shadows.

Hutton stepped forward to nick the straps of the light cotton top. But Jenna's soft voice stopped him.

"Enough."

Hutton stepped back. "Then you continue, my dear."

She felt all eyes on her as she slowly unbuttoned the chemise. One young, full breast, then the other, emerged in the firelight, her pale areolas constricted in the chill air, her small, fine nipples erect.

At first Hutton was transfixed. What a natural beauty she was. But it was not her firm breasts that mesmerized him, or the graceful line of her neck or the vulnerable slant of her waist where the white band of the pantalet hugged softly.

No. It was the way she stood. Unashamed. Not defiant, not proud. She met degradation with amazing serenity.

Then a dark frown knitted the white eyebrows of the viscount as he realized why. Her self-possession came from a prior possession. Jenna was undressing for the bastard.

Her eyes had not wavered from Ian's. The very air between them seemed warm with a strange current of intimacy. The fire had begun to crackle soothingly and lent a bizarre coziness to the message understood only by them.

Disturbed, Hutton stepped in front of her.

Jenna's eyes fell on Hutton then. "There is no one else," she said softly. "No matter what happens."

Hutton pressed the knife blade flat against the mound of her breast, near the tip. "I have a gift for making common acts feel new and real, my love. Do not dismiss me yet," he said, watching her nipple tense harder at the cold threat.

"You know nothing new." She bent her head to look at the metal blade that indented the smooth whiteness around it. "Rape is ancient. So are your methods." Her voice was quiet.

Something in her certainty disturbed Hutton.

"It takes two people to create passion," she said softly. "You will be alone. Always."

Hutton began to tremble, the knife edge vibrating hard against her flesh.

"You're ruining your chance, Parrish!" Ian's voice was low-toned but urgent, aware of the madness that gripped the man with the knife. "Just as you did with my mother."

Hutton whipped the knife away from Jenna and began to advance on Ian. "You dark Norman bastard. You've haunted me almost as much as your mother has. She was the only woman I ever cared for. The only one worthy. If she had not spread her wealth so generously, you would have sprung from me!"

The knife gleamed closer. "Dear, unmerciful God. I did," Ian whispered.

Hutton's hand cracked across his face with a sound that seemed to stay in the air between them. "You lie." Hutton's eyes twitched.

Ian shook his head, trying to clear the fog. Blood dripped from inside his cheek. "She was an adulteress only once," Ian whispered. "With you. It was more than enough for her."

The hand lashed his face again.

"The birth records! Your age!" Hutton seethed.

Jenna's voice came anguished into Ian's fog. "Ariel staged an elaborate lie. She wanted to protect Ian."

Hutton grabbed a fistful of Ian's hair and jerked his head back, searching for signs. The bastard's eyes had always been Ariel's. And they looked at him now, fiery with outrage, just as Ariel's had when she closed the door on his pleas.

But there were subtle clues. The shape of the forehead, the turn of the mouth. Hutton let the flat of the knife rest there on Ian's lips as he scanned the rest. His bones, the broad, solid build that Hutton would have had with an active life at sea.

He removed the knife and released Ian's head with disgust. Dear God, he could have had this instead of a pallid slug like Connell to carry on the Parrish name.

But he had moved too fast. Repaid Ariel for her rejection. And now he found he had missed thirty years of building an empire no one could equal. With a son like Stonebridge, he could have had the combined wealth and power of both houses.

Damn! He ran his fingers through his hair and shook his head.

"It is a sign," Ian said with difficulty.

"Of what?"

"Of how careful you must be this time," Ian said, dazed, praying that he could buy Jenna some time. That she would not be treated as Carolina had. "You cannot hurt Jenna. She is your chance to begin again."

Hutton stepped close to Jenna, flinging a lock of her dark hair over her shoulder so it would not cover her breast. "But what if she carries *your* beginning!" Hutton shouted, grasping Jenna's pantalets by the waist and slicing the material to the crotch. "What if your seed is sown here." He placed his hand flat against her abdomen, low, so that he could feel the soft borderline of her hair.

Before Ian could move, Lindstrom's hand yanked cruelly on the rope binding Ian's hands.

Hutton could feel Jenna's whole body tense. But she remained still, so icy still. She knew Hutton was eager for her to struggle.

"If Jenna carries my child," Ian said carefully his eyes locked on the viscount's hand, willing it not to move lower, "you have no better heir."

Hutton's eyes tightened in warning.

"I carry two legacies. Yours. And Ariel's. Perhaps, this time, you will have a link to Ariel that you can live with."

Unexpectedly Hutton removed his hand and turned to Ian.

"She should have told me," Hutton said softly. "It could have been different."

All he could see reflected in the bastard's dark eyes was the glint of firelight off the blade in his hand.

"Then again, perhaps not." Hutton pursed his lips thoughtfully. He turned and tilted Jenna's face to the firelight. He could see his trespass still burning in her face.

"I won't make you stay for the rest," Hutton said to Ian, his thumb slowly stroking Jenna's chin.

Hutton turned to Lindstrom. "Take him now."

The Swede pulled Ian to his feet. Ian stumbled, leaning against him as he walked.

"Where will you take him?" The words came out unevenly as Jenna struggled to stay calm.

"To the mine portal. Then he will be lowered into the pit. Alive. He must be able to think there in the blackest dark God makes. To speculate on what I am doing. Then, when Stiles arrives with the explosives, Sir Ian Stonebridge will die a quick and fiery death. But no one will know," Hutton smiled. "For I am paying to have you 'sighted' at regular intervals all around the world. Your brother will never inherit your estate. And it will give me plenty of time to find a way to call Stonebridge Hall due on its mortgage."

Ian stopped at the door, holding on to the frame.

"A remarkable study in revenge, is it not?" Hutton said.

"Thorough." Ian's breath came in uneven bursts.

"No more so than yours, my son." Hutton gave a mock bow.

"The same hell—awaits you," Ian said, his eyes strangely bright.

"Not tonight," Hutton whispered.

Ian breathed deeply and gathered his strength. For it took every ounce of his willpower to look at Jenna then. He could not have left her more vulnerable. There was nothing for them to say, no words he would let the monster savor. Slowly he tightened his bloodied hand into a fist, tapped his heart once and opened his hand.

He left.

Her heart was so still she felt cold as ice. Neither she nor Hutton moved. She heard the sounds of boots scuffling against the dirt, the soft thump as Lindstrom placed Ian in the wagon, the light metal song of the harnesses as the horses fidgeted, the crack of the whip as Lindstrom yelled "Haw!" the raw, final scraping of the wheels as they left the rocks in the yard behind.

Breathing was an effort for her.

Taking advantage of her stillness, Hutton sat down and took off his boots. Then he unbuttoned his pants and slipped them off. His shirt hung to his knees like a nightshirt. As he began to unbutton it, she backed away, stepping closer to the fire.

She picked up a long, black iron poker from the hearth.

"We can fight, if that is what you wish," he said.

"What I wish is not possible," she said, her voice breaking.

A sudden scratch against the house. Outside the window.

"Stiles?" Hutton called.

No answer.

Warily, Hutton went to the door and looked out. He backed up immediately, the cold end of a long-barreled shotgun in his stomach.

"Get back." A man in black pressed steadily forward until Hutton's back was against the wall. The voice, soft, vaguely familiar, was muffled under the black executioner's hood of the Red Bow Bandit.

"Stonebridge?" Hutton was incredulous.

"No. Guess again, you slimy scum of Satan."

Jenna stifled a cry of joy. Father.

"Find some clothes," he told Jenna softly.

She ran past Hutton and pulled Leona's nightgown off a hook on the wall. The garment slipped cleanly over her head. As she lifted her hair from under its neck, the gun blast sounded. Jenna screamed and turned.

Hutton doubled over with a rough, startled cry. The Earl had fired point-blank into Hutton's belly. Without warning.

"Bleed long and well." The earl removed his hood so Hutton could see his face.

Hutton gasped, but could not speak. His face was a gri-macing mask.

"Father!" Jenna ran to him. She hugged him so tightly her arms ached from the strain. The tears began as she smoothed his gray frizzled hair back from his ears. "Thank God you came," she whispered.

"A doctor," Hutton choked, twitching on his side, his fingers grasping at slippery masses escaping from the wound.

Jenna squeezed her eyes shut so she would not see the growing pool of blood that was beginning to stream over the floorboards toward the door.

"Sshhh. You are safe now. Finally." The earl's voice was soothing. But strangely detached. Even as he stroked her hair, she felt a chill of unreality. "I knew I could save you, Charlotte. He did not touch you, did he?"

"Father?" Jenna drew back.

He grabbed her shoulders. "Did he?"

Horrified, Jenna shook her head.

"Thank God." He hugged her tight. "I knew I would arrive in time. I have saved the mine act, too. How the miners cheered me tonight. I played the Bandit. And they cheered. Hutton has lost. The mine act will be law."

"Yes," Jenna choked.

"But all I ever wanted was to make you safe, Char—"

There was the crack of a rifle. Without knowing it, Jenna screamed. Her father was thrown forward against her, the bullet entering his back high.

She fell to the floor with him, welcoming the black oblivion.

Stiles rushed over to the fallen Bandit and rolled him over. "God damn!" he spat. It wasn't Stonebridge. He had killed the bloomin' earl. If the miners ever found out, they'd string him to a tree.

"Stiles—" Hutton's voice was high-pitched, wild, like the squeak of a kitten about to be drowned.

The stench of bile and half-digested food made Stiles wrinkle his nose. "Ain't nothing to help you now, you twisted son of a bitch. 'E blew the guts right outta ya."

"The gun! Quick!" Hutton squealed, crawling madly toward Stiles.

The foreman stepped back in disgust. "No bullets to waste on a man who wanted to slit my gullet."

"No," Hutton croaked, turning to his back as he pressed two hands to his wound, trying to hold in the entrails and wet tissue behind his fingers. "Don't—leave," Hutton gurgled.

"Ya left me a goddamn mess 'ere!" Stiles shouted as he threw the limp body of Jenna over his shoulder. "Yer such a smart bluenose toff. Patch things up, yer own bloody self."

Stiles trod out into the night. Near the cottage, a donkey brayed a raucous request to be unharnessed from Stolley's cart. "Noisy bastard!" Stiles spat as he lay Jenna roughly on the dirty wooden cartbed.

"C'mere," Stiles said, as he jerked the earl's tall gray stallion across the yard. "I always wanted me a decent animal to mount." He smiled and tied the gray's bridle to the black rail of the little wagon.

Inside the cottage, Hutton racked his mind as his teeth clenched tightly. The barn, he thought. Leona. Stolley. Inch by gasping inch, Hutton crawled to the door. At the threshold he hesitated, then bit his lip and slid forward, screaming as his body raked over the two steps.

The ground was cold against his face, a small hill of dirt mounted at the corner of his mouth. He could taste the grit.

Raising himself on one elbow, he began to claw his way toward the barn. He kept one hand over the hole in his belly, but parts of him still slid out. Minutes passed. He could not keep the pain at bay so he howled with it, keeping up an anguished rhythm.

Ten feet from the barn. Only ten feet.

The scratching came from the darkness to his right. Then closer. Light crackling as claws roved the brush beyond the barn.

He swallowed the blood that gurgled in his throat and inched forward, aware of the wet sniffing noises in the air.

Then one growled.

Wild dogs.

He groped blindly for a rock to throw. The growls grew deeper, longer. He could see them now. Yellow eyes glowing in the light of the full moon. Their noses quivering with the scent of blood and flesh.

"No," he whispered, grasping for the grimy masses that now trailed down his leg.

The dogs, wild whelps of a mixed-breed mastiff, had roamed far and were hungry. The slick bloody scent was too strong. They could not wait for the animal to die.

Hutton screamed as they descended on him. Mercifully, the pack leader's fangs closed on his throat. And the noise died.

One by one the sated dogs pulled away. They regrouped in a pack on the moor, licking each other's muzzles, grooming themselves clean.

A mile down the cart path from Leona's cottage, Ian's head jostled in the straw that pillowed it, a new bruise swelling on his cheekbone. He could only smile inwardly. For he had heard the shots.

And he had seen the dark shadows creeping alongside the house. It had only taken a small pool of spittle landing on Lindstrom's face to keep the giant occupied, unaware of the intruder.

He could sleep now. The Red Bow had come.

Chapter 24

The wagon creaked to a stop on a slope near the mine portal. Ian awoke fuzzily to an eerie weightless feeling as his body slid down toward the end of the wagon bed. He tensed to stop the slide, then quickly closed his eyes again, feigning sleep. He had glimpsed the open moonlit sky, the stars ghostly pinpricks in a vast fabric. Crickets trilled loudly in the coolness.

Ian felt the raw thump of the wooden brake setting its stop against the wheel. Then the wagon dipped to one side as Lindstrom stepped over the back of the seat and onto the wagon bed.

Ian lay dead still, his hands still tied, consciously relaxing to lessen the impact of the blow he expected. The Swede hovered. Ian could smell the stench of his rotting teeth and the vague sour-sweetness of ale drunk early in the day.

"Bloody bastard. Wake up!" Lindstrom shouted. His massive hand encircled Ian's neck and raised the limp torso off the wagon bed.

A sound from the other side of the hill made the Swede pause. The uneven rumble of wagon wheels grew louder. Lindstrom dropped Ian quickly and climbed over the seat, rummaging on the floorboard for the pistol.

"It's me!" Stiles's voice yelled. "It's me! We got a change 'o plans."

Ian lay still, one side of his face in the stiff straw, unable to turn his head. He heard a rickety, wooden cart draw up next to Lindstrom's wagon. A testy whinny and snort came from the back of the cart. An unharnessed horse. If I'm lucky, Ian thought, the animal will also be lacking a rider. And God knew it was time for his luck to turn.

As Stiles talked to Lindstrom, Ian learned it was the earl who had stalked in the Red Bow's disguise tonight. And that he was dead. But the earl had left Parrish doubled on the floor, a point-blank belly wound streaming blood and slippery entrails.

"The ole bugger screamed for me to kill 'im," Stiles said. "I tole him a man with no guts can't give me orders!"

Stiles guffawed. But Lindstrom remained silent. And Ian sensed the tension between them.

"We do it like 'is lordship said." Lindstrom's voice was slow and rough. "We put 'im in the pit."

"You stupi—" Stiles's words were cut off. Ian could hear the foreman choking for air.

"We put 'im in the pit," Lindstrom said again.

After a while Stiles's voice came again, hoarse. And much quieter. "I got the girl with me. She's all passed out. Pretty as an angel."

Ian's heart beat faster and his senses sharpened.

"Connell wants 'er," Stiles said. "He'll pay good money. 'Specially when 'e finds out the ole devil didn't have time to wet 'is whistle."

Thank God. Ian's face tightened in a grimace of relief.

Lindstrom's voice was rough, decisive. "First we get rid of the bastard. Help me bring up the basket. Then we'll rouse 'im."

As they walked away, Ian could hear Stiles's grainy voice speculating on how much Connell would pay. The voice receded. Then a screech rent the quiet night as metal gears grated against one another. Lindstrom was twisting the winch that raised the elevator basket to the top of the portal.

As soon as the rumble began, Ian raised himself up cautiously.

They were in a clearing of squat sheds and scattered pieces of wood and rail. Two hundred feet from the wagons, the tall, skeletal frame of the pulley rose over the mouth of the pit.

Ian could see Lindstrom, his back to the wagon, methodically grip and pull the line, the earsplitting noise as welcome a cover as cannon fire. Stiles stood peering down the shaft.

Ian eased himself off the lip of the wagon. The moonlight showed him a nearby pile of broken tools. He had to inch his way. His leg had stiffened badly. He spotted the head of a pickax and lowered himself beside it, rubbing and pricking at the rope that bound his hands. Soon the cord gave way. As he rubbed life back into his numbed wrists, he scanned the mine site for possibilities. A storage shed sat fifteen feet from the wagons. He carried the sharp, heavy ax head with him as he explored.

He found a large black bucket half filled with carbide rocks near the outside wall of the shack. He went inside, feeling his way through the darkness, his fingers roaming lengths of rope, bags of rusty iron nails and piles of wood. He quickly grabbed two bags of nails. If the gray horse was carrying a canteen, they had a chance. He could—

There was movement near the wagons. A flash of white caught the corner of his eye.

Jenna.

* * *

As silently as she could, Jenna inched her way out of the old wood cart, twigs and swatches of bark snagging at her gown. Her father's gray stallion was tied to the back of the cart. The animal calmly nosed in the crevices of the flatbed as Jenna eased past. She gathered the long skirt of Leona's nightgown over one arm and crept quickly over to the straw-packed bed of the neighboring wagon.

But there were only dark stains in the light straw. Jenna grimaced and bit back a moan. Dear God, she had counted on Ian being here.

She knew she had to go for help. The miners of Glencur would be home for the rally by now. She would ride to the mine camp. Carefully she ducked back along the slatted side of the wagon and moved across to the cart. The stallion was pawing nervously at her quick movements. She reached up to stroke his neck as her fingers worked frantically to free the reins. Then a silent cry welled deep in her, driving her heartbeat faster.

Ian.

Instantly she cupped her hand across Ian's and pressed it hard against her mouth. She felt its warmth, smelled its heady musk of dried blood, sweet straw. Gently he pulled her head back against him and she turned her cheek to brush the bare heat of his chest. Still fevered. Still alive.

He whispered close to her ear, his face pressed against the soft cushion of her hair. "We have a chance, my love. If we're quick."

She nodded and pulled his hand away as she turned. Her face spoke silently of a night filled with sadness.

"Your father is dead," he said softly.

She looked down at the bloodstains on the white nightgown she wore.

"Check the horse's saddlebags for a canteen and matches," Ian said. "Those buckets." He pointed to the shack. "They're carbide."

Jenna remembered her father's warning about the mineral when she was a girl. Carbide was used to fuel the miners' lanterns. The carbon rocks oozed a volatile gas when mixed with water.

She could not take her eyes from Ian. He had sunk back against the wagon wheel, his breath uneven.

"You will not die," she said to him, her face pale but confident.

He was too drained to smile. He could only concentrate on the sight of her. Her hair tangled wild as a woodland gypsy, her eyes demanding an answer, her gown wrapped tightly around the curves of her body so it would not billow and be seen. Somehow she had remained untouched by the worst of Parrish's madness. Was that not a sign there was a future for them both?

Ian pushed himself upright.

Her hand rested one moment on his chest, a touch that left a sweet mark of coolness on his warm skin. He turned and scooped an armful of straw from the wagon bed and gestured for Jenna to do likewise when she finished rifling the saddlebags.

Then he limped to the storage shed in rhythm to the wail of the pulley.

Quickly he pried the lid off a large tin bucket and dumped in the loose nails he had scavenged. All but two. Then he tamped the lid tightly back in place. He used the flat side of the ax head to drive a nail hole in the top and the bottom of the bucket.

Ian placed the bucket on a small pile of rocks so it was raised off the ground. Underneath he placed handfuls of straw. Jenna brought more, and he made a long, curving trail of the dry grass from the bucket to the other side of the shed.

"There's water. A little." Jenna shook the canteen she held.

"A match?"

Jenna opened a small pouch. Tears stung as she withdrew her father's cherrywood pipe and a tiny cloth bundle containing two matches.

"There were no weapons? A crossbow?"

She shook her head.

"Get the horse. Then release the brakes on the wagons." She nodded and hurried away.

Quickly Ian set the canteen upside down on the bucket so the water trickled through the nail hole. When it was drained, he plugged the top hole with a nail and the one underneath with a twist of grass.

Thank God the pulley still screeched. In a few minutes the gas would build inside the can.

He waited. Hurry, Jenna, he thought. It was nearly time to set the fire. He looked for her. She was walking slowly, upright, leading a horse across the stretch of rock-strewn ground toward him. Her white gown billowed.

Why would she—?

Quickly he belly-crawled into the shadows around the back of the shed.

"Come out, Stonebridge. Or she gets a bloody taste of what I gave you." It was Stiles's voice.

Ian didn't move. Stiles would need Jenna unhurt in order to bargain with Connell.

"He's barely alive," Jenna said loudly to Stiles. He was following closely. She let the reins drop so that she and Stiles walked clear of the animal. "Your friend was thorough."

"'Alf-dead men don't build firetraps, now, do they?" Stiles gestured at the trail of straw and the carbide bucket.

"You idiot, I did it," Jenna said, walking on slowly, leading him past the corner of the shed.

"Hold it here, Miss High-and-mighty." Stiles grabbed her hair and yanked her backward against him. "It's bad manners to lie to a man holdin' a gun to yer back."

"Keep me alive or you're a dead man," she hissed.

"What da ya mean?" he said, pulling harder.

She would not answer. Gradually he released his hold and she stepped away from him, glad to be clear of his stench. His clothes were rank with a winter's worth of sweat and coal grime.

"The miners are on their way here," she lied. "They know you helped kill Bilpo. You are the dog who licked Parrish boots and shorted the miners their pay. They will tear at you, Stiles until you're nothing but chunks the size of coal nuggets." She stepped backward slowly as she talked.

"But I will tell them you helped me," she added softly, cajolingly.

He followed stiffly, a cautious frown narrowing black-bead eyes. "I don't believe ya. Why would they come tonight?"

"You gave them the signal," she smiled. "The winch. My father told them. 'Gather at the portal when you hear the basket raised,' he said. 'And you'll know it's time for vengeance.'"

The rifle was still leveled at her chest. But she had increased the distance between them. "I can tell them you saved me from Parrish." She was nearly even with the corner of the shed.

"Stop it," he said, stepping forward to keep the rifle close.

She inched backward. "If you kill me, no one will keep

them from mixing your entrails with the sows' slop tomorrow."

"I oughta cut out yer tongue ta save Connell the grief," Stiles said, lowering the gun in disgust.

Then Ian's hand shot out from the shadows and Stiles's gargling cry carried on the night air. The ax head punctured the back of his trigger hand, driving the nose of the rifle into the ground.

The screech of the pulley stopped suddenly.

Ian swung the piece of iron full force against Stiles's jaw and the foreman folded to the ground.

"The horse!" Ian said. Jenna ran to grab the reins as Ian limped to the start of the straw trail. He fell to one knee, grimacing at the twist on his other leg, and hurriedly ran the match head along the shed.

It broke. The sulfur end was swallowed by the shadows.

"Stiles!" It was Lindstrom's voice. Deep. Demanding. And only a hundred feet away.

"Get clear!" Ian shouted to Jenna. Then he breathed deeply and pressed the remaining match to the shed door. He flicked it slowly this time. It flared to brightness. He placed it in the straw and it caught easily. The fire wound slowly around the edge of the shed toward the bucket.

"Ian!" Jenna called. She was safely beyond the shed, in the dip of the hill, tugging on the reins of the nervous horse. "Now!"

Ian could see the shape of Lindstrom fifty feet away. He had to get him closer.

Ian limped into the clearing so Lindstrom could see him. "Don't worry!" he called, as if to Jenna. "Lindstrom is too fat to run after you!"

Lindstrom's answer whizzed close to Ian's cheek. The Swede still carried the pistol. Ian dived and rolled over and over toward the tall pile of broken tools. His eyes were tightened against the racking pain in his leg. He could not see when the fire reached the bucket and licked its underside where the nail hole gave access to—

The blast. It pounded like a crack of thunder, erupting sooner and stronger than Ian expected. Ian felt the nails rain furiously, futilely, against the mound of metal discards. He heard the terrified squeal of the wagon horses as they reared, the creak of the flatbed bouncing over the rocks as the horses fled.

A subdued neighing rose from the hill behind him as the debris subsided. He raised himself up to see Jenna uncurling slowly from a crouch. She had tied the bedroll blanket over the gelding's head.

Jenna started to run toward him, but Ian stood shakily, a broken ax handle in his hand, his arm out in warning. The dry wood shack near the carbide trap was beginning to burn like paper. Where was Lindstrom?

Ian dragged his stiff leg along slowly as he emerged in the clearing.

"Stone—bridge." The voice was raspy and deep. And genuinely weak. It came from the ruins near the fire. "Help me."

Dear Christ, Parrish's beast still lived! And he wanted Ian's help! With anguished disgust, Ian flung the ax handle away. It sailed beyond the ruins, down the slope toward the portal. When it landed, the crack of a pistol cut through the noise of the roaring fire.

"Did I get you, you devil's son?" Lindstrom fired again and laughed.

Ian could see the giant now, standing uncertainly on two feet, shrinking back from the flames. The fire illuminated the top half of his body, blackened and burned. His face had caught the exploding nails. Ian could see only blood.

The Swede, Ian realized, could see nothing.

Lindstrom stumbled away, gasping with pain, his thick arms sweeping the night air as he groped toward the mine portal. "Where are—you?"

Ian watched until the Swede was out of sight in the swale near the pulley. Then he turned and limped to the grassy slope where Jenna waited.

She walked to him slowly, hesitating, not knowing where to touch him. His body was blood darkened in too many places.

He reached out, breath shaky, and ran his grime-streaked thumb down the soft, clean curve of her cheek. She was safe. Finally.

"Go now," he said, his voice drained of feeling.

She shook her head. "Help is coming. The miners." She gestured across the valley where the flaming tops of torches and erratic bobbing lanterns inched across the moor.

Then she sat down in the grass and smoothed the night-gown across the dip of her lap. "A pillow," she said.

With control he didn't know he had left, Ian lowered himself to the ground beside her and fell back into the small pocket her crossed legs created for him.

He could feel her fingertips roam lightly across his closed eyes, brushing his eyelashes, tracing his cheekbones, his nose, traveling down to his lips. Her fingers rested there a long time.

She is feeling the breath escape my lips, he thought. Then, unexpectedly, before sleep overtook him, he felt the rain. Soft sweet drops. They reminded him how thirsty he was.

Chapter 25

A month passed, and Lancashire was ready to greet the summer solstice.

Jenna had buried her father under the shady oaks of Shadow Glen, beside her mother. Two dozen members of Parliament arrived with Uncle Ronstead, Aunt Enid and Lady Whitston to pay their last respects.

The rapid inquest into the bloody deaths of Lords Hutton Parrish and Arthur Thornton had been less grueling then she expected. After interrogating Stiles and the blind Lindstrom, investigators left Jenna to her grief and did not press her for details about what happened in Leona's cottage.

The authorities tried to question Ian. But he was fighting fever and a raging infection that kept his leg from healing. He had few moments when he was lucid and free of laudanum sleep.

She had spent only a few days at his bedside. Her brother Phillip, and even Lady Whitston reminded her how unseemly an act it was for a distraught gentlewoman and daughter in mourning. She would have continued, though, changing the dressings and mixing the poultices prescribed by the Jamaican Betts and the Thorntons' physician, Edward Falmon, had Ian himself not sent her away one quiet morning before dawn.

He had called out for her in the darkness, his voice soft, as if he knew she would be close.

The fire was cold, no embers glowed. There was no light for her to see his face. Her hand swept softly over the bed-clothes to find his shoulder, his beard-stubbled cheek, his forehead. She brushed back strands of his hair.

"I want you to leave," he said.

She was silent. Across his brow Ian could feel the slow chill that ran through her hand.

"Why?"

"You have seen me helpless too long." His voice was dry.

She drew her hand away, knowing it was not the weakness of the sickroom that hurt him. It was the futile struggle that night in Leona's cottage. She remembered his heartsick gesture at the door as he was forced to leave her with Parrish.

"You did not leave me defenseless," she said quietly.

"Only you would face a sadist from hell naked as an egg and call yourself evenly matched," he said.

Her voice was soft. "There was nothing you could do."

He did not reply.

Her heart pounded. He meant it. He didn't want her with him now.

She knelt on the small stool next to the high bed, leaning closer to him. His breathing was shallow but even.

"Ian," she said quietly in the darkness. "I will love you even if your leg is lost."

She knew the fear was choking him. Each time they changed the dressings he checked the wound for gangrene. "Do not stumble on your pride," she said.

"With one leg gone, it's easier to do," he whispered. But there was no humor in his voice.

She knelt beside him, unwilling to move. She placed her hand flat against hs bare chest. His skin was so hot and dry.

She raised herself higher to lean over him and run her hand gently over the tight, rounded muscle of his shoulder, down along his taut belly, reassuring herself of his solid warmth.

As she bent over him, her long hair cascaded forward and swept across his chest, soft as a silken scarf. His hand suddenly pressed the nape of her neck with a strength she did not expect, and she was pulled tightly to him, her face pressed desperately to his cheek. The sweet-sour tinge of fevered sweat clung to the crease of his neck.

"Ian—" she whispered, her lips kissing the hollow below his ear. She relaxed against him, waiting for the words that would bid her stay.

But minutes passed. His hand slipped away from its resting place at her nape. She felt his grip on her loosening, smoothing absently across her neck. Quickly she turned her head so her lips would catch the glide of his hand across her cheek. But the broad cup of his palm was already gone. There were only his fingertips barely brushing the fullness of her lips.

She pulled away silently and rose in a rush for the door, before his lips could form a word.

"Good-bye."

Jenna spent the next weeks helping the new Earl of Glen Manor repair the monetary chaos he and his father had created.

From the day of the funeral, Phillip kept his claret bottle close at hand, roaming to and from the dinner table with his hand around its neck. He and Jenna had made a tense but civilized journey to London to settle her father's bequests. She had even found Phillip slightly interested in talk of irrigating old fields and revitalizing the farm yield on tenant properties.

In London she met with Lady Whitston to enlist the well-connected widow's help. Connell Parrish was single-mindedly pursuing a murder charge against Ian. But within a week, Lady Whitston had circulated rumors in the right ears that worked magic on the political sensibilities of Judge Harcourt. The case was cycled for dismissal.

Jenna notified Connell through her solicitor that she would be fighting to return Ethan Durrell to his great-aunt, Leona.

At home she dealt with both domestic and county problems. She fired the butler Eaton, Parrish's spy, and hired the two eldest Grawlin children as domestic servants.

The miners were a more serious concern. Jubilant at passage of the Mine Safety Act, the union workers quickly grew apprehensive when they realized the start-up of the Parrish Colliery depended entirely on Jenna's willingness to bargain with Connell Parrish. The Parrish vein was mined out. Shadow Glen's coal would be the livelihood for a hundred workers and their families. But if Shadow Glen's old surface shaft became the entry portal, the forest would be destroyed.

Alexander McBryde traveled from London to plead the miners' cause. "Why not strike a deal with Connell Parrish to use his portal and your coal?" McBryde asked.

"Get the financing in order, and someone who will negotiate controlling interest of the company for us. Connell is to have no say in day-to-day operations, nor in policymaking," Jenna said, tired of all talk of coal and money. "Then the colliers can have their mine."

Woodenly, she managed the estate, calling in an accounts clerk from Lancaster to help sort out the wreckage her father had left. She was no longer driven to handle the details herself. She wanted rest. She wanted time. And a chance to touch the memory of Sarbin's Crown.

She slipped out of the house one morning, properly dressed in a black riding habit, and rode Dulcy to the grave site in Shadow Glen's forest.

The summer sun streamed warm and dappled through the leaves. She walked past the dark, grassless mound where her father lay. Past the tall granite stone that marked her mother's resting place. Jenna paused there, reached inside the bodice of her riding habit and drew out the silver locket that held the bloom from her mother's wreath.

The petals were black now. She placed the crumpled pieces on her mother's gravestone.

"Father was not as helpless as he seemed," Jenna whispered to her. "None of us are."

She wound her way across the wide swale and down to the mossy bank of the stream where she had hunted with Stolley. Little brown sparrows scolded a squirrel away from their nest in the birch branches above her head. She looked up the hill, to where she had first seen the dark stranger advancing through the brush to catch a thief so many weeks ago.

He would not move so agilely now. His leg was saved, but stiff, healing badly.

She sat down on the outcropping above the brook. Ian would be home tomorrow from London. He was visiting a doctor who advised surgery to repair the muscle Parrish had slashed.

They had not spoken since the morning she left his bedside. They had no need to talk.

Too much is understood between us, she thought, her head resting on her drawn-up knees.

"The shadows make it hard to find a huntress in mourning."

His voice. It came from the hill behind her. Her heart quickened as she looked up. Ian stood at the top, a towering figure in black day coat and boots. She had to raise one arm to shield the glare of the sun. Its angle behind him made his outline a blur.

She walked slowly toward the brush-covered slope. "You are back early," she said, her riding hat in hand, its veil catching on a wild bed of sweet william.

He did not answer. Only waited, looking down on the gleam of the sun in her thick ebony hair. The stylish drape of her riding skirt over slim hips. The white lace collar that rose to the sweet, delicate hair nestled at the nape of her neck. The creamy pink of cheeks his lips had kissed fervently in the mindless heat of their lovemaking. God, how he had missed her.

"What did the doctor advise?" she asked.

"The surgery could do more harm than good." He stepped forward, closer to the edge of the grassy knoll, his wounded leg bent slightly at the knee. "It will heal. But I will never be able to run a poacher through the woods."

"Then I am safe," she smiled up, stepping across a small swale to the foot of the incline.

"If you want to be." His tone made her choice clear.

Jenna hesitated a moment, knowing her answer would take her much farther than the top of the slope. Then she lifted her skirt and began to climb the steep hill. Surefooted, she angled her path upward.

He watched the easy grace with which she took the hill. She could be at home in a London ballroom—or on a ranch in the American frontier. They both knew she was giving him the power to choose which.

She was a few feet below him now. He stepped down, his right leg stiff, and reached for her. His hand, strong and cool, clasped over hers and he pulled her upward, steadily at first, until her waist was close enough for him to encircle. Then his arms swept her supple body to the length of him, his senses aching for the feel of her firm, rounded breasts against his chest as his hand pressed hard down the column of her spine, molding her closer, ever closer.

She gave a small cry of breathlessness. And he turned his attention to lips that waited as impatiently as his own.

But his hands could not stop exploring her, remembering her. Fingers stretched wide and searching, he grasped either side of her bodice, cradling the delicate frame of her ribs. Gently his hands kneaded lower, to the sharp inward curve at her waist, the sweet softness around her navel, then upward along the velvet front of her gown, smoothing slowly over her breasts.

The kiss, never gentle, grew into a tearing, desperate sign of their hunger. They pushed away, breathless. For a moment.

Then Jenna stepped slowly toward him. His touch had awakened a searing awareness inside her, as if something raw and pulsing had been sleeping fitfully, waiting only for the searching claim of his hand on her breast, his tongue atop hers.

One hand reached up to stroke the strong angle of his jaw. Involuntarily her slim fingers glided higher, past bristling sideburns to the softness of the long black hair at his temples. Her nails raked a path there, then entangled long strands in her fist. She shook her head, at a loss for words, painfully aware of how many weeks they had been apart. Her fist clenched harder and she pulled his head down toward her.

She felt his hand cradle the small of her back as he bent over her and lowered her gently to the ground. The soft summer grass yielded to the weight of her head, her shoulders, her hips.

His coat and vest were tossed away, landing in a heap near the trunk of a dappled larch. With a control that surprised him, he gathered her warm body against him. "What shall I promise you?" he whispered.

She said nothing for a long time, savoring the feel of him, the safety of his embrace, the unmistakable heat surging between them. "Anything but a lifetime of choosing drawing-room curtains for Stonebridge Hall," she said.

"A proper lady would accede to such a fate," he said, unbuttoning the front of his shirt. "Fortunately, you are much too singular and inventive a woman to saddle me with such an easy, predictable life. All in all, not a very marriageable woman."

"But a lovable one?"

"Exactly what I told the vicar," he said.

"So. You will have a real fiancée," she smiled. "You are sure we can perform marriage without conspiracies and masquerades?"

"Of course, love," he said, reaching behind her to begin unhooking buttons, one by one. "We need only discard our costumes. . . ."

Dear Reader,

I would love to hear from you. Your comments, observations and feelings about *Dare I Love?* are important. Please write to me care of Warner Books, 666 Fifth Avenue, New York, NY 10103.

Regards,
Gillian